DEMANDING
Diamonds

Eileen Ann Brennan
Tiffany Bryan
Amanda Sidhe
Desiree Holt
Margaret L. Carter

ELLORA'S CAVE
ROMANTICA PUBLISHING

What the critics are saying...

ɛɔ

A GIRL'S BEST FRIEND
Eileen Ann Brennan

Outstanding Read! "Natalie and Steve make hot, steamy and smoldering sound like a tepid bath. You will definitely need something cold to drink hmmm maybe you should just sit your butt in a tub of ice—that might be a better idea! Don't miss *A Girl's Best Friend*; this little fantasy is much too much fun to pass up!" ~ *Simply Romance Reviews*

4 Hearts "A fun, sexy and highly addictive story that I know will entertain many readers to come." ~ *Night Owl Romance Reviews*

Rated 4 Excellent! A GIRL'S BEST FRIEND is a wonderful paranormal romance. Eileen Brennan gives a great short story, and shows us diamonds are truly A GIRL'S BEST FRIEND. The characters are strong and believable. You can't help but cheer Natalie and Steve as the clock ticks down, and the Chemistry between them is hot." ~ *The Romance Readers Connection*

BEJEWELED AND BEDEVILED
Tiffany Bryan

5 Dark Angels "Tiffany Bryan absolutely swept me away with this phenomenal story. BEJEWELED AND BEDEVILED is a kick butt BDSM romance that left me breathless. I loved everything about this story. […] I really enjoyed the premise of this storyline. I am very much hoping that this is going to turn into an ongoing series so I can find out the other women's fantasies also. Full of smoking hot passion and an unbelievable romance, BEJEWELED AND BEDEVILED is a keeper to be read over and over again." ~ *Dark Angels Reviews*

BEYOND THE VEIL
Amanda Sidhe

5 Rating "Amanda Sidhe's *Beyond the Veil* was an absolutely engrossing and thoroughly enjoyable read. The author deftly weaved a fascinating story of spirits, curses and intense passion peppered with a smidge of bondage. [...] *Beyond the Veil* was a great short story full of steamy hot sex with a dash of romance for good measure. Ms. Sidhe's writing continues to impress me and I'll be on the watch for more from her in the future." ~ *Just Erotic Romance Revciews*

DIAMOND LADY
Desiree Holt

4.5 Lips "Desiree Holt's *Diamond Lady* should come with warning signs, this book is extremely HOT. Panty changer alert time! Desiree Holt brings bondage, hot sex, and emotions together in *Diamond Lady* to make the perfect story. [...] *Diamond Lady* is a quick, but powerful read, I for one want to see more like this from Desiree Holt in the future." ~ *Two Lips Reviews*

HEART DIAMOND
Margaret L. Carter

"*Heart Diamond* is literally an erotic ghost story. Through the connection of Tim's ring he is able to visit and make love to Roseanne as a ghost. Will that be enough for Roseanne since it isn't permanent? The sex scenes with Roseanne and the ghost of Tim are very unusual but sensual. The ghost has some interesting tricks. [...] This story is kind of creepy and fun all at the same time and I enjoyed it. Ms. Carter defiantly has a creative imagination!" ~ *Manic Readers Reviews*

An Ellora's Cave Romantica Publication

www.ellorascave.com

Demanding Diamonds

ISBN 9781419958649
ALL RIGHTS RESERVED.
A Girl's Best Friend Copyright © 2008 Eileen Ann Brennan
Bejeweled and Bedeviled Copyright © 2008 Tiffany Bryan
Beyond the Veil Copyright © 2008 Amanda Sidhe
Diamond Lady Copyright © 2008 Desiree Holt
Heart Diamond Copyright © 2008 Margaret L. Carter
Edited by Ann Leveille, Briana St. James, Helen Woodall, Pamela Campbell.
Cover art by Syneca.

This book printed in the U.S.A. by Jasmine–Jade Enterprises, LLC.

Trade paperback Publication February 2009

DEMANDING DIAMONDS

ଞ

A GIRL'S BEST FRIEND

Eileen Ann Brennan

Dedication

∞

To Mike, my one true love, and Diann, my head cheerleader.

To Gail, Lena, Lisa, Sheila and Tracy. You are all truly "A Girl's Best Friends"!

Trademarks Acknowledgement

∞

The author acknowledges the trademarked status and trademark owners of the following wordmarks mentioned in this work of fiction:

ESPN: ESPN, Inc.

Menudo: Menudo Entertainment LLC LTD

Nike: Nike, Inc.

Starbucks: Starbucks U.S. Brands

Wal-Mart: Walton Enterprises, Inc.

Chapter One

ဢ

Natalie Phillips lay in bed waiting, wondering if her mysterious dream lover would join her, afraid he would but more afraid he wouldn't. For the first time in weeks sleep eluded her. How could she relax and fall asleep when her heart pounded in anticipation? Inhaling deeply, she counted to ten, held her breath for a moment then counted again as she exhaled. She tried again. Nothing. You'd think eight years of yoga would be of some help. Evidently not tonight.

She tossed from her back to her side. Not a sliver of light glimmered in the pitch-dark room so that wasn't the problem. Drat. If she didn't fall asleep soon she wouldn't be able to handle tomorrow's big project. Not that that was a bad thing. She really didn't want to do it anyway. Maybe that's what was keeping her awake. Dreading tomorrow.

She punched her pillow and rolled onto her stomach. Would he visit her tonight or was it over? If only she could fall asleep… If only she could fall asleep…

Did you think I would not come to you? That I had tired of you? That will never happen, mi amor. *You are mine and I will bring you the most exquisite pleasures you will ever know.*

His hot words sent shivering tingles through her body, which centered in her pulsing clit as he settled his solid muscular form on her back. The springy hair on his chest tickled her flesh as he aligned his body on hers. She let out a sigh. He'd come. Relief followed swiftly by excitement washed over her. It was ridiculous that she would want him, crave him, but when he was with her she didn't care who he was, how he got here or how improbable the whole situation was. She cared only about receiving the pleasure he offered and giving what she could.

He nestled the length of his thick cock between her buttocks, spreading her for his enjoyment. His elbows rested near her shoulders and he lifted his chest, easing his weight on her but wedging his cock more firmly within the hot crease of her ass. She squeezed her cheeks. A sharp sense of triumph filled her at his hiss of satisfaction. The thought that she pleased him elated her and increased her confidence. She could be his match in their carnal games.

His tight, flat abs snugged against her back as his lips seared a path from her shoulder to her ear.

Ah, mi corazón, *what you do to me. Tonight I will take you someplace special, someplace we have never been before.*

She squirmed at his erotic promise even as he rocked his pelvis against her ass, pushing her mons rhythmically against the mattress. The large pendant around her neck pressed into her breasts but she ignored it, concentrating instead on the vibrant and forceful man covering her.

Her heightened senses detected the soft sprinkling of hair on his legs, the gentle slap of his balls against her pussy, the pulsing friction of his cock as it burned a trail of heat down her cleft. Her nipples, already taut with desire, rubbed against the fine cotton sheet. They tightened further, making her gasp at how quickly he could bring her to the edge of insanity. At the urging of his long fingers she spread her legs, inviting him to continue, to increase the motion.

Yes, tonight will be very special.

He lifted his weight, removing his cock from between her cheeks, and knelt in the V of her stretched legs. The cool air of the room assaulted her heated body, shattering the euphoric feeling. She uttered a small whimper of protest.

Never fear, mi amor. *You will have your fill of my cock tonight…and so much more.*

He brushed the sides of her breasts with the back of his knuckles. The motion only made her yearn to feel his hands cover her breasts, squeeze them until she cried out. He shifted his weight and kissed a slow, leisurely path down her back, nipping her shoulders, licking her ticklish side, trailing his tongue along the length of her spine until she thought she'd go mad from the sheer pleasure of it. His every touch brought a new vibration to her already thrumming clit. Knowing his heavy cock would soon be buried deep within her dripping pussy, her panting body sizzled with impatience. She licked her dry lips, wondering what he could possibly mean by "so much more".

He kneaded her butt, caressing her, soothing her even as her fevered excitement expanded and she teetered on the brink of climax. No, not yet. It was too soon. More. She needed more. His lips lingered at the small of her back then moved lower to explore the firm globes of her cheeks.

Ah, cariño, *you have a glorious ass. Small and well shaped.* He nipped her and she came off the bed with a start.

And delicious too. His lips curved into a wicked smile against her skin. She wanted to tell him how much she liked that and to keep doing it but no words came.

With a palm still cupping each sensitive cheek he urged her onto her knees then urged her to lift her butt. She complied with eager expectation when she felt his finger trace a path down her cleft, a finger that was suddenly slick with a scented oil as it circled her tender, puckered opening. Hot blood thrummed through her veins at his gentle massage. Would he really…? Wouldn't he ask first? She rotated her butt to extract the most pleasure from his motions. No, he wouldn't ask. He'd already know what would please her. Just like he had every other night. Anticipation flooded her senses. She flinched when he eased a single digit into her ass.

Easy, mi amor, *we will both like this very much.*

His voice held a husky, rasping tone and his playful mood of a moment ago seemed to have deserted him. He rotated his finger, allowing her to become accustomed to his invasion. At first a burning sensation brought tears to her eyes but she took a few deep breaths and the discomfort receded.

Slowly he inserted another finger, spreading her, drawing out her trepidation. She closed her eyes and concentrated on the sharp, spicy scent of the oil, feeling it trickle down the valley between her cheeks, imagining it dripping from his swollen cock, his heavy balls. Then his massage changed tempo and he began to finger-fuck her, slow at first and then with more and more drive. She cried out at the sweet pressure and he inserted a third finger.

That's it, querida. *Tell me you want this. Tell me you want more. Beg me.*

His panting breath fanned across her arched back and his free hand gripped her buttock but she was powerless to answer, powerless to beg as he wanted—as she had done so many nights before. The musky scent of his excitement surrounded her, heightening her senses to an unbearable peak.

You do not beg? It does not matter. You are mine.

His thick muscular thighs pushed her legs wider. Then his fingers left her tender portal. For an instant she wanted to cry out, to object, until she felt the demanding head of his cock probe her puckered opening. His hands gripped her buttocks, separating them, spreading them to fully accept his pulsing erection. Slowly, with infinite care, his throbbing head breeched her tight back entrance.

His groan shattered the silence of the room but he held himself, allowing her to become accustomed to his thick cock. Her body bucked in protest at the invasion. She clasped the sheet, almost shredding it with her nails. No man had ever taken her this way, dominated her this way. And yet she was torn between chagrin at her submissive position and a feeling of sublime satisfaction at the pleasure she could give him.

Relax, mi corazón. *Did I not promise you would have your fill of my cock tonight? Is this not a special place, a special joining?*

She waited, the air in her lungs fighting to get out. Somehow her body remembered to breathe. Certainly her brain was too occupied to undertake such a mundane activity.

She exhaled and gulped precious air. The only other sounds were the deep guttural urgings from her lover. It must have taken supreme determination to remain immobile. She snatched another deep breath.

More. She needed more of him. This was not enough. Tightening her muscles, she rocked gently back, signaling him that she was ready to continue.

At this slight urging it was as if the entire reserve of his control had been spent, depleted. In one swift, breathtaking moment, his cock surged into her, impaling her firmly on his throbbing length. She gasped then bucked, pushing her ass to meet his hilt. Never before had she felt such an indescribable sensation, such a feeling of fullness.

So tight. So snug. Stay with me.

His long fingers massaged her buttocks as his thick cock withdrew and thrust, withdrew and thrust, each stroke coming rapidly upon the last. Her chest tightened, her body tensed, the sound of her labored breathing played counterpoint to the sound of flesh slapping flesh. A spiral of heat rose from deep within, surrounding her, drowning her.

Now, mi amor!

His burning seed shot through her and she buried her face in the pillow, screaming as the pulsing waves of an exquisite orgasm overtook her.

In a tangle of sweat-soaked sheets Natalie awoke, hanging off her bed—naked and alone. She drew in a deep, steadying breath before opening her eyes. Her heart rate was somewhere between thumping madly and cardiac arrest. "For the love of Pete. You better get a grip, girl," she muttered, dragging herself back onto the mattress. This really was getting out of hand. Perspiration layered a thin sheen on her skin and the throbbing between her thighs continued to pulse with a need for more stimulation. Her dream lover had made another appearance, taking her with an intensity that had her crying out as he once again brought her to a shuddering climax. But like every night he'd gone too soon, leaving her alone and craving his touch. She rolled her eyes at the sight of her naked body and kicked the remaining sheets toward the footboard. Had she yelled like the other night? What if Gran heard? The thought brought her swiftly back to reality. Gran hadn't heard her. Gran wouldn't hear anything anymore.

Natalie swung her legs off the bed and sat for a moment, dangling them, waiting for feeling to return. No, Gran hadn't heard and Gran wouldn't have the coffee made or her bagel toasted either. Life without Gran may have produced Natalie's wildly sexy dreams but she would have traded all those wonderful moments with that marvelously talented dream man for one more day with her beloved grandmother.

But as they say, life must go on. Natalie stood and headed toward the bathroom down the hall, not bothering to put on her robe. What was the point? No one would see her. She climbed into the claw-footed tub and drew the bright purple shower curtain. Gran had allowed Natalie to pick out the color when she came to live here at age seven and purple it had remained in one shade or another for the next twenty years.

Twisting the porcelain knobs, she jumped back from the expected cold spray then lifted her face. As much as she loved them these dreams simply had to stop. Fantasizing like this couldn't be healthy. Yeah, like she had any control over her subconscious. But the timing was just too weird. She grabbed the shampoo and lathered up and rinsed then did the conditioner thing as she tried to wipe her brain clear of the night of ecstasy she'd just experienced — again.

The dreams had started the night of Gran's funeral over a month ago. The service had been small, only Gran's bingo buddies, as they called themselves, and a few of Natalie's close friends had been present since there was no other family. They'd all returned to the house but once respects were paid and the will was read everyone left, leaving Natalie to fall into bed exhausted and drained. That's when they'd started.

A man. A dangerously dark, handsome man appeared in her dreams and made love to her. Not just close-the-door and isn't-this-sweet love but wild-monkey-sex-swinging-from-the-ceiling-fan love.

And the damnedest thing was he wouldn't go away. Every night since Gran's funeral he'd visited her bed and brought her orgasm after orgasm. Not that she couldn't do with all the orgasms she could get but, damn, this guy was insatiable. Then too, she never would have imagined her dream man as a rugged Latino with eyes that turned to black velvet when he made love but now she couldn't imagine anyone else. Natalie shivered as if someone had walked across *her* grave.

She turned off the water, grabbed a towel and was about to slather on a glob of skin lotion when the melodious chimes of the doorbell reached her ears.

Slapping the skin lotion on her thighs, she rubbed it in and hustled to her room. Grabbing her thick terrycloth robe, she hurried downstairs just as a loud banging began on the door. No need to look through the peephole—only one person attacked a door like that.

"Hey, Shanice. I don't believe this. Nine o'clock on Saturday morning? Shouldn't you be asleep for another three hours?" Natalie's friend from the next street over stood on the porch, bouncing on her toes, her dark braids keeping time with her little running steps as she jogged in place.

"Hey, girl, it's spring, it's warm and it's a beautiful day. You want to do some miles in the park this morning? My shoes are just begging for a run."

Natalie leaned against the doorjamb. "Where are you getting this energy?"

"My energy, or rather my guilt, comes from not one but two slices of cherry cheesecake I gobbled down last night. You wanna run or what? Go get changed. I'll wait."

More than anything Natalie wanted to join her friend. Running had worked before to clear her mind of the dream man but now she pushed her own wants to the side. "I'd love to but I promised myself I would go through Gran's papers and stuff today. I've put it off long enough."

Shanice stilled her hopping. "Whoa, sounds serious. You want me to stay and help? I don't mind but please say no."

Natalie laughed. Shanice was a true friend but couldn't stand anything that smacked of "touchy-feely". "Actually, I need to do this by myself so you're off the hook. But I'll collect on your guilt later."

"I've no doubt about that. Look, you gonna be home tomorrow? I may come by after I get off my shift. Mama's back on her 'when are you gonna get married so I can have some grandbabies' kick. She's making me nuts."

"Hey, you can hide here any time you want."

"Thanks, girl. We can get a pizza and trade excuses on why neither of us has a man in our life." She gave Natalie a wide smile. "Well, if you're sure you can't come, I'll catch ya later." With a little finger wave, Shanice was down the porch stairs and jogging toward the park.

Natalie closed the door and retraced her steps to her bedroom. She had a man in her life, only not the kind she could tell her friend about. She grabbed a pair of panties and running shorts from a pile of clean laundry and slipped them on. Digging deeper, she found a sports bra. If she finished her project she'd reward herself with a run later.

Not bothering with shoes, she wandered down to the kitchen to make a pot of coffee. Somehow hers didn't taste as good as Gran's. She found some sensible bran cereal in the cupboard and poured herself a bowl. Peering into the refrigerator, she noted the milk was a week past the expiration date. One whiff and it was down the drain. She stood by the sink, eating her cereal dry while she waited for the coffee.

It was all a delay tactic. She'd been putting off cleaning Gran's room for a month. What was a few more minutes? Somehow as long as Gran's stuff was where she left it, Gran wasn't really gone. Right?

With a grimace she put her bowl down and poured her coffee. Wrong. Gran was still gone and the sooner Natalie cleaned the room the sooner she could get on with her life. With a determination in her step she didn't quite feel, she grabbed her coffee mug and marched upstairs to Gran's room. The closed door stopped her. Was she ready to face the memories on the other side? Not really but it was now or never.

She turned the knob and pushed. The lingering scent of Gran's perfume assailed her senses.

Oh, Gran, I miss you so much. She sucked in her lower lip and swiped the tears before they could overflow. *I can do this. Help me, Gran.*

Sunlight streamed through wide arched windows decorated with tailored navy drapes. An equally sedate spread covered the antique white bed. Matching furniture dotted the large bedroom. Everything about the room suggested understated elegance—just like Gran.

Natalie's gaze went immediately to the long bureau and a double picture frame. Gran's wedding picture was on one side. She was radiant, gazing with such love and devotion into Granddad's eyes. And why not? Granddad had been one hot hunk in his day.

In the other picture Gran wore a classic portrait drape. That photograph had always puzzled Natalie. Why would Gran keep a picture of herself as a young woman on her bureau? Natalie thought it was there for Granddad but the portrait remained after he'd passed away five years ago. Gran wore the same enamored expression in both photos but Granddad wasn't in that one. In fact, Gran said it had been taken the day before they'd met. It was as if Gran could see him waiting for her in the future. The love and joy in her eyes was breathtaking.

"Oh my God." Even though Natalie had seen these pictures hundreds of times she'd never actually *looked* at them. Her hands shook. She placed her coffee mug on the bureau and picked up the frame. That necklace. Gran wore it in both photos. A large diamond pendant in an ornate, almost garish, setting hung from her neck on a thick gold chain. It seemed so at odds with her conservative, sophisticated taste.

The room closed in around Natalie until only the picture in her sweaty palms existed. It wasn't the gaudy piece of jewelry that had her heartbeat doing double-time. No, it was where she'd seen that diamond before—around her own neck each night while her dream lover brought her to unspeakable heights of ecstasy.

Chapter Two

ဢ

Natalie hugged her knees to her chest as she sat on her own bed, staring at the pictures beside her. Once she'd realized where she'd seen the necklace she couldn't get out of her grandmother's room fast enough. What on earth was going on? Did her subconscious simply plop that necklace into her dream? It hadn't registered that she wasn't entirely naked in the dreams until she saw the picture. Maybe she'd been too preoccupied with the wild sex and how the blatantly provocative man made her feel to pay attention to anything else.

How come she'd never seen Gran wear the necklace except in these pictures? Was it still in the house? Was there some link between the necklace and the dreams?

She lifted her chin in determination. *Well, I'm not going to find any answers hiding out in here.*

Heaving herself off the bed, she forced her feet back to Gran's room. The door stood open just as she'd left it when she'd run out. Now it beckoned, urging her to return.

Her gaze darted to the stately armoire in the far corner of the room. Gran's jewel box would be tucked in the bottom drawer. When she was little Natalie had never been allowed to play with the contents in that box. Gran had kept another box of everyday jewelry on her bureau and Natalie had spent hours playing "fairy tale princess" with those pieces.

But the box was now hers. Except for a few sentimental bequests she'd been left everything in Gran's will.

Natalie went directly to the armoire and opened the drawer. A faint musty scent of Granddad's cigars filled her nostrils. A fist gripped her heart as images of her grandparents ricocheted in her mind. They'd been so happy together, made for each other. She shook off the feeling and knelt to reach into the drawer. Moving her fingers through several items of Granddad's clothing that Gran must have kept for the memories, Natalie found it. There, under an old sweater, the shape of a hard oblong box. Tugging it out, she smoothed her fingers over the inlaid design of diamonds strung across the lid.

She pushed the delicate latch. Locked. She shook the box. If the weight hadn't given it away already, the rattle and clinking demanded the jewelry box be investigated. Running her hand around the drawer, she searched for a key. Nothing.

Now where would Gran hide a key? Someplace easy to remember and readily accessible. Of course. The other jewelry box. Setting the locked box on the floor, she rose and went to the bureau. The lid offered no resistance and she fingered through the items in the box. Memories flooded back at the sight of the familiar pieces but no key appeared.

Natalie's gaze wandered around the room. It settled on a lamp next to Gran's reading chair. She strode to the lamp and lifted it. As Gran would say, bingo. With her heart thumping like a bunny's foot she grabbed the key and returned to kneel beside the box.

Well, here goes.

Her fingers shook and it took her three tries to insert the delicate key. She held her breath. It turned. The latch clicked and the lid eased open on its own. The top layer contained a removable tray that held an assortment of earrings, broaches and rings. Her heart lurched as she recognized Granddad's wedding ring.

The necklace. Look for the necklace.

She lifted the tray. Several black velvet bags snuggled beneath. Her hand hovered. Which should she open first? *Well, duh, try the largest.*

Picking it up, she jiggled it. A promising sound jingled back. She loosened the drawstring and spilled the contents onto the thick white carpet.

The magnificent piece lay before her, glittering in the sunlight that streamed through the windows. She sucked in her breath until it hurt…and stared. The heavy gold chain with thick links almost a half-inch long shimmered but it was the stone that held her attention. A square-cut diamond so large it had to be fake. Did they have cubic zirconium back in the Forties? How old was this thing? Was Gran the first owner? Natalie wasn't any authority on expensive jewelry but this piece was old, very old.

She picked up the chain and examined the intricately twisted links. Yes, very old and very well crafted. The diamond dangled in the sunlight. Prisms of color danced across the walls and ceiling, adding a touch of whimsy to the staid, serious bedroom. No doubt about it. This sucker was the real thing. It had to be at least a gazillion carats it was so big.

The gem seemed to call to her. She reached. Her shaking fingers connected with the smooth glittering surface. Gingerly, she stroked the diamond. Though she expected it to be cool from lying hidden in a dark drawer it was warm to her touch as if it had recently been held in a closed palm.

"It's about time you figured it out, *mi corazón*. I've been waiting for you."

Natalie whirled at the sound of the deep masculine, lightly accented voice then fell back onto her bottom. There, kneeling behind her, his powerful thighs spread to shoulder width, was a man. *The* man. The one from her erotic dreams. She'd know that lean, muscled body anywhere. She'd explored every inch of his powerful, rippling physique with her mouth, her hands, her eyes. Now he appeared as he always did in her dreams—naked, hot and with a cock as hard as a steel pipe.

She scrabbled backward on the floor, still clutching the diamond, until she bumped into Gran's reading chair.

"Don't be afraid, *mi amor*. I won't harm you."

He held her gaze and she knew he spoke the truth. His face was just as she dreamed it, high cheekbones, sharp angular nose, smoldering ebony eyes with thick black lashes — and a mouth that was pure sin. A lock of his casually long black hair fell across his forehead, emphasizing his strong Latino heritage.

"Who...who are you? What do you want?"

"You already know who I am and you know what I want." His voice was low, seductive, sending liquid desire fluttering to her stomach and a sweet moisture between her thighs.

This was crazy. How could her body betray her like this? She gathered her scattered wits and went on the offensive. That's what you did in an emergency. Right? "Look, pal, I don't know who you are or how you got here but you and your malfunctioning wardrobe better leave or I'll call the cops." As much as she liked the sight of his lightly haired chest and that lovely trail that drew her attention to his sex, nothing good could come of a strange naked man popping up in her house.

At her words he spread his fingers on his hair-sprinkled thighs and laughed, not just a chuckle but a hearty, no-holds-barred laugh. "You're going to call the police when it was you who called me in the first place?"

"Huh?"

He nodded toward her fist that clasped the diamond to her breasts. His smile was so tender that under any other circumstance it would have melted her heart. Right now though, it made her more wary.

"It's simple. You are the owner of the necklace. You touched the stone. I answered its call."

Natalie frowned, opened her fist and raised the diamond to eye level. "You mean this necklace is like a magic lamp or something? I rub it and a naked genie appears?" *Oh brother. The guy really is nuts.*

"No genie. Just the man who has been waiting for you. You know me. We've made passionate love dozens of times. Every night your heart calls to mine and I visit you the only way I can—in your dreams. But now, finally, you have found the stone and I can come to you."

She stared from the diamond to the man kneeling before her, holding out his hand, his eyes imploring her to trust him. Could he be for real? If what he said was true he'd simply appeared out of thin air because she'd touched an old diamond. She'd love to believe him. Everyone could use a little magic in their lives.

Her dreams of him had been so vivid, so real. He'd made her come time after time, night after night until she'd started going to bed as soon as the sun went down so she wouldn't miss a minute in his arms. Here he was, and if that stiff hard-on was any indication he was ready to start a new dream.

No doubt about it. She was the one who was nuts. Could this be some sort of delayed reaction to Gran's sudden death? There had been no warning. A heart attack when Gran jumped up after winning the jackpot at bingo. Of course. This whole thing was Post-Traumatic Stress Disorder, brought on by being in Gran's room. That was it. This guy wasn't here. He was just her imagination running amuck. She could prove it very easily. Hallucinations weren't solid, right?

Her deafening pulse pounded in her ears as she cautiously pushed off the soft carpet, rose to her feet and smiled at the man. No point in being rude to her delusions. He held out his hand again and a look of ravenous hunger burned deep in his eyes. A hunger so strong she wanted to surrender to its call.

Steeling her resolve, she marched toward him. She'd pass through him. That would prove he was as real as Peter Pan. She'd march downstairs for a fresh cup of coffee to steady her frazzled nerves.

She bumped into a rock-hard body and lost her footing. The man caught her and swung her around so that he cradled her in his formidable arms. The contours of his unyielding pecs against her breasts, the smell of his aroused masculine scent as he gathered her close left her no doubt he wasn't an illusion.

"Now do you believe I'm real?" His firm, warm lips grazed her ear then scattered light kisses along her jawline and across her cheek. She pulled back and peered into his dark eyes. The hunger was tempered now by a look of affection, touched with a hint of triumph. "If you find this too hard to believe, *mi corazón*," he rasped, "pretend I'm still a dream, a dream who wants you, needs you, cannot exist without you."

His gaze lingered only a moment before his sensuous mouth closed over hers. Oh God, he felt so good—just like always. She shut her eyes and gave herself over to the familiar taste, scent and feel of him. Excitement pooled in her belly, shooting that same titillating thrill to her pussy.

If she was having a breakdown, this was the way to do it. He skimmed his tongue along hers before plundering deeper to stroke the sensitive recesses that only he knew. His powerful arms crushed her to his chest, catching her hand that held the diamond necklace between them. It bit into her palm but there was no space to adjust it.

When he released her lips to trail a string of open-mouthed kisses down her throat she forgot about necklaces, breakdowns and everything but the glorious sensation of his mouth and hands roaming over her heated flesh. Was she dreaming again? Was she hallucinating? It didn't matter. He was here.

One powerful hand pressed against her back, holding her locked to his torso while his other hand found the waistband of her running shorts. In one swift move they disappeared along with her panties. The bright sunlight streaming through the window warmed her exposed skin before his touch heated her from within.

He lifted her as if she weighed no more than a feather then angled her so that she straddled his powerful thighs, spreading her legs wide while he continued to run his lips down her throat. His thick cock stroked her belly and she undulated, pushing her mons against the solid ridge. She arched her pelvis so that her slick folds enveloped the length of him and the tip of his cock rubbed against her clit. A forest fire of desire consumed her and she pushed herself harder against him. He held rock still, allowing her to pleasure herself with mindless abandon. A thin sheen of sweat on his chest was the only indication that his control was slipping.

Her aroused state increased with the knowledge that he strained to hold himself in check so that she could use his body to bring them both impossible sensations. The hardened peaks of her nipples scraped along his chest through her sports bra, sending a new wave of searing heat to her pussy. All the while his lips slid along her throat, her shoulders. As if he couldn't decide what he wanted more, his tongue continued to seek her mouth and delve deeply, coiling the tension within her.

"Open for me, *mi amor*. I need you much more now that I'm not a dream but flesh and blood."

With her free hand Natalie wove her fingers through his silky hair, urging him to continue his sweet assault. He grasped her hips and leveraged her above his cock and slowly, in an oh-so-familiar motion, she slid down his penis until he was buried in her up to his hilt. She shivered at the hard, thick sensation of him, so unmistakable, so unforgettable. Her soul mate? Her lover? The label didn't matter. He was the man who made her universe stop and her world tilt.

She nipped his neck and clenched her thighs tightly against his hips. With a groan rumbling low in his throat they fell into a rhythm more intense than they'd ever had in her dreams. Nothing they had done before prepared her for this. He seemed to thrust deeper, pull back longer and fill her so completely all control was swept away in the storm that raged around her.

His strong arms held her locked against him as if he feared she would disappear should he ease his hold. Ragged breathing echoed loudly in her ear and she buried her face in the crook of his neck.

"Come for me, *querida,* come for me." His hoarse whisper sent her over the edge and into a shattering maelstrom. He gripped her hips, thrusting harder and faster, drawing spasm after spasm from her, extending her climax.

A sharp thrill shot through her at the sound of his strained shout. She tightened her muscles around him as his cock twitched and jerked deep inside her. He pumped himself into her, pulling her to a new level of awareness of her own body's need for him.

"*Mi amor, mi amor.*" He thrust again, surging into her with a staggering force, then froze in the final moment of his orgasm. She clenched her muscles tighter and dug her nails into his shoulder. Time became endless as they rode out the magic together.

With a satisfied growl he lay down then rolled and tucked her beneath him. She spread her thighs so he was cushioned between her bent legs. Sweat glistened on his body as they lay on the floor in a pool of warm sunlight. She smoothed her hand down his taut, muscled back. Cupping his buttock, she looked up at him. His expression had eased somewhat from the urgency of his climax but his eyes remained closed. He lowered his lips to catch hers in a gentle, lingering kiss.

"You are mine," he said between soft nibbles.

She sighed and gave herself over to the tender moment. In her dreams he'd always been loving and affectionate after sex and apparently he was no different now. She stroked his hair with her free hand. Her other hand still clutched the necklace between them. Now that the passion had subsided, new impressions leapt forward. The glorious feel of his weight cradled between her thighs, his warm breath on her cheek…the diamond biting into her palm.

Hmm. She wiggled her arm free from between her breasts and his chest and opened her fingers. As if in slow motion, the diamond slid from her hand. Her lover's head shot up, a look of disbelief then sadness washing across his features.

"No, *mi corazón*. Do not release the stone."

Natalie blinked. Then blinked again. She really was going nuts. She had to be. Why else would she be lying on the floor of her grandmother's bedroom—naked and alone?

Chapter Three

Natalie tore into her room and threw the necklace onto her bed. She'd used her running shorts to pick it up off the carpet in Gran's room, retrieved her panties and dashed back to her own private sanctuary. Being naked in her grandmother's bedroom was too creepy, having sex there—imaginary or otherwise—was just plain wrong.

That didn't happen. I fell asleep and it was all a dream. Right?

If it had all been a dream why was she sweating and her heart pounding like she'd just run a marathon...or had an orgasm? She stood rooted by the bed staring at the magnificent diamond where it sparkled in the morning sunlight. Next to it lay Gran's picture, where she'd left it earlier. Natalie had no doubt this was the necklace in the picture. But could it be magical? Seeing it around her grandmother's neck gave it an air of legitimacy. Maybe there was something more to it, maybe she wasn't hallucinating.

She wrapped her arms around herself and a silky sensation grazed her elbow. She glanced down at the panties in her hand. Jeez, she was still half-naked. She'd bent to put them on when a not-so strange, moist feeling between her legs registered. *Oh crud.*

She held her breath. Her stomach clenched and a shiver of alarm crept up her spine. With a hesitancy born of dread she inched her fingers between the folds of her pussy.

Oh my God.

She withdrew her fingers and stared at the creamy substance. No, this couldn't be happening. This wasn't her own natural wetness. This was a man's...

"Oh my God! He *is* real!" She sank to her knees on the deep pile carpet. It wasn't a dream. She'd not only had sex, she'd had *unprotected* sex with...with...some sort of genie of the necklace. Could she get pregnant from an illusion? No, of course not. She was on the Pill. Could she get a disease? After all, she didn't know who that genie had been with.

Even as the words entered her head she discarded them. In her heart she knew he hadn't been with anyone except her. The way he'd come to her in her dreams, the way he touched her, the caring look in his eyes. No, he wasn't the type of genie who slept around. He'd only been with her. The thought warmed her and she almost smiled. He was everything she'd ever longed for in a lover, everything except for the fact that he wasn't real. Or was he?

She looked at her wet fingers then the necklace lying innocently on the bed next to the pictures of Gran. Okay. She needed some answers and it appeared the only way she would get them was from the genie of the necklace. But first things first.

She took a quick shower and dressed. This time in jeans and a conservative button-down shirt. No easy access for roving fingers.

Sitting cross-legged on her bed, she glanced at her grandmother's pictures. *Oh, Gran, I wish you'd told me about this necklace*. She ran her fingers around the edge of the picture frame, delaying the inevitable. Would it be better if she just dropped the necklace back in the jewelry box and hid it in the bottom drawer? Probably. Did she want to see her dream lover again?

She leaned her head back and studied the blank ceiling. A warm glow wound its way through her, invading her with the feel of his insistent hands on her body, his hot mouth on her throat, his hard cock pumping inside her. *Yes. Yes, I want to see him again. Very much.*

She glanced at Gran's picture. "Well, here goes." Her fingers trailed down the length of the chain but stopped before reaching the diamond. They lingered on the antique gold, hesitating. Inhaling and exhaling to steady her nerves, she closed her eyes and brushed the stone with her fingertips then clasped it tightly in her palm.

"Why did you leave, *querida*? Why did you release the stone? I was afraid you wouldn't call me back."

The hurt and pain was plain in his husky baritone. She opened her eyes to find him lounging next to her on the bed as he'd appeared before—naked. He skimmed his knuckles across her cheek, sending a trembling surge straight to her pussy. The deep timbre of his voice had shivers racing down her spine. Yes, she did want to see him even if it meant she'd be on the next express train to the loony bin.

"I didn't realize I had to hold on to the diamond to keep you here."

"You don't have to hold it. As long as it touches some part of your delicious flesh I can remain with you. Here." He sat, crowding her, reaching for the buttons on her blouse.

She slapped his hands away. "None of that. I need answers not sex."

He eyed her skeptically, a hint of humor playing around his sensuous lips. "Really, *mi corazón*?"

"Well, no—yes, oh, stop it."

"I was only going to put the necklace around your throat so that the stone could nestle between your beautiful breasts, and then you would not have to hold it like a hungry cat clutching a little bird." Raising his hands, he indicated the buttons. "May I?"

She shrugged and suppressed a shudder of anticipation. "I guess so," she responded, sucking in her breath. Yes, she did want to feel his hands on her again.

He bent over the task and his fingers gently tugged the fabric. His warm breath rippled across the tops of her breasts and her nipples hardened into taut peaks as if his fingers instead of his breath massaged them.

He chuckled. "You may say you need answers instead of sex but your body tells me something else. It wants more than my fingertips grazing your breasts. I think it would like to have my mouth taste those luscious peaks, and perhaps lick every inch of your golden flesh." He placed a soft kiss between her breasts and guided her hand, which still grasped the diamond, to her chest. Brushing her hair over her shoulder, he leaned closer, reaching behind her neck to fasten the clasp. He directed her fingers to snuggle the diamond against her breasts.

"Your hair reminds me of sunset, fiery and wild. I love the feel of it against my body when your mouth explores me." He placed another kiss on her cheek before leaning back. A look of mild surprise crossed his features. "I embarrass you? Your face is now as red as your hair."

Of course she was embarrassed. They both knew he referred to her dream of several nights ago. She had explored him with her mouth—his hard, hot cock, his sensitive balls, his tight, sculpted ass, every intimate inch of him. And here he was live and in person and the length of his pulsing cock left no question that he'd like to rerun that dream.

She reached behind herself for a pillow and covered his erection. "You know, this would be a little easier if you wore more than your birthday suit. It might keep my mind—I mean, your mind, on the matter at hand."

He tossed the pillow aside and her gaze strayed again to his thickened cock. This would take all her willpower but she needed a few answers before she jumped back in the sack with him.

"What do you want me to wear?"

She gulped and shifted her eyes to his face. "Anything. Just so it's something."

"Then imagine me wearing whatever you want. I only come to you like this," he circled his cock with his fingers, "because this is how you want me, how you imagine me."

Her cheeks, already red, now flamed. Yes, she did always imagine him naked and hard and ready. Even now it seemed impossible to think of him any other way. She closed her eyes and tried then giggled as an image of him in a black leather thong danced across her mind.

"Is this what you mean by covering up?"

Her eyes popped open and her breath caught in her throat. A large bulge encased in black leather rested between his thighs. Two thin straps disappeared around his hips. It was one of the sexiest sights she'd ever seen. Raw desire unfurled in her belly and her fingers itched to stroke the sac, to feel the leather, hot from his excitement, to run her tongue down his length.

He snorted and her eyes shot to his. That little mischievous smile played around his lips as if he knew what she was thinking, what she really wanted.

If this was how things worked she'd better imagine something else—fast. Before her eyes the thong morphed into a pair of worn jeans and a black t-shirt. She gawked. "This is incredible. Hmm, on second thought…" The t-shirt vanished to reveal his well-contoured chest and six-pack abs. "Nice. Just one more thing." The button on the jeans opened and the zipper slid down an inch. "There. That should do it. No point in covering everything worth looking at."

He looked down, scratched his navel and laughed. "At least it's more than the thong. I felt like I should be posing for a beefcake calendar. Do you think I could make it as Mr. January?"

She smiled at his humor. Could he be any more perfect? Well, except maybe for the genie part. "I'm sure you'd make a wonderful Mr. January. Now back to business. You still haven't told me who you are."

He took her hands in his, turned them up and kissed the center of each palm. "But you already know who I am, *mi corazón*. I am your one, your only, true love."

She almost laughed except his expression was so serious, his kiss so gentle. One and only true love? Jeez, that sounded like something right out of *The Princess Bride*. Did she get dropped into a fairy tale along with getting a necklace with a genie? "One and only true love? That's quite a claim. Where did you get that idea?"

"Every night when I come to your bed."

She couldn't deny that. She lived for the nights in his arms. But how could she have a one true love who disappeared when she took off a piece of jewelry? "I don't get it. How can you be my one true love when I don't know anything about you? I don't even know your name. By the way, what is it?"

He looked puzzled then thoughtful. "That's part of the challenge. I don't know."

* * * * *

Natalie paced the floor beside her bed, trying not to look at her dream man. "You say you're my one true love but I have to *find you* if I want to stop you from fading away when I take off this necklace? But you don't know who you are? No name, no address, no nothing. I just don't get it. What's there to find? You're sitting smack in front of me." She stopped and faced him, arms akimbo. "Just what kind of a secondhand genie are you?"

He laid the pictures of her grandparents, which he'd been studying, on the bed but continued to lounge. A sheepish expression crossed his face and he shrugged. "I am what I am. I had no choice." He glanced at Gran's wedding picture. "No, that's not true. I had a choice and I chose you."

Her anger faded. No, she wasn't angry. How could any woman be angry with such a charmer? His boyish expression of apology traveled straight to her heart and gave her a warm cozy feeling. She might be perturbed at the circumstances but she certainly was not angry with the messenger. "I'm sorry I snapped at you. You're caught up in this...this...*situation* as much as I am. Right?"

He nodded and patted the bed next to him. She went to him and sat, leaning to rest her head against his chest. His pecs bunched and he wove his fingers through her hair, anchoring her in place. She sighed. When he held her like this, how could she not buy into the whole bizarre story? Her body recognized his touch and in some secret undefined way so did her mind.

She walked her fingers across his abs and circled his navel. "Okay, we can always make up a name for you and so what if I have to wear a blockbuster diamond around my neck for the rest of my life to keep you here. There are worse things. What if you were the genie of a lamp? Wearing that could get awkward."

"It would certainly be a unique fashion statement." He squeezed her and a rush of tenderness washed over her. Hot, handsome, humorous. He really was the perfect man of her dreams.

"Unfortunately, *querida*, it is not that simple."

Her fingers stilled. "What? Is this where the three wishes come in? Or is there a catch? Fairy tales always have a catch, don't they?"

"I should mention there are no wishes, this is not a fairy tale and I am not a genie."

Natalie snuggled closer and let her fingers wander below the open waistband of his jeans. "I kind of figured that."

He grasped her wrist and placed it on his chest. "But you're right. There is a catch. I'm real and I'm here with you now in this form but I also exist outside in the world as a living, breathing person who has a body and a name and a place to live that has nothing to do with a diamond."

"But you *are* living and breathing." She playfully yanked at his chest hair.

"Ouch!"

"See. You're real." She slid her hand to his zipper and began to lower it.

He released her and bounded off the bed. "I can't talk when you do that. Let me try again."

She leaned on her elbows, unable to ignore the sense of panic building low in her belly. His worried glance did nothing to ease her escalating concern. Whatever this catch was it had to mean trouble. Catches always did. "Do you turn into a frog or a hideous monster at midnight?" She tried to keep her tone light and teasing but it fell flat.

He frowned at her, zipped and buttoned his jeans and shoved his hands into his back pockets. "Be serious. I am real in that you can see and hear and feel me but I am just the essence of another man. Somewhere out in the world there is a man who is me. You have to find that man. His body is the mate to my soul. He is your one true love."

Natalie wrinkled her brow. "I don't get it. I thought that honor belonged to you."

"It's complicated and I'm a little fuzzy on how it all works but you are now the owner of the diamond, correct?"

"Yes. I inherited it when my Gran died." *Wait a minute. That was the night he started to appear.* "You showed up in my dreams the night of her funeral—after her will was read. Is that what triggered it?"

He shrugged. "Most likely, if that made you the owner. Now in order for the diamond to work you must locate my counterpart in the real world. Then I, er, *we* will be yours forever."

She sat upright. "What? Is this some kind of fairy tale ménage à trois? What do you mean *we*?"

Anger flashed in his eyes and his mouth flattened to a thin line. "Do you think I would share you with another man? That I would stand by and let another man touch you? You are mine." As fast as an attacking panther he was on her, leaning over her, his fists jabbed into the mattress on either side of her shoulders, his face a mere inch from hers, his eyes narrowed to alarming slits.

"You... Are... To... Find... Me. Do you understand?" His whispered growl was more telling than any shout.

"Y-yes. I got it."

His eyes opened wider then flickered down to her mouth. His lips moved to hers. She shifted slightly to give him easier access, tension fluttered in her stomach. He hovered for an instant, drawing out the anticipation. She waited. The ache to have him touch her grew so quickly she would explode if he didn't take her. She slid her arms around his shoulders and pulled him down on her, his weight crushing her into the mattress. Their lips met at the same time their bodies melded together. She spread her thighs and he nestled himself between them.

Something sharp bit into her shoulder. She shifted but that only made the pain worse. He moved with her and his weight pressed her harder into the object. Hating to lose the feel of his lips on hers, she broke the kiss.

His mouth trailed across her jawline to nip her earlobe. "Wait. Stop." She clasped him by the shoulder and pushed.

He leaned back then leveraged himself off her to lie next to her. "Did I hurt you, *mi amor*?"

She sat and twisted to see the problem. The closed frame with Gran's pictures lay on the bed beneath her shoulder. Natalie rolled her eyes. It was bad enough she'd had sex on Gran's bedroom floor. The least she could do was not have it on top of her grandmother's picture.

Rubbing her shoulder, she picked up the frame. "Say. If I inherited this diamond from Gran does that mean Granddad was a genie of—" His frown and winter cold eyes stopped her. *Right. No genies.* "What I mean is was Granddad like you? He was Gran's one true love, wasn't he?"

"Probably." He pushed himself off the bed and moved to lean against the doorjamb. "Were they happy together?"

"Happy? They were ecstatic. Here, just look at their wedding picture." She turned the frame and opened it.

He stepped closer. "Nice-looking couple but I prefer the one of him not wearing the monkey suit. He looks more relaxed in casual clothes."

"Casual cloth—? What are you talking about?" She turned the picture then dropped it on the bed and clutched the diamond where it rested between her breasts. Her heart pounded and a wild rushing sounded in her ears. *Oh my God. This is impossible.*

Staring back from what should have been the single picture of her grandmother were both her grandparents. Gran still had that moony expression on her face but she no longer stared into space. Granddad now posed in the exact spot where she looked.

"Something wrong?"

She pointed to the open frame. "H-how come he's in the picture now and he-he wasn't this morning?"

"Maybe he was there but you couldn't see him. You've never looked at it while wearing the necklace, have you?"

She shook her head and studied her granddad. He seemed thoroughly at ease with his hand resting on Gran's shoulder.

"Maybe that picture was taken before your grandmother found him."

The husky tone of his voice brought her out of her fog and a tiny smile brushed her lips. "Gran always said he'd been right under her nose but she never noticed him. I assumed he'd grown up near her, not that she needed to own a diamond to see him."

"Which reminds me. You need to begin your search, otherwise you'll never find me." He held out his hand and pulled her into his arms.

She skimmed her palms up his chest and glided them around his neck. The rough texture of his chest hair prickled her fingertips and she buried her head in the crook of his shoulder, letting the heat of his body surround her. "What's the rush?"

Her nipples puckered at the touch of his lips on her temple. There was a lot to be said for this one true love thing.

His arms wrapped her in a blanket of sensuality, tugging her close to feel the hard thrust of his erection against her stomach. Genie or not his body was hot and hard in record time just like any red-blooded male.

"I hate to stop just when things are getting interesting, *cariña*, but there is another *catch* to the diamond you should know about."

"Why don't you explain it to me while you take off my clothes?" She gently clasped his earlobe between her teeth and tugged. A wicked thought popped into her mind. In the next second he was naked—just like she imagined him.

"Very funny." He ran his hands down her back and clasped her bottom tighter to him. "The catch is, *mi amor*, we're running out of time. If you don't find me before the sun sets twice, I will vanish like smoke in the wind."

Chapter Four

ဢ

Natalie raced around her room. "I don't believe it. You knew I had only two days and you didn't say anything? We should have been figuring out how to find you — with, I might add, the pathetically miniscule amount of information we have. Instead you let me screw away half the day." She stopped and fixed him with what she hoped was a smoldering stare. She hadn't had much opportunity to smolder during the day lately. "Not that it was a bad thing."

If she was going to meet her one true love she had to look halfway decent. She needed to change her clothes, brush her hair, put on some makeup and who knew what else. And she had to do it fast. She glanced in the mirror over her bureau. Her hair wasn't too bad and the jeans were okay but the tailored shirt had to go. Something a little more revealing, more eye-catching was needed. Eye makeup! Eye makeup and blush!

Her mysterious man lounged on her bed. She caught his heated look in the mirror and smiled. At least he had a reflection so he wasn't an evil vampire kind of genie. That had to be good news.

He stroked his hard cock as he watched her. Whether he was issuing an invitation or just doing a mindless guy thing it still had the same effect.

"So where do we start?" she asked.

His cock jutted from his body as his eyes focused on her breasts. "Obviously we go where there are a lot of people. That will improve our odds."

She tamped down her rising lust and strode to the closet. Pulling out two blouses, she held them up for his inspection. "What do you think?"

"The green. It matches your eyes perfectly. And," he added with a gleam in his eye, "it will let me look at your delectable cleavage."

Little butterflies invaded her belly at his words even as she tried to ignore them. He was one smooth guy but she needed to keep her mind on the mission. She unbuttoned her blouse to change into the flowing emerald green top.

"Don't stop there, *querida*. We can spare a few minutes more, can't we?" He dropped his knee on the bed to give her a better view of his straining erection as he continued to stroke it.

No doubt about it. This was an invitation she wanted to accept. "As much as I would like to I think I'd rather find the real you so I can have you and that lovely hard cock for the rest of my life. You know, it would help if you'd put some clothes on so we—" She stopped at his twinkling look. "Oh, sorry. I forgot."

The temptation to imagine him again in that thong almost got the better of her but she dressed him in worn jeans, and this time left on his black t-shirt.

"It doesn't matter if I'm dressed. No one can see me but you."

"Another catch, huh? This just keeps getting better."

"I think so." He adjusted his crotch in the now too-tight jeans.

So much for sarcasm. "Well, you still have to wear something or I'll be too distracted." She finished changing her blouse, turned back to the mirror and quickly applied her makeup. "I realize you don't know your name but I have to call you something. It's getting a little weird." *Like this whole thing could get any weirder.* "Any preferences?"

A small smile curled his lips. "You can call me *mi corazón*, my heart, *mi amor*, my love, *mi cariño*, my darling, *mi —*"

She laughed. "I was thinking more along the line of 'Bob' or 'Harry' or 'Steve'. Something a little less mushy."

He frowned. "I can't say I'm fond of Bob or Harry but I could live with Steve."

"Then Steve it is." She rather liked that name — simple, solid yet sexy.

He continued to lounge on her bed like he hadn't a care in the world. Wasn't he concerned about what would happen if she failed?

"For a guy who is searching for his one true love you show a distinct lack of enthusiasm. What happens if I can't find you? That vanishing catch seems pretty yucky. What really happens to you? Do you go somewhere like a bus terminal and wait?"

"I don't know what will happen but I imagine it will not be pleasant. The diamond will acquire a new companion for the next owner. It's rather single-minded and handles only one woman at a time — the current owner. As I understand it I'll simply fade away."

"No! That is not going to happen." She jumped on the bed next to him and wrapped her arms around him. "We *have* to find you. I am not going to spend the rest of my life without you."

He stroked her hair and kissed her forehead. "What will be will be, *cariña*. We think we can change destiny by our actions but we are only small, insignificant specks in the vast wheel of the universe."

She slid off the bed and grabbed his hand, pulling him with her. "That may be so but this insignificant speck is going to do whatever she can to make sure you are her destiny. Come on. It's a gorgeous day. Why don't we walk downtown? People will be out shopping or enjoying the park. I know we'll get lucky. You'll be waiting for me on the first corner."

Three hours later Natalie plopped into a wrought iron chair at an upscale Cuban café. The outside patio teemed with customers but she managed to snag a table by the street so she could keep an eye on the steady stream of passersby. The aroma of dark pungent coffee mingled with the faint colognes and perfumes of the patrons—an interesting yet pleasant mix.

"Steve" slouched in the chair opposite her. As their search had lengthened his previous lighthearted attitude sobered. Her attitude wasn't much better. They'd walked their feet off through town and several times around the park.

"Maybe we're going about this all wrong. Maybe we should try a really high traffic area like the mall or—God forbid—Wal-Mart. Though I've got to tell you my ego's going to take a major hit if you're the cashier in the express aisle there."

A shadow fell over the table and she glanced up to see a young waiter eying her suspiciously.

"Can I get you something, *bella doña*?" He placed a cocktail napkin in front of her.

"Yeah, I'll have a cappuccino, low-fat, grande."

The waiter's eyebrows wrinkled.

Steve chuckled. "What? You think this is Starbucks? There are no low-fat cappuccinos here. Tell him you want a *café con leche* before he throws you out. You'll like it. It's a bold coffee with scalded milk."

She grinned sheepishly at the waiter. "On second thought make that a *café con leche*." She turned to Steve. "Do you want one too?"

The waiter coughed. "Thanks for the thought but you don't have to buy me anything. I get all I want for free. My uncle, he owns this café."

Steve chuckled. "Remember, *cariña*, he cannot see or hear me."

Natalie wanted to give herself a head slap for forgetting *that* catch but it would probably only make things worse. She shot the waiter another self-conscious grin. "Oh, okay, never mind then."

The waiter, who had to be ten years her junior, flashed her a wide smile. "You're new here. I've never seen you before. I get off in a couple of hours. Why don't you hang around and maybe we can, ah, go somewhere then. I know a great place where we could get to know one another."

Steve's burst of laughter didn't make her feel any less dopey. "Try to get out of this one, *bebé*."

As if this day wasn't strange enough, now she was fielding come-ons from an adolescent Don Juan who addressed all his comments to her breasts. "Um, yeah, we'll see. I'll just have the *café con leche* for now. Thanks."

"Coming right up, *señorita*." The waiter gave her a parting wink that might have been sexy coming from someone who wasn't wearing a Menudo t-shirt and his baseball cap on backward. On this kid the wink looked like a nervous tic.

"Stop laughing," she hissed, swiveling her head to see if anyone was watching. They were.

"Sorry, *mi amor*, but you had such an expression of shock I couldn't help myself. Who knows? Maybe that was your one true love not yet out of puberty."

"Spare me, please." A thought struck her. "You do eat and drink, don't you?"

He gave her a thoughtful look. "I can't say that I do. I'm not hungry even though I've haven't eaten all day. But I can't seem to shake the urge to order a beer."

Hmm, probably just a guy thing. "Do you feel the urge to watch ESPN?" She fiddled with the cocktail napkin, ripping off small pieces from each corner.

"What?"

"Never mind. Bad joke." She scanned the street, zeroing in on every tall, dark-haired man that walked by. Nothing.

With each passing minute her heart sank. She wasn't at the panic stage yet but the impossibility of it all settled around her. How could she find a man she knew nothing about? Where did she even begin her search when all she knew was what he looked like?

A large warm hand covered hers and she stopped tearing the napkin. "Don't be discouraged, *mi corazón*. We will find him. Forget what I said about destiny. I cannot believe the universe is so cruel to give us the diamond and then withhold its promise."

"Here you go, *mamacita*." The waiter placed a cup with a steaming liquid in front of her. He made a tsk-tsk noise with his tongue and scraped up the pile of torn napkin. "I talked to my uncle. If it slows up he'll let me off an hour early."

Steve barked a laugh so loud she was sure everyone in the café heard him. *Catch or no catch.*

Natalie forced herself not to roll her eyes. "Actually I'm supposed to meet someone. I should have mentioned it before. You haven't seen a tall man, longish black hair? Mid-thirties?" She glanced at Steve and her heart lurched. His loving expression reached out and caressed her. Her voice faltered. "His skin is the color of melted caramel and he has deep, jet-black eyes with little gold rings around the pupils that glimmer when he —"

"Damn. The guys said I was dreaming. No way a *bella ángel* like you would make a pass at me."

Natalie shot a look at the disappointed waiter. She'd totally forgotten he was there. "Oh, I'm so sorry. I didn't mean to —"

"Hey, it's for the better. My girlfriend, if she found out I was sharing myself with a hot *mamacita* she'd cut me." He shrugged. "I haven't seen your date but you just described almost every Latino man in the city. Dozens of them stop here every day."

She wrapped her fingers around her cup as the realization hit her. "I guess I have. Never mind. Come to think of it, I'm not sure he'll be here." She bit her lower lip to ward off the urge to cry. The kid was right. Her search was hopeless.

"Well, if you change your mind," the waiter tossed over his shoulder, "I can always tell my girlfriend you're my teacher and I'm working on extra credit." He gave her the eye-tic wink and sauntered inside the café.

Steve pried one hand from the cup and entwined his fingers with hers. "The day is not over. Drink your *café*. You'll feel better."

"But what if I don't find you and you disappear? What am I supposed to do knowing that for the rest of my life anyone I date, anyone I'm at all attracted to is not meant to be with me? Evidently this is a one-shot deal. Anyone else is a runner-up."

"Shhh. People are staring."

Natalie lifted her head and shifted her attention around the enclosed table area. Yup, she was the center of attention. She snatched up the coffee cup and put it to her lips. "I guess they don't get too many crazy ladies in here," she muttered before taking a sip. The aroma of the rich, dark mixture brought to mind Sunday mornings sitting here drinking coffee and reading the newspaper with Steve or whomever he turned out to be. The coffee warmed her as it slid down her throat.

The sun hung low in the sky, bringing a slight chill. She shivered. In a few minutes the first sunset would be over. She closed her eyes but the tranquil picture of endless Sunday mornings vanished. Now she sat alone in the café, her hair gray and her face lined with wrinkles because she'd refused to accept any man who was not her one true love. A deep sadness washed over her. *No, I won't let it be that way.*

She opened her eyes and placed the cup on the table. Steve still held her hand. The look of concern in his unfathomable black eyes strengthened her resolve.

"Come on, we're going back to the house, get my car and head to the mall. We still have one more sunset and I *will* find you."

Chapter Five
ဢ

"Don't be sad, *mi corazón*, we have time."

Natalie shuffled up the stairs to the darkened front porch, fighting the tears that edged her eyes. She would not cry. She would not give up. They'd searched the mall until it closed then wandered into Wal-Mart where—mercifully—Steve's counterpart was not stocking shelves. After that they'd hit every bar and dance club they could find.

"We have tonight together." He stood behind her as she turned the key to open the door. His heated breath grazed her shoulder before he lifted her hair to nibble just above the heavy chain of the necklace.

"I can recognize cajoling, you know. You're trying to distract me."

"Is it working?" His voice was low and husky, sending shivers of promise down her spine. When she stepped inside he crowded in behind her, shutting the door and pulling her into his arms.

She lowered her head to his chest. "Yes. It's working."

His hands slid under her blouse and caressed her nipples through the fine lace of her bra. Already puckered from the chill night air, they throbbed at his touch. His mouth found hers and he invaded as he had so many times in her dreams. Only now she was caught up in another dream. Her nightly lover was real and yet he wasn't. Despair washed over her. Unless a miracle occurred by this time tomorrow he would be gone.

"*Querida*, forget your thoughts. I am here now. Kiss me. You know what I want," he rasped, nibbling her lower lip. "Put your tongue in my mouth. Let me taste you."

Natalie ignored the ache in her heart and gave herself over to the moment. Her dream lover was here and she needed him more than ever before. Darting her tongue into his mouth, she stroked the inside of his cheek for only an instant before his tongue found hers to dance and duel in an erotic ballet.

He wove his fingers through her hair, holding her in place to slant his mouth across hers. Wrapping his other arm around her, he pulled her flush against him, rotating his hips so she could feel his hard erection. His assault was both demanding and gentle as he guided her through a familiar seduction. Her body blended with his, welcoming every caress, every contact with his sleek, tight muscles.

In one motion he turned, pressing her back against the front door, and leaned heavily into her. Her mind whirled as she drank in the feel and taste of him. He sucked her tongue farther into his mouth then stroked and circled it with his own as if begging her to understand his desperate need to possess her.

The heat coiling in her belly threatened to ignite into a blistering inferno when he again pressed his heavy cock against the soft notch of her thighs. Desire as luminous as her diamond enfolded her, threatening to consume her. She pulled her mouth from his and sucked in a deep lungful of air. His harsh breathing echoed in the front hall. When he placed his forehead on hers and aligned every inch of their bodies her mind spun out of control. The intimate contact with both his body and his spirit proved he belonged to her just as passionately as she belonged to him.

His hands found her hips then slid up her back. In a second both her blouse and bra disappeared into the darkness of the hallway. His palms hovered a whisper above her sensitized nipples. She arched to brush the burning tips against his hands but he pulled back.

Why wouldn't he stroke her, lick her, suck her? She was about to clasp his hands and pull them to her breasts when another dream crossed her mind. With a whimper of need she knew why he waited.

"Please, touch me. I need to feel your mouth on my breasts. Please," she pleaded, with the remembered knowledge that the more she begged the more aroused he became. "Suck me. Do whatever you want with me. I'll do anything to please you."

With a strangled growl his mouth came down on her breast. His teeth clamped around her distended nipple and tugged. Her fingers entwined in his shaggy hair, anchoring his head. His hand came up and caressed her other breast with a gentle, loving touch. Moisture pooled between her yearning folds and her clit throbbed with a delicious agony. Pleasure-pain shot through her as he roughly nipped one nipple and pinched the other.

"Oh God, don't stop." Pleasure like she'd never known tore through her. He rolled her nipple between his fingers and pulled. All the while his mouth sucked and teased the other. Natalie squirmed, squeezing her thighs together to lengthen the sensations rocketing to her clit.

"You are greedy tonight, *mi corazón*. Have no fear. I will give you everything you want." He lifted his head and trailed his hot tongue around the diamond before kissing his way along the heavy gold chain to the delicate crook of her neck. His heated words seared her and she let out a low murmur of need.

The soft fabric of his t-shirt scraped her sensitized nipples. Shirt? He still wore his shirt? She imagined him without it and immediately his aroused flesh melded with hers.

He chuckled. "The shirt is gone but you left the jeans? Don't you want to feel my naked body against yours?"

Oh, she did. But first she wanted to be naked, to feel the worn, soft denim against her bare thighs, his hard, straining cock fighting the zipper as it pulsed against her belly. "But I'm not naked," was all she could moan through her kiss-swollen lips.

"A situation easily remedied." He smoothed his large hands across her stomach to unbutton her jeans then traced small circles below her navel as the zipper slowly lowered.

She arched her back then wiggled when he scraped his fingernail across the top of her thong. "Oh, *bella querida*, what you do to me." He knelt and hooked his fingers into the belt loops of her jeans, pulling them to the floor. The sensation of the cool air in the hallway meeting her burning flesh sent a tingling shiver to her clit. Her slick hot juices flowed between her folds and she ached for his mouth to find her wet slit.

In moments she wore only her thong. She inhaled in a vain attempt to steady her nerves. Wrong move. The scent of Steve's hot, aroused body filled her, surrounded her, enveloped her. Oh God, how she needed this man.

He leaned up on his knees, placing a soft kiss in the center of her thong, then flicked his tongue along the lacy edge and inhaled deeply.

"The scent of your pussy beckons me. It arouses me as much as your touch." His hot breath lingered over her sensitized flesh.

She spread her thighs wider, silently begging for more. Silky puffs of air fanned her mons but he didn't move. He was close, so close but remained motionless.

"What are you waiting for?" Gasping and flushed, she barely recognized the strangled cry as her own.

He answered in a rough growl. "You know what I want, *bebé*."

Her muzzy brain heard but couldn't process his statement. She thrust her hips closer to his panting mouth. He had her in such a frenzied state she couldn't remember anything, couldn't comprehend anything except her desperate need for his touch.

"Not until you beg me, *cariña*," he growled.

"Please. Eat me. I want your lips between my thighs. I want to feel the heat of your tongue licking my pussy, your fingers sliding inside me."

He answered by nipping her through the thong. The sheer lace offered no resistance when he pulled back. A soft ripping sound reached her ears and then fevered lips brushed her moist thatch. He nuzzled her, blowing wisps of blistering air across her slick folds. Anticipation burned through her, roiling low in her belly before erupting in an inferno that threatened to consume her.

Two sweat-slicked hands clasped her thighs, widening them. Another rip sounded and her thong hung by a thin band from her hips, leaving her pussy exposed beneath the remaining shreds of lace.

"*Bella, querida, bella.*"

His damp palm stroked down her calf to clasp her ankle and lift it, angling her trembling thigh over his shoulder. Leaning heavily against the door, she sighed and squeezed her eyes closed. "Please…"

His fingers spread her glistening folds and she reveled in the intensity of his motions. A rough fingertip grazed her clit, sending a tremulous shudder through her entire being. "Please. I can't wait any longer."

Soft lips replaced the fingertip as he gently kissed her engorged clit. Instinctively she arched toward his mouth. The pressure of his rough tongue increased and he demanded more. He sucked her clit, pulling the stiff nub with his lips. His fingers circled around her leg and delved into her dripping folds from behind. He worked her pussy with his relentless mouth and invading fingers just as he had done so many times in her dreams. The growls from deep in his throat had her shifting and stretching so she could offer him more of her burning flesh.

She gripped his shoulders tighter as his heated tongue lapped the length of her channel before centering once again over her clit. Her nails bit into his hard, dampened flesh. She couldn't stop herself. The sensations he pulled from her were too extreme, too acute for her to feel anything but the intense eruption building deep inside her. He captured her overly sensitized clit between his teeth and tugged. Wave after wave of surging pleasure crashed over her. She clung to his shoulders, riding out the surge of the glorious climax.

Just when she knew her trembling leg muscles would fail her he grasped her hips to pin her against the door. He stood and she rocked against him, craving the feel of his body. His mouth slanted over hers, raw and demanding. The taste of her own essence greeted her when she opened her lips for his onslaught.

"My jeans. Get rid of my jeans." His groan held a note of desperation. In her mind's eye she pictured him naked and suddenly his thick cock pulsed against her mons. His sac hung low, brushing her thigh, heavy with need. She reached, skimming her hand down the length of his hard cock to cup and gently massage his balls.

He rested his head in the crook of her shoulder. Arching his back and spreading his legs, he allowed her better access to his heated flesh. "You make me *loco, cariña*." They stood in silence with only the sound of their strained breathing filling the hallway. She slid her other hand between them to clasp his cock as it throbbed and pulsed against her. How she loved the feel of his sex. Primal instincts took over and she pumped him, running her thumb over the velvet-soft tip of his cock. She moistened her finger with a drop of slick hot fluid and slathered it over his swollen head.

"Much more of this and I will come on your belly." He gripped her wrists and guided her hands to his shoulders then skimmed his palms over her breasts and down her sides to cup her bottom.

When he bent his knees to lift her she braced her back against the door and wrapped her shaking legs around his lean hips. The smooth head of his cock probed her pussy before gliding halfway into her dripping slit.

He held himself still, driving her mad with a heated longing for more. The words were on her lips to urge him to hurry when she remembered. "Please..." she pleaded, "please, I need all of you. Please fuck me hard. Let me know you're real."

With a growl from deep in his throat he pulled out to the tip of his engorged head and thrust in up to his hilt, grinding his pelvis against hers. She cried out at the exquisite invasion and clamped her muscles tightly around him, pulsing her insides in rhythm with his throbbing cock. A wild, trembling need took hold of her, a primitive need that demanded he give her every part of himself.

"I am real and I want it hard too." He drew back his hips, breaking the silent dance and thrust into her again...and again.

She clung to him, burying her face against his shoulder. A slick sheen of sweat covered his body and she flicked her tongue, tasting the salty result of his arousal. His excitement permeated her every cell as he drove into her, each plunging motion stronger than the last. Her legs locked around his hips. His fingers dug into her bottom, pulling and pushing her with each demanding thrust.

The familiar whirlwind took hold of her soul, lifting her higher and higher until her body shattered into a thousand diamonds of light. She clung to him, drawing out every shock wave and crying out with the raw intensity that filled her. Through the fog of her climax his strangled shout rumbled in her ears and his hot, thick seed filled her.

* * * * *

Natalie rolled over to stare at the sleeping man beside her. He lay on his stomach, his face turned away, an arm draped across her breasts. His wiry hair tickled where his legs entwined with hers. Dark hair brushed the nape of his neck and she imagined a lock of it falling across his forehead. She inhaled a slow breath, taking in the scents of sex and satisfied male.

Looking down the length of his body, she admired the rippling muscles of his taut, sleek back, his tight, sculpted butt and the steely contours of his thighs. He'd made love to her throughout the night. She didn't always understand his whispered endearments or the low, guttural comments he made in Spanish but she did understand he needed her. Yesterday he'd called her many tender names but it wasn't until he'd rasped *te amo*—I love you—in her ear that she understood how deeply his feelings ran.

Last night had proven she could not go on without him. No one could replace him. A fierce sense of possessiveness welled up inside her. She didn't want to settle for some "also-ran". She wanted Steve or whatever his name turned out to be. And if she couldn't have him then she would end up the wrinkled, gray-haired old woman she imagined at the café yesterday.

But what could she do in one day? Not even a whole day—only 'til sunset. Maybe she could wear the diamond and hold on to him at sunset. Maybe then he wouldn't vanish. But what if he did?

Get a grip, girl, you're working yourself into a panic. You need to think this out logically.

That was it. She needed a clear head. A run. That always worked. But what if he woke up? He'd want to come along. She imagined him wearing only running shorts and Nikes...and then he was. Her breath caught in her throat. He was so irresistible she wouldn't be able to concentrate.

He stirred, his Nikes scraping against her naked calf. Quickly she imagined him naked again, hoping he'd remain in dreamland, light sleeper that he was. Every time she'd rolled over last night his hands were on her, his lips nibbling her, murmuring his need for her, whispering promises in Spanish. She'd have to sneak out without waking him.

Forgive me, my love.

She reached behind her neck, unfastened the clasp and removed the necklace, careful not to touch the diamond.

His sleeping form shuddered. His head snapped toward her. His eyes flew open. The look of disappointment and betrayal in them as he vanished had her reaching for the magnificent gemstone. She stopped. It was only for a short time while she gathered her wits.

Quickly, before she changed her mind, she placed the necklace under her pillow. She jumped into her running attire and was out the door in five minutes.

She pounded her way toward the park. The crisp late-morning air stung her lungs and she welcomed every sharp breath. The sun slanted through the new spring leaves emerging from the branches overhead, casting spidery shadows on the asphalt path. With each step her thoughts cleared and she focused on the situation.

That she was madly in love was a given. As insane as it seemed "Steve" was somehow the soul of the man she was destined to find happiness with, and she was more than okay with that. How to find the body to go with that soul remained the issue.

Another thought struck her. Shanice planned to crash at Natalie's later to hide out from her mother. But what if Natalie didn't find Steve's counterpart before then? This could be their last time together. As much as she wanted to help her friend, she wanted to be with Steve more. Maybe she could say she had a headache? She tossed out that idea the minute it crossed her mind. No way could she lie to her best friend by no way could she not be with Steve. She couldn't leave him in necklace limbo. She had to put the diamond on the minute she got home.

But could she handle Steve and Shanice in the same room? Could she even hold a conversation without revealing Steve's presence? What if Steve started talking or touching her? She'd had a difficult time maintaining her composure in front of that waiter yesterday when Steve was with her. She'd sure never fool Shanice.

The questions pounded through her brain to the beat of her shoes pounding on the running path in the park. With each step another problem swirled through her thoughts.

An hour later she still hadn't solved either of her dilemmas. Cooling down with a walk through town, she spied the café from yesterday. The heavenly aroma of fried dough and cinnamon with an underlying scent of rich coffee wafted in the air. She glanced at her watch. Shanice's shift wouldn't end until late afternoon but Steve was sure to be upset when she returned. A nice cup of coffee and an order of *churros* would go a long way toward fortifying her. Not that he would do anything but a large dose of guilt had followed her all morning. She wasn't quite ready to face his disappointment in her for taking off the necklace.

The outdoor yard held a mix of patrons—small children with their indulgent parents, seniors enjoying the spring morning and other runners rewarding themselves.

She stood at the little gate, searching for a free table. Sunday morning business was even more brisk then Saturday afternoon—not an open table in the place. Oh well, maybe she could get an order to go.

"*Mamacita*, so you have changed your mind and come back to proposition Naldo."

Natalie turned in the direction of the voice. Her waiter from yesterday squeezed through the closely placed tables to reach her, pointedly looking her up and down. "Legs as long as yours should be illegal."

She would have felt self-conscious in her little neon pink running shorts and white sports bra but the twinkle in his eye and crooked grin gave his silly advances a certain ludicrous charm. She also noted several other runners similarly attired.

"Your timing is good…and bad. My girlfriend, she is off with her family but my uncle, he will never let me leave with this crowd to be served."

She laughed at the mischievous look in his eyes. "I guess this just isn't my day."

"You will stay so I can appreciate your fine, er, outfit and together we will look for that man who did not come yesterday." He shook his head. "Such a fool."

"I'd love a cup of coffee but it looks like you're full." She gestured, indicting the packed tables.

"Is not a problem. Come. My uncle is taking a break. You can sit with him. I'll tell him you are a regular. He'll never know you're not. He always loves to talk with his regulars." He gave Natalie his odd little wink. "And he will be delighted to have such a *bella doña* share his table." He turned, leaving Natalie little choice but to follow.

They wove their way to the far corner of the yard where she spied a lone man at a small table. His back was to her but there was no mistaking those wide shoulders, the lean hips snugged into a pair of worn jeans and that midnight hair which hung just below the collar of his European-cut navy blue shirt.

The waiter placed a hand on the man's shoulder and leaned in to say something. The man nodded, stood and looked around.

Natalie's stomach clenched into a hard knot. Two dark eyes, eyes that had stared at her in shock and disbelief only that morning, collided with hers. This really was right out of a fairy tale.

Chapter Six
🔊

The beginnings of a smile froze on the man's lips. His piercing black eyes widened then narrowed as if they betrayed him and he could no longer believe them. His gaze drifted downward from her face, inspecting every inch of her, lingering on her breasts, her bare midriff. When he reached the apex of her thighs his eyes flared ever-so slightly before continuing down her legs. Under his scrutiny Natalie's whole body shimmered with excitement. Her nipples tightened, pushing against the soft fabric of her bra.

"Uncle, I know she is a vision of beauty but your manners," Naldo chided.

The man shook his head as if clearing it and with a wave of his hand offered her a seat. "Please, *señorita*, I would be honored to share my table." His lightly accented voice washed over her, reminding her of warm, dark honey. The deep, rich timbre vibrated with her very essence, sending a coil of sensuous longing snaking through her.

Naldo nudged her with his shoulder. "*Bella doña*, my uncle will not bite. Please, sit."

"Yes, of course." In a daze Natalie took the offered chair. Okay, she'd bought into the whole "find the real genie of the diamond" game but in the back of her mind there had always been a niggling doubt. Except here he was—just as Steve had said. His hungry assessment of her and the spark of desire growing in his eyes now left her breathless.

Natalie could only nod when Naldo said he'd bring her a *café con leche* like yesterday and hustled off.

The man extended his hand. "My name is Esteban Santiago. Thank you for gracing my café with your lovely presence." His lips curved into a welcoming smile.

Natalie placed her hand in his. It was large and strong and sent a spasm of electricity straight to her heart. Feeling a bit absurd, she introduced herself to the man she'd spent the night with and had last seen in her bed that morning. Steve had been right. The resemblance was exact. The only thing missing was the sense of familiarity. Despite the look of hunger in his eyes this man had a reserved, almost formal bearing.

"Naldo said you were a regular. Evidently I am spending too much time in the back. I beg your pardon for not meeting you before now. However, there is something strangely familiar about you. As if I've known you in some other…way." His dark eyes raked her body, leaving no doubt as to what that other way was.

He doesn't know me. He doesn't know I'm his one true love. Well, now, this is awkward.

She gave him her best and brightest smile. "Really?"

"Yes, I have a distinct impression of meeting you somewhere else…away from the café… I have this odd feeling you have visited — Never mind, that is quite impossible."

So on some level he knew her but not the way Steve did. Could it be the necklace? She had to touch the diamond before she could see Steve. Could it be that with Esteban she had to touch the diamond for him to know her?

"Um, perhaps you've seen me around town? I've lived here most of my life. Over in the big yellow Victorian house on Windemere?" *Stop babbling!*

His expression changed from sexy to thoughtful. "Big yellow Victorian? Yes, I know it. Nice neighborhood."

He hadn't released her hand but grazed his thumb back and forth across her knuckles. She should pull away but it seemed the most natural thing for him to caress her. Tiny sparks ignited low in her stomach, threatening to explode into sensations she wouldn't be able to hide.

His dark eyes pierced her with an unmistakable promise that stole her breath away. He brushed his knee against her bare thigh and raised a slanted eyebrow. The worn fabric of his jeans reminded her of last night when she'd been naked and Steve hadn't.

The heat swelling between her legs burned white hot. Her clit tingled in answer to his unasked question. It wasn't her imagination. He wanted her even though they'd just met and she knew he was hard and ready — just as she was wet and ready.

He held her gaze like a predatory animal when it has cornered its prey. She should be afraid. He intended to share more with her than simply a table. Her eyes locked with his but there wasn't an ounce of fear in her. Instead she wanted nothing more than to be drawn in to that hungry stare. Yes, she could easily drown in the deep pools of his midnight eyes and never notice or care. Raw need, riveting and hot, shone in those eyes.

His strong fingers no longer toyed with the back of her hand but entwined with her fingers in a lover's grasp. His hands had the rough texture of a man who earned his living. A man who knew his own worth and was not afraid of working up a sweat to see that a job was done right.

Her nipples hardened into rigid peaks. If he didn't do something to ease the pulsing desire that surged through her there was a very real possibility she'd make a fool of herself in the next few minutes. The man of her dreams sat across from her and she could almost feel the waves of male desire cascading over her. He had to realize something extraordinary was happening between them.

He shifted in his chair and Natalie instinctively knew his jeans had become too tight. "I am grateful the café was crowded this morning and that my nephew — Ah, here he is."

"You looked like you could use a glass of water after your run, *mamacita*." He placed it in front of Natalie along with a *café con leche* for each of them. "I thought you could use a refill, Uncle."

"Thank you. You're a good boy, Naldo." Esteban reached and ruffled Naldo's spiky hair. "But you must address the *señorita* with more respect. Such endearments are perhaps a bit too forward coming from one so...inexperienced." Esteban lifted his dark, sensuous eyes to Natalie, leaving her no doubt he considered himself experienced. As ludicrous as it seemed she had the distinct impression Esteban was laying some sort of claim to her, as if he were jealous that any male, even his goofy nephew, would become friendly with her.

Naldo laughed. "I simply take after you, Uncle. I cannot help but appreciate a *bella doña*. She is a feast for the eyes of a poor beggar."

The boy's presence had served to rein in her rampant lust and Natalie couldn't help but smile at his outrageous comment. To cover her amusement she picked up the glass of water.

Still laughing, Naldo reached to remove Esteban's empty cup. The boy's elbow jarred her hand, knocking the glass and spilling it down her front.

"Forgive me! I am such an ox!" Naldo grabbed a stack of napkins from his apron pocket.

Before he could help her Esteban snatched the napkins from his hand and waved him aside. "Don't touch her!"

"It's all righ—" Natalie's gaze clashed with Esteban's. The look of naked lust he returned brought a halt to any further comment.

"I'll tend to our guest. Get a towel and clean the table...please."

Wide-eyed, Naldo looked from her to his uncle and back to her. With an apologetic nod he hurried off. From the corner of her eye she noted the appreciative expressions of male patrons at nearby tables, who had been distracted by the accident. She also noted a few glares directed at both her and the men by their female companions.

Esteban's dark eyes seemed to turn blacker as he focused on the water dripping down her breasts. He licked his lips but otherwise remained frozen in place. Her nipples puckered not only from the icy shower but from the inferno blazing in his eyes.

Her saturated sports bra clung to her breasts and she suddenly remembered what liquid could do to white fabric. Tearing her eyes from his, she shot a quick glance at her bra. Yup, totally transparent. She closed her eyes and willed the heat that was creeping up her neck to disappear. It refused and continued its relentless march upward until her cheeks flamed. Somehow she didn't mind Esteban staring at her dark areolas but now she understood the covert glances and dark looks coming from the other tables.

Crossing one arm over her breasts, she reached for the napkins clutched in Esteban's hand. At her touch he snapped out of his stupor and stood, shielding her from ogling glances with his body.

"Come." He drew her up from the chair. Wrapping a protective arm around her shoulders, he angled her into his chest. His warm body enveloped her in an intimate cocoon. Nothing had ever felt so right as leaning against his muscled chest. It was as if she'd finally come home. His crisp blue dress shirt hinted of spice and coffee and some indefinable male scent that made her want to cling to him and never let go. Being in his arms felt…felt… It felt exactly like being in Steve's arms.

Esteban hustled her into the side door of the café. Avoiding the main seating area, he led her through a sunny hallway lit by skylights. Stopping before a rich mahogany door, he opened it and drew her inside. It clicked closed and they stood together, alone in his office. She assumed it was his office but could not take her eyes from his to check.

He still held her pinned to his side. She no longer needed protection against curious patrons but she couldn't move away. His heart thudded in time with hers and her heightened awareness of him shifted every one of her hormones into overdrive. He was so male, his presence so overpowering.

He snuggled her close, so close she could see the individual hairs in the shadow of his beard. His warm breath fanned across her cheek and he raised his hand to tuck a stray strand of hair behind her ear. A droplet of water dripped onto his fingers and dribbled across the back of his hand. He seemed to remember where he was and released his hold, stepping back slightly.

A large dark blotch stained his shirt where he'd held her. "I'm sorry. I've gotten your shirt wet."

He waved a dismissive hand. "It is nothing."

His eyes wandered leisurely down the length of her body just as they had when he first saw her. In her current condition she felt exposed, naked. She knew he was her true love but he didn't. Until she had a chance to explain she didn't want him to think she'd let just any man peruse her so intimately. She turned away. How did she tell a man she'd just met that he was destined to belong to no one but her? That his very soul had selected her to be his mate for the rest of his natural life? However she did it, it was guaranteed to be one strange conversation.

"Excuse my impertinence, *señorita*. I have no excuse for my behavior except as I have said, I feel we have met before."

Natalie smiled over her shoulder. "You never know." She shivered at the thought of where they had met before—her bed.

"My manners are deplorable. You are not only soaking wet, you are freezing in this air-conditioning." He strode across the office to what appeared to be a closet. "Here. Put this on."

He held up a dress shirt identical to the one he wore and indicated she should step into it.

"But you need to change. I got you soaked."

"Come. I will not have every man out there gawking." His lips turned up in a sheepish grin. "Myself included."

A warmth flowed through her veins and surrounded her heart. Yes, she could very easily love this man. Moving as if in a dream, she stepped into his waiting arms and slipped into his shirt. He placed his hands on her shoulders and turned her to face him.

"You look good in my clothes." He bent his head so close a lock of his hair grazed her forehead. His fingers moved to the shirtfront and he buttoned the top button. When he worked the second one his fingers brushed her breasts. He stopped, his hands hovered. Heat pooled in her belly. Her nipples puckered and her breasts grew heavy. She willed him to cup her breasts, to pull her into his arms and kiss her like he did in her dreams.

His breathing grew harsh, ragged in the silence of the room. She raised her head and found him staring at her through hooded eyes. His gaze shifted from her eyes to her lips. Her knees shook under the intensity of his stare and he grasped her shoulders, steadying her. She clutched at his forearms as he lowered his mouth.

A loud crash sprung them apart. The office door slammed against the wall.

"*Papi*! *Papi*! There you are!"

Esteban released Natalie just as a tiny girl no more than five years old tore across the office and launched herself at him. He caught the child and her thin short arms went around his neck.

"*Papi*, I've been looking for you! Were you hiding from us? *Mami* is so mad."

Natalie froze. *Papi*? *Mami*? Her stomach knotted and her lungs stopped working. Esteban was *married*? She stared at him as he tried to contain the wiggling child. It was like herding cats. Impossible.

"Come on, *Papi*. We have to go. *Mami* is waiting."

Natalie's notice darted to the door where a sophisticated woman leaned against the jamb. Her folded arms and malevolent stare confirmed she was the child's mother — and Esteban's wife. With a disgusted grunt she turned and left.

Natalie returned her attention to the man who only moments ago had turned her world upside down. The child wiggled from his arms and now stood, tugging his hand to make him leave. Even through his swarthy complexion a hint of red tinged his cheeks. This couldn't be happening. He was *hers*. How could he have a family?

"Lucinda, where are your manners? Tell the pretty lady you are sorry."

The child took one look at Natalie, scrunched up her face and burst into tears. "*Mami* is mad. I want to go. Now!"

"I am so sorry. She is usually a pleasant child." Natalie glared at him, unable to speak. He'd just been caught flirting by his wife — no, it had been much more than flirting. He'd been seducing her — and he was apologizing for the little girl's behavior? The son of a bitch *should* be apologizing but not for the child.

He picked up the struggling girl but she continued to squirm. "Will you stay? You need to dry off. I'll send Naldo with a coffee. I will be back shortly."

Natalie bit back a caustic remark and shrugged her shoulders. It was just as well, she probably couldn't say two words without giving in to the overwhelming urge to imitate the child and start bawling herself.

"Please don't go. I need to talk to you." His expression pleaded more than his words and Natalie let the last piece of her broken heart fall to the floor. With an imploring look over his shoulder he carried the squirming child toward the door.

The woman reappeared and threw Natalie a nasty glance then turned and huffed away.

Natalie sucked in her lower lip and stood silently, watching the man of her dreams walk away with his family.

Chapter Seven
ജ

Natalie dragged her feet up the front porch steps and into the house. The stairs to the second floor loomed before her. With a shake of her head she climbed them as if going to the gallows. She'd been swatting away tears since she'd darted out of the café to hide in the anonymity of the crowded park but now she let them flow freely. It had all been a fairy tale from the start. Nothing had been real. How ridiculous to think an old necklace had anything to do with finding the man she would love.

In her bedroom, she glanced at Gran's pictures on the bureau. Sure enough Gran still had the goo-goo-eyed expression and Granddad was nowhere to be seen. She ran her fingers over the blank space where she'd seen her grandfather. "I guess it doesn't always work, does it?" she said to the picture. "Is that why you never told me about the necklace? Still, I'm glad you found Grandad."

The rumpled bed caught her attention. Images of last night flooded back. It had been the most spectacular night of her life, especially since she'd believed it was only the first of many. She'd been so sure she would find Steve's counterpart.

Steve had vacillated between unrelenting passion and aching tenderness but always with the intent of bringing them both pleasure. He'd given and taken and talked of their future together even as she spiraled out of control. She had given of herself in a way she'd never done before, leaving her inner being behind and abandoning herself to his wants and desires.

A picture of Steve's shocked face as she'd taken off the necklace that morning shot through her mind. The hurt and accusation in his eyes paralyzed her now. How could she let him go? Her heart ached at the thought of telling him they couldn't be together, that another woman had found him first. Whether that woman was his one true love didn't matter. She was the one with a child, his child.

More than anything Natalie wished she'd never found the necklace or that she'd left it in the bottom drawer and never touched the diamond. Then she wouldn't know about the wonderful man she couldn't have.

She could still put the necklace back. She didn't have to face him, didn't have to see the anger then the desolation in his eyes when she told him.

The bed came back into focus and she pushed the gutless thought aside. Of course she had to tell him. She couldn't have him fade away thinking she didn't want him.

With all the enthusiasm of attending her own funeral, she shuffled to the bed and lifted the edge of her pillow. The diamond shimmered, mocking her as if it knew she had no choice but to let its spell envelop her. Grasping the ends of the chain, she focused on the side of the bed where she'd last seen Steve before he awoke and vanished. His tousled hair hung like a silken curtain over his forehead, his strong jaw needed a shave and his spiked lashes were way too long and full for any man.

She blew out a deep breath and palmed the diamond.

"Why did you do it, *querida*?"

The bed remained empty. The deep, rich voice came from behind. She began to turn then stopped when his arms encircled her, so strong, so comforting. She closed her eyes, savoring the moment, memorizing his gentle touch, his distinct male scent, how the hard planes of his body molded so perfectly against her. What could she say? No words came so she rested her head on his muscled chest and lived in the moment.

"Why were you gone so long, *mi amor*? You have wasted most of the day."

Should she tell him the abject dread she'd felt about returning? That she'd slunk around the park, crying and not caring who saw? That she'd sat on a bench and stared at nothing, trying to dull the pain in her heart?

"We are running out of time." He placed a soft kiss on her temple.

She could only shake her head at his statement. No, time didn't matter anymore. Their luck had already run out. Shrugging off his embrace, she wrapped her arms around herself and opened her eyes.

"We need to talk—" Her words stuck in her throat. Instead of being naked or in the t-shirt she'd imagined him in yesterday he wore faded jeans and a dark blue dress shirt—in a European cut. She closed her eyes again as a wave of desire washed over her. She'd conjured him up wearing Esteban's clothes. And why not? Wasn't she still wearing an identical shirt? Esteban's shirt?

Quickly, before she could stop herself, she undid the buttons and tossed the shirt on the floor. She didn't need any physical reminders of the man she could not have.

Steve's eyebrows shot up at her actions but she was grateful he didn't press for an explanation. "Talk about...?" he encouraged instead.

"I found him, er, you, er, you know what I mean. I found your counterpart in the real world."

"So the diamond has worked its magic once again. Where is he? We must connect so the diamond can complete its purpose." A sexy smile spread across his face and his eyes took on a smoky seductive glint. He took a step toward her but she avoided his outstretched arms. If he touched her she'd go to pieces.

"It's not that simple. There's a complication."

"The diamond will overcome any complication." He continued his advance so she gave him a look that said "keep your distance". He stopped.

"It's going to have to be a pretty talented diamond to overcome this complication." Her heart slammed against her ribs and a lump choked her throat as she formed the words she still couldn't believe. "You're married. You have a daughter." *There. I actually said it out loud.*

"What? That's impossible. You're mistaken." A dark shadow of incredulity and shock crossed his face and the need to comfort him overwhelmed her. She fought the urge to smooth her hands up his broad chest and around his neck, to rest her head on his strong shoulder again and make the world disappear. Instead she clutched the diamond in her hand and fought against emotions that threatened to bubble over and turn her into a blubbering wreck.

"I saw them this morning...at that café...the one from yesterday. He introduced me. Your daughter's name is Lucinda. She's the most darling little thing." Natalie suppressed a sob. "She looks just like you."

"This can't be. I am meant to be with you." Bewilderment, denial and finally anger chased across his face.

She steeled herself against the unbearable ache in her heart at his reaction. "You're married and I can't be responsible for taking a father away from his child even if that man is supposed to belong to me. I'm sorry."

His eyes blazed and he slammed his palm against the wall. "Where is he? I'll get to the bottom of this. I will not be denied a life of happiness because of some fool."

"It's over, Steve. He's married and there's nothing either of us can do about it. His name is Esteban Santiago. He owns the café."

The corner of Steve's mouth quirked into an ironic grimace.

"What?" she asked.

"You say his name is Esteban. Funny how that worked out."

"Esteban? What's so funny about that?"

"The name you gave me. Steve. Didn't you know that Esteban is Spanish for Stephen?"

She shook her head. "What does it matter?" Turning her back, she fought her own battle with hopelessness, already knowing it was a lost cause.

His heaving breaths filled the room and his arms closed tightly around her, anchoring her back to his front. "*Te amo, mi corazón.*" His rough voice betrayed the depths of his despair.

She knew it was wrong—flat-out wrong—to act on her impulses with another woman's husband but at this moment she didn't care. Steve was supposed to be hers. Right? They still had time before sunset. She couldn't let that time go to waste knowing this would be their last hour together. If that made her a bad person then she was a bad person.

"Put this on me—please. I won't take it off again." She held up the necklace.

His rough fingertips skimmed across her shoulders. Taking the ends of the necklace, he fastened the chain and nuzzled her neck, blowing hot kisses across her shoulders.

Raising her arm to hold his head in place, she wove her fingers through his silky hair as he stroked his hands up and down her sides before sliding them around her naked belly and pulling her against his muscled body. The hard ridge of his cock pressed into her bottom and she shuddered in anticipation.

"I cannot believe the diamond has betrayed us, *mi amor,*" he rasped, continuing to nuzzle and flick his smooth tongue along her throat.

She tilted her head in invitation and pressed her bottom against his swollen penis, allowing her growing need to take over.

A loud chime sounded from the first floor, followed by a demanding knock.

The chime rang again…and again.

"Someone is making a lot of noise downstairs." He trailed his lips down her neck, nuzzling that sensitive spot at the base of her throat.

Natalie's muzzy brain surfaced as the banging increased. "Huh? Oh, it's probably Shanice. We made plans for tonight."

His arms tightened. "You were going to leave without touching the diamond? Without saying goodbye to me?" He ground out, his tone accusatory.

"We made plans *before* I ever found the necklace. I could never have let you go like that."

The knocking escalated into a continuous banging.

Natalie shrugged. "She's usually not that aggressive except when she needs to use the bathroom." Taking a cleansing breath, she extricated herself from Steve's embrace. "I'd better go answer the door. She's not likely to give up if she really has to go."

The doorbell chimed again in rhythm with the drum solo on the door.

"I'll get rid of her and be right back," she whispered, grazing her lips across his cheek, not trusting herself to touch his mouth.

"Make sure she uses the bathroom downstairs. I'll be in the one up here, soaking in that big tub, waiting for you to join me." His devilish grin sent a shiver racing up her spine then back down to tingle her clit with anticipation.

"I'll be right back, my love." She darted down the stairs to open the door before Shanice beat it down.

"All right, I'm coming. Keep your pants—" she swung the door open, "on...?"

"Actually, I had no intention of taking them off—unless you would like me to?" A small smile played across Esteban Santiago's lips. His eyes seemed to hold a hint of relief.

Natalie's knees gave out and she slid against the doorjamb to keep from falling over. It was enough to make her head spin. Didn't she just leave this same man upstairs? Hot and hard and ready to overwhelm her senses with his intimate caresses if only for the last time? And here he was on her front porch with no idea how she felt about him or what erotic times they had shared in each other's arms. How much did her poor little brain have to take?

Esteban moved quickly to catch her, easing her into the house and shutting the door. Rays of dimming sunshine slanted through the upper window, highlighting the chiseled planes of his concerned face.

"Is something wrong? You look like you've seen a ghost." His strong arms curled around her, attempting to steady her. She swayed at his familiar touch. When his rough palms grazed the skin on her back, shards of delicious pleasure shot through her veins, quickening her heartbeat and moistening her pussy—the same reaction she'd had upstairs when Steve touched her.

"I'm okay. I'm just…well, I didn't expect to see you again."

"I asked you to wait. I had…some business to attend to."

Yeah, I saw your business. Who the hell did he think he was coming on to her like this? She should toss him out on his ear and lock the door behind him. No good could come from the way his fingers burned into her flesh, the way her nipples hardened at just the sight of him and the way her pussy dampened and begged for his touch. Most definitely she should get rid of him but her treacherous body ignored the 911 from her brain.

Staring up into his handsome, caring face, all that registered was he belonged to her. The diamond had given him to her. Esteban's gaze explored her face as if searching for someone he remembered from another time, another place. In that moment she knew without a doubt she loved this man. Loved him in whatever form, by whatever name he called himself.

His eyes darkened and his hold on her arms tightened. "The instant I saw you I was drawn to you. I feel you are special to me, as if I've waited for you all my life." He stretched his hand to touch her but hesitated, wordlessly asking permission.

At her almost imperceptible nod his hand traveled up her arm to her shoulder, skimming across the strap of her sports bra to cradle her cheek.

Natalie lost herself in the warmth of his fingers, the delicious scent she knew was his alone—exotic, rich coffees mixed with the faintest aroma, reminiscent of cigar smoke, and tinged with the growing scent of his arousal.

His tall, lean frame hovered within inches of her. Any second he would close the gap and press his hard, muscled chest against the taut tips of her nipples, his hot swollen cock against her pelvis. He bent his head and a ghost of a breath caressed her lips. She parted them, skimming her tongue across her upper lip, preparing herself for his invasion.

His eyes glittered at the sight of her tongue so she repeated the motion across her lower lip. He moved closer. His lips brushed hers when he spoke. "Ah, *cariña*, I want to lose myself in you."

His mouth crushed hers and he leaned full against her, sandwiching her between his aroused, hard body and the front door. He didn't bother with any tentative, exploratory motions. No, he attacked as if he knew what she needed, what she expected, taking her mouth in a blistering kiss. She slid her arms around his back, the smooth texture of his dress shirt humming across her palms. Reaching higher, her fingers traced the line of his muscled back until they dug into his solid shoulders.

His burning tongue dueled with hers, sweeping and twirling until she trembled and writhed against him. Tension coiled deep inside her. He rotated his hips, pressing his hot straining cock against her mons, all the while never letting up on the assault against her mouth. His hand slid beneath her bra, pushing it over her breasts. He cupped one globe and, squeezing it, sent another surge of desire through her. His fingers found her taut nipple and pinched, sending a frenzy of pleasure through her clit. He worked his cock harder, pushing, rubbing, finding her fiery center. He knew every movement, every action that sent her whirling toward a bottomless spiral. All she could do was hang on as her body exploded in a breathtaking crescendo.

Chapter Eight

SO

Natalie opened her eyes to find Esteban's smoky black ones watching her like a python ready to strike. The planes of his face were a study in agony and exultation, his stiff erection, still encased in his soft jeans, pressed against her skimpy running shorts, his warm breath came in labored rasps. Slight beads of sweat formed on his upper lip and she had the primal urge to flick her tongue and taste him. Unable to break the eye contact, she stared into his dark pools, still layered with passion and satisfaction. He didn't move, didn't blink as if waiting for her reaction.

Heat flamed up her neck. Had she totally lost her mind? She'd just had door sex and climaxed with a stranger, a man she'd met that morning. And fully clothed! Well, almost. What the hell had she been thinking? No matter how she rationalized it he did not belong to her. He was someone's husband, someone's father. She had no right to touch him. She pushed away and leaned against the wall.

His gaze lowered and his hungry stare smoldered with desire. The band of her sports bra gripped her chest. *Oh, for Pete's sake*. She tugged the bra, covering her naked breasts. When it brushed against the distended nipple he'd fondled a sharp, titillating sensation streaked to her pussy, extending the aftershock of her orgasm. She held her breath and closed her eyes, willing the surging waves to continue.

Her pussy tingled and if he didn't leave soon she'd forget her resolve—again. She touched her lips, swollen now from his kiss, waiting for the delicious feelings to pass. Reluctantly she opened her eyes and fought to put the decadent experience in his arms behind her. "You have to go."

"I'm sorry. I don't know what came over me. When I touched you I went crazy. That's never happened before." He shielded his eyes and rubbed his temples. "I should be whipped for doing that."

She knew what had come over him. The diamond's magic. "Look, forget it. Just leave."

"No. I can't. I apologize for not returning to the café. I called but Naldo said you'd already left. We had an accident on the way to the airport. Nothing serious but by the time everything cleared up Lucinda and her mother had missed their plane. We had to rebook. The wait was endless." He waved his hands in a typical male sign of frustration. "I've been going *loco* trying to find you."

Anger washed away her embarrassment. Was there no end to this man's audacity? "Trying to find me? You've got your nerve. What do you think I am? Some cheap plaything to amuse you while your wife and daughter are out of town? Get out of my house. Now."

His head snapped up. "Wife and—? I'm not married. Maria is the mother of my child, yes, but we were never married." He drew himself up to his full height as if it would add more weight to his words. "I am not proud of my indiscretion but I am proud of Lucinda and love her very much. As her father I am a large part of her life but Maria? She has no use for me and I have none for her. Everybody knows that." His eyes narrowed. "Especially the *regulars* at my café."

He turned away, shaking his head, and gripped the hall banister with both hands. In the fading light she watched the muscles ripple beneath his fitted shirt, his anger thick in the air. He dropped his head to his chest as if trying to regain his composure. "You berate me for thinking I'm merely amusing myself with you but it is all right for you to think I am the kind of man who would ignore his marriage vow."

Esteban's reprimand was lost. She clung to those two words—*never married*. "You're not married?" Did that tremulous squeak really come from her?

His fingers tensed on the banister then released it. He spun around and speared her with an icy stare. A lock of jet-black hair fell across his forehead. "Of course not. I could never dishonor a wife that way," his voice softened, "or you."

He wasn't married. A daughter wasn't a problem. She could handle him having a daughter. But he wasn't married. For the second time her knees wobbled and gave out but this time Esteban was not as quick and she grabbed the arm of the hall bench and slumped into it. With three quick strides he sat beside her and gathered her in his arms. "*Querida*, are you all right?"

"You're not married."

A slight smile touched the corners of his mouth. "I'm sure I would remember if I was." He squeezed her lightly and folded his arms around her. It felt so right, so perfect, she never wanted to be anywhere but in them.

"Wait a minute, how did you find me? Why are you here?"

"Yellow Victorian on Windemere? It took a while but I finally remembered." The smile faded. "As to why I am here, I hesitate to tell you. You'll think I'm crazy, that I've escaped from some asylum."

"Tell me, please," she whispered not daring to hope. Did he know? Could the diamond's magic have reached out to him?

He tucked her head under his chin as if he didn't want her to look at him. "When I saw you in the café this morning you reminded me of someone. I knew you from somewhere but I couldn't quite place you. When I'd found you'd left I was consumed with a burning need to find you but I didn't know why." He stroked her hair and his warm breath caressed her temple. As she waited his heart hammered beneath her ear, letting her know how her closeness affected him.

"Go on," she encouraged.

His voice lowered to a raspy growl. "For the past month I've had dreams. Strange dreams...erotic dreams. A mysterious lover comes to me and fulfills my every need, physically, emotionally, even spiritually. I've never felt so complete, so...at one with myself as I am with this dream lover."

He leaned back, his expression a montage of confusion, embarrassment and raw desire. "When you opened the door just now I realized where I'd seen you before. You're the woman who haunts my nights, the siren who calls to me and takes me to the heights of ecstasy with her touch. All my self-control, my restraint deserted me. I don't understand. I've never lost my mind like that."

"It's not you." She stroked her hand over his rugged jaw, scraping the stubble of his five o'clock shadow. So she'd guessed correctly. He hadn't recognized her at the café because she hadn't been wearing the necklace but now... How could she tell him they were both caught up in something neither could control?

"And that necklace. You wear it in my dreams." Disbelief rang in his deep voice. He ran his fingers lightly over the stone. "How can it be real? I thought I imagined it."

A fluttering in her stomach sent a sharp prickle to her every nerve ending. Esteban saw the diamond in his dreams. The diamond seemed to have a mind of its own. Steve had alluded to its magic.

"Oh my God! Steve!"

Her eyes shot to the darkening window and her heart leapt to her throat. Extracting herself from Esteban's embrace, she grabbed his hand. "Come on! Hurry!"

She darted up the stairs, dragging him behind her. Running down the hall, she burst into the bathroom. The tub brimmed with water but no Steve. She released Esteban's hand and dashed back to her bedroom. "Steve? Steve, where are you?" The sun had not quite set but it was close. Had something gone wrong? Had he vanished already?

Esteban strode into the room on her heels. "Who's Steve?"

"Steve, oh Steve, my love, please still be here."

"I did not think you would return, *mi corazón*, I was afraid you wished to spare yourself the pain of my departure." At the sound of his voice, she turned to find him lounging on her bed, naked. Quickly, she imagined him in Esteban's clothes.

"What is going on here? Who are you talking to?" Esteban's voice rumbled his anger.

"He can't see you, can he?"

"No, *mi amor*," Steve bounced off the bed and stood before her. "Just like before, only you can see and hear me."

"Can't see who?" Esteban's concerned voice turned mystified. "Are you all right?"

She clasped Esteban's hand. "You know how a few minutes ago you were afraid I'd think you were nuts? Well, I'm hoping you won't think the same about me." Esteban's brow wrinkled but she turned back to his look-alike. The resemblance was extraordinary, right down to the lock of hair falling on their foreheads.

"Oh, Steve, it's okay. He has a daughter but he's not married. He never was. We can be together."

Steve's mouth split into a wide grin and she wanted to wrap herself in the warmth of that smile.

"Natalie? What's going on?"

Her head snapped back to Esteban. It was difficult to separate them. They were different parts of the same man. A man she'd fallen in love with in her dreams. Now that love spilled over into the real world where Steve was somehow a part of Esteban's inner essence and Esteban was the embodiment of Steve's spirit. She reached up and smoothed the lock of Esteban's hair back in place, only to have it stubbornly fall across his forehead again. Oh yes, she loved this man just as she loved the man who'd come to her in her dreams and awakened a new level of awareness in her, showed her how much she had to give.

She concentrated on Esteban's face. The diamond would link them together for the rest of their lives. A true happily-ever-after fairy tale.

"We will be deliriously happy, *mi corazón*. We will have a wonderful life," said Steve. "All that is left is to let the diamond finish its magic before the sun sets. Not a minute too soon either."

Steve's comments snatched her from her thoughts. "What do you mean 'we'?" She turned to stare at him.

"Do you need to sit?" Esteban's deep, rich baritone echoed in her small silent room. He wrapped his arm around her and led her to sit on the bed.

What exactly could this magical diamond do to Esteban? Steve said he was the soul and Esteban was the body but didn't he already have a soul? She couldn't allow anything to interfere with his central being, his inner self. "Will Esteban still be the same man?"

"*Cariña*, we're running out of time. The sun is setting."

"Just answer me. Will he still be the same man? Will he know what's happened to him?"

"Yes."

Natalie let out a long breath.

"And no."

"Stop playing games with me."

"He will not know what happened but he will be the same man. He will have the same memories, the same life but he will have more, so much more than he could ever dream. He'll grow old in the bright sunlight of your love."

"Wait a minute, would he still love me without the diamond?" Maybe she didn't need all this magic and hocus-pocus. After all, Esteban seemed more than attracted to her anyway.

"I'm not some gigolo." Esteban's grip on her arm tightened. "I don't care about any diamond necklace. I'm interested in you, Natalie, and why you appear in my dreams."

Oh great. She'd wounded his masculine pride. "I know. I'm sorry. I didn't mean it that way." She looked past him at Steve and raised an eyebrow, not daring to ask the question again.

Steve's expression saddened. "Remember, *querida*, fairy tales always come with a catch. The magic of the necklace has brought you together but unless you accept that magic, the necklace will keep you apart. He will be infatuated with you for a time then it will fade. He will leave you and spend the rest of his life going from one woman to the next, searching for something but he will never find it. It will elude him like a shadow on a cloudy day. You will grow old and bitter with the knowledge that you could have had everything but chose to throw it away. This is the only chance you both have to find happiness."

She turned to the strikingly handsome, confused man beside her. "Esteban? You know how strange it was finding the woman from your dreams? There are more strange things about to happen." She glanced out the window, only faint rays of sunlight filtered through the night sky. She turned, not even trying to keep the desperation from her voice. "I know we only met this morning but I promise I will love you and cherish you for the rest of my life. This is our only chance at a fairy tale romance."

Esteban's eyes darted from Natalie's face to the diamond necklace. "So this is why you come to me in my dreams? Because you love me?"

"Yes," she said with as much conviction and love she could squeeze into that one small word.

"I have to warn you. I am not successful with romance. Every relationship I have ever had has fizzled out."

A sense of sadness washed over her. So it had started already. He'd wanted to commit to someone but the diamond interfered. It wouldn't allow him to find a lasting relationship with anyone. She brightened. *With anyone except me.*

Smoothing her fingers across his cheek, her eyes locked with his. "I promise you, Esteban Santiago, this relationship will not fizzle out. Ever."

He raised an eyebrow. "I think I understand." He studied her face and seemed to come to a conclusion then grasped her hand. "I am not an impetuous man, Natalie, but I can sense something important is happening here. My dreams, finding you, that necklace. It's all culminating now, isn't it?"

She nodded, unable to summon any words. *Oh, thank God, he understands.*

"All right then, I will go with my gut instinct, with what's in my heart." He brought her hand to his mouth and kissed her palm. His dark eyes remained riveted on her face. "I too promise I will love and cherish you. Whatever happens in our lives I want it to happen to us together."

She tore her attention from Esteban and turned her head to watch Steve approach. He bent and brushed a soft kiss across her lips. "*Te amo, mi corazón.*"

She stared transfixed by the love shining brightly in his eyes. The diamond nestled between her breasts warmed then grew hotter. She flinched but her gaze never faltered. The diamond glowed, bathing the bedroom in a soft, warm radiance.

"*Te amo, mi corazón. Siempre.*" *Always.*

The diamond flickered. In the dimming light Steve's image wavered then seemed to evaporate into Esteban. The glimmering diamond winked out, leaving her room in total darkness.

Natalie sat on the bed, the stillness and absolute silence of the room settled around her. An overwhelming sense of loss engulfed her as the surface of the gem cooled against her breasts.

"*Te amo, mi corazón.*" A strong, firm hand gripped hers, entwining her fingers with his.

"Esteban?" Her heart leapt at the sound of his voice, husky with desire.

Soft, firm lips nibbled at her temple. "I'm here, *mi amor.*" His heavy breathing cut the darkness and his arms wrapped around her with a sense of comfort that chased away her feelings of desolation.

"That was quite something." His lips trailed across her jaw and down the long column of her throat. "One moment." He leaned away and with a click the room was bathed in a muted light. "I need to see you. I need to know I am not dreaming."

He held her at arm's length. "Ah, there she is. The *bella doña* who comes to me in my dreams and makes me wild with wanting her."

She searched his face. Passion-laden eyes stared back at her but even as they smoldered she caught a hint of a familiar twinkle.

"Esteban? Is it really you?"

"Yes, *mi corazón*, it is. Or rather, it is all of me now." He traced a finger along the necklace chain until he stroked the diamond. Each facet seemed to sparkle brighter at his touch. "You have made me complete."

His words sent shivers racing up and down her spine. She slid her palms over his chest, the muscles rippled beneath her hands. He gathered her close, surrounding her with his presence. She sighed and snuggled tightly into his intimate embrace, feeling the diamond wedged between her and...her one true love.

Epilogue
Three months later

&

Thunder rumbled outside, waking Natalie from a delicious dream. Stretching, she opened her eyes as the early summer storm splashed bullets of water against the windowpanes.

"I was wondering how long you would keep me waiting, *cariña*."

Espresso-colored eyes scrutinized her face. Esteban leaned on his elbow beside her, his head propped in his hand. The fingers of his other hand drew lazy circles on her naked stomach as a muscular knee wedged between her thighs.

"Good morning. *Te amo*." *I love you*. It seemed so natural to say those words. Words he said so frequently to her. And, oh, how she did love him. She cupped his cheek and drew his lips to hers. His kiss, soft at first, quickly deepened, igniting a fiery coil of passion through her veins that soon had her squirming beneath him. He broke the kiss and resumed playing with her navel, leaving her breathless and craving more.

"I was afraid you would sleep away the entire day. That would leave me a very frustrated man if you did."

She slipped her hand around the corded muscles of his neck and threaded her fingers through his silky hair. "It's your own fault for keeping me up half the night."

"I don't recall you protesting. In fact, didn't you wake me that last time?" His deep, sexy voice brought another shiver of anticipation to her throbbing clit.

Weeks ago she may have blushed at his statement but now she merely threw him a wicked grin. She had no modesty, no reservations when she was in his arms. He'd made it clear he wanted all of her, that there could be no holding back. "How late...?" Her eye caught a glimpse of the bedside clock behind him. "Oh my, shouldn't you be at the café?"

Esteban continued to trace his mesmerizing pattern up her torso, circling her breast then working his way to the edge of her areola. She ached to feel his touch on her nipples but his fingers detoured to the sensitive valley between her breasts to outline the diamond pendant that glittered there. She knew it aroused him to think his dream lover had come to life and she took every opportunity to act out his fantasies—just as he brought hers to life. The diamond necklace was a solid reminder of how much they had both gained when it brought them together.

"Go to the café? Are you trying to get rid of me?" He leaned over and dropped a quick kiss on her nipple, tugging it with his teeth before releasing it and pulling away.

She sighed. "You know I'm not. It's just that they might need you. Saturdays are always so busy." She ran her hand over his broad chest, outlining the sharp planes of his pecs. The soft hair tickled her palm. Playfully she followed the path of hair that narrowed from his chest past his flat, tight abs to his groin and fingered the springy nest at the base of his aroused cock. His groan of satisfaction sent another wave of desire through her, moistening her, readying her pussy for his inevitable taking.

"They can survive without me for one day," he growled, shifting and settling his weight on her. She spread her legs wider and welcomed him between her thighs. His heavy cock pressed against her belly, flexing, testing.

"That's what you said last week." She slid her palms up the length of his powerful arms as he leveled himself on his forearms. Pausing to squeeze his rock-hard biceps, she once again marveled at his blatant masculine strength, so potent, especially in tender moments like this.

"So is it a crime for a man to want to spend a rainy day in bed with his wife?"

She smiled at his logic. "You said that last week too...husband."

His dark, expressive eyes smoldered at that word. She knew they would. It was a word that never failed to bring out the possessive nature of her hot-blooded Latino male.

"Well then, *querida*, it seems to me that since the café did not come crashing down last week there is an excellent chance it will remain standing today."

As if emphasizing his words, a clash of thunder so loud it seemed to be right over their roof sounded. He raised his hips and with one swift thrust buried his length inside her. All thoughts of the café and thunder fled her mind as he held himself immobile and stared into her eyes. She stared back with all the love and desire she held in her heart, telling him with her eyes what she had told him with her lips and her body so many times.

"Being one with you like this is my greatest joy, *mi amor*." His lips pressed a soft kiss where the diamond nestled between her breasts. "You have convinced me." With infinite care he slowly rocked his hips, giving her a taste of the passion that would soon flair between them.

A sudden disappointment rose in her chest. "Convinced you? To go to the café?" She wanted—no, she needed—another rainy day in bed with this man, the man of her dreams.

"No, *mi corazón*." His thrusts quickened and his hands cupped her face in a possessive cradle as he lowered his lips to hers. "You've convinced me fairy tales really do come true."

The End

BEJEWELED AND BEDEVILED

Tiffany Bryan

℘

Dedication

To my hubby, Jeff – the Sir Geoffrey in the very first novel I ever wrote and the man who brings me roses for no other reason than to cheer me up and express his love. There are so many things to thank you for, but since space is limited I'll just list a few. All the support and inspiration you've given throughout the years. The hours you spent lounging at my back, nagging me for the next pages of my current work so you could read them. Your unwavering and fierce support of my writing. Never once complaining about the money spent on the pursuit of my publishing dream. For being a great dad to our children. But mostly for giving me the peace of mind in knowing that no matter what life throws my way, your loving hand will be extended for me to reach for.

I love you – Wifey.

Acknowledgements

જી

To the most wonderful bunch of friends and critique partners a writer could hope for. Thank you all for your constructive input and support throughout the years.

Kathy Fuller, Chris & Kathy Kraft, Nelson Kirsch, Chris Nolfi, Christy Carlson, Jane Sabo and Kim Porter.

Special thanks to: Mary Ann Chulick who knew when a good swift kick was in order. Raelene Gorlinsky for the opportunity to submit to EC. Briana St. James, my editor, for helping make this story the best it could be.

Trademarks Acknowledgement

The author acknowledges the trademarked status and trademark owners of the following wordmarks mentioned in this work of fiction:

Gucci: Gucci America, Inc.

Trilliant Cut (aka Trielle, Trillian, Trillion): Henry Meyer Diamond Company of NY

Velcro: Velcro Industries B.V.

Chapter One
༄

SEXUAL BOUNDARIES—Are yours real or imagined?

Kayden Starling moved her gaze from the top of the centerfold article in the four-month-old issue of *Tell it Like it Is* to the short questionnaire on the adjacent page.

Name A Sexual Act That Both Fascinates and Repels You.

If you'd be willing to try it with complete anonymity—all related expenses paid—and will agree to a confidential interview, reply to the P.O. box provided below.

From the thousands of entries submitted, six lucky readers were handpicked.

Kayden knew because *TLI* was her baby. The survey, her brainchild.

What the hell had she been thinking!

She didn't regret the inspiration. It was the best idea she'd had since the magazine's inception two years ago. It was the getting personally involved part she was doubting.

The project had hatched from a conversation thread on TLI's new blog of things you'd never be caught dead doing in regard to sex.

Kayden couldn't help but smile. Give a group of women an open forum of obscurity, real or alcohol induced, and the subject inevitably turned to sex.

They were high on the issue's success and it was under the proverbial alcohol-induced umbrella that the six women who comprised TLI's executive staff were enticed into making a personal pact of their own. The general nightclub roundtable consensus—*Why the hell should the readers have all the fun*? If six follow-up issues were as good for sales as projected, wouldn't twelve be even better? Irrefutable pocketbook logic no woman contemplating her next pair of Gucci winter boots and matching bag could resist.

So they'd enthusiastically tossed their names into the bowl containing those of the lucky readers picked.

Kayden leveled a jaundiced eye at the fishbowl rimmed with genuine birthstones at the corner of her desk. Purchased at the Bling Your Pet shop on the first floor of the building, it held the remaining ten names for the drawing. A reader, the first name to be drawn, was currently mink-deep in her taboo sexual fantasy of being a rich man's mistress.

Kayden's name had been drawn next.

The very reason the owner of Club Kimberlite, Chicago's most exclusive BDSM and submissives training club, was waiting in the lobby to see her.

A situation that caused her heart to pound and her pussy to throb. Kayden was hard-pressed to say which reaction caused her the most concern.

She loved strong, dominating men. Hell, she netted them like a pheromone-soaked spider web. It was when their dominance spilled out of the bedroom into her everyday life that her independent nature balked.

He was a Master Dom with an impeccable reputation, she highly suspected the only time the word *boundaries* entered his thoughts was when he was walking over them.

A stickler for her magazine's reputation, she'd done extensive research. The information on the elusive Mr. Hunter Trielle had been much harder to come by than the details of his reputable establishment. But Kayden had found enough about the man to feel, if not comfortable, at least completely safe with the situation.

She glanced at her notes, still up on her computer screen. *Kimberlite* – a rock in which diamonds are formed.

An apt name for a club reputed to produce the "jewels" of the submissive world.

Out of the corner of her eye, she caught the time display at the bottom of her screen.

Six o'clock.

She drew in a deep breath and let it pass through her lips in a slow exhale.

Even if the man had showed up unannounced, without a single attempt to get an appointment, three hours was a long time to keep him waiting. Not a great way to start off with someone you were about to give carte blanche over nearly every aspect of your life and body. Even if it were only for two weeks.

Her gaze dropped to the notepad beside her phone.

Fourteen days.

Three hundred and thirty-six hours.

Twenty thousand one hundred sixty minutes.

One million two hundred nine thousand six hundred seconds.

But who was counting?

After another calming breath, Kayden closed the file and shut down her computer.

Her attempt to reach the intercom button was curtailed by a soft knock on her door, followed by a curvy, petite form slipping into the room.

The tiny smirk on the copy editor's face made Kayden sigh.

"You can't keep him waiting forever." Trista's pink, glistening lips morphed into a grin. "Come on, smile. Unlike the rest of us, you won't have to spend any more time agonizing over your decision."

"You're so full of crap. All you've been talking about this past week is rigging it so your name is picked next so you can pack yourself off to your secluded week of ménage a trois."

Trista shrugged and sauntered over to plant herself in front of the desk. "I'm trying to psych myself past the *repels* stage and focus on the *fascinates*." She stuck her hand into the fishbowl for a quick swirl through the folded, multicolored paper penises. "And it seems to be working. I get so wet thinking about it, I had to lay in an extra supply of batteries for my *Big Boy*." She expelled a weighty sigh.

Kayden laughed, and with usual after-hour abandon, pressed the intercom button and spoke loudly. "Shayla, get my broker on the line. Ask him to sink a bundle in whatever brand of batteries Trista uses in her vibrator." Sitting back, Kayden grinned.

Until the reason for the goofy smile on her friend's face sank. She dropped her forehead onto her desk. "Any chance in hell he didn't hear me?"

"Nope," Trista emphasized with a loud pop of her lips.

Groaning softly, Kayden sat up. "Anyone else out there?"

"Just Consuela. This is the third time the old crone's been up to vacuum the lobby. Between her and the foot traffic from nearly every female in the building tramping through on some trumped-up errand, including subscribing to TLI, your procrastination is wreaking havoc on our rug fibers."

"You're kidding?" Kayden sat up straighter.

Her friend shook her head. "The upside is we just broke the record for single-day subscription sales."

"I suppose that's something."

"He's gorgeous. With a capital *G*." A dreamy sigh followed the statement. "It seems no one is impervious to his strong, silent charms. Hell, this is my third trip through and I've lost track of the times Morgan, Kendra and Harley have given Shayla a break from her secretarial duties to keep him company while he waits. And I gotta tell ya, not one of us would have a problem kneeling at *that* man's feet with mouth open wide."

"Yeah well, I appreciate the offer and if I find myself in need of any help, I'll be sure to call."

Trista ran a tongue across her lips, kicking up the shine. "I know I speak for the group when I say, night or day, you got my number."

Kayden rolled her eyes. "All right, point taken. Give me five minutes and have Shayla show *Mr. Gorgeous* in."

Exactly five minutes later, her door reopened.

Resigned to her self-inflicted fate, Kayden looked over the top of her secretary's curly red head to the tall, dark-haired, gut-wrenching hunk behind her and became immediately ensnared in his piercing amber gaze.

One thought went through her mind.

She was about to go skinny-dipping in some very dangerous waters.

* * * * *

"Mr. Trielle." Kayden stood and extended her hand over the clutter on her desk, catching Shayla's thumbs-up as she quietly exited.

"Hunter." Instead of offering his right hand, he used his left to capture hers and draw her out from around her desk. He held her gaze for several intense seconds before indulging in a slow, arousing perusal of her body.

Feeling exposed down to her darkest secrets, she warded off a shiver and gave free rein to her irritation. "Would you like me to strip and turn around? Wouldn't want you to miss anything. That's why you're here, right? To size me up?"

"An enticing offer, *Kayden*." He released her hand. "If I thought it stemmed from anything other than a feeling of vulnerability, I would take you up on it."

She frowned. "It has nothing to do with vul—"

"Don't." His voice stern, he cupped her chin in a grasp that was no less commanding for its gentleness. "I will tolerate many things during your training. Lying...is not one of them. Neither to me, nor yourself." He loosened his hold to run his thumb over her lips, leaving an electrifying fizz in its wake. "Not until you learn the limits of my tolerance and the consequences for exceeding them."

Caught in his compelling gaze, Kayden fought the urge to rock up on tiptoes and offer up her mouth for his plundering pleasure. The thought of where else he might plunder caused a flood of sensation between her legs. "Now why don't we sit and discuss my terms for our agreement. Then perhaps we'll revisit your generous offer."

Freed of his hold and potent gaze when he turned to take the chair in front of her desk, Kayden felt both relieved and bereft. It wasn't until she was firmly reseated in the position of power behind her desk that his words registered. "*Your* terms? What about mine?"

"I am well aware of your terms, Kayden. You were quite meticulous in spelling them out during our e-mail exchanges. Normally, I would never have agreed to participate in anything like this. But you intrigued me."

"Yes, it is an intriguing concept. Everyone thinks so."

He shook his head. "Not the idea...*you*. The reason I decided to make this surprise visit instead of having you come to me."

"I don't understand."

"People's reactions are influenced by environment. I needed to see you in yours. Get a true sense of your wants. Your needs. Learn what I need to know to be sure we'd be a suitable match."

"You're kidding, right? We've been together all of what," she glanced at the clock on the wall, "fourteen minutes and you're saying you know me? Not likely."

"It has nothing to do with time. I just needed to look into your eyes."

"You expect me to believe that?"

He took a deep, measured breath, drawing attention to his impressively wide chest. Knowing she would feel the pleasurable weight of it in the not-too-distant future made her breasts tingle.

"Are you saying you *don't* believe it?"

Not entirely sure she didn't and remembering what he'd said about lying, she opted for a change in subject. "Maybe it would be best to get on with your terms. It's getting late and you probably have something—someone—back at your club that needs your attention."

"As luck would have it, I'd only recently returned from a much-needed rest in the Philippines when I came across your interesting request. I hadn't committed to training a new sub yet."

She almost asked if it was his arm that needed rest from whipping women into submission, but she doubted he'd see the humor in it. Taking measure of the bronzed, healthy-looking and extremely fit man sitting across from her, Kayden was seriously beginning to question her so-called luck.

This was a game, nothing more. Her body wasn't supposed to be humming along to the tune of the power he seemed to exude without so much as a quirk of his little finger. Unnerved by her reaction to him, she attempted to regain some control by saying, "It must be nice having a private island hideaway to escape to."

One dark brown eyebrow rose slightly.

The satisfaction she felt by his apparent surprise made her smile. A fair hand at reading people herself, she'd sensed he wasn't a man easily impressed.

"You would have had to dig long and very deep to find that bit of information. Was it curiosity about me personally or can I assume you research everything this thoroughly?"

"Everything."

"Club Kimberlite?"

She nodded.

"The submissive lifestyle?"

Another quick nod.

Only to regret it when a predatory smile touched his lips. "Excellent. Then I will expect much more from you as you already have a fair knowledge of what I'll require of you."

"I never said I knew everything. And I'm sure the experience is a far cry from reading about it. That would be like slapping a collar on a dog, snapping on a leash and expecting it to heel its first time out."

He didn't so much as blink at the deliberately crude parody she'd drawn. Why she felt the need to crack his calm veneer, she wasn't sure. Nor was she sure it was wise. She suspected it was a sudden case of nerves and that he was pressing her beyond her comfort zone way too quickly for her liking.

"You know I don't expect that of you, any more than you expect me to believe after your in-depth research, you think that's how a Dom perceives his sub. They are loved and cherished as well, if not better in some circumstances, as most wives. That a large majority of couples living this lifestyle are, in fact, happily married to each other."

"You're right. I'm sorry."

"A perfect opportunity for your first lesson. A *sincere* apology is always accepted."

She got the uneasy feeling there was a *but* lingering somewhere after that statement. Deciding this might not be the best time to have it clarified, she asked, "Exactly what are your terms?" A rhetorical question, since she had a fairly good idea.

The corners of his mouth lifted a fraction. "There's only two. The first—your choice of a safe word. And I think you know what the other one is."

"Total submission." She didn't bother to make it a question.

His smile widened. "Do you agree?"

Did she? She could back out. No one was holding a gun to her head. But if she did, she'd possibly be throwing away the best opportunity she'd ever have to lay to rest a deeply buried fear she'd harbored for years. And what better man than the charismatic, supremely confident one patiently waiting for her answer to test it against. "Yes," she said with the feeling of just having consigned her soul to the devil. "I'm all yours. For the next two weeks," she added hastily.

He shook his head. "Four weeks. More if I think necessary for you to gain full knowledge. After all, you wouldn't want your magazine's integrity taken into question."

"Four!" She rose from her chair. "I never agreed to that. I have a business to run."

"*Yes*, you did commit to that...and more when you agreed to my second term. I will allow you ample time to confer with your staff whenever needed. Having done some research of my own, I'll admit to being impressed with the qualifications and caliber of the women you've chosen to help run your company. Intelligence and beauty are a combination few men can resist. And after all, I am but a simple man."

Kayden smothered a snort. Simple her great-aunt Winifred's fat ass. But if she didn't agree, she'd have to start from square one. And that she wouldn't do. Impeccable both in reputation and screening measures, validated by the rigorous medical and psychological exams required of anyone wishing to partake in this particular club's training, his was number one. And she never settled for number two.

"Okay. Just tell me when and where to show up with my bags."

He leisurely unfolded from the chair. "I like to start off slow and I also believe in a reward system. Your first gift, for agreeing to place yourself under my tutelage, will arrive tomorrow. I hope you will like it. You'll receive further instructions then. For now, all that remains is for you to come here and kiss me goodbye."

She hesitated before saying, "Yes, *Master*."

"Hunter," he corrected as she made her way over to him. "If and when I want you to call me Master, I'll let you know."

"Yes, Hunter." Refusing to portray a lamb going to slaughter, she stretched up to wrap her arms around his neck, pressed her lips to his and, with an enticing slice of her tongue, slipped into his receptive mouth.

Had he not wrapped his arms around her waist and pressed her tight, she most likely would have melted to the floor.

Holy shit, the man could kiss. A strong, laying-my-claim kiss that rocked her world and made her grateful for the few seconds of steadying support he provided before pulling away.

"One more thing before I leave."

Unable to form a coherent word, she nodded.

He hooked her chin onto his index finger. "If you ever keep me waiting again, for any reason, your delectable ass will take the brunt of my displeasure."

Chapter Two
∽

When the elevator doors opened to TLI's lobby at nine the next morning, it took Kayden several seconds to realize the high-pitched whirring noise she heard was not the byproduct of sleep deprivation.

She'd spent half the night fretting over her relinquishment of control. The other half in the throes of some very erotic fantasies centered around the heartthrob Dom to whom she'd literally given a free pass to every nook and cranny of her body. The two hours since awakening in a sheet-twisted sweat she'd wasted trying to figure out which caused her the most apprehension.

Knowing either would take deeper thought than she was currently capable of, she focused on the more mundane issue of noise.

Since it usually took building maintenance days to get to any reported problem, whatever had them up drilling this early didn't bode well for the quiet, appointment-free morning she'd contemplated.

Not in any particular hurry to hear whatever bad news awaited her, she peeled her slumped body away from the back wall of the elevator and trudged through the spacious area that served as both waiting room and secretary's office.

Halfway there, one of her other senses kicked in. *Was that the smell of coffee being freshly ground?* Her brain cells perked up at the heavenly aroma of a rich, strong blend.

She wasn't sure how much of the office's slush fund Shayla had blown on what apparently was a new espresso machine, but whatever it was, Kayden's exhausted body was casting its vote for *who gives a shit, it's worth every damn penny.*

Hastening her steps, she breezed past Shayla's unoccupied desk and into her office. "You might've just earned yourself a raise, Shay—"

Her sluggish brain taking its good old time to shift gears, words failed her as Kayden swiveled her gaze between her shoulder-shrugging secretary and the man looking every bit like a five-star restaurant maître d'. It wasn't until he'd packed down the finely ground beans, attached the silver cup to the gleaming stainless machine, switched it on and straightened to look her way that she found her voice. "Who the heck are you?"

"Good morning, Miss Starling. Chalmers, at your service." He dipped his head in greeting. "Mr. Trielle is a firm believer in starting the day off with a good breakfast. "Please, have a seat." He glanced in the direction of the small, round conference table in the corner of her office. Usually groaning beneath stacks of old projects to be filed with only a small space at one edge to work on the current one, it was now buried beneath a white linen tablecloth and an assortment of fine-dining paraphernalia.

"I don't eat breakfast," she grumbled, prying her gaze away from the small, black-velvet box propped against the White-House-worthy five-arm candelabra. "Where's the stuff from my table and how did you get up here?" Legit questions, since she knew it hadn't been her secretary. Accustomed to Kayden's cluttered work style and a habitual night owl like herself, Shayla wasn't prone to arriving much before her starting time.

"Since the folders were clearly marked, I took the liberty of filing them away. You'll find the rest of your papers there." With an economical movement of his hand, he indicated the wide ledge that ran the length of the windowed wall facing Lake Michigan. "Mr. Trielle says clutter is not conducive to serenity."

Had the intrusive Mr. Trielle been present, Kayden would have informed him it wasn't the clutter that was playing havoc with her serenity, it was him. Along with all the things she anticipated he was going to do to her.

"Mr. Fuller was kind enough to give me access to your office. Under Mr. Trielle's assurance that should there be any ramifications, they would fall squarely on his shoulders."

Struggling to dispel the image of those wonderfully broad shoulders and how far she'd have to spread her legs to accommodate them, Kayden was slow to process the rest of Chalmers' statement. "Mr. Fuller?"

"Jimmy," Shayla supplied.

"Remind me later to have a little talk with our security guard."

"I assure you, Miss Starling, that won't be necessary. Mr. Trielle—"

"It's Kayden. And this is my office. Not Mr. Trielle's."

Instead of voicing the contradiction revealed in the slight shift of his expression, he said, "Very good, Miss. If you will please sit, I'll serve you breakfast." He turned and lifted the silver dome off the platter sitting on the cart behind him.

Kayden nearly closed her eyes and ummmed over the mouthwatering smell of eggs, Canadian bacon and...oh crap, was that a Belgian waffle beneath a mound of fresh strawberries supporting a white, fluffy mountain of whipped cream? The scrumptious sight almost made her cave. But she needed to bring home the point that this was her place of business and no one was going to come in here and dictate to her.

"I told you, I don't eat breakfast."

Before he could say anything, Shayla's stomach growled and drew their attention.

"Sorry." She smiled sheepishly. "Guess the small bowl of cereal I had before rushing out of the house didn't quite do it."

"I have the perfect solution." Kayden turned to Chalmers. "Shayla can eat the breakfast while I sit with her and have my coffee. Then you can inform Mr. Trielle that the meal was thoroughly enjoyed. Problem solved. Come on, Shayla, let's sit down." Intending to set her purse on the desk, noting it too had been cleaned, Kayden was stopped in her tracks by his next words.

"I'm sorry, Miss. Mr. Trielle was specific in that *you* eat the breakfast. He believes that one's body —"

"Look, Chalmers. Your loyalty to Mr. Trielle is commendable, but maybe I didn't make myself clear earlier." Kayden fought to keep the irritation out of her voice. "This is not Mr. Trielle's office. And this," she poked herself in the middle of the chest, "is not Mr. Trielle's body."

The last part netted her a raised eyebrow. Okay, so what if he did know of her arrangement with his boss. This was her turf. Over *this* world, she was master.

About to tell him as much, she noticed both his and Shayla's gazes fixed on something over her shoulder. *Shit.*

"Good morning."

The deep, quiet voice that flowed into the room curled down her spine and infused heat into every crevice of Kayden's body. Chin lifted, she spun to confront her nemesis.

Smacked with the realization the man looked every bit as handsome, commanding and sinfully sexy as she remembered, her throat constricted, cinching off her words.

"Perhaps it was *I* who didn't make myself clear yesterday." His gaze never leaving hers, he said, "Chalmers, the staff's breakfast should be arriving at any moment. Why don't you confer with Shayla on how best to have it served?"

"Very good, sir."

"And Shayla," Hunter said as he shifted slightly to let them leave. "Would you be kind enough to hold all of Miss Starling's calls?"

"Kayden?" Shayla, God bless her loyal soul, turned to her for confirmation.

After a defiant hesitation, Kayden nodded. "I'll let you know if I need anything."

* * * * *

Once assured of their privacy, Hunter stood where he was for several long seconds, his gaze fixed on the stunning, stiff-chinned woman in front of him as the need to reach out and grab her diminished. An urge that had more to do with the lust hardening his cock than the sparks of open defiance in her sapphire eyes.

He hadn't been completely honest with her yesterday when he'd said one look into her eyes was all he'd required to assess their suitability. He'd known long before that. Blatant to him from the intriguing revelations hidden between the lines of her over-explained e-mails, she'd given every indication of being the kind of challenge a man of his high expectations would relish. So he'd accepted her offer. Not for the sake of some article. And sure as hell not for the sake of readying her for another man's benefit. He was doing it because she would belong to him. Not for a month. Forever.

"Look, I think we need to get something straight," she said, legs slightly parted, fists jammed onto her nicely rounded hips.

Hunter was sure it would make her even more agitated to know rather than appearing powerful, he pictured her naked, her wrists clamped to a thick leather waist restraint, ankles to a spreader bar. A position that left her helplessly exposed for his personal pleasure.

"This is my office. You said I'd have ample time to confer with my staff."

"I believe the exact phrase I used was *allow you*." He walked over to the table and pulled out her chair. "And you agreed to *total* submission."

Her eyes lit with another spark of defiance but instead of acting upon it, she took several deep breaths and relaxed her stance.

"Yes, I did agree. When I'm at your establishment."

"There is no wiggle room in the word *total*. If you check the dictionary, I believe you'll find it means complete...utter...absolute."

"I'm not disputing that," she said, holding her ground. "I assumed—"

"Assuming anything is no longer an option available to you. If you have the slightest question or doubt about anything, you will check with me for clarification."

One fine eyebrow arched up. A sure sign her defiance was once again about to ignite. "You're serious."

"Emphatically. Now unless you intend to renege on your word, come here and I'll serve you breakfast."

She didn't immediately comply. Not that he expected her to. A strong-willed woman in a position of power, she was used to having people answer to her. The role reversal wouldn't come easy. She would likely resist every step of the way. Rather than irritate, the thought pleased him more than she would know.

Her deep, resigned breath accentuated an already impressive cleavage as her breasts swelled into the constricting space of her partially unbuttoned shirt. Like a near-white moon nestled in a midnight sky, the dark blue silk of her shirt provided a stunning contrast to her pale skin.

Knowing every inch of that sweet flesh now belonged to him, to explore whenever, wherever he wanted, should have tempered his need to see her stripped of everything but the remnants of her stubborn pride. It didn't.

"I have *never* gone back on my word," she said, slowly moving toward the chair.

"I can't tell you how pleased I am to know that." She was halfway seated when he said, "Don't sit."

She straightened.

"Are you wearing pantyhose or stockings?"

"What? Yes, pantyhose."

"Take them off and give them to me." He held out his hand.

Her eyes widened. "You expect me—"

"Kayden." He let his disapproval ring through. "I refuse to believe you are ignorant of the fact that, as your Dom, I expect obedience. Not after boasting of your detailed research. Therefore, if you continue in this vein, I'll assume it's because you want me to punish you. If not, I'd strongly advise against making me wait longer."

Having made an art form of studying the subtle nuances of a woman's body, Hunter didn't miss the slight tensing of her jaw. He had no problem with her harboring a bit of resentment. He expected it at this early stage. Welcomed it. Years of experience had taught him the subs that proved most difficult were always the most gratifying.

He extended his hand farther. "For earning my displeasure, I'll take your panties too."

"My—" She glanced at the door and turned back. "What if—"

He narrowed his eyes.

She captured her bottom lip between her teeth and slipped out of her shoes.

Silently applauding her restraint, he made a mental note to take her shopping. Practical and low-heeled, the shoes did absolutely no justice to her trim ankles and shapely legs.

He knew she was worried about someone walking in. He could have eased her discomfort by letting her know he'd reached behind him to lock the door when Chalmers and Shayla had left. And he would have, if he hadn't gotten the impression she enjoyed pushing him.

She was going to be deliciously difficult to train.

* * * * *

Kayden bit the inside of her cheek to keep from arguing further. Lord knows what he'd ask for next. Most likely her skirt. Then she'd be two measly articles away from naked.

Not that she would have minded had the circumstances been different. Trista hadn't exaggerated when she'd said Hunter was gorgeous. Over six feet of well-packed muscle stuffed into a black turtleneck that intensified the gold hues of his eyes and beige pants that hugged a trim waist and thick thighs. Had he not already been rich, he could've made a lush living modeling for any number of top men's fashion magazines. With the rapidness of a photo shoot camera, her mind pictured him in various stages of undress. Tux. Polo and jeans. Just jeans. Swim trunks. Naked.

Her thoughts came to a screeching halt. Damn. Fully clothed he could have half the female populace of Chicago dropping their panties with the crook of his finger. She could only imagine their reaction to seeing him naked. That she would soon have that privilege—

Already off balance trying to get one foot out of her pantyhose, she teetered and threw out her hand to catch the back of the chair. Instead, she latched onto a thick, solid forearm when Hunter thrust out his arm.

Startled, she looked up.

When she was stable, he withdrew his arm and asked, "Better?"

She nodded.

"Among the many things you will need to learn is that when I ask a question, I will expect a verbal answer. It will eliminate the chance of misunderstanding in the future. Another is that from today on, in all things, you will look to me for support. I will always be here to catch you."

"I'm not used to depending on—"

"You will be." He skimmed the backs of his fingers down her cheek and along her jaw.

Oddly calmed by the tender gesture and not quite sure what to say in response to his declaration, she focused on her task and freed her other leg. Silently bemoaning the loss of her pantyhose, she offered them to him.

"Thank you." A small smile stretched his lips as he accepted them, balled them up and, with a light toss, made a perfect two-pointer into her waste can.

"Hey." She stepped forward.

He grasped her wrist. "Leave them."

Kayden shot an annoyed glance at his hand before transferring it to his face. "Those were brand new."

His brow rose in warning.

"Fine. I'll leave them. I have plenty more at home."

"Where they will stay," he stated evenly. "As long as we are together, you are forbidden to wear them. Now the panties."

Shaking her head, she stepped back.

Still in possession of her wrist, he reeled her back in.

Braced for a scolding, she was struck motionless when he laid gentle hands on her forearms.

"I wonder what it is you are so afraid of." He slid his hands up and over her shoulders to bracket her neck. "That you won't like submitting..." He lightly traced the rims of her ears with his thumbs, his eyes warming at her resultant shiver. "Or...that you will?"

He claimed her mouth for a mind-numbing kiss. Had he not, Kayden would've said that for someone who supposedly knew women so well, he was way off base this time. Of course, it would have been a lie. The truth was he was much too close to the truth for comfort. Because in a forgotten place, deep down where she'd buried it a long, long time ago, stirred the scary suspicion that he was right. Then as now, unwilling to face her fear, she surrendered to his kiss, the slow, languid swipes of his talented tongue. His large, capable hands spreading warmth as they slid down over her arms, then under them to capture her hips and draw her close.

The unexpected nudge of the long, solid ridge of flesh that met her stomach made her gasp.

He pulled his head back, his soft, throaty chuckle stirring butterflies in her stomach. "The sooner you stop fighting me, the sooner we can get beyond the basics and onto the more...pleasurable aspects of your being my submissive." Holding her still with his hands, he put his mouth next to her ear and whispered, "You want that, don't you? To have your pussy played with—filled." He nipped her earlobe at the same time he thrust his hips.

Kayden swallowed a moan generated by the simultaneous stimulus of his warm breath, deep voice and obviously eager cock. Want it? Wanting wasn't the issue. She'd wanted him since he'd set foot in her office. Before that. Since she'd unearthed a rare newspaper photo taken at a charitable event to establish college scholarships for underprivileged women. How a dull black-and-white picture could project so much power and charismatic sensuality defied logic.

Until she'd met him.

She wouldn't be one bit surprised to find a trail of panties when she left the building tonight, hastily discarded by the women he'd passed on the way in. He was screw-the-preliminaries-come-here-and-fuck-me sexy.

Hell no, wanting wasn't the issue. She had no problem relinquishing her body. It was her vehemently protesting independence that was dragging its feet.

"Kayden."

The distinct crack of command in his soft voice brought her gaze up to his.

"You have much to learn in a short time. Attention is key. And although I have no intention of being a jailer to your thoughts, when I am with you, I expect your focus to be wholly on me. From today until the day we part company, our pleasure and displeasure are irrevocably linked. Do you understand?"

She caught herself mid-nod. "Yes." The word was clipped.

His expression unchanging, he gave her ass a stinging taste of his hand.

"Ow!" She flattened her hand over her left butt cheek to disperse the light burn.

The intercom chimed. "Kayden, are you okay?"

Hunter's mask broke to reveal a hint of humor as his eyebrows went up.

This time it was Kayden's *upper* cheeks that flooded with warmth.

"I'm fine, Shayla. Thanks for checking."

"You're sure?"

Feeling a bit more relaxed knowing reinforcements were only a closed door away, Kayden took a calming breath. "I'm sure."

"Okay." A single bleep announced the connection closed.

Hunter sighed and reached up to run a finger along the side of her face. "You can't imagine how disappointed I am right now."

Sure she could. But she doubted he was half as disappointed in her as she was in herself. After all, she was the one who'd initiated all this. Wanting to experience, if only for a short time, what it felt like to give one hundred percent to a man. To expose herself fully. No secrets. No shame. Free to express her deepest needs and desires without fear of censorship.

And now that she had the opportunity, she was blowing it—big time. *Way to go, Kayden.*

"I'm sorry." Ashamed of her behavior, she hung her head. "I don't know why I thought this would work. Maybe we should call it quits." Shaking her head, she took two steps back. "It will mean a setback for this particular article, but there were several other women interested in submission. Maybe..."

"Kayden, enough." Responding to the added authority in his voice, exactly as she had the last time, her gaze flew to his. Hunter fought a satisfied grin. "This agreement is between you and me. Non-transferable." He clutched her shoulders. "Again, this is your fear talking. If you're looking for the coward's way out, say so and I'll walk out that door. Think your answer over carefully, because this is the last time I'll allow you this option. If you tell me to stay, it's for the duration."

Her expressive eyes shooting blue flames, she stepped back, breaking contact. "I am not afraid and I am *not* a coward!" Her words went from alto to an impressive soprano.

The intercom chimed again.

She snapped her head in its direction. "I'm fine! Damn it." She took a quick breath. "Sorry, Shayla. I'm fine," she said more calmly. "And from today on, anytime Mr. Trielle is in my office, assume we don't want to be disturbed," she leveled a mild glare toward him, "no matter what you hear."

"You got it, boss." The intercom bleeped.

Her chest rose and fell with her agitation. "Answer enough for you?"

"Pretty speech, but you know it's not. Say it." Reaching out, he again grasped her shoulders and pulled her close. "And you may want to think about what tone you use when you do."

She took several deep, calming breaths, tempting Hunter to look down at her luscious cleavage. With a stern reminder that there'd be plenty of opportunity to bury his face between her beautiful breasts later, he retained the needed eye contact.

"Yes, Hunter. I—"

"Master. Just so there's no mistaking exactly what you're agreeing to, *this* time, it's Master."

There was a long pause, during which Hunter could see the struggle going on behind the glimmer in her mesmerizing eyes.

"Yes…Master. I belong to you." Another slight pause. "To do with as you will."

Having gotten exactly what he'd wanted, Hunter couldn't help himself. With no desire to be gentle, he firmed his grip on her shoulders and yanked her up to meet his kiss. It was the first of many ways he intended to claim her, mark her, stamp out any lingering doubt that she belonged to him. And would stay that way. Her journey to reach the same conclusion began here…now.

For several long moments, he devoured her mouth. It was the sweetest mouth he'd ever tasted, warm, wet and welcoming. He could have gone on kissing her forever. But they'd more important things to do.

With one last long, slow swipe of his tongue, he broke the kiss and moved back. He dropped his gaze to her toes, inched it up her long slender legs, paused in the vicinity of her pelvis and, with a slow, crawling perusal, reconnected with her gaze. In silent command, he held out his hand, palm up.

Without hesitation she reached up under her skirt and wiggled out of her panties.

They were black, to match her skirt, a small bit of lacy fabric. When she got them past her knees, she latched onto the arm at his side. Catching his gaze momentarily, she balanced on one foot then the other, removing her underwear more quickly than Hunter would have preferred, and placed them in his hand. He drew some consolation in the fact that someday soon she would perform a striptease for his pleasure.

A very slow, sexy one that would expose all her beautiful assets and give him time to appreciate each one the way they deserved. The thought of how many ways he would take her afterward made his cock so hard it threatened to shatter his control. And it was way too early in their relationship for that. He knew eventually she would learn exactly how much power she had over him. But it wouldn't be today.

"Are you throwing those away as well?" She glanced toward the trash can.

"These, I'll keep. I may want you to put them on for me some day. Just so I can have the pleasure of taking them off." He tested the delicacy of the fabric between his fingers for several moments before bringing them up to his nose to inhale her scent. After a quick kiss to the crotch, he carefully tucked them into his pants pocket.

Her eyes followed his every move, a good indication of her attentiveness. Since her awareness of his movements and body language were as important as hers to him, it was a pleasing step forward.

"Your smell is positively intoxicating." He smiled at the blush that dusted her cheeks. "But like the pantyhose, this is another item of clothing you will no longer need."

"So you can have access to my pussy?" she stated bluntly with raised chin.

"No." Capturing her chin between thumb and forefinger, he lowered it slightly. "So I can have access to *my* pussy."

To drive home his point, he stepped closer, slipped his hand under her skirt and indulged himself in a slow, sampling caress up one trim thigh and cupped her.

"This," he buried his finger between her folds, pleased by her soft gasp, pleased even more to find she was damp and slick, "and every other luscious inch of you now belong to me. And I believe in taking very good care of what's mine." He wiggled his finger.

Just as she melted into his caress, he pulled out with a steady, quick glide over her G-spot. "Starting with a good, nutritious breakfast." Ignoring her soft, needy moan, he clasped her wrist and, seating himself, pulled her sideways across his lap, cradling her back with his arm.

"Breakfast? But I thought…"

"I know what you thought." He held back a smile at her bemused, slightly disgruntled expression. God, she was just all kinds of beautiful. Sexy as hell. Not the in-your-face sexy, but a combination of earthy sensuality and naiveté that brought men to their knees. And if he wasn't careful, that's exactly where he'd end up. "We'll be getting around to this," he splayed his hand over her lower thigh and, with a firm slide, pushed her skirt up high enough to graze her soft curls with his thumb, "soon enough."

Chapter Three

Kayden sucked in a breath. Talk about being between a rock and a hard place! Hunter's long, hard cock cutting across the back of her thighs and his thumb toying with the hair between her legs. Her pussy throbbing in wanton need of either.

She canted her hips. His thumb bumped her clit. Maybe if she moved a little more…

"No." His hand clamped her thigh, stilling her. "I'll tell you when it's time."

Now! Now would be a great time, she wanted to scream. *Couldn't we just forget all this in-between bullshit and get to the you-master, me-slave, tie-me–up-and-fuck-me part?*

A light pull on her pubic hair got her attention.

"Have you ever shaved here?"

"No."

"We'll take care of that tomorrow. Are you aware it heightens the senses?"

If her senses were any more heightened, there'd be a new skylight in the roof. "So I've heard."

"After tomorrow, you'll know it for a fact. One more thing before we get started on breakfast. Have you chosen a safe word yet?"

"Not yet."

"Good. Because after some serious thought, I've decided to choose for you."

"Isn't that against some sacred BDSM rule or something?"

"I think it best we clear something up so you don't go into this with another misconception. There are no hard-and-fast rules. This is not a board game, which comes with an instruction manual. There are, however, many tried-and-true guidelines with respect to safety and comfort. All to cultivate trust. As I said earlier, without trust this relationship will fail. Have I given you reason to distrust me?"

Kayden was surprised to find her answer required little thought. "No."

"Excellent. Then your safe word will be *Diamond*. Do you know what Trielle stands for?"

"A triangular cut of a diamond. Trademarked by the Trillion Diamond Company, the word *Trillion* is also sometimes used to describe the diamond's shape." She looked into his eyes. "Everything about you revolves around the gem. The name of your club, the month you were born."

"And Triangle, what does that symbolize?"

"Point up, male power. Point down, female power."

"Diamond?"

"Passion. Energy. They're believed to enhance relationships, increase inner strength and provide the wearer with balance, clarity and abundance." She paused, wary of the road he was leading her down.

"Don't stop there." His lips eased into a knowing smile. "I'm curious to see if you've discovered something I'm not aware of."

Kayden sighed. "The word diamond derives from the ancient Greek *adamas*, meaning *impossible to tame*. And they're renowned for their superlative physical qualities, especially their *hardness*." Deciding to share some of the discomfort she was experiencing, she shifted her hips over the huge erection she was sitting on.

If not for the slight tightening of his thighs, she would have thought he was impervious to the gesture. Miffed at his iron control, she vowed to crack it before their agreement came to an end.

"*Hard*, as in durability and strength," he clarified. "The perfect safe word for you."

"But all that relates to you. Not me."

"Precisely. Through me, you will find your strength. Your balance. With me, you will find your safety. The indestructible rock behind your back." With his free hand, he tucked her hair behind her ears and cupped her neck to bring her lips to his. "Your safe haven." The promise was a warm breathy whisper. "What's your safe word?"

Kayden swallowed the lump in her throat. "Diamond," she murmured softly against his mouth.

"Diamond," he confirmed, the low, strong tones sending a tingle across her lips.

The pressure of his hand was light, non-threatening. His lips, when they met hers, soft and requesting—demanding nothing. So why in hell did Kayden feel compelled to give him all?

Unnerved by the thought, she broke the kiss and turned her head. "I can't..." She bit her lip.

He dropped his hand to give her thigh a light squeeze. "Can't what?"

Thankfully her stomach chose that moment to growl, saving her from answering. "Can't...wait to eat. I'm starving." She reached for the silver dome covering the plate.

His hand covered hers. "Look at me."

Prepared to be chastised for her lie, she turned.

"Running from the truth won't change it."

"What truth?" she asked tentatively, assuring herself the queasy feeling in the pit of her stomach was the result of hunger, not that he was intuitive enough to have guessed her secret longings.

"The truth you will come to terms with sooner or later. The one you'll willingly share when you're ready. But as I doubt very much it will be this moment, I think we should proceed with today's training session. Lean back."

Relieved to be let off the hook, Kayden relaxed into the curve of his strong arm.

"You are not to lift a finger unless instructed." Hunter reached over and uncovered the plate. "Spread your legs. Keep them open," he instructed, setting the lid aside. "You're mine now. I expect to have easy access to your pussy *whenever* I want it, *however* I want it. First we'll appease your hunger. Starting with a bit of cream." He skimmed a healthy dab of white fluff from the top of the waffle and brought it to her mouth. "Some for you."

Imagining it to be his cock, Kayden dutifully, slowly sucked the cream from his finger. His amber gaze heated as it tracked her lip's progress.

"Very nice. Now some for me."

Expecting him to help himself to some whipped cream, she couldn't stop the gasp when he stroked his hand up her inner thigh and slid a finger deep inside her.

"Wet and warm," he said, swirling his finger before pulling it out. His eyes locked on hers, he inserted it into his mouth and sucked it clean. "Just the way I like it."

Next he fed her a plump red strawberry, and while she chewed, marveling at the sweet juice that exploded over her taste buds and trickled down her throat, he took one for himself.

Kayden almost choked on a swallow when he ran his strawberry between her pussy lips in a long, slow stroke before popping the berry into his mouth.

"Another?"

She wet her lips. "Yes, please."

His gaze warm and intent, he dipped the very tip of the small plump fruit inside her wet channel. Rotated.

Kayden fought to hold back a moan, losing the battle when he brushed the textured berry up, over her clit, circled once, twice, and then rode it through her swollen folds. After several tantalizing moments, it found its way into her mouth.

If he kept this up, she'd expire before they got to the waffle.

"Open your eyes, sweetheart."

Open? Crap, she hadn't even realized she'd closed them. When she lifted her lids, it took a moment for his smile to come into focus.

"Here," he said, pressing a fork into her hand. "I think you can manage the rest on your own."

"You're done eating?" she said, trying not to let her disappointment show.

"Not entirely. I have every intention of stealing a little nibble now and then." He shifted sideways slightly to allow her easier access to the plate. "Go ahead and eat."

The first bite of waffle hit her palate at the same time he drove two fingers deep inside her. She caught the fork between her teeth and his hand between her thighs. One look at his stony expression had her releasing both.

"You expect me to eat while you're doing *that*?"

"Yes." Applying more pressure, he rotated his fingers, slightly withdrew them. Added a third.

Moaning, Kayden caught her legs mid-close.

"I'll expect that of you. And much more. I'll slip my fingers…or anything else inside you whenever the mood strikes me. And you'll not utter a single sound of complaint. Not because you'll be afraid to. Because you'll come to love it. Open your legs wider and continue eating. Close them again and you'll find yourself face down over my legs."

"I—"

"No more talking. The only times I want to see that pretty mouth of yours open is when you're putting food into it or when I ask you a direct question. I'm running out of both time and patience."

He was running out of patience? He could have fooled her. The man must have King Kong restraints on his temper. Some day, when she knew him better and was feeling more courageous, she'd test his limits. Running her tongue over suddenly dry lips, she cut off a generous portion of waffle and stuffed it into her mouth. The quicker she got this over with—

His thumb brushed her clit.

Stomach muscles knotting, she whimpered around the food in her mouth.

He nipped her shoulder.

She gasped.

Hunter smiled against her arm and kissed where he'd nipped. "Women have no idea how much those sexy little feminine sounds turn a man on. A breathy gasp, a throaty whimper. Especially when he's caused them. You do it especially well. I'll have to make sure you do it often. Keep eating."

Keep eating? She could barely keep breathing. All she wanted to do was toss down the fork and concentrate on the delicious sensations spiraling up from between her legs. But determined to stick to their agreement and be a good little *sub*, she cut and speared another piece of waffle.

As it touched her lips, his fingers curled inside her.

Screw it. Tossing the fork onto the plate, Kayden leaned back into his arm and spread her legs. Not the least deterred by his knowing chuckle, she thrust her hips, impaling herself deeper.

"I can see we'll need to work on your self-control." He used his thumb to toy with her clit. A light, gliding tease. "But since this is your first day and I'm feeling magnanimous, I'll give you what you want."

Personally, at that moment she didn't give a damn what he was feeling. It was what she was feeling that mattered. And a little laughter at her expense wasn't going to deter her from getting it.

"Hook your heel on the table."

An order she was eager to follow if it would help him get the job done.

When his fingers remained unmoving, she pumped her hips in encouragement.

He chuckled again. "I said I would give you what you want. I didn't say it would be on your terms." He withdrew his hand.

She groaned.

"There are few sights more beautiful than what I'm looking at right now. You... open, willing, waiting for me to give you pleasure. A sight I could stare at for hours. Unfortunately, our time today is too limited for such an indulgence."

He smiled at her little sigh of relief.

"I suppose you think that's a good thing. When in actuality it's not. Making love should never be rushed. Once you learn the pleasures to be found in denial and self-control, you'll look back and wish I hadn't given you what you want so readily."

Bringing his hand up from between her legs, he lightly swiped his thumb over her bottom lip, leaving behind a hint of moisture and the musky scent of her own arousal. Kayden swiped her tongue slowly across her lips, taking great satisfaction in the way his eyes darkened as he followed its movement.

He bent his head, retraced the path his thumb had taken with his tongue then lingered to nibble. His tongue invaded her mouth at the same time his fingers invaded her pussy.

Her moan of pleasure passed from her mouth to his when he started a slow, steady, synchronized rhythm that set both her body and mind on the path to sweet oblivion.

When his magical thumb came into play, circling, sliding, lubricating her throbbing clit with her own juices, it only took a handful of masterful strokes to bring her to the edge, another two to make her shatter.

Seconds later, left unashamedly spread, panting and satiated, she thanked God her *Oh God* had been captured by his mouth.

She couldn't remember when she'd ever been brought to an orgasm so quickly. It usually took forever. More than likely it was a combination of not having had one in a very long time, the nature of the situation she'd placed herself in and her strong attraction to the man. She refused to believe any man could be that talented.

But as she lay there in the afterglow, eyes closed, her inner muscles still fluttering around his deeply imbedded fingers, she hoped like hell he was.

* * * * *

Hunter was loath to take his fingers from her sweet, hot pussy, but he only had a half hour before he had to leave. Not once in the ten years he'd been meeting Simon, his best friend and fellow Dom, at their health club for their morning game of racquetball had he failed to show up on time. That he was tempted to cancel today didn't set easy with him.

His intuition about Kayden had been dead on target. He knew from the start she would prove to be a distraction. He just hadn't thought she'd prove to be this much of one, this soon.

With great reluctance, he withdrew his fingers from her moist, silky depths, took her foot off the table, grudgingly closed her legs and helped her sit straight.

"Better?"

"Hmmm. Yes Sir."

He smiled at her dreamy expression, planted a brief, affectionate kiss on her forehead and reached across the table to snag the small black box leaning against the candelabra.

"This is for you." He placed it into her hand. "The reward I promised for agreeing to our arrangement."

She didn't tear into it as many women would, instead studied it with a skeptical eye reserved more for a boxed snake. Locating the trailing end of the bow, she pulled until the white ribbon dropped into her lap, then peeked inside.

His heart warmed at the appreciative breath she drew.

"They're beautiful."

Opening the lid all the way, she pulled out the white-velvet inset displaying the earrings. He took the box from her and placed it on the table.

"Onyx and diamonds." She turned to him. "Your birthstone."

"And yours."

"I was born in December. My birthstone is turquoise."

"On the modern and traditional charts, yes. On the mystical chart, it's onyx."

She raised a brow. "It appears I'm not the only one who has done his research. What else have you learned about me?"

More than you can imagine. "Most likely no more than you learned about me."

She gave him a cynical look before returning her rapt attention to the earrings. "These must have cost a small fortune." She traced her fingertip over the substantial, triangular diamond embedded in a teardrop field of black onyx. "I've never worn anything this opulent. Are you sure you want to loan them to me? What if I lose them?"

"Not a loan. A gift. One of many you'll be receiving over the ensuing weeks. As far as losing them…" He shrugged. "They're insured."

He could see she wanted to object. That she refrained gave him hope that she was capable of change, albeit grudgingly. A good start. Although her constant questioning of his every action would have to end soon.

"Give them to me and I'll help you put them on."

"Wouldn't it be better to save them for a special occasion?"

He sighed heavily. "Kayden, what were you told about obeying me?"

"I'm sorry." She placed the earrings in his hand. "I won't—"

"Too late." He returned them to the box. "Apparently words are not enough. Stand up."

Grabbing her waist, he helped her to her feet. "The ruler on your desk, bring it to me."

She looked between him and the object requested.

"Your hesitation just cost you two additional swats. Instead of five, you'll get seven."

"But—"

"Ten."

"Ten!"

"Fifteen. Care to try for twenty?"

Compressing her lips, she turned and headed for her desk. Her skirt, still hiked above her thighs, gave him a tantalizing glimpse of the firm, pale ass he was about to pinken. He was so going to enjoy this. He glanced down at his watch. Too bad he couldn't prolong it. Stay around to savor it.

He would next time. And there would be a next time. Of that he was sure.

The best he could hope for now was to leave a lasting impression. Something for her to think about, give her pause before she opened that soft-lipped little mouth of hers and questioned him.

Chapter Four

ഗ

Kayden picked up the ruler from her desk. She couldn't believe she was going to allow Hunter to turn her over his knee and spank her. Even more astonishing was that she wasn't all that upset about it. The spanking was a recurring topic during the infamous after-work roundtable discussions and Harley and Morgan had confessed to love having their asses paddled and dared the rest of them to try it. Kayden's adamant "No way!" came back to haunt her. Having the opportunity to find out if spankings were as big a turn-on as her friends insisted land in her lap, or more accurately *over* Hunter's, she wasn't about to wimp out.

"Twenty."

Shit! Pivoting, she marched back to him.

"When I tell you to do something, don't think, just do it." He held out his hand.

The challenging glint in his eyes made her check the temptation to slap the thin, twelve-inch piece of oak into his palm. Knowing full well there'd be dire consequences should she succumb to the foolish notion, she laid it gently across his palm.

"Thank you." He stood, spun the chair with his free hand and resettled with knees slightly apart and feet firmly planted. "Pull your skirt up around your waist." Not willing to risk his adding additional swats, she immediately complied.

"I'll instruct you in the position I prefer only this once. I will rely on your intelligence to remember. In the future, after you've handed me the implement of your punishment, I will expect you to present yourself accordingly. Without complaint or hesitation. First you will kneel in front of me."

Kayden made a quick descent to her knees.

"Not like that. Slowly, gracefully. Stand and try it again. You are feminine to my masculine. When you are with me, you will leave behind the trappings of the independent modern-day woman."

Had it been any other man who made such an archaic statement, she would have laughed. But damn it, he was the epitome of masculinity and every latent particle of femininity inside her was on high alert and anxious to please. So she stood and knelt again. With all the grace of a prima ballerina. His pleased smile was the equivalent of roses tossed at her feet.

"Very nice." He balanced the ruler between his hands. "Kiss it."

She touched her lips to the cool, impersonal piece of wood, suspecting it would be much too warm and personal in very short order.

"Rise." He offered his hand for balance and drew her over to the right. "Lie across my knees, palms flat on the floor and spread your legs."

"More," he instructed, using the flat of the ruler on her inner thigh to guide her legs the right distance. "Comfortable?"

Was that a trick question? Her naked ass in the air, her most private parts exposed for his intimate viewing. The man certainly had a warped sense of humor. "Yes, Hunter."

"Hunter is never present during punishment."

"Yes, Master."

Expecting to feel the sting of the ruler, Kayden jumped when he palmed her ass. His large, warm hand covered her entire right cheek, his light squeeze sending a surge of warmth across her flesh.

"You have a beautiful ass. Much more suited to kissing–"

She sucked in a breath when his lips brushed her butt.

"And nibbling—"

Her lungs emptied it in a rush when he nipped her.

"Than spanking."

She clenched her ass in anticipation of the smack. Received a chuckle instead.

"I'd say this is going to hurt me more than it hurts you, but you know how I feel about lies. On the other hand, who will enjoy it more is up for grabs."

Enjoy it! Was he nuts?

"Ow!" The first whack to the unprotected half of her ass caught her off guard.

"Considering where we are, it might be wise to keep a tight rein on your vocal cords. Unless you desire an audience."

Damn. She'd almost forgotten.

"Stay still," he ordered, sliding his hand up to press her shoulders down.

She braced for the second swat. It didn't help. Jarred by the crack of wood meeting flesh, had it not been for his holding her in place, she would have arced up again.

The next three landed in random, sharp, ass-heating succession. Not all together unpleasant.

The next five, each harder than the last, sent a flash of heat both up her back and down her thighs. Instinctively, she closed her legs, earning her a firm whack across the back of both thighs. She immediately spread them back open.

"Just so you know, those two don't count. Close your legs again, I'll add five more."

Sonuvabitch. "Yes, Master."

"How many was that?"

How many? He expected her to keep count? "Eight. No, ten."

"Which?"

"I...I don't know."

He ran a gentle hand over her ass. "I suppose we'll have to go with eight just to be sure." Two more connected.

Somewhere between the thirteenth and fourteenth—she knew exactly because she was now keeping very good track— another sensation just below the threshold of pain flickered to life. Arousal. She scrunched her eyelids. *Damn, it was true.*

Hunter must have sensed what she was feeling because he stopped. Hell, with the unhindered view he had of her pussy, he could probably see the effect it was having on her.

Her assumptions were validated when he skimmed his hand over her ass and down to trail his fingers through the moisture between her dewy, plump lips. She clenched her teeth to keep from shuddering.

"Should I stop the punishment or continue? This once, I'll leave the decision up to you."

Bastard. He knew damn well she didn't want him to stop. He just wanted her to say it.

He flexed his finger, sliding the tip easily into her wet, aching pussy, reminding her of its presence. Not that he needed to. She was very much aware of his finger, of him, of the potential pleasure awaiting her if she told him to keep going.

Cursing him for his smug knowledge and herself for her weakness, she said, "No, Master. Please don't stop."

He never made it to twenty. Four more hard, well-placed smacks and she was rocketing over the edge, buffeted among the waves of an enormous orgasm. Were it not for the thick, solid thighs supporting her, she would have crumpled to the floor.

Physically exhausted, struggling for breath, Kayden hung limply over his lap. How the hell this man could bring her to such an explosive orgasm so quickly without so much as the tiniest flick of her clit was downright amazing. If he was that good with a scrap of wood, she couldn't wait to find out what he could do with the massive hard-on cutting across her diaphragm.

Her face-down position allowing Hunter freedom of emotion, he let his mask of control slip and took a few moments to appreciate the beautiful sight her brightly striped ass presented. The emblazoned *MINE* he'd imprinted on her milky flesh, a temporary symbol of ownership in lieu of the real one to come later, brought a smile to his lips. How he would love to trace the letters with his finger. But didn't dare. One feel of her warm backside would have him hauling her up and pinning her to the desk with his dick before she took her next breath. With the Herculean self-control he was known for, he avoided looking at her glistening labia as he grasped her shoulders and stood her up.

"Give me the earrings." Suppressing a grin at her hasty compliance, he followed her to her feet. "Turn your head."

Removing the small gold hoop from her ear, he replaced it with the new earring. Moving her head back the other way with a light pressure on her chin, he exchanged the other.

She raised her hand to toy with the earring. "Thank you."

"You're welcome." He pressed his lips briefly to hers. "Those were for yesterday." He reached into his pocket and pulled out another small black box topped with a miniature white bow. "This is for today." Pulling her hand away from her ear, he placed the gift in her palm.

"I don't understand. You just punished me. Now you're rewarding me?"

"The punishment was for what you did wrong. The reward is for today's progress. Open it."

She lifted the lid. "It's stunning." Her hushed tones went straight to his loins. Extracting the delicate ankle bracelet from its white-velvet bed, she discarded the empty box onto the table. Suspended between her long, slender fingers, she stared admiringly at the three onyx hearts—one large, flanked by two smaller ones— linked by a delicate gold chain. A Trielle diamond, his namesake, in the center of each. The only cut of diamond that would adorn her body from this day on. Though she wasn't aware of it yet.

"Lean against the table and put your foot on my thigh." Spanning her small waist, he guided her there with gentle pressure and waited patiently while she braced to keep a small distance between the table's hard edge and her tender ass. Once she was comfortably situated, he relieved her of the jewelry and patted his thigh. "Right foot."

There was a flash of uncertainty in her eyes before she took her lower lip between her teeth and did as he asked. Hunter was impressed. Especially since he suspected it was more determination than a true lack of self-consciousness. It showed her grit. She would need plenty of it in the days to come. Time was not a luxury in this relationship. He would push her harder and faster than he had any other woman he'd ever trained.

He ran his hand up the back of her leg from ankle to knee. Paused to nibble her inner thigh, savoring the telltale quiver of her tender flesh. Then he fastened the anklet around her trim ankle and adjusted the gems to the outside of her leg.

"Like it?" he asked, raising his head.

"Very much." She twisted her leg to better see the hearts. "Thank you, Hunter." Her lips spread into a beautiful smile.

"Whatever jewelry I give you is for you to wear. Especially when you are with me. Some will be visible to the public." He reached up to graze the back of his knuckles over the tops of her breasts. "Some will not." He slipped his hand inside her bra and captured a pebbling nipple between his fingers. He squeezed until she bit her bottom lip and then released the elongated tip. "*All* will be for our mutual pleasure. But none will carry more meaning than the last piece I present you with. That one alone will be yours to accept or reject."

"What is —"

"I'm afraid we've reached the conclusion of your first day of training. As it is, I left myself precious little leeway to be on time for my appointment." Lifting her leg by the calf, he set her foot down on the outside of his and stood. Planting himself between her wide-spread thighs, he cradled her pussy in his hand and leaned in, causing her to arch back over her unfinished waffle. "Much too late to appease my growing appetite, but I find I can't leave without helping myself to one last, delicious morsel."

He curled his middle finger and slid it into her wet channel for a quick, probing sampling. Sealing his lips to hers to muffle her enchanting little mewls, he used his unoccupied hand to reach behind her and pluck a strawberry off the plate.

Breaking the kiss, he pumped his finger a few more times and, satisfied he'd stirred enough of her juices for his purpose, he replaced his finger with the tip of the strawberry. After several swivels to collect some of her body's sweet cream, he extracted the fruit and popped it into his mouth. A few appreciative chews and it was gone.

Intent on her face, he licked his lips. "My last instruction before I leave is that you are not to touch yourself here," he rode his finger through her drenched pussy lips, "without my permission."

"You intend to leave me…wanting!"

"An exercise in restraint and obedience I expect you to adhere to. Don't disappoint me."

"How will you know?" she asked a bit too smugly for his liking.

"I'll ask. Are you prepared for the consequences should I discover you lied to me?"

The spark of defiance in her eye faded to a dull glimmer. "No."

Bracketing her head gently between his hands, he kissed her forehead and then her lips. "I won't be able to see you for the next three days because of some business matters of my own I need to clear up. I will, however, be in touch. Expect a call from my personal assistant later today to coordinate a time for you to visit the club's private spa tomorrow for your hair removal. Any questions before I leave?"

"None that can't wait."

"If you think of any, you have my private number. As of today, I'm available to you twenty-four hours."

She raised a brow. "What if it's very late? I'm something of a night owl."

He chucked her lightly beneath the chin. "That will change, since I'm an early riser."

Her brow rose even farther.

Hunter traced the feathery arch with his thumb. "Careful, love, your control is slipping. Now I really must go." He planted a firm goodbye kiss on her lips, and after helping her get her clothes back in order, he took his leave, fully aware of the emotional havoc he left in his wake.

He'd wait until he was comfortably settled in his limo and on his way before he called her.

* * * * *

Kayden looked down at what remained of her breakfast. She distractedly trailed her finger through the mixture of strawberry juice and wilting whipped cream framing her half-eaten waffle and, sticking her finger into her mouth, sucked it clean. A mistake, she realized, when instead of taking her mind off her unsatisfied needs, it only served to remind her of another finger dragging through another set of lips, leaving behind a trail of sticky sweetness.

She let her head fall back and moaned.

With the hopes of diverting her thoughts, she made her way to her desk, trying to ignore the slight tackiness between her thighs. That she knew a few talented swipes of his tongue would have taken care of the problem didn't help matters.

No way would she make it through the day like this, especially without benefit of underwear. Deciding he couldn't possibly have meant she couldn't wash herself, she veered off to the small private bathroom in the corner behind her desk.

She closed the door, flicked on the light and gave each of the brass handles on the sink a half crank. Hiking her skirt up to her waist, she soaked a washcloth and, deciding it best to start with the least sensitized areas, cleaned her inner thighs.

She rinsed the cloth, widened her stance and, holding her breath, flattened the cloth against her aching pussy. The steamy warmth felt like heaven.

Kayden stood that way for several moments, not daring to rub. She knew if she applied just the right pressure in just the right spot, a couple passes of the soft terrycloth over her clit would give her the release she craved.

She closed her eyes and immersed herself in the moist, soothing heat.

What would one little white lie actually hurt? It was her hand, her pussy.

My pussy. Hunter's possessive proclamation rang in her head, causing her eyes to open.

"Not technically," she said to the mirror image frowning at her. "It's not as if I'm cheating on Hunter with another man." The woman staring back didn't look convinced. Glaring, Kayden flipped her off.

The distinct ring of her private line filled the air.

She started guiltily and dropped the rag. "Shit." Tugging down her skirt, she snatched up the cloth, flung it into the sink and went to answer the phone.

"What are you doing?" The sound of Hunter's deep voice had the same effect as looking up and seeing flashing lights in her car's rearview mirror. Her heart sank into her stomach.

"At the moment, talking to you."

"Before that."

She could hear the smile in his voice. *The bastard.*

"Tidying u—" Deciding word games would gain her nothing, since it was more than likely he'd been through hundreds of scenarios just like this one, she took a fortifying breath and said, "Washing myself."

"Just washing?"

"Yes Sir." She was relieved to be able to answer honestly.

"But you were tempted to do more, weren't you? You wanted to stuff your fingers inside your wet, neglected pussy, slide them over your throbbing clit, get yourself off?"

Major bastard! Kayden squeezed her thighs together. "Yes Sir."

"What stopped you?"

"The phone, Sir."

There was a long pause. "Hmmm. That does create a dilemma. I'll have to decide which one outweighs the other— your honesty or your thwarted disobedience. I think the best thing to do is see how well you follow my instructions over the next three days and then decide."

Three days to agonize. That alone would be punishment enough. Patience never had been one of Kayden's strong suits. Sighing silently, she plopped down in her chair. She shot back up on a very audible hiss and ran a tentative hand over her burning bottom.

"The tenderness won't last too long. A few hours at most. Don't expect the same lighthanded consideration the next time your sweet, firm little ass is presented for my displeasure."

That he was so sure there would be a next time didn't cause Kayden as much concern as the tidal wave of lust that roared up and hit her squarely between her legs. "I'll keep that in mind, Sir."

"So will I, sweetheart. So will I."

There was a wealth of promise in his low, deep tones, laced with a sensual sinister quality that sent a hot rush of yearning through her body.

"The next time you're tempted to touch yourself, call me. Be lucky enough to catch me in the right mood and I just might let you get yourself off."

Yeah right. Like she believed that. "Yes Sir."

"I'll see you in three days," he said just before hanging up.

She had barely enough time to digest that threat when the phone rang again.

Her hair removal appointment was set for three o'clock the next day.

Chapter Five
✤

Standing in front of the floor-to-ceiling mirror, Kayden let the fluffy white robe slip from her shoulders and waterfall to the heated, black-marble floor beneath her bare feet. There wasn't a single nuance in the cozy, intimate dressing room that didn't appeal to one's senses. Or more accurately, one's sensuality. Low lighting, soothing music, warm woods and some unique, exotic scent filtering through the ventilation system for supreme serenity. And it was working. Thank God!

The woman who stood in the mirror now was a far cry from the one who'd entered the luxurious spa four hours ago.

Who knew getting your most private hairs yanked out by the roots could be such a non-traumatic experience?

Instead of the anticipated waxing, she got sugaring. An ancient Egyptian method used in the harems, she'd been informed by the highly trained, *naked* technician. All the women in the inner sanctum of the club were completely naked, with the exception of those wearing collars around their necks.

The initial few yanks to remove her hair had shocked more than hurt, after which the technician had settled into an experienced, gentle rhythm. Once her privates were denuded, her legs were given the same treatment.

Seduced by the soothing effects of the tea she'd been given earlier and the slow, seductive melodies pouring through her earphones, overall, it was not the traumatizing experience Kayden had expected.

The last hour of her visit, she was treated to the most amazing massage. It was during that time something occurred to her about the women's collars. Made of different materials ranging from leather to fine jewelry, studded with various precious gems of varied sizes and shapes, they were all stunning. But there hadn't been a single triangular cut gem or diamond in sight. What that meant and why it pleased her, Kayden wasn't quite sure, and lulled into a state of supreme relaxation by the masseuse's extremely talented fingers, she'd forgotten all about it.

Until now.

The mere thought of diamonds brought Hunter to the forefront of her mind. She skimmed her fingertips over the smooth surface of her mons, liking the feel and the look. It was amazing how one small change could make her feel so incredibly sexy. She couldn't wait to feel Hunter's hands on her. Better yet, his mouth.

Away from the intensity of her job, with four hours of uninterrupted time to think, she'd decided to wholeheartedly throw herself into her forbidden fantasy and she couldn't wait to start.

Turning, she walked over to the tufted white lounger and the two gift boxes sitting there. One open—one not.

The first had been presented when she'd arrived. She'd expected something along the lines of a bracelet to match the other two items he'd given her. This piece did indeed have two heart-shaped pieces of onyx with a triangular diamond in each center, but instead of being centered on the long, sturdy gold chain, the gems dangled from the base of two onyx cylinders crowned with rubber-tipped gold clamps. There was no doubt as to the adornment's purpose. Her nipples tingled in anticipation.

She'd always wondered what nipple clamps would feel like. Apparently she was going to have to wonder a bit longer. The accompanying note from Hunter specifically stated she was to bring them with her so he would put them on.

The second box had been in the dressing room when she'd gotten back. It was too large to contain jewelry and Kayden's curiosity had been peaked.

The white cross-ribbons and bow attached only to the lid had made it easy to get to the surprise nestled within the ebony and white swirled tissue paper.

A black leather thong.

The barely there garment folded onto itself and Kayden didn't notice the stenciled H and T in the small triangular patch that formed the front until she held it up. Centered over her freshly denuded skin, it would be a gleaming reminder of exactly who it was that now owned her pussy.

Though it wasn't as disturbing as the two thin leather strips that would pass through her legs and travel up the crack of her ass to connect to the thin leather waist strap. Threaded through a succession of diamond-studded onyx beads, the sizes and variations of openings between the two strips were completely adjustable. The endless possibilities of what exactly the adjustments would be used for caused Kayden's imagination to fire along with her libido. But she doubted there was anything she could dream up that Hunter hadn't already. Like if several beads were lined up perfectly over her clit, walking would become a whole new experience. And if positioned that way during sex—

"Ms. Starling?"

Startled, Kayden nearly dropped the thong. "Yes?"

"Sorry to disturb you." The congenial voice of Hunter's personal assistant filtered through the door. A tall, willowy brunette, Elizabeth had greeted Kayden upon her arrival and given her a tour of the expansive spa. "Before you leave, Mr. Trielle—"

"He's here?" Kayden fought to keep the excitement from her voice.

"No, Miss. He won't be back until tomorrow. But he sent you something and I wanted to make sure you stopped by my office on your way out."

"I'll be there in a few minutes." Swallowing her disappointment, Kayden was about to drop the thong back into the box when she glimpsed the tip of yet another box beneath some dislodged tissues.

The length of a bracelet box, but three times as thick, she had a sneaky suspicion what it contained. With equal parts apprehension and excitement, she lifted the lid to find a gleaming black onyx dildo. Intrigued by the flared base, she pulled it out for a thorough inspection. Upending it, she discovered a magnificent diamond deeply embedded in the bottom. At this rate, by the end of their time together, he'd have spent a small fortune on her. Though reported to be filthy rich, she found it hard to believe Hunter spent this much on every sub he trained. Especially one who was only temporary. So why then was he investing so much in her? Not wanting to dwell on a question she was determined not be an issue, she repacked everything, got dressed and went to see what Hunter had sent her.

* * * * *

Fairly certain the large, white florist box contained flowers, but learning not to second-guess Hunter, Kayden waited until she was home to open the box.

Thank God!

Oh there were flowers. The most magnificent red roses she'd ever seen. And not one, but four *bracelets*, each circling a dozen shiny green stems. But unlike the previous jewelry, their black and white theme came in the way of two-inch leather, each adorned with diamond studs and a highly polished silver ring. Kayden didn't have to be a BDSM enthusiast to know they were used for wrist and ankle bondage. Thick swatches of Velcro for easy on and off, the sturdy restraints were a far cry from the flimsy, amateur ones found in adult store bondage kits.

Her heart pulsed and accelerated at the thought of her splayed in sexual sacrifice, helpless and vulnerable to anything Hunter wanted to do to her. She clamped her thighs to restrain the sudden flow of her juices.

Ironic how she'd dreaded the day when she'd turn her body over to the Master Dom and now couldn't wait for it to get here.

It wasn't until she'd carefully freed the thornless stems from the restraints and transferred the flowers to two glass vases and two plastic water pitchers that she discovered the instructions and another highly intimate gift. A set of three. In graduating sizes.

Clearly, her mouth and pussy weren't the only orifices Hunter intended to find pleasure in.

Chapter Six

ഓ

Yanked from sleep by Beethoven's Fifth, Kayden threw her arm in the direction of her nightstand and snatched up her cell phone. She didn't bother looking at the display to ID the caller. Having programmed the tune to this particular number, she knew who it was.

"Uhmmm." She executed a one-armed stretch. "Good morning, Hunter."

"Good morning, love." The deep tones that poured through the phone reached out and gave her slumberous libido a solid shake. "You knew who it was and still answered the phone?"

"You expected me not to?"

"To be perfectly honest…I had some doubts. There were times when you gave the impression of not being one hundred percent invested in this endeavor. And I need you to be one hundred percent."

"You can stop worrying."

There was a long pause. "Yes, I believe I can. You sound different this morning — more confident. I'm proud of you."

He was proud of her? No one had ever said that to her before. Not even her mother. It wasn't that her mom didn't love her. Working two jobs and making sure that even if her own wardrobe was lacking, her daughter's was up-to-date enough not to be ridiculed by classmates, her mom was too tired at the end of the day to expend any energy on emotional nurturing. That Hunter had said the words shouldn't have mattered. The warm feeling that spiraled up from her stomach to spread through her chest said just how much it did.

"Did you like your gifts?"

The loaded question blew through her sappy thoughts like buckshot. Sitting up, Kayden jammed her pillow against the headboard and nestled her back into it. "They're...interesting."

"Interesting! That's all? They didn't turn you on? Get your pussy juices flowing?"

"A little," she admitted tentatively.

His deep, sexy laugh spilled through the phone. "Only a little? Not good enough. Have you ever indulged in any ass play?"

Any lingering fatigue vanished at the blunt question. "No," she answered, ignoring the scintillating spasm of her sphincter muscle. "I never had the desire t—" She sank her teeth into her bottom lip. Not entirely true. She'd often fantasized about what it would feel like and had considered purchasing a small butt plug while on a recent vacation to New Orleans. The only thing in her bag when she'd left the Bourbon Street shop was a basic seven-inch, pink plastic vibrator, a large tube of lube and an economy pack of Mardi Gras beads. The latter a waste of money, since the girls at the office didn't believe for one second some guy had tossed them down to her from a wrought iron balcony because she'd bared her tits.

"You're awful quiet, Kayden. You didn't fall asleep on me, did you?"

No, not yet, but she was certainly hoping to. Naked, her leg thrown across his thick thigh, her ear pressed against his wide chest, enjoying the strong beat of his heart. A delicious shiver shook her body. "I'm still here. And no, I've never tried it because I never found anyone I trusted enough to make me want to."

Several moments of silence ticked by. "Do you trust me enough?"

The answer came easily. "Yes."

"Good. Then are you ready?"

"For what?"

"Anything I ask of you?"

"Yes, Master," she stated adamantly, wanting him to know just how serious she was.

"In that case, get up, hang up, leave whatever clothes you're wearing on the bedroom floor, go to the door and buzz me in."

Kayden pulled the phone away from her ear and looked at it like an alien being. *Hunter here*? A quick scramble off the bed and peek through the white mini-blinds covering her bedroom window revealed a black limo down at the curb.

"Kayden!"

The distant command had her plastering the phone to her ear. "Sorry. I'll be right there."

Flipping her cell closed, she yanked her oversized, smiley face sleep-shirt over her head and tossed it to the floor. Doubting she'd need the unsexy garment in the foreseeable future, she kicked it under the bed and dashed into the adjoining bathroom. After a fast swish with mouthwash and a lame attempt to confine her sleep-mussed hair, she made a beeline to her front door, giddily savoring the thought that Hunter had contacted her a day earlier than he'd said.

* * * * *

Hunter closed and pocketed his cell, leaned his head back against the seat and slowly released the breath he'd been harboring deep in his lungs. Used to holding himself detached, he'd forgotten how intense needing to hear the right answer from the right woman could be. He wasn't comfortable second-guessing himself—another thing he hadn't done in a very, very long time. But now that he was absolutely certain he hadn't pushed too hard too fast, he knew exactly how to proceed from here.

Sitting up, he hit the button to roll down the window between him and his chauffeur. "I'll let myself out, Ray. Make yourself comfortable for a while."

"Sure, boss. No problem." He leaned to open the glove compartment and flashed the magazine he plucked out.

Catching a glimpse of naked, bound and gagged women, Hunter shook his head and left the car.

He'd barely made it to the building's front door when Kayden buzzed him in.

After a relatively short elevator ride up to the sixth floor, he was surprised to find her apartment door slightly ajar, but no Kayden in sight.

He let himself in and the sight that greeted him took his breath away.

She was in the perfect kneel-up position. Balanced on her knees, legs spread perfectly to allow him a cock-hardening view of her naked pussy. Her back was straight, both her chest and head high, eyes lowered. Her arms were down, hands resting on her thighs, palms up. Telling him without words she was open to his wishes, while at the same time letting him know once again how extensively she'd researched the lifestyle. He had to steel himself against scooping her up, tossing her across the first available piece of furniture and burying his dick deep inside her hairless cunt to take them both to the heights of ecstasy and back.

"Welcome to my home, Hunter."

"You're beautiful." He let the statement hang unembellished as he soaked in her breathtaking sensuality and allotted time to harness his rapidly mounting desire. She was pure perfection. He'd lost count of the times he'd envisioned her exactly this way.

Except for one thing.

Closing and locking the door, he walked over to softly stroke her cheek. "Don't move," he warned when she turned her face into the caress. She instantly stilled. He smiled and reached up to remove the clip holding her hair haphazardly atop her head. An obvious hasty attempt to tame it. But he didn't want tame. He wanted wild and natural.

Freed from its imprisonment, the luxuriant black mass tumbled from her head, over her creamy shoulders and spilled halfway down her slender back. Gathering up a thick section, he brought it forward and laid it alongside her breast, grazing the tender flesh with the back of his hand as he did. Her slight shiver knotted his gut.

"Unless I specifically request otherwise, you are to wear your hair down."

"Yes, Hunter."

He flicked the tip of her earring with his finger, setting off a display of dancing lights. They were perfectly faceted, like all the others he'd given her and those she'd yet to receive. "Where are the rest of your gifts?"

"On the dresser in my bedroom. I'll go get—"

"No. Stay as you are. Location?"

"Down the hall, last room on the right."

Anxious to conclude his business on the West Coast and return to her, Hunter had taken the redeye back, leaving no time to change. In no particular hurry, now that he was here, he took his time removing his coat, suit jacket and tie, neatly folding and laying them across the back of her couch. All the while enjoying the way her graceful back tapered into a trim waist and flared again into a lust-inspiring, heart-shaped ass. That he would be the first to explore the hidden treasure between the two pale, smooth globes pleased him immensely. His hard dick was more than ready, but Hunter knew she needed to be prepared first. In her current receptive state of mind and positioned as she was, what better time than now?

Unable to resist the gnawing need to touch her, he walked up behind her, bent to press his cheek to hers and helped himself to a handful of her sweet ass. "Don't move," he reminded softly, slipping his hand between her legs and trailing his finger from the opening of her pussy up between her butt cheeks.

Her clipped, throaty whimper when he pressed lightly against the rosebud of her ass sent heat coursing through his veins. He pressed again, feeling the warm, textured ring of flesh contract beneath his touch. "One day, very soon, I'm going to fuck you up this tight little ass of yours. Do you want that?" His face was so close to hers, he heard her soft swallow.

"Yes. I want that very much."

He'd expected the *yes*. The *very much* was a pleasant surprise. That she was so willing to embark on this new adventure made him wonder if she'd be this receptive to everything else he'd planned for her. Already hard to the aching point, Hunter hadn't thought his dick could get any harder. That she was not only willing but eager to experiment made the swollen flesh almost painful.

"Then the sooner we start preparing you, the sooner that time will come." He softly nipped the sensitive muscle where her shoulder and neck met and when she spontaneously cringed, he swatted her ass. "I said not to move. Or your ass will be feeling more than a little discomfort today."

He nipped the same spot. Satisfied when she held steady, he rose and headed down the short hall that led to the back of her apartment.

More interested in getting back to Kayden than her taste in decorating, he made a cursory glance of her blue-walled, cluttered room, his eyes lingering for a few seconds on her recently vacated bed, its mussed lemon-yellow sheets and the scrunched pillow leaning against the headboard. The lingering indentations proclaimed it a feather pillow. That he also preferred feather meant one less thing she'd need to bring when she moved in. Her comfort was of great importance to him. After all, she'd be there a long time.

He moved his gaze to the dresser flanked by two windows. The items he sought were lined up neatly in the center, surrounded by a colorful clutter of perfume bottles and innumerable makeup and hair paraphernalia.

Apparently neatness wasn't high on her priority list. Considering his well-ordered life, that would definitely change. Shaking his head, he stepped over several pairs of carelessly discarded shoes, a skirt, two crumpled tops and a pair of jeans as he made his way across the room. Selecting what he needed, he retraced his cautious steps and headed back out.

* * * * *

Kayden locked her spine against the shiver that threatened upon Hunter's return. Eyes downcast, concentrating on keeping her breaths steady in light of the unknown, she watched his shadow on the rug.

"Stand and look at me."

She rose as gracefully as she could without benefit of support and faced him.

"Put this on." He presented the thong across his palm. "When you're done, I want you on hands and knees, legs slightly spread."

When she reached for the scrap of leather, he withdrew it.

"Not yet. There's something I want to do before you cover that lovely, smooth pussy of yours."

Compelled by his golden, commanding gaze, and wanting to show her readiness to embark on this sensual adventure with him, Kayden relaxed.

Eyes locked with his, she concentrated on his touch, the light, feathery sensation as he ran the back of his large hand along her jaw and down her neck. The heightened awareness when his hand rode the valley between her breasts and continued on with a slow glide over the slight swell of her stomach.

Always a bit self-conscious of her not-so-flat stomach, she sucked it in.

His hand stilled.

She caught her lower lip between her teeth and dropped her gaze. "I'll work on it."

"Kayden, look at me."

Her eyes came up to collide with his contemplative gaze.

"Work on what?"

"My stomach. It should be firmer." She held steady under the shadow of mild disapproval clouding his eyes.

"I'm glad this came up now. We can deal with it and get it out of the way."

Her stomach clenched tighter.

"There are only two people you have to please. *Me* and *you*. If you're doing it for yourself, that's fine. If it's for me, you're wasting your time. I love your body—just the way it is—soft and slightly rounded, the way a woman's body should be."

He splayed his hand over her stomach, his large hand warm and soothing. "Relax."

Kayden slowly unclenched her muscles.

He caressed her stomach. "Although I subscribe to healthy living, physical perfection is a commercial illusion. We all have flaws, real or perceived. I will place enough demands on your mind and body without your adding to them. The only area in which I will expect near perfection is your obedience to me. Can you give me that?"

"I'll do my best."

"Don't try too hard."

"But you just said—"

"I know what I said. But if you never slip up, I won't get the chance to spank that gorgeous ass of yours and I so want to have the pleasure of doing that again." The corners of his mouth tipped up.

Since Kayden wanted that too, it was a lost cause to hold back the pleasure struggling to claim her lips.

"Ahhh, liked being turned over my knee, did you? Well, let's see if you like this as well." He claimed her mouth at the same time he palmed her naked mound.

The abruptness of the move caught Kayden off guard. Her small squeak of surprise turned into a low moan of pleasure as the heat of his hand warmed her flesh. Having her hair removed had indeed made the area more sensitive, but she hadn't really realized how much until Hunter's big hand covered her.

Her moan grew louder when he ran his middle finger between her damp folds, rode it back and forth through the wealth of moisture several times, then dragged his finger back through her cream-slick labia and up over her sensitized clit. When he rasped his fingernail against her unguarded nub, she gasped and pulled away.

He palmed her crotch and jerked her back.

Thrown off balance, Kayden threw her hands up and caught hold of his shoulders, bringing them nose-to-nose.

"Pull away from me again and we'll be getting around to that spanking a lot sooner than I'd hoped. Though I wouldn't suggest it. Your ass will be dealing with enough tonight without adding the burn from punishment."

If there had been any doubt as to what he intended, that cryptic statement obliterated it. After tonight, the only thing her ass would be a virgin to was Hunter's masterful cock. Not that she was complaining. She was ready for that. If not physically, mentally. But she was hoping for a little front action as well and she wasn't thinking of the artificial kind. Sure, he said he liked to take it slow, but after having made up her mind to enter into this wholeheartedly, Kayden was more than ready to get the proverbial ball rolling. Dare she make her feelings known? Was that even allowed? There were some things her research was vague on. Oh to hell with it.

Drawing a deep breath, she looked him in the eyes. "Permission to ask something?"

He nodded. "Granted."

"I'd like to step up the learning process."

His only reaction was an intense study of her face. As silent seconds ticked by, Kayden began to worry.

"What exactly do you mean by *stepping up*?"

"Before you leave tonight, I'd like you to make lo—" She shook her head. *No that's not what this is about.* "I'd like you to…fuck me."

"You would, would you?"

The glint of devilment in his eyes made Kayden's heart race and her toes curl into the deeply piled, beige fibers beneath her feet. Damn, the man was sexy. Her libido made a beeline for the top of the Richter scale at the thought of being claimed by this enigmatic Dom. Hell, if he, with all his experience, didn't know how to turn a woman on, where did that leave the rest of the male population? Probably in Earth's sub-basement.

"If I grant your request, what will I get in return?"

"Anything you want."

"Anything?" One dark brown eyebrow spiked, accentuating the sparkle in his golden eyes. "Hmmm, right answer. Brave, but do you really mean it?"

"Yes."

"We'll see."

Kayden didn't even try to stop the small, throaty mew that bubbled up when he crooked his finger and pushed it inside her. It found its way easily into her wet and ready depths. So did the second finger. He was a tall man with big hands, Kayden was looking forward to a third. Instead he withdrew, stepped back.

Swamped by frustration, it took a moment to realize what was dangling in front of her face. The thong. A spiral of excitement rapidly replaced the disappointment. Taking the minuscule scrap of fabric, she slipped it on and, without waiting to be asked, got down on hands and knees.

"Legs wider," he said, giving no indication he'd been pleased by her voluntary obedience.

She didn't need the prompting of his hand halfway up her inner thigh to spread them, but she welcomed the warmth and comfort of his solid touch.

The wider stance caused the straps of the thong to dig deeper between her swollen lips, the beads an added pressure wherever they touched. Kayden fought a needy whimper. She was just giving herself a silent pat on the back when Hunter slowly slid his hand up between her legs, running his finger over the two beads wedged between her juice drenched folds and pushed in slightly.

She moaned and moved into the touch. The next thing she felt was his hand landing hotly onto her ass.

Kayden sucked back a protest and resumed the correct position.

"Good girl. Disobey again and you'll be unwrapping your next present sooner than planned."

Ninety-nine point nine percent sure what the *present* was, and not in any particular hurry to test her perceived psychic abilities, Kayden vowed to hold her pose no matter what. Trouble was, she had a sneaky feeling Hunter wasn't going to make it easy for her.

"Then again, maybe a visual reminder will help," he murmured next to her ear.

The stream of breath that delivered the soft, sensual threat triggered an array of goose bumps that started at the back of her neck to fan out over the rest of her heated flesh.

Then he was gone, along with the heat his big muscular body generated. Kayden mourned its loss. A girl who burrowed deep under the covers at the first sign of a snowflake and dreaded the long Chicago winters, she knew Hunter would make the perfect bedmate. Although the sultry summer nights might pose a problem. An image of a spacious, air-conditioned room, drenched in soft, early morning light came to mind. Their naked limbs entwined on a large bed.

Problem solved.

It was easy to picture a long string of lazy Sunday mornings, waking up next to him. A smile took up residence on her lips. For all of two seconds.

What would possess her to entertain the idea of a future with a man she barely knew, and who barely knew her? Overwhelmed by an onset of unease, she cringed. Was it possible Hunter could be the one man who might know her much too well? Dare she—

A package appeared on the floor in front of her.

Happy to be yanked from her disturbing thoughts, Kayden focused tenaciously on the mental lifeline the familiarly wrapped gift provided.

The next thing to come into view was a pair of black-clad legs, followed quickly by a panty-wetting set of muscular thighs when he hunkered down in front of her.

Lust. Sex. Two additional and very welcomed distractions.

"Look at me."

Hunter's soft command cut short her admiration of the way his black dress pants strained at the seams, but didn't prevent her from checking out the enticing bulge nestled in his crotch. *Good grief, the man could pack the space behind a zipper like there was no tomorrow.*

Dragging her gaze up to his, she was greeted by a heated gleam of awareness.

"You'll have more of my cock than you can handle before too long."

He didn't know her as well as he assumed if he thought that. She suppressed a smile.

He cupped her chin. "That little glint in your beautiful blue eyes tells me you doubt my words."

Curse the too sexy devil. Could he read minds as well as bodies? She'd have to be more diligent in hiding her emotions.

He pressed his thumb to her bottom lip, tugged gently and then released. "Believe me, sweetheart, when I tell you that before I'm through with you, you won't know which you want more—for me to stop...or continue. I didn't gain my reputation because of my mastery over a female's body alone. You might want to keep that in mind. I only come when I'm damn good and ready. I'll make you orgasm a dozen times before I find sweet release in your body."

A dozen! Seeing no downside, her pussy swelled in anticipation, but the skipped heartbeat was due wholly to the challenge. Kayden made sure those were her only reactions. He wasn't the only one with a reputation to uphold. Hers was twofold. She never made the same mistake twice—unless it suited some purpose—and she always accomplished what she set out to do. And making him lose control just skyrocketed to the top of that list. First step to accomplishing that goal was learning all his rules before she could break them and implement a few of her own.

He released her chin and took the lid off the box. "I hadn't planned on giving you this so soon, but after your positive reaction to the introductory spanking session in your office, I changed my mind."

Kayden stared at the flogger. Though no great surprise, her reaction to it was. Both her breathing and heart rate went into overdrive. She might have mistaken the reaction for fear, if not for the mounting desire she felt deep in the pit her stomach. A feeling that intensified when Hunter picked up the flogger. Innocuous curled on its bed of snowy satin, it looked ten times more threatening stretched across his large, open palms.

"How do you like the handle?"

Kayden tore her wary gaze from the long, soft leather tentacles at the business end. Handle? Her body jerked and her eyes widened. Easily nine inches of solid onyx with two rings of staggered diamonds around its wide circumference and a single row lengthwise along the top, it was obviously a dildo. And she was pretty damn sure the gems' placement wasn't to assure his grip. Nor was the flare at the base a hand guard. But like the other toys, it was made to be held in place by the openings provided by the adjustable beads on her thong.

Swallowing to clear the large lump in her throat, she whipped her gaze up to his. He couldn't mean for her to carry that around inside…

One look into his unyielding, fiery eyes said he did.

From his pocket, he extracted and pressed a button. The leather tentacles retracted. Another press and they lengthened. "Adjustable for whatever length of skirt you're wearing. If you're wearing one," he added on a devious purr.

How fucking considerate of him! Well hell, she did say she'd let him do *anything*.

"It didn't seem cost-effective not to make it a multi-purpose punishment tool."

Had she not feared a test run of his new gadget, she'd have snidely told him that even with two purposes it was an extravagant investment, considering their temporary relationship. Was he a major stockholder in a friggin' diamond mine?

She hadn't realized she'd voiced the question until he smiled. "Not a stockholder. Part owner. My family owns one." His smile widening, he hit another button on the remote. A low hum reached her ears. There was no doubting what kind of punishment that meant.

Determined not to give him the satisfaction of a reaction, she bit the inside of her cheek. She was quickly discovering that researching the BDMS lifestyle was a far cry from the actuality.

He laid the flogger out full length, placing the handle in the box, trailing the loose ends slowly through his hand to spill over the side of the box onto the carpet. Almost a loving gesture, like stroking his hand along the silky length of a woman's hair.

If he were trying to put her at ease, he was falling way short of the mark. She knew damn well, placed in his powerful, capable hand, the only affection she'd experience was the biting kiss of leather against her tenderized flesh. Given her penchant for rebellion, there'd be no skipping a formal introduction to the damn flogger—before she and Hunter parted company, she added belatedly.

He tucked the remote in his pocket and stood. "If the mood to disobey becomes unbearable, feel free to run with it." He winked and moved around to her feet.

She closed her eyes and suppressed a groan.

The intimate stroke of his hand across her ass turned it into a silent whimper.

"Normally, I would hold off initiating a new sub to this form of pleasure. But after one look at your lovely ass, I knew I couldn't deny myself its use for very long. We'll start small and work our way up," he palmed and squeezed her cheeks, "as soon as you tell me you're ready."

Why was he asking? Wasn't it supposed to be that she just showed up—naked—and he made all the decisions? Where was all that guilt-free psycho-babble she'd read about? She scrunched her eyes. Took a quick shallow breath. Somehow she knew Hunter didn't operate that way. Because when it came right down to it, that scenario was a deception. An easy way out. Ultimately, every choice, conscious or subconscious, had to be hers. The ultimate one, to gift him with her unconditional submission. Only then would Hunter take full control.

Since she had no major hang-ups about what he was asking of her, she had no problem consenting. She'd heard too many of her girlfriends say how wonderful it felt to have a man's long, thick cock up their ass not to. She just hadn't found the right man to share the intimate experience with...until now. The man who was patiently awaiting her answer.

She drew a calming breath and let it out gradually. "I'm ready."

"Would you like a drink of water first?"

Her heart tripped at the unexpected consideration. "I'm fine. Thank you for asking."

"Don't sound so surprised." The long, gentle stroke of his hand down her back warmed her insides. "Your comfort and pleasure are of the utmost importance to me. Secondary only to my own. The only time that will not apply is when you are being punished. Then it will be your *discomfort* that takes precedence."

He knelt behind her, his thick thighs forcing hers even farther apart.

Her earlier bravado aside, Kayden locked her elbows in preparation of the embarrassment she anticipated. Was shocked when it never materialized. Totally vulnerable to his gaze and touch, she felt sexy, wanton and more alive than she'd felt in years. Hit with a sudden charge of sexual expectation, her legs and arms trembled. Before they failed her altogether, she was bracketed between Hunter's steely arm and wide solid chest. She melted into the warmth. Cool met hot. She shivered. God, the man exuded enough body heat to melt the polar ice cap.

"Take a slow, deep breath," he said, obviously misconstruing her reactions as he relaxed his hold. "It's only natural to be a little nervous."

"I'm not...nervous...I'm—"

"Excited? Turned on?"

"Yes."

He gave her an encouraging squeeze. "Not half as much as you soon will be."

No idle promise, Kayden was sure.

He released her to glide his hands teasingly up and down her outer thighs, up and over her ass, back down. "This might be a little cold, brace yourself."

Kayden closed her eyes and stoically endured the tug and tightening of the thong as he hooked it with his finger and held it aside. Then the cool flow of the lube as he painted a line between the globes of her ass, stopping shy of her pussy.

He used the tip of his finger to spread the gel, with an occasional pause to test the resistance of her anal entrance.

Kayden concentrated on relaxing to make the initiation easier.

His finger breeched the tight opening and slid partway in.

She sucked in a sharp breath.

"Easy," he said, holding his position. "That was the hard part. The next step will be easy."

So says the man with the thick finger. After several seconds and no real pain, only a slight burning sensation that wasn't entirely unpleasant, she realized he was telling the truth.

He alternately withdrew and advanced in small increments, going deeper and deeper each time, until he settled into a rather pleasurable rhythm that Kayden wasn't merely tolerating, but enjoying. So much so that instead of dreading the addition of a second finger, she was anticipating it.

Given Hunter's capacity for torturous teasing, she knew it would be a long, long time in coming.

Chapter Seven
Ꮹ

Hunter knew from the little quivers in Kayden's body, combined with her escalating breaths, that she was impatient for more. Something he was prepared to give her—when he was damn good and ready.

There was a first time only once and he'd every intention of savoring it. As he would the many other pleasurable firsts he intended for her. But breaking in a virgin ass was a particular favorite of his. And since this particular ass would now and forever belong to him, he was determined to make it a memorable occasion for them both. Not an easy task, considering his rock-hard cock was clamoring against the steel teeth of his zipper with a bid to replace his finger.

Studiously ignoring his jealous dick, Hunter concentrated on the fantastic feel of her tight little anus and the way her much paler flesh looked as it rode smoothly over his tanned finger. It wasn't until his knuckle was swallowed and the last flutter of resistance disappeared that he deemed her ready for more.

Placing his left hand flat in the small of her back to anchor her, he crossed his second finger over the first and introduced them both halfway with one long, steady push.

She gasped.

Detecting no genuine pain in the soft sound, he went in for a deeper sampling.

Her low, melodious moan hit Hunter straight between the legs as he pressed down with his other hand to keep her from arching up.

"Oh God."

"Is that a good 'Oh God' or a bad one?"

"A very, very good one, Sir."

Smiling, he slowly rolled and swiveled his fingers to stretch her a bit more, pulled partway out, then delved deeper.

She moaned again. Louder.

He moved from the hand on her back to cradle her throat, draped himself over her back and lifted her head up to gain access to her ear. "If you think this feels good..." He ran his tongue over the outer ridge, punishing her with a quick nip to her lobe when she attempted to shy away. "As I was saying, if you think this feels good," he seated his fingers, absorbing the vibration of her needy whimper with his chest, "wait until you feel my cock deep inside, stretching you, filling you. You were made for this, sweetheart. And so much more." Uncrossing his fingers, he pulsed them open and closed within the gloving, warm confines of her body. He paused to savor the heat and silky texture, then withdrew.

"Nooo."

Her sweet, desperate protest cut another slice in the weakening reins of his constraint. Sensing impending freedom, the unruly beast caged within the confines of his suit pants roared to life, insisting it was long past time to move to the next phase.

Needing to taste her, he used the hand at her neck to twist her head enough for a greedy, thorough possession of her mouth. "Don't fret, love. I have no intention of leaving you wanting." He planted a row of tiny kisses along her jaw, up to her ear. "At least, not *this* time," he whispered in a soft, ominous tone and reached down for the larger of the two butt plugs he'd coated with lube earlier.

* * * * *

Though Hunter's threat didn't bode well for the future, Kayden decided to stay firmly rooted in the promise of the here and now. Her friends hadn't lied. Ass play *was* a colossal turn-on. Looking past the initial soreness, she anticipated the day she'd be able to accommodate Hunter's long, thick cock. Just not today. As pleasurable as it was to have his fingers invade her, having sat in his lap, there was no denying the man's wealth in the family jewels department. And although her pussy was up to the challenge, her slightly tender butt was not.

The wet tongue in her ear and the beads on the thong being pressed into her clit dispersed Kayden's attention to those particular parts of her body.

"Ummm." The sound purred from her throat as she closed her eyes and focused totally on the dual sensations. Hard, wet bead. Warm, soft tongue. "That feels— *Fuck*!"

Caught off guard by the unexpected seating entry of the butt plug and the flash of pain as her muscle expanded and contracted over the flared base, the only thing that prevented her springing from the floor like a scalded cat was the reassuring weight of Hunter's chest.

"Breathe, Kayden." The command was terse, the kiss he placed on the side of her neck whisper soft. "You're fine."

Her vehement denial died quietly when, a moment later, the pain mellowed to a mild, throbbing discomfort, followed quickly by an unbelievable feeling of fullness and unexpected pleasure.

"Better?"

She nodded.

He nipped her shoulder.

"Yes," she yelped and after expelling a small sigh, said more quietly, "You could've warned me."

"If I had, you would have tensed and felt even more discomfort."

His quiet self-assurance streamed into her ear on a warm, calming breath. Blanketed by the warmth of his large, strong body with the steady thud of his heart against her back, Kayden let her body go lax.

"In time, you'll learn to trust I know what's best. Your body and mind are riddled with roadblocks. Most imaginary. Based purely on assumption, fear of the unknown or the taboos placed on us by a narrow-minded society. It's my job to find the best way to dismantle them."

Bearing down lightly, he rolled the bead located over her throbbing clit, its journey made easy by her slick juices. "Sometimes slow." He increased the pressure, rolled the bead again.

Kayden's breath hitched.

"Sometimes fast," he whispered, just before his other hand pressed on the base of the toy he'd inserted.

Hit with an unexpected ripple of pleasure, the breath rushed from her lungs on a fractured whimper.

It wasn't until his muted laugh penetrated her sensual daze that she realized she'd canted her hips and was pushing back, like a cat in heat. She didn't care. She'd be his willing cat any time, any place, for however long he wanted her.

Shock gripped Kayden's body. No, this was *temporary*. The stern, silent reminder did little to allay her anxiety.

"I think it's time to move this somewhere else."

Grateful to be pulled from the disturbing depths of her thoughts, Kayden focused all her attention on Hunter. The delicious graze of his finger on her needy cunt as he slid back a bead to secure the butt plug. The giddy sensation of being airborne when he stood and scooped her up against his warm, solid chest. The heady feeling of excitement when he headed straight for her bedroom.

Finally! She was getting her wish. He was going to fuck her.

* * * * *

Maneuvering around the clothing on her bedroom floor, Hunter stopped short of the bed, eased Kayden's feet to the mauve carpet and turned her to face him. Bracketing her face between his hands, he lowered his head and devoured her mouth, familiarizing himself with the satiny texture, the taste.

She melted against him, the combination of soft, pliant breasts and rigid nipples playing havoc with his fading self-control. When she raised her arms to encircle his neck, he broke the kiss and, capturing her wrists, lowered her arms to her sides. "Do you have a travel bag?" He released her and took a half-step back.

Clearly confused by his request, she was slow to answer. "Yes. Over there. Already packed." She pointed at a fairly large piece of navy designer luggage next to her night stand.

"Anything smaller? An overnight bag?"

"Yes. But aren't you going to fu—"

"Are you questioning me?"

She dropped her gaze, but not before he caught the unmistakable glint of dissatisfaction. "No Sir." She sighed softly and let her head sag, causing a thick, heavy section of her raven hair to slide over her shoulder and cover one breast.

Her questioning him wasn't the only reason he'd cut her off. He disliked her using the word *fuck*. A crude, unsophisticated word. Not that he was hypocrite enough to say he hadn't used it, or fucked more than his fair share of women. It was simply not a term he wanted associated with what the two of them would share. She was expecting him to take her to bed. He had every intention of doing so. Only not hers. When they made love the first time, it would be in *his* bed.

With a gentle prolonged stroke, he brushed her hair back over her shoulder and lifted her chin. "Where's the case?"

"In the closet. Top left."

He touched his lips to her forehead and went to retrieve it. Returning, he unzipped it and set it on the bed.

"Bring me whatever toiletries you think you'll need."

When he deliberately failed to address the confusion clouding her gaze, she turned and walked into the adjoining bathroom.

During the symphony of drawers opening and closing, bottles clinking and plastics clacking, Hunter went to the dresser and gathered up the other things he'd given her and packed them. When he was done, he looked up to find her standing a foot away with an armful of female beauty products.

"On the bed," he instructed before she could dump them into the case.

Hunter selectively picked through the small, colorful mound of items, coming away with only a pair of round, plastic containers. Tossing the full pack into the case, he held up the one missing a single birth control pill. "Protection and cycle. Very important things for a Dom to know."

Admiring the pink flush that crawled up from her chest to tint her cheeks, he pitched the open packet into the case, zipped it shut and picked it up. "Everything you'll need, you'll find at my place. If not, I'll send someone to buy it for you. So unless there's anything you want to present for my consideration, it's time to go." He moved to her side and placed his hand in the small of her back.

When a light nudge failed to move her, he looked down and met her inquiring gaze.

Rather than waste time on another lengthy discussion on total obedience, he said, "You're entering a new life. One in which all your needs will be fulfilled by me. It has been my experience that the transition is much easier if you bring little of your previous life with you. At least, not at first. The option to negotiate will depend on how quickly you adapt. But because you weren't planning on coming to me until tomorrow, I'll allow you to choose one item to bring with you."

Hunter followed her searching gaze as it touched on items around the room. Some dismissively, others longingly, like her pillow and the clothes hanging in her closet. Shoulders squared, she started for the living room.

Fairly sure she was headed for the front coat closet, Hunter trailed behind at a leisurely pace. When her brisk steps slowed to a more tentative stride, he grinned. She'd forgotten about the butt plug. As she continued on, the two-carat triangular diamond centered in the base winked merrily from between her pale, firm cheeks. Presented with such a delightful homing beacon, Hunter and his hungry, eager cock were happy to follow.

Kayden was halfway across the living room when he emerged from the hallway. Instead of heading for the closet, she veered left toward the kitchen.

His licentious thoughts mulled by curiosity, he picked up his pace. Entering the room, he found her in front of the small oak-topped island, facing him.

Off to her side, he caught sight of a multicolored handbag. He should have suspected.

"Are you sure that's what you want to bring? I doubt there's much in your purse you'll need."

She frowned. "I've no intention of taking my purse." She stepped aside and slapped her hand on the object next to it. "This is what I'm taking."

"Your laptop?"

Her cocky nod was barely completed when the laughter bubbling in Hunter's throat broke to the surface.

God, she was a treasure. And he was pretty damn sure this wouldn't be the last surprise in his future. A future that was starting…right now!

* * * * *

Kayden smiled in reaction to the deep, throaty laugh that filled her kitchen. It bounced off the white maple cabinets to surround her and enhance the cozy feel of the small space. Handsome by any woman's standards, Hunter was simply devastating when humor lit his face and his golden eyes sparked. Liking the warm tingly sensation she felt clear down to her bare, red polished toes, she vowed to make sure he laughed often during their time together.

Ten minutes later, they were in the elevator. His chauffeur, facing forward, his back to them, carrying her overnight bag and laptop. Hunter carrying her. Snuggled against his broad chest and surrounded by the warmth of his heavy, wool overcoat, she buried her face against his shoulder, hoping like hell she didn't run into any of her neighbors.

A sneak peek when the doors opened revealed the small white-marbled lobby to be blessedly empty. Halfway through, Hunter stopped. The light tap of the chauffeur's footsteps echoed in the high-ceilinged space as he continued on.

"We'll give Ray a few minutes to put your things in the trunk and come back to hold open the doors. We don't want to risk you catching a cold."

The smile in his voice when he kissed the top of her head brought Kayden out of hiding to glance down at her curled, bare toes. When the man said she wouldn't be allowed to bring *anything*, she hadn't taken him literally. She wouldn't make that mistake again.

When Ray returned, Kayden snuggled tighter against Hunter to provide a smaller target for the slicing, winter wind.

The coordinated exchange from one comfortably heated environment to the next was accomplished within a matter of seconds.

All in all, not a bad way to travel. A girl could get use to this type of TLC.

Fully expecting to be settled in the soft black leather seat next to Hunter, she was surprised when he kept her in his lap.

"Comfy?" He smoothed a section of wayward hair back over her shoulder.

"Yes."

"Good. Reach over and hit the second button up from the left on the panel in front of you," he said as the limo moved smoothly into the steady stream of Saturday Chicago traffic.

Fully aware she'd be exposing half her body if she did, since her arms weren't actually *in* the sleeves of his coat, she glanced at the back of Ray's head and then at Hunter.

He captured her chin between his thumb and finger. "From this moment on, you're mine — completely. So I suggest you start acting like it."

"For the next month," she felt a deep need to clarify. Bathed in the golden heat of his unflinching gaze, she fleetingly wondered whose benefit the reminder was for.

"Until the day our relationship ends."

His choice of words caused her pause. But since the outcome would be the same no matter how it was worded, she took a bracing breath and reached for the button.

As feared, the coat fell away, leaving one breast bare.

There was a soft hum, followed by the appearance of a darkly tinted window slicing away the view of the driver. Her prayer that it complete its ascent before Ray looked into the rearview mirror proved unnecessary as his eyes never left the road.

The light pressure of Hunter's hand against her cheek returned her attention to him. "The only man that need concern you is the one whose lap you're sitting in. What other people see," he slid his hand down the length of her neck, over her shoulder, across her chest to firmly cup her breast, "or think doesn't matter." He slackened the arm behind her back so she lay more still. "Open your legs."

Holding his gaze, she let her outer leg drop to the floor, the butt plug shifted at the sudden change of position. She sucked in a breath and raised her hips.

"Does it hurt?"

"No," she admitted, warmed by the concern in his voice. "It just takes a bit of getting used to." She settled back down, shifting to find the most comfortable position.

"You will. In time." He reached down and palmed her pussy, extending the tips of his finger to lightly pump the plug. "You'll come to love having something in your ass. A toy," he pushed with a light steady pressure and held, "my cock."

Stirred by both the physical stimulus and his words, Kayden moaned. Yes, she wanted that. Couldn't wait. If the small plug generated this kind of pleasure, she could only imagine what something bigger would do. In an attempt to enhance the pressure, she thrust her hips.

"Like that, do you? Let's see how much."

She barely had time to bemoan the loss of his touch when he dragged his finger up through her slick folds and slipped easily inside her welcoming heat. He played awhile— pumping, sliding, twirling until she wanted scream.

"Tell me what you want," he demanded with quiet authority, as if he couldn't guess by all the wriggling and writhing she was doing.

"Another finger. Please, Hunter, use two."

The slow, penetrating glide of the second finger nearly drove her mad as it stretched and filled. Once embedded, she couldn't believe how full she felt. Had it not been for the toy in her ass, she would have begged for another of his long, thick fingers in her hot, aching pussy. But there was no space left.

When he didn't move, she began softly pumping her hips. God, she was so close to coming, why wasn't he moving? She pumped harder. Closed her eyes.

"Be still."

Be still. Was he kidding? Focused totally on her building orgasm, she bucked her hips, driving his fingers incredibly deeper. Oh God, yes. Once more—

The sudden emptiness shocked her eyes open. He'd pulled out!

"When I tell you to be still, I mean still."

Not until she blinked him into focus did the sternness in his voice register. "But I was so close to —"

"I know exactly how close you were. It doesn't matter. You'll come only when commanded or granted permission. You may think it cruel at first, but will soon learn the longer you wait, the more gratifying it will be and the more you'll appreciate it."

Her attempt to close her legs and sit up was aborted by a heavy hand on her thigh. "I said I didn't want you to orgasm. I didn't say I was done playing."

Chapter Eight

 හ

By the time they pulled into the private underground parking lot beneath Club Kimberlite, Kayden was so hot and worked up she'd slipped back into cat-in-heat mode. Complete with yowling. For at least the last fifteen minutes of the ride.

Before that, she vaguely remembered being able to string two coherent thoughts together. Like being fairly certain the dark-tinted glass kept the chauffeur from seeing anything, but having serious doubts about the soundproofing in the limo. But subjected to Hunter's sweet, manipulative torture, her concerns for embarrassment had gone the way of her pride, preempted by her escalating frustration and the desperate need thrumming between her legs. She'd never been so turned on in her life. And God love the man for his consummate skill, she knew it wouldn't be the last time.

Snuggled back inside Hunter's coat, hugging her overnight bag, Kayden was barely aware of her surroundings as he carried her the short distance to the elevator that led to his private quarters above the club. All her focus was centered on her deprived pussy and the tip of the big stiff cock prodding her side. With any luck, it would shortly be prodding where she most needed it. That he was as turned on as she was brought her some measure of satisfaction. Her concentration wholly on her unrequited lust and the steady, effortless rise and fall of the large chest she was pressed against, the trip to his bedroom was a blur of black, white, glistening crystal and shiny chrome.

The man really needed to put some color in his life.

The fleeting thought vaporized when he let her feet drop to the dense, white bedroom carpet.

"On the bed," he commanded in a low voice, taking her bag and stripping his coat from her shoulders.

"As you wish." She added a bit of sway to her hips for added enticement and reaching the foot of the bed, she turned. "How do you want me? Back or stomach?"

The sexy little smile that lifted the corners of his mouth made her belly do a double flip.

"On your knees. Facing away from me. Show me how ready you are."

Thinking of the limo ride, she zeroed in on his muscular right thigh.

Like the wet spot on his dress pants from her overflow of pussy juices wasn't proof enough?

Not about to point that out, she obeyed without question. Whatever it took to get her laid, she was more than happy to do.

He wanted proof? She would damn well give it to him.

Back in cat-mode, like a kitty having its back lovingly stroked, she undulated up onto the black brocade bedspread until she was nearly nose to button with the round, red, tufted throw pillow at the head of the bed, the only bold splash of color in the room. Hands planted in line with her shoulders, she eased her knees apart. Going for maximum spread, she almost did a nose-dive into the pillow. It was while she was stabilizing herself that she realized, in light of Hunter's earlier disclosure, the twinkling stones comprising the triangular button in the center of the pillow were most likely a conglomerate of small diamonds. Sure he couldn't see her, she rolled her eyes, until she realized she could use the tiny gems as a focal point. Better them than the picture she presented, all spread open, swollen and glistening from the probing and teasing he'd done earlier.

It only took several seconds to come to the conclusion it was a fruitless exercise. Hunter had done too good a job in making her aware of her body and its needs. The taunting

175

fullness in her ass accentuated the keen emptiness on the other side of its thin wall. Amazing how quickly she was getting use to the small onyx intruder. She often wondered why many sex toys were tapered when a man's cock was not. More than likely because they didn't have a wide, strong pelvis behind it, determined to keep it in place. *That* picture made her insides clench and an unavoidable moan to escape.

In the process of unbuttoning his shirt, Hunter's head came up at the small, soft sound coming from the bed. After his first initial long look to make sure she'd followed his instructions…

Hunter frowned. When the hell had he last lied to himself? So long ago, he couldn't even remember. He'd looked his fill, wanting nothing more than to walk over and plant his aching cock so far up inside her, it would form a memorable acquaintance with her womb.

He forced his concentration back to removing his clothes, determined to take his time. It would serve as a lesson of patience for her and allow him the time needed to get in the right mindset. It was a wasted endeavor. Watching his fingers work their way down his shirtfront only reminded him of where they'd last been. Sliding around inside her wet, snug pussy until the first flutters of an orgasm forced him to pull out. The little frustrated sounds she'd made as she'd squirmed in his lap had gotten him so hard that he'd come dangerously close to taking her in the limo. Thankfully, by the time his control threatened to snap, they'd been too close to the club to do the first time they'd make love any justice.

He curled the fingers of his right hand into his palm to stave off the strong urge to bring them up to his face. The smell or taste of her right now would demolish his plans to take things slow.

To remove himself from temptation's path, he moved across the room and into his massive walk-in closet. The dimmed can-lights along the ceiling's perimeter automatically brightened. Hunter glanced up to where one touch of a button would retract several concealed panels to reveal the necessary apparatus for a variety of suspension devices. A man who made his own rules, he wasn't about to follow some preconceived notion that *dungeons* needed to be dark and dreary. When he took control of a woman's body, he wanted enough light to see every subtle change in expression and body. Especially when it was *his* woman.

He was eagerly looking forward to bringing Kayden in here, relishing the fascination on her face when he showed her all the room's cleverly hidden secrets. Her bold, curious nature wouldn't allow her reaction to be anything less.

On his way to the back of the closet, he bumped his fingers along the row of dime-sized diamonds along the underside of the two-inch granite lip of the six-foot-long island of drawers. He pressed the last two and went to stand in front of the first section of the mirrored back wall that slid open.

Retrieving the butt plug remote from his pants pocket, he activated it.

A soft squeal followed by a delicious tortured moan flowed to him from the bedroom.

He smiled.

Reaching back, he placed the control on the island, stripped off his rumpled clothes and tossed them into the built-in clothes bin. He passed his hand over the electronic eye to close that section and moved over to the next. He took several moments to admire the onyx and diamond collar displayed there. One of two very important gifts he would bestow upon Kayden when the time was right. The rare, red, flawless ten-carat triangular diamond in each matched to perfection.

He didn't have to close his eyes to imagine how this gift would look on her. Blessed with an innate eye for detail, Hunter had made sure the satin it was displayed on matched Kayden's creamy skin tone. Hunter ran his fingertips over the collar's cool smooth surface before grabbing the box that contained the toe ring he would put on her after he claimed her scrumptious body.

He returned to the bedroom as quietly as he'd left, pleased to see Kayden was still in the exact position he'd left her in.

His cock pulsed at her open, receptive position. If every sub came to him so well prepared and determined, his training numbers would double. Though, if things turned out as he'd planned, those days were numbered. At least where other women were concerned.

Taking out the toe ring, he slipped it onto his left little finger and set the box down on the glass wall-table beside the closet's entrance.

On his way to the bed, he confiscated the nipple clamps from her overnight case and, crawling up behind her, positioned himself between her legs. "Rise up on your knees. Slowly." Governing her ascent by hooking his arms beneath hers, he slipped his cock between her legs and rode it over the beads on her thong, pressing harder when he reached the ones over her clit.

"Please, Hunter." She paused on a stuttering breath. "I don't think I can wait much longer."

"Not *much* longer." He thrust and canted his hips, enjoying the moist heat against the top of his straining cock, the clench of her soft ass against the tautness of his stomach and the strain of her leg muscles as they protested being held open by his.

Lowering his hands to cup and test the soft, pliable texture and warm weight of her breasts, he bent his head to lay a trail of teasing kisses along her shoulder, nosing her hair aside to get to the fragrant niche behind her ear. There, he filled his lungs with her heady scent. With few exceptions, one of the first things he demanded of a sub was to change her perfume. Not Kayden.

Unlike too many women catering to their own tastes by wearing an overpowering sweet floral fragrance more apt to stiffen a man's nose than his cock, she exuded a subtle, musky scent. One that entrenched itself into a male's subconscious. Indulging in another whiff, he switched his grip on her breasts to a slow, massaging pull, inching his way to the tips, until he captured her pebbled nipples in a tempered pinch.

He rolled, tugged, squeezed, increasing and decreasing the pressure, using the slight changes that passed to his body from hers to gauge the level of pain she could endure. When he was certain where her current boundaries lay, he reached down for the nipple clamps. "Have you ever worn nipple clamps?"

"No Sir."

"Tomorrow, over breakfast," he nuzzled her neck, "we'll discuss your sexual preferences and dislikes." He traced his tongue along the lower edge of her ear, delighting in her tiny shiver. "Reach back and grasp my shoulders. Don't let them down until I tell you."

When he felt the soft, light weight of her hands, he plucked and played with her left nipple until it kernelled and lengthened enough to attach the first clamp. Once in place, he screwed the onyx cylinder until she hissed a small breath between her teeth, waited until she relaxed, then gave it another quarter turn.

She whimpered but didn't protest.

Perfect.

After attaching the second one, he ran his hand down her quivering stomach to the front of the thong and using his fingertip, traced through the stencil of his initials. Dipping his finger lower, he rotated the first bead over her clit. It rolled easily. A sign of how ready and excited she was. A good thing, since he was more than ready. "I believe the time has come to get rid of the thong."

Chapter Nine

છ

Her patience strung to the breaking point, Kayden closed her eyes and took a sharp, deep breath. Her lungs emptied on a hiss when the motion enhanced the pinch of the clips dangling from her nipples. She froze, letting the snippet of pain fade.

Hunter's hands moved to her hips.

Damning him and his cursed fortitude, she concentrated on the warmth of those big, supporting hands and shallowed her breathing. She bit back a demand that he remove the clips. All too sure he would know the reason had little to do with pain itself, and everything to do with the invisible hotwire link straight to her pussy and the shocking aftermath of pleasure.

His hands skimmed up and down her sides several times, painting a trail of warmth. "You okay?"

"Yes," she whispered.

"Put your hands back on the bed."

More mindful of the clamps, she moved slowly. The chain swung away from her body and her sensitive nipples took the full weight of the thick gold links. Her muffled moan turned into a yelp when Hunter's palm landed across her ass.

Jarred forward, the chain swung out sharply and snapped back. Her next moan was full blown.

"Much better." The lack of sympathy in his tone was contradictory to the soothing hand he ran over the spot he'd abused. "How can you expect me to learn your limits if you continually suppress your reactions?"

He couldn't have just asked? Riding out the ripple of pain rolling across her ass, she fought the urge to turn and glare.

"Or was I mistaken in believing the clamps tight enough? Would you prefer I tighten them more?"

"No."

"I didn't think so. Now let's get this thong off."

The process of widening the opening around the butt plug, sliding the skimpy thong down her hips and removing it after instructing her to lift one leg and then the other amounted to no more than a few seconds and left Kayden feeling a bit cheated that he hadn't lingered a bit longer to tease and play.

"Relax." He rubbed his hands methodically over her back, kneaded the back of her neck and shoulders, massaged her upper arms and unhurriedly worked his way back.

Kayden arched into his soothing touch. "Mmm." The kiss he placed at the base of her spine ignited a spiraling tingle that fanned out over her flesh.

"I had initially thought to remove your new toy before granting your request to be...fucked. Considering how well you've taken to the small amounts of pain I've administered so far, I've reconsidered." He palmed, squeezed and spread her ass cheeks, running his thumbs beneath the flared lip of the plug.

Kayden internal muscles seized at the light tug, an instinctive reaction to hold the plug in place. In the hours she'd worn it, she'd discovered she liked the erotic feeling of something in her ass. "Leave it in."

After a prolonged silence, she hastened to say, "*Please*, leave it in."

"Better. Remember your manners and you'll get everything you want tonight," he passed the tip of his finger teasingly through the puffy lips of her pussy, "and so will I."

"Hunter, p...leeez." She lowered her shoulders and raised her butt. The rasp of his fingernail lightly over her clit had her sucking in a breath and coming back up.

"One more question, sweetheart."

Kayden bit back a frustrated scream.

"What's your safe word?"

"Diamond," she nearly screeched and then did when he shoved the full length of his cock inside her in one long, slippery lunge.

There was a flash of pain. Fast on its heels came a swift tidal wave of burning pleasure, making her grateful for the strong hands at her waist that kept her ass pinned to his pelvis and thwarted her attempt to pull away. She'd never experienced anything like it. Not the feeling. Not the man.

She could too easily get addicted to both.

The addiction to the *feeling* wasn't what scared the living crap out of her.

"Stay with me, love. I'm far from done with you."

For a paralyzed moment, she thought he could read her thoughts. When his pumping hips fell into an easy, cadenced rhythm, she relaxed and emptied her mind of all thoughts of permanence. Not a difficult task, since the rhythmic in-and-out glide of his long, thick cock was pushing her rapidly toward a long overdue orgasm.

Filled both front and back, with the only separation a thin wall of sensitive tissue, Kayden knew blessed oblivion was just around the corner. She closed her eyes, shutting off one of her senses to elevate the others and better experience every facet of this first-time experience. She wanted to remember everything, down to the tiniest detail.

The smell of their mingled arousal.

The roll of his powerful hips as his pelvis pushed off her ass.

The way his firm stomach bumped against the base of the plug, forcing it deeper.

The hot, glorious glide of his claiming penetration as her pussy swelled open to welcome the lusty invasion.

At the first flutters of her impending climax, she opened her eyes. As much as she craved the explosion, she wanted to prolong and savor all the wonderful sensations thrumming through her body a bit longer.

Apparently, Hunter wasn't of like mind. As if he'd known what she was doing, he curled his body over hers, captured her clit between his fingers and pressing his face to hers, whispered, "Come for me. Now."

One pinch was all it took.

Her orgasm hit with the intensity of a category five tornado. Blindsided, picked up, spun and spit back out, she was allowed precious few moments to catch her breath inside the eye of the storm before she was flipped onto her back and staring up into Hunter's smiling face.

"Not bad for starters," he said, grabbing hold of her ankles, raising them to his shoulders and plunging into her again.

* * * * *

Cocooned in Hunter's long wool coat, surrounded by his masculine scent, Kayden stared sightlessly out the cab's backseat window. She couldn't even remember what lie she'd fabricated for the club's security guard to get him to call her a taxi. She doubted he would've been so amenable had he known whose bed she'd just slinked out of. Whatever the excuse was, it must have been believable. Much more so than the lies she'd been telling herself. The best one yet, that since she didn't have a cowardly bone in her body, the reason for her sneaking off in the wee hours of the morning could be laid squarely at the feet of her stiff independence.

Stiff? Ha! It was folding like a sapling in a hurricane. No, not folding, bending. Giving itself over to the stronger, dominant force and loving every submissive minute of it. That was the real truth. And it was scaring the hell out of her.

She'd awakened in the middle of the night, draped cozily over Hunter's large, rock-solid, warm body. More content than she'd ever felt in her life, she was tempted to close her eyes, snuggle down and drift back off. Mother Nature had other plans. She'd reluctantly peeled herself off Hunter and padded from the bed in search of the bathroom.

If she hadn't taken a good look in the mirror after washing her hands and face, she would probably still be at Club Kimberlite.

The sight of the starry-eyed, wild-haired, sated female reflected back would have taken her to her knees were it not for Kayden's tenacious grip on the marble sink. The woman she'd glimpsed had never looked happier. A woman who'd been fucked sore, suspended from hooks in the closet ceiling and flogged into a mind-blowing orgasm — twice, fingered in both her pussy and ass, at times simultaneously, and commanded to her knees to suck Hunter's mouthwatering cock until her jaw ached. Then, and only then, allowed to savor the taste of his tangy come.

Kayden didn't want to know who that deranged woman was, but whoever she was, the shameless hussy was staying back at the club and *this* woman was going home to resume her hectic, sexually deprived but safe life.

Two hours later, her flaming, tear-stained cheek mashed against the taxi's cool back window, Kayden was ready to kill someone. The most likely candidate, the asshole who hadn't properly secured the load of drywall in the back of his pickup truck. The smashed and scattered pieces now sucking up the winter slush in the middle of I-90. At this early hour, in any other city, it wouldn't have been such a major problem. But this was Chicago. Traffic was never light.

On second thought, maybe she should be thanking the *asshole*. He'd given her a reprieve from the submissive she-devil riding her conscience, sabotaging every logical, mental argument Kayden had erected in her path.

Once unearthed, it wasn't easy to ignore the truth, but if she caved and admitted deep down that she'd always secretly yearned to be that sexually submissive woman in the mirror, she'd then have to acknowledge the fear that she'd just walked out on the only man she could trust with that knowledge.

Oh God, what if — "Damn it."

"Sorry," the driver said, straightening from his sharp swerve to take advantage of a miniscule opening in the faster moving lane next to them. "You okay?"

Kayden caught the man's concerned gaze in the mirror and burst out in hysterical laughter.

For the rest of the way, she could've sworn the man drove with one eye on the road and one in the rearview mirror. Hell, who could blame him after her maniacal display. Her hair bed-tossed, wearing a man's overcoat and clutching onto her overnight bag like it contained money from a bank heist, he probably thought she'd escaped from a mental institution.

Given all that, it was no big surprise that when they'd arrived at her apartment building and she asked him to wait until she ran up to get her money, he'd eyed her skeptically and shook his head.

Desperate, she'd searched Hunter's coat, hitting pay dirt in the inside breast pocket.

"Thanks for bring me home safely." Freeing the wad of money from the diamond-studded, gold money-clip, she peeled off several large bills into the man's pudgy walnut-toned hand. When his thick black eyebrow flew up, she added another hundred.

What the hell, the driver had earned it, having to put up with her lunacy. And Mr. Hotshot I-own-a-diamond-mine Trielle could well afford it. Besides, it was his fault she found herself in this mess, both physically and mentally.

If she hadn't been so upset, she would've planned her escape better. Money being at the top of her essentials list.

She'd hold the expensive clip and the rest of his loot hostage in exchange for her forgotten laptop.

By the time she trudged into her apartment, dropped the coat and bag next to the bed and tumbled onto the sheets, she was more than ready to embrace her exhaustion. There'd be plenty of time to sort through her emotional turmoil in the lonely days ahead. Plenty of time to decide which of the two women warring inside her would reign supreme and take her rightful place in the world.

Chapter Ten
ഇ

Without knocking, Simon stepped into Hunter's office, took one look at his friend's appearance and laughed.

Unfazed by the glare targeting him as he strolled into the room and plopped himself in the chair in front of the desk, he hooked his booted foot on the opposite knee and relaxed back. "Sorry, pal. But I can't remember you ever looking so—"

"Disheveled," Hunter supplied.

Simon crunched his nose. "Actually, scruffy was what I was going for. The last time I saw you like this was after that three-week cabin stint with that nympho sub you trained for Romeo Luigi." Simon whistled. "I'd have liked to have been a fly on the wall for that one."

Hunter lips twitched. "With most women, the challenge is to get them to leave their legs open, making them accessible to their men. With her, it was teaching her when to keep them closed."

"Whatever happened to her anyway?"

"Romeo married her."

Simon sat up straighter. "No shit?"

The men shared a laugh, though Hunter sobered much faster.

"She's really got your guts tied up in knots, doesn't she?"

There was no reason to clarify, since they both knew it was Kayden they were speaking of.

Blowing out a deep breath, Hunter raked his fingers through his hair, adding little to the damage already present.

"Why don't you just go and get her? If your instincts about her being submissive are right—and I can't imagine they're wrong—she'll obey."

"It would work on another woman, not Kayden."

"Why, because she's strong, independent and bullheaded? You've broken tougher."

"I don't want to break her. And, yes, she's all that, but mostly she's afraid to face the truth. And knowing her as I do, trying to force her to face that she was born to be a submissive will only make her deny it more adamantly. If she's to be my wife, she needs to come to me of her own free will…without doubts."

"So you're just going to sit here in your self-imposed misery and wait?"

"I didn't say that."

"Then what are you going to do?"

"I've already done something. I've sent her a gift."

* * * * *

"Well, aren't you going to open it?" Trista asked, seated with Morgan, Shayla, Kendra and Harley in a semicircle around Kayden's desk.

Kayden stared down at the thin, flat box sporting a big white bow as if it contained anthrax.

It had been two whole, long soul-searching weeks since she'd come to work the Monday morning after escaping Hunter to find her laptop already returned. She'd looked at it and broke down. Immediately surrounded by her five supportive friends, she'd spent the next hour sobbing out a slightly abridged version of why she'd walked out on her fantasy. Denied a few very important details in relation to her true feelings, they'd unanimously supported her decision to forget Hunter.

Until last night.

When during one of those cursed alcohol-induced roundtable discussions, exactly like the one that had gotten her into this whole mess, she'd confessed there was the teensiest possibility she was falling in love with him. After a lengthy silence, she'd squinted through the martini haze clouding her vision. When she'd finally fine-tuned all five of their shocked expressions, she'd attempted a quick backpedal by saying, "But that's crazy, right? No one falls in love at first *sex*!" She'd been the only one who'd laughed.

"Well?" Kendra prompted, tapping out a Morse code routine on the edge of the desk with a long, glittery-red fingernail.

Resigned to the inevitable, Kayden sighed. "Okay." She lifted the lid off the box and stared down at the envelope. Not that there was any doubt who'd sent it. If there had been, the bold H T next to the large triangular diamond embossed in the left corner would have laid it to rest. Setting the envelope aside, she extracted the black velvet box inside.

When Shayla helpfully pushed the outer box aside, Kayden set the other in its place and opened the hinged lid.

Struck speechless by its contents, she gave the box a half-turn so the others could see.

Comments flew in rapid succession.

"It's beautiful."

"I've never seen a red diamond before. Must be worth a small fortune."

"Does he have a single brother?"

"Breathtaking."

"Are you going to keep it?"

It was the last whispered question by Morgan that drew Kayden from her mind-spinning stupor.

"I...I think I should give it back."

Trista folded her arms on the desk and leaned in. "Given who the man is and what he represents, I believe your *taking* it back is the point. I also think it's not your everyday run-of-the-mill necklace. And I'm not referring to the gargantuan red diamond."

No, not a necklace, a collar. Three impressive rows of half-inch onyx squares linked together by dozens of small, brilliant triangular diamonds—points down to symbolize female power. Her gaze dropped to the mind-staggering triangular red diamond, hanging off the center bottom onyx—point up. She ran a marveling finger over the unique gem.

Having shared a good portion of her research with her friends, she wasn't surprised when Shayla asked, "What do you think it means?"

"You mean other than, thank you, Lord, there's hope I won't have to marry a computer geek in my search for a rich husband?" Harley's attempt at humor earned her five sour looks, which she shrugged off.

"I think it means Hunter acknowledges and respects her female power," Kendra said in hushed tones.

Kayden smiled at her insightfulness. "And the lower placement of male power signifies the female power is not subdued, but an extension of."

"Are you going to go back to him?" A die-hard romantic, Shayla's eyes glittered with hope.

"I'm not sure." She picked up the envelope and stared down at the lettering across the front. Not her name, but ONYX. "I'd like some time alone to think."

Once the others had filed out after a round of supportive hugs, she opened and read the letter. She expected to find an explanation for why he'd written onyx. What she found was…

Deny it all you want. Deep down, you know what you truly are and running away won't change the fact that you are and always will be submissive. My submissive.

—H

* * * * *

190

There was no knock on his office door before it swung open, so Hunter didn't bother looking up from the article he was reading in the latest issue of TLI. He didn't even know why he was reading it. Except that he somehow felt a connection with Kayden when he did.

"If you've come to gain some perverted amusement at my expense, Simon, you can just turn your sorry ass around and head back the way you came." Having reached the end of the list of the ten top things women look for in a man, Hunter snorted and flipped the page.

"Something wrong with the article?"

The soft feminine voice had his head snapping up. "Kayden?" He drank in the sight of her. "How did you get in without—"

"Actually, Simon was on his way in, but when he found out who I was, he convinced your assistant to let me surprise you."

Closing the magazine and sliding it aside, Hunter hit his intercom button. "Elizabeth."

"Yes Sir?"

"Is Simon still there?"

"Yes Sir."

"Then tell him not to go far. I don't want to waste time tracking him down when I come to kill him."

Hunter pulled his finger off the button, cutting off a stream of robust, male laughter.

Kayden's lush lips turned up at the corners, eliminating all thoughts of Simon.

"Don't get up," she said, forestalling his attempt to rise. She stepped farther into the room. Focused on her cherished face, it wasn't until she moved that he noticed the large, cloth bag she was carrying by the handle.

She came as far as the chair in front of his desk, stopped and set the bag on the seat.

"Why are you here?" Hunter kept both feet planted on the floor and his clenched hands on his thighs, resisting the unsophisticated urge to lurch to his feet, vault over the desk and capture her in his arms.

"I'm here for a couple of reasons. I have some questions and a few things to give back to you."

Having a pretty good idea what one was, the hope that bubbled up in his chest at first seeing her deflated.

She flipped her hair over her shoulder and bent over the bag. The diamond from the earrings he'd given her winked back at him. He drew some consolation from the fact she apparently didn't intend to return *all* his gifts.

"Your coat." She straightened and laid the pile of neatly folded black wool on the corner of his desk. "I would have sent it back with the money, but it was out being cleaned. Thank you for the prompt return of my laptop."

"You're welcome. I know how lost I would feel without mine, given the business material it contains." Jesus, was this how it was going to end? A string of mundane senseless bullshit and then bidding each other polite adieu? He hoped to God not.

"Now a question," she stated softly with a touch of hesitancy.

If she asked if they could remain friends, Hunter knew they'd probably be taking him out of there in a straitjacket.

"Why ONYX on the envelope instead of my name?"

Hunter very slowly expelled the breath he'd been holding. Why tell her, when he had the gut feeling she wouldn't be staying? He shrugged. "It doesn't matter anymore."

"Why not?"

"Because you're not staying." He voiced his thoughts.

She mimicked his shrug. "If I were?"

"Are you?" He cursed the acceleration of his heart.

"It depends on your answer."

He let out an audible sigh. "Don't toy with me, Kayden."

"I don't recall you having an aversion to toys." A sly little smile crested her lips.

Hope warred with fear, the latter a feeling he wasn't particularly fond of or familiar with. That went double for his floundering emotional control. An uncomfortable, all too frequent state when it came to the woman standing in front of him.

Determined to end this sooner than later if the only thing she came here to do was return the collar and leave, he decided to tell her the truth.

"I'm good at what I do because I have an instinct for knowing what it is a woman really wants and then using that knowledge to gain what I want. Although I've led many women down the road of *total* submission, it's not the path I'd intended for the woman I plan to spend the rest of my life with."

The corners of her silky black eyebrows dipped and the skin above her nose crinkled. "It's not?"

"No. Not one hundred percent of the time. That's why the word *Onyx*."

The crinkles became more pronounced.

Distracted by how adorable she looked, it took him a few moments to regroup his thoughts. "It would work the reverse of a safe word. Instead of freeing you from submission, it would initiate it."

The crinkles disappeared. "So any other time, you would lead a fairly normal life?"

The short breath he pushed from his lungs was half self-mocking laugh. "As normal as can be expected, living with a man accustomed to getting his way in everything."

Her expression gave no insight into her thoughts when she said, "Thank you for explaining that to me. I appreciate your honesty. I know it wasn't easy. Before I leave...there's one more thing I need to return to you."

The hot ball of emotion churning in his stomach since she'd walked in began to froth. He shot a surreptitious glance at the decanter of cognac on the wet bar to his left.

"Goodbye, Hunter," she whispered softly and, reaching halfway across the desk, set down the black-velvet box containing the collar.

Not a total shock. But it still hurt like hell.

When he didn't return her goodbye, she gave a tiny, sympathetic smile and turned.

He kept his gaze on her as she walked to the door, taking in every miniscule detail of her unhurried steps, her alluring shape, grace of movement, the slight sway and exact shade combination of her long, luxurious black hair as it whispered softly across her back. All the things he intended to cement in his memory, along with every precious moment he'd ever spent with her. The very last thing he noticed was her small, delicate hand as she turned the knob to let herself out.

A second before the door closed, an image flashed of him groveling on the knees of his two-thousand-dollar Italian suit. How pitifully ironic was it that God had graced him with the unerring ability to read women, yet he had so misread the one he wanted most.

Weary, he let his head drop, only to have his gaze slam against the box she'd left. Hunter reached out his hand then pulled it back.

He'd get his secretary to remove it.

He swiveled his gaze between the small black intercom unit on his desk to the wet bar and the dark amber liquid beckoning him.

After the collar was gone from his sight, he'd work on numbing the pain in his heart. Temporary though the oblivion may be, he sorely needed it at the moment.

Chapter Eleven
ဢ

Several more minutes ticked by before Hunter summoned the energy to request his secretary to come get the collar Kayden had left and lock it way.

His hand was halfway to the button when the intercom bleeped.

"What is it, Elizabeth?"

"Sorry to disturb you, Sir. There's a lady here to see you."

Not interested in any other woman except the one who'd just walked out of his life, he said, "Express my apologies and ask her to make an appointment. Then cancel anything else on my schedule."

Rather than her usual ready agreement, there was a moment of silence followed by the hushed tones of a conversation. "She's rather insistent, Sir. She says you'll definitely want to see her."

An internal sigh rose and fell in his chest. "Why?" he asked, scrubbing his hand across his eyes. "Who is she?"

"She says her name is Onyx, Sir."

Hunter's hand fell away from his face. This time the prolonged silence was on his part. "What did she say her name was?" he asked, with more enthusiasm in his voice than he was comfortable with.

"It's...*Onyx*, Sir." The clear, sultry answer floated across to him from the other side of his office.

Heart expanding in his chest like a dehydrated sponge tossed into the Atlantic, Hunter looked up to find Kayden, eyes aglow, a sultry self-confident smile on her lush red lips, leaning against his door, the diamonds from her ankle bracelet and toe ring drawing attention to the bare foot she had pressed high up on the door. She pushed off and sauntered toward him, one hand hidden behind her back, the other working loose the ends of the belt on her ankle-length, blue winter coat. Halfway across the room, the front of the coat separated, giving him a glimpse of the heaven he'd despaired ever laying eyes on again. One sexy little roll of her shoulders and the garment hit the floor.

His thundering heart shot a deluge of blood straight to his cock. Hunter gripped the edge of his desk to brace against the sudden aching fill.

She was wearing every present he'd given her—nothing else.

His gaze narrowed on the shimmering gold chain dangling from her creamy breasts, held there by the nipple clamps that clung tenaciously to her pouty, engorged nipples. The mesmerizing, shimmering sway of the chain, the result of Kayden's enticing, loose, long-legged strides.

The devious little witch. Had he known she was naked beneath her coat before she'd left, she would've never left this room unfucked.

Shoring up his declining restraint, he slowly rose to his feet and came around the desk to meet her.

She stopped directly in front of him. Her clear, bright gaze held his for several seconds before she bowed her head, brought forward what she'd concealed behind her back and sank gracefully to her knees. "I should never have left the club...you, the way I did, *Master.*" Stretching the flogger between her hands, she presented it up to him. "I'm ready to accept whatever punishment you feel justified."

Deeply touched by the revealing gesture, Hunter made no attempt to contain the smile that claimed his lips.

Taking the flogger from her hands, he flung it aside. It hit the wall with a light slap.

Kayden flinched but otherwise held her head-bent position.

The last thing he wanted to do right now was beat her. Especially when all he wanted was to answer his escalating need to yank her up and wrap her in his arms. But before he did that, there was something he needed to know.

"Stand," he said, cupping her shoulders and gently pulling her to her feet. "Look at me."

She raised her head.

"Why did you give back the collar? You're wearing everything else."

"Permission to be Kayden, Sir."

"Granted." An easy request to fill since it was Kayden's free-willed answers he was looking for.

"Are you so sure I'm wearing...everything?" she asked, a devilish sparkle springing from the depths of her beautiful blue eyes.

Holding her gaze, he relaxed his control enough to allow her a glimpse of the lust raging through him.

Her eyes widened and then she smiled.

Looping the back strap of her thong around his index finger, he gave it a sharp tug. The resultant gasp when she came up on tiptoes and canted her hips to relieve the pressure on the butt plug made him grin. "I'm sure. But on the off chance I'm wrong..." He tugged again, eliciting a soft squeak. "I have every intention of checking later. Now answer my question."

"I gave you the collar back because," remaining up on her toes, she wound her arms around his neck, "it would mean more if you put it on me. I read somewhere it's a symbol of a Dom's pledge to protect, love and cherish. And my accepting it symbolizes my willingness to surrender, be devoted and loyal."

"Similar in meaning to an engagement or wedding ring." He reached into his pants pocket to pull out the little box he'd carried around since the day she'd left, flicked up the lid with the tip of his thumb. "Like this one."

"Oh...my...God."

He eased his grip on the thong's strap to accommodate her descent to flat feet.

She tilted the box for an admiring look at the red diamond. An exact match to the one on her collar. "Are you asking me to—" Her stunned gaze swung to his.

"Marry me?" he helpfully supplied. "Yes, I am."

"Why?"

He chuckled and, untangling his finger from the strap, used that arm to give her a brief squeeze. "Because...I fell in love with you before I even met you. I knew from your e-mails you were destined to be mine. Meeting you only confirmed it. And because with *Onyx* wearing my collar and *Kayden* wearing my ring, there will never be any doubt as to whom either belongs to."

"Oh Hunter."

The soft, warm emotion gleaming from her eyes nearly melted him into a puddle.

"You won't need any physical proof to be sure of that. You'll find the answer here." Bringing his hand from around her back, she pressed it over his heart. "And here." She moved his hand to the identical spot on her chest. Removing her hand, she cupped the back of his neck. "And here." Levering back up on her toes, she pulled him down to meet her lips and whispered, "I love you," just before sealing her pledge with a passionate, soul-melding kiss.

BEYOND THE VEIL

Amanda Sidhe

ഔ

Dedication

ഔ

For Shane Swift, a wonderful friend and an inspiration.
Thank you for everything.

Chapter One

ဢ

The faint light from the single naked bulb hanging on a chain from the exposed wood beam ceiling in the basement of the Warren Mansion Museum barely cast enough of a glow for Carolyn Bennett to see the faded, hand-drawn map in her hand. The map which she'd just found in a hidden compartment while restoring Celia Warren's dressing table, which had brought her down here into the dark belly of the mansion. What it led to, she could only guess.

Her best guess, of course, was Celia's infamous diamond wedding ring. The one she claimed allowed her to commune with spirits on the "other side". The one she said she used to speak with her grandson, Bruce Warren, after he mysteriously and tragically died at the age of thirty-three. Legends of the ring's power aside, the artifact itself would be a boon for the museum and as its curator Carolyn understood the importance for both the collection and for visitor revenue if she could locate that famous diamond ring.

Carolyn squinted at the map and then around the unfinished basement. They used it for storage but mostly on the south side of the building. The north side, where the map led her, contained an old brick fireplace. She counted the bricks along the right hand corner until she came to the seventh from the bottom. That brick didn't look any different from the others. Frowning, thinking she must have misread the map somehow, Carolyn pulled on the brick. It slid out of place by half an inch. With a growing smile of excitement, she wiggled the brick until it popped free from the fireplace. Behind it a crumpled envelope filled a small void in the mortar. Carolyn drew it out, trying not to rip it.

Something gave it an odd bulky shape in one corner and Carolyn's heart raced. The flap was not sealed, or had come unsealed over the years, and so Carolyn opened the envelope. The folded note she ignored for now. It was the diamond ring she pulled out first. Even in the faint light, the gold and diamond of the ring sparkled. "Thank you, Celia." Carolyn slipped the ring on her left ring finger and admired it.

Even though she was already kneeling, the sense of falling swept over her. Carolyn reached out but lost her balance before she could grab anything. She landed on her bottom on the basement floor.

"Not a terribly graceful entrance," a strong male voice interrupted the silence, "but certainly I can forgive that in such a beautiful woman."

Carolyn spun around, getting to her knees. There, in the flesh, stood Bruce Warren himself. Just like in photographs she'd seen of him, he wore tan drop-front trousers and a pleated-front shirt—without the detachable collar—of the style popular in the pre-civil war South. Ever since she'd first laid eyes on the portrait of him in the hallway upstairs Carolyn longed to reach through time to touch him. Those deep blue eyes penetrated her, stripping her soul bare. His loose blond hair brushed his shoulders, inviting her to touch it. His strong yet handsome face held a confident, almost triumphant, expression. Those pictures and portraits hadn't done him justice. In the flesh, so to speak, his movie-star good looks and solid body had Carolyn's skin tingling.

"So it is true," Carolyn chuckled to herself. "Your grandmother's ring did allow her to see you." She got to her feet and brushed the dirt off the seat of her slacks. Even standing straight she had to raise her chin to meet his eyes. "You were over six feet tall. Very unusual for the men of your era." Her gaze roamed back down his body. It was easy to see how Bruce Warren had gained the reputation as the most dashing man in Louisiana. There wasn't a thing about him that didn't make her want to drool. His wide, muscular chest begged to be fondled, or even licked. Those full, expressive lips just made her want to bite them. Too bad he wasn't real. Carolyn placed her hands on her hips as she regarded this rather solid-looking ghost. Ghosts didn't scare her as they did most people. History fascinated her. Being able to see and speak to the people from the past intrigued her.

Bruce crossed to her suddenly, reaching her in two long strides. The hungry, demanding way about him set her heart suddenly racing in fear and desire. She'd barely managed to take a half step back before his arms circled her. Bruce crushed her to his chest, stealing her breath. His mouth covered hers. Her lips parted in surprise, allowing his tongue to drive between them. Feeling overwhelmed, yet safe, in his arms, Carolyn surrendered to him. Surrendered to the plundering kiss.

She wrapped her arms around his wide shoulders and held tightly to him, as much to keep him close as to keep her from sinking weakly to the floor. Besides the coolness of his body, nothing about him seemed the least bit ghost-like. The moisture from his mouth mingled with hers as their kiss deepened further. Even his chest expanded as he breathed. Most noticeably, his thick cock, trapped in his trousers, jabbed into her stomach.

Her own body responded instantly to Bruce. Some magnetism he possessed snared her. There was no right or wrong, just sudden and intense need. Her sensitive nipples rubbed hard into his chest, sending echoes of pleasure through her. She wrapped one leg behind his calf, as if to prevent him from retreating from this commanding embrace. If not for his powerful arms supporting her back, the force of his kiss alone would have knocked her down. There was barely an inch of the front of her body that did not mold perfectly into him. He had to know, from her responsiveness, that she would not resist him.

As he drew back from her mouth Carolyn leaned forward, reluctant to end the single most intense kiss of her life. Bruce tangled his fingers in her hair and gently forced her neck to arch back. Her swollen lips remained parted, ready and wanting more. "I'm sorry about this," he murmured.

"About what? Kissing me?" Carolyn drew herself even more forcefully against him, showing him that she wanted more. Needed more. Certain beyond all logic and reason that Bruce could fulfill it, fulfill her, in a way nothing else could.

"No. About this…" He reached behind him and drew out a length of leather cord. Using her hair to control her, Bruce peeled her off him and turned her around. He forced her to lean against the basement wall. His hand moved from fisting in her hair to gripping the back of her neck. Bruce pressed his body against hers, pinning her to the wall.

Carolyn closed her eyes. Her body felt alive, sandwiched between Bruce and the wall. Every place they touched felt incredible. Their thighs. His hips against her bottom. She knew from letters she'd found about Bruce's occasion forays into bondage play. That had been one of the things that had specifically interested her in his history. He released her neck and both his hands found her wrists. With practiced skill, he bound her wrists together with the leather cord. Whether or not she should have resisted him, she did not. Lightly, she tugged on the bonds and a slow smile spread on her lips. Not too tight but definitely secure. She laughed softly, "Nice."

Bruce gripped her upper arms and closed his body around hers, nearly covering her completely. His breath tickled the hairs by her ear. "Mmm. You like this?"

Carolyn leaned her head back what little she could until it rested against his shoulder. In just a whisper, she admitted, "Yes."

His hips moved, grinding his cock into her soft ass. "You want that?"

Carolyn closed her eyes. Bruce's scent surrounded her as his body did. He filled her senses like no man had before. He'd been a personal obsession of hers since coming to the museum.

Strong, indomitable, some even said cursed, but above all delicious. And he was here now. Ready to give her what she wanted most.

Flexing, Carolyn rubbed her bottom back into Bruce's crotch. "I want it very much."

His voice growled against her cheek. "I have not been with a woman in a very long time. Do you understand what that means?" With a sudden thrust of his hips, Bruce shoved his erection hard against her ass.

The erotic need he charged her body with vibrated through every inch of her. She indeed understood his warning. So long without the touch of another. Decades without that vital release. Turning toward him as much as she could, she murmured, "Don't be gentle."

That was all the encouragement he needed. He pushed himself off her. Carolyn felt his fingers curl in her long, auburn hair and his hand gripping the leather around her wrists. Easily, he hauled her away from the wall and turned her around. She barely had a chance to realize that the basement had changed. The storage crates no longer filled one side. A workshop with the leatherworking tools from Bruce's generation lined shelves along the wall. A bare wooden table stood alone in the center of the room. None too gently, Bruce dragged her to the table and bent her face down over it. He pressed her against the table, his hand between her shoulder blades.

He reached around her and roughly unfastened her pants. Releasing his grip on her upper body, he drew back enough to grab her waistband and yank it down. He knelt to lift one of her ankles and stripped the pants from it, leaving the other as it was, with the cloth bunched around it.

Carolyn felt teeth biting into tender flesh of her ass cheek. She gave a little yelp in surprise, but not in protest. He didn't break the skin—at least she didn't think so—but she imagined that he might leave a mark. The very thought of him marking her made her wet with excitement. In the next moment he rose and once more towered over her. With a sharp smack on her ass, he said, "Spread your legs."

The spank made her core clench, sending tingles shooting through her entire body. The sting of his hand on her ass heated her flesh. She was so stimulated and hungry for his touch, Carolyn rocked herself against the table. "Oh, fuck yeah."

She widened her stance so that, bent over as she was, Bruce had perfect access to her pussy. Turning her head, Carolyn watched him unfasten his trousers. The front flap dropped, unveiling his huge cock. Bruce used his hand to slide his head up and down her wet slit. "You do want this, don't you?" he growled. "You are soaked."

"Yes," she admitted, resting her cheek on the smooth wood of the table. Her need demonstrated by the tremble in her voice as she repeated, "Yes."

Before she could claim a steadying breath, Bruce shoved himself hard and deep inside her pussy. She gasped, suddenly and completely filled by his massive cock. Bruce roared out a triumphant cry. Using the bonds around her wrists, and her hair as handles, Bruce tugged her up off the table, changing the angle of her body to where he wanted it to be. He yanked her back onto him until he buried himself to the hilt in her flesh. Each time he withdrew and pushed her away Carolyn inhaled and each time he pulled her back so he slammed deep into her she bit back a scream of pleasure.

"That's it, woman. Take me into your depths." Bruce shoved her back down to the table once more. He rammed into her over and over, showing no mercy and she didn't want him to.

"Yes! Yes!" she cried out. His body pounded so deep inside her. He didn't spare her one inch of his throbbing erection. The smacking sound as his hips slapped into her ass filled the basement. This was fucking, pure and simple, and it was glorious. Carolyn's body fed on his pleasure. Her insides felt like hot oil, slick and steaming. The bliss of her orgasm built within her fast. For all her wanting it, no one had taken her this way before, as if a woman of intelligence could not possibly desire the conquering sexuality of a man of primal power.

Bruce pulled out suddenly and Carolyn whined in protest, her core suddenly empty of his gigantic cock. He laughed, "I'm not done with you yet."

Bruce pulled her up from the table by her hair. He spun her toward him. The smile he flashed her made her weak with lust. So handsome. So hungry for her.

Easily, Bruce lifted her and sat her on the edge of the table. He pressed himself between her legs, keeping her thighs wide. His hand grasped the scooped neck of her silk shirt. With one sudden jerk he ripped it right down the center.

Arching her back, she offered herself to him. Her legs wrapped behind his thighs, encouraging him to find her wet center once more. "Bruce! Take me! Take me as you want me!"

He reached inside the cup of her bra, pushing the material aside. Roughly, he grasped her breast around the base, making her hard nipple stand out even more. He bent to her and took her nipple into his mouth. He sucked hard. His teeth nibbled on her just short of pain. The sensation exploded through her and Carolyn thought she might come right then. "Ah! Yes! Oh, Bruce!"

He lifted his head from her breast and clamped it on her throat. She surrendered to his love bite. He rolled and pinched her nipple hard with his other hand, charging her over and over with erotic delight. Once more, his cock pressed to her pussy. With a hard thrust he drove it into her.

Unable to grab him with her bound hands, Carolyn closed them into fists. Her arms jerked, wanting to embrace this mountain of a man. She could do nothing. Nothing but take all he had to give her. With increasing speed, Bruce pistoned into her soft core. At the very moment she felt him swell, her orgasm hit her like a thunderbolt. It tore through her even as she heard Bruce's growling cry. The force of his cum shot deep into her. She could feel his seed filling her. Her orgasm made her convulse. Her pussy flexed in spasms around his erection. It echoed through her again and again, sparing no fiber of her body.

He pounded into her several times more, slowing bit by bit as the storm passed through them both. His cock slid in and out of her easily on their combined juices. At last he stopped, fully inside her. He held himself for several breaths, not moving and yet throbbing like a pulse in her core.

Bruce gripped her thighs as he finally dragged himself out of her. Strange how real, how alive, he seemed. Candlelight glistened on the perspiration on his brow. His breathing was ragged from effort. The fact that he breathed at all seemed different from what she would have expected from a ghost. Carolyn believed in magical and supernatural things. She'd spent too much time in Louisiana's voodoo country to think anything less. Even still, there certainly seemed to be more to this ghost than met the eye.

His gaze settled on her chest and she suspected it had more to do with avoiding her eyes right now than checking out her body. He gripped her upper arms and helped her to sit up. "I am tardy in asking this. You know my name. What is yours?"

Carolyn rested on the edge of the table and smiled at Bruce even though he still did not look her in the eye yet. "Carolyn Bennett."

"Miss Carolyn, taking you as I did might have seemed ungentlemanly of me but I am afraid it is not the worst trespass I will commit against you." Finally, he met her eyes and the seriousness of what he wanted to say weighted heavily in them. "I have been alone here for a very long time. Do you have any idea how lonely 'alone' truly is?"

It would be unfair of her to even pretend that she could understand what he was trying to explain to her. "No. I can't imagine how awful that must be."

"Miss Carolyn, forgive me." He tilted his head as if searching for some comprehension within her, some forgiveness perhaps. "I can't let you leave. I can't. Do you understand?"

"There is something you don't understand, Bruce." Behind her back, Carolyn's fingers closed around the ring she wore. "You can't keep me here. I don't belong here. I am sorry you are dead. But I am alive."

With that, she tugged the ring off her finger.

Chapter Two

ဢ

Bruce vanished like the ghost he was. That was not all that vanished. The table beneath her vanished, as well. So too did the strap around her wrists. Carolyn dropped to the floor, her hands catching her so her bare butt did not hit the ground too hard. Looking down she found her pants and panties still wrapped around one ankle. Her shirt remained ripped down the center.

After a second she let the ring fall to the floor next to her. The ring did more than simply allow communication with Bruce Warren. Being with him had not been merely a dream or vision. Raising her arm she could see, even in the pale light, the marks the leather strap had left on her wrist. If he had decided to kill her to keep her with him it might very well have worked. Not that she could be sure he had meant to do that. On the other hand, she couldn't be sure he didn't intend to either. Certainly he'd had no qualms about seeing her trapped with him, wherever that was.

Hearing movement in the room above, Carolyn knew Greta had returned and now puttered around in the kitchen. Quickly, she pulled her pants back on. Nothing could fix the silk shirt, unfortunately. Carolyn replaced the brick she'd removed from the fireplace. She gathered the map and returned the ring to the envelope. Holding her shirt closed with one hand, she quickly and calmly hurried from the basement up the stairs to her third floor bedroom. After changing clothes, Carolyn sat at Celia's antique cherry writing desk and regarded the envelope once more. Tipping it over, she let the ring slide out onto the desktop. Careful of the fragile parchment inside, Carolyn pulled out the note and unfolded it. The ink had faded but Carolyn could still make out the flowing handwriting.

"I weep knowing that my grandson will suffer when I am gone. Only I and one other know the curse that keeps him trapped here and I don't trust the deceiver with this ring. I hide it in the hopes that the powers will see to it that the one who holds the key to free Bruce shall one day find it.

"I have enchanted this ring so that when it is held in a closed fist Bruce can be heard and felt as a ghost is meant to be heard and felt, upon the cold breeze. Worn on a chain about the neck the ring allows Bruce to appear to the one who wears it as if he walks in our world. When it is worn on the hand the bearer walks in Bruce's prison.

"While I know much of the secret of the curse that binds my Bruce to this home, only the deceiver knows the key to free him."

Carolyn read the note again. So Bruce had been cursed? Why curse someone who was already dead? It didn't make sense to her. It was a mystery. One she was determined to solve. *That place is haunted.* Those had been her grandmother's ominous words. Still, it hadn't stopped Carolyn Bennett from packing her office plant and family photos to leave her position at the Cincinnati Municipal Museum when she learned of the opening for a curator here. She'd grown up in Ohio, but she spent every summer here in Louisiana with her grandmother, only a twenty-minute walk from the Warren Mansion. The property had been private then, no trespassing allowed, but Carolyn still found herself drawn here. Drawn to stand outside the gate and stare at the mansion and daydream about what it must be like inside, somehow feeling that she belonged in there. Her grandmother knew the "old ways" as she called them and often had feelings that came true. Carolyn didn't have her grandmother's skill, but the one thing she knew for certain was that she belonged here. For four years now Carolyn had been the museum's curator. Truly, she felt like it had been destiny.

For now she hid the map and the note in her desk. She found a simple gold chain and slipped the ring onto it before placing it into the pocket of her slacks.

Still turning the situation over in her mind, Carolyn descended the huge mahogany staircase that curved up from the main floor. Against the wall, beneath the upper stretch of the open staircase, a formal sitting area was arranged opposite a huge fireplace. A portrait of Bruce Warren hung above the heavy mantle, guarding the main passageway of his home.

Carolyn smiled unconsciously at the image of the man towering over her, as she often did. Bruce certainly was a good specimen, with good bones and a well-built physique. In the portrait, his blond hair had been carefully combed and she imagined herself running her fingers through it to ruffle it up. The eyes of the portrait snared her in their Caribbean blue grasp. The same ring she now possessed dangled from a simple chain around his throat in that portrait. With a master's hand the artist had captured the glint of light sparkling spectacularly off the diamond. The dainty band was far too thin for a man's hand, even if a man had fingers fine-boned enough to wear it. She knew the diamond itself was a round cut, three-quarter carat in a distinctly Edwardian style openwork crown setting. Floral silhouettes adorned the band with almost no sign of wear. Even in the oil of the painting, the ring shone with polished brilliance. Clearly the rendering with such exacting care indicated the importance that the ring held to its owner, she thought as she fondled the ring on a chain in her pocket.

Regarding Bruce once more, Carolyn decided that the historic but stuffy suit would have to go. Had she been the portrait painter he would have appeared much differently. She wanted to see him wild, riding a horse or, better yet, sweeping her up to carry her off to his bed. His shirt would be unbuttoned to the navel so she could run her hands on his hard chest. Her fingertips would trace the grooves of muscle across his broad torso. With his lust-hazed eyes gazing deeply into her own, Carolyn's hand would travel lower. Rubbing the rough woven fabric of his tight britches, Carolyn could imagine the delight with which she would discover his obvious need for her. He would remain restrained only for a moment longer before she would unfasten the buttons to free the pure masculine force harnessed inside.

Carolyn slipped her hand into her pocket and withdrew the ring, keeping it tightly enclosed within her fist. Holding it up before her, she concentrated on the closed fingers, able to feel the shape of the ring against her skin.

Mingled floral scents swirled on the air around her. An unseasonably cool breeze stroked like fingers along her cheeks and combed back her hair. Carolyn closed her eyes and relaxed into the comforting caress of the air. She could almost picture invisible hands gliding down her arms and then back up her quivering stomach. The icy touch circled her waist like arms hugging around her. A cool pressure spread down her rear as if someone had walked up behind her so that their bodies touched. Carolyn sucked in her breath, noticing the scent had changed to masculine cologne. The chilled air breathed a trail of tender lover's kisses up her neck. Carolyn rolled her head to the side invitingly. Nothing in this affectionate touching tasted the slightest bit threatening. Rather the sensation carried a gentle coaxing. A sweet summoning. A distant melody inviting her to seek its source.

She saw nothing even though she felt hands moving up her body, rubbing over her stomach, ribs and finally grasping her breasts. The sensation of a man grinding his stiff cock against her bottom made her gasp. Going with the motion, she pressed back into what felt like a solid form behind her.

One of the ghostly hands moved from her breast and snaked down her body. Shakily, she exhaled. The growing sensations carried her away like a dream until she no longer questioned them. It just felt so glorious to be touched this way. The pressure of the hand lowered to follow the curve of her body. The fingers slipped between her legs and she leaned forward even more, bracing herself against the mantle to keep her balance. Carolyn closed her eyes and moaned. The swirling circles of pressure on her pussy aroused Carolyn in magnificent ways. A wonderful ache spread through her like a drop of watercolor on silk, soaking into the fibers of her being. Her clit swelled as her nether lips rubbed over it again and again. Her panties grew tacky with her juices, sticking to her crotch, begging to be torn away.

"Bruce," Carolyn moaned.

"Carolyn." The whisper, husky with desire, vibrated down her nerves.

"Is that you, Carolyn?" Greta's elderly voice drifted from the kitchen along with the heavenly scent of her home cooking.

With her fingers tangled in the chain, Carolyn opened her hand. The ring fell free. It came to a dangling stop at the end of the chain. The breeze vanished once more. Bruce's touch faded as well.

Still tumbling her thoughts through her mind and with the echoing ripples of Bruce's touch lapping at her body, Carolyn made her way into the kitchen. A gnomish elderly woman with an apple-shaped body on her four-and-a-half-foot frame toiled busily in the updated kitchen. Like every other room in the mansion, the kitchen gleamed spotlessly. Homey smells of chicken and dumplings bubbled up from the pot on the stove. The little woman balanced on her tiptoes atop of a small wooden stepstool so she could peer inside. With a motherly smile, she glanced over at Carolyn. She twittered in a high-pitched warble, "Set the table for me, dear. Why don't we have iced tea? I have some in the refrigerator. Use the glasses drying in the rack."

Something about Greta's mix of fairy godmother and grandmotherly qualities always had Carolyn assisting in the kitchen obediently. For as long as anyone could remember Greta had been the caretaker of the Warren Mansion and had a way about her as if she owned the place.

Greta spooned the chicken and dumplings into the two bowls Carolyn held. She glanced up at Carolyn and her smile immediately faded. "You look a little flushed, dear."

"I just…" had sex with a ghost? She set the bowls on the table as she thought how to answer a concerned and inquiring Greta. Carolyn shook her head and forced a smile. "I just had a weird morning."

Greta twinkled a grin at Carolyn. "You must have seen Bruce."

Greta could always see through her. Even so, some things she just couldn't share with her. "I… Well… I don't know."

"Bruce is not among the living, dear."

"I know." She chased a dumpling around in her bowl. "I know it in theory anyway."

Greta reached out and gripped Carolyn's wrist. "Are you in love with him?"

The dumpling dropped off Carolyn's fork. Before she could retrieve it, it rolled off the table and landed on the polished wooden floor with a splat. "You must be kidding," Carolyn said, more to herself than to Greta.

Greta laughed as she watched Carolyn wipe up the mess. Rocking herself, she clapped in her amusement over Carolyn's graceless reaction.

"My family has been the caretakers here since almost the beginning. It was mere months after Bruce built this home that he crossed the veil to the other side. Only those close to him have actually seen him since then." Greta ate a bite and then added, "I've seen how you look at his portrait."

Carolyn didn't reply. The rest of the meal, she half listened to Greta chitchatting about the history of the mansion that Carolyn herself already knew so well. How did she really feel about Bruce? More than just infatuation. More than just lust. Could she be in love with a ghost, like Greta thought?

* * * * *

Two hours later, Carolyn sorted through the scatter of notes spread on a large table in the study. According to Celia, only "the deceiver" knew the key to free Bruce. Whoever that was had to be long since dead and beyond questioning. Her only hope—Bruce's only hope—was to find some clue to who that had been or what the key was among these old documents.

After three hours, Carolyn sat back and rubbed her face hard. She'd been through all of this countless times before and had not seen anything that seemed the least bit helpful. Taking a chance, she withdrew the ring from her pocket. After considering it for a moment, she slipped the chain over her head.

She glanced around the room, looking for Bruce and not seeing him. The floor-to-ceiling windows illuminated the room with bright afternoon sun. Antique porcelain figures without a hint of dust, thanks to Greta, glimmered on the shelves. Even the table she worked at was in good shape for its age and gleamed like new with fresh polish. Gently, she stroked the nicks and dents with curiosity. That was the lure of antiques for her. She wondered about the history each piece remembered in its scratches or lovingly worn surfaces. Was the nick she touched now from a careless soldier's sword hilt when he sat at this table? Had Bruce been frustrated at a long ago offense and struck the table with something? Had he propped his booted feet on this table and accidentally marred the wood with his heel? What stories could this one object tell her?

"You are paying that table an inordinate amount of affection." The rumble of a male voice broke the silence and throbbed through her like the percussion of a bass drum. His joking and suggestive comment woke her out of her reverie and Carolyn jerked up straight in her chair. She twisted to see Bruce lounging against the doorframe, long and muscled even in repose. The looming appearance of so intimidating a figure as he sent her heart pounding. His straight blond hair accentuated the strong bones of his face. Carolyn's gaze locked on the righteous blue of his eyes.

As she began to rise, he held out a palm indicated she should stay where she was. "Don't let me disturb you, even if you are making yourself at home in my chair."

"Bruce." Carolyn rose despite his protest, instantly the need for him washed through her once more. She wanted nothing more than to feel his touch on her body. Only, could she trust him? Would he try to draw her once more into his realm and lock her away there?

"You don't trust me, do you?" he strode to her. His focus locked on her mouth as if he meant to ravage it in a ferocious kiss. "Perhaps you are wise not to."

Carolyn stiffened like a fawn before a stalking timber wolf, shocked by his sudden and threatening approach. Her arms were raised—whether to embrace or ward off Bruce she wasn't sure. Her mouth opened to speak just as Bruce faded to a transparent mist. His approach didn't slow and before she could express her shock he pressed against her like a cold wind. Pressure without form passed right through her. The shock of a soul foreign to her body drifting through her crumbled her resistance.

Bruce filled her like Christmas filled a loving home. Despite the warm weather outside a breath of crisp winter air chilled her lungs. The rich, masculine scent uniquely his own opened her senses and her heart to possibilities she'd not dared to dream of. The taste that flooded her mouth hinted of ginger and vanilla. The sensation of a second heart beating inside her chest, but in perfect rhythm with her own, transcended any claim on logic and skepticism.

A moan escaped Carolyn as Bruce passed out of her body on the other side. A loneliness that surpassed her own familiar solitary existence tore her heart with the abandonment of a soul lost to the world, trapped in space and time. With dawning realization that not her own but Bruce's sorrow clenched her soul, Carolyn turned toward him. Such beauty and such sadness mingled in his heart. The urge to hold him, to comfort him, swelled inside her. Before she could speak, something covered her mouth. Bruce reappeared, more handsome now that his soul had been naked against hers. His liquid kiss deepened as his lips and tongue melted into hers as though he were not completely solid yet.

Never before had Carolyn been kissed with such commanding desire as Bruce did. Never before had a man wrapped his arms around her as Bruce did now with demanding need. Her surrender happened so naturally that Carolyn didn't stop to question it. Did the trees question why they swayed in the breeze? No. They simply did as they were made to do, to bend and dance and celebrate the insistent force of the wind.

Closing her eyes, Caroline gave herself to Bruce. She gripped his powerful shoulders, not to push him away but to draw him closer. When his kiss broke from her mouth only to trail down her neck, Carolyn arched into his attentions. "Yes," she breathed, "Oh yes."

He supported her with his broad hand at the small of her back. Bruce's talented lips closed over the sensitive pulse in her neck and he sucked hard, eliciting a moan from deep in her soul. Her body pressed into his, breasts nuzzled up to his solid chest, hips danced against his, her knee slipped between his legs so that her core slid wantonly against his thigh, giving him wordless permission to plunder her further. And she dearly wanted him to go further. "Don't stop," she gasped.

Bruce slipped a hand between their bellies. With a sensual glide it traced up her stomach and into the valley between her breasts. With nimble thumb and forefinger, he flicked open the buttons on the front of her blouse revealing her beige, lacy bra underneath. His hand dipped inside the cup, forcing aside the fabric so that it outlined rather than supported her. Her heavy orb filled his palm and widely spread fingers. Softly, he fondled her, massaging lightly in circles so her tight nipple rubbed tantalizingly under his caress. Sparks skated along her nerves until her entire breast came alive with excitement like electricity. The building arousal did not stop there. It twisted and trailed through her body like vines over a trellis and blossomed with tingling need between her legs.

Still supporting her back easily with one arm, Bruce leaned Carolyn back into the desk. Her bottom rested on the edge as he dipped her back, forcing her breasts to thrust upward. His lips broke from her neck with a hungry gasp and his cool tongue glided down the slope of her body until his mouth closed once more, this time consuming her nipple and a mouthful of her breast. Carolyn cried out in shock at how cold his mouth was over her warmth. Only if Bruce had an ice cube in his mouth could his tongue become any colder. Her nipple tightened even more at the chill and attention. Clutching him, Carolyn's fingers tangled in his hair. Her leg hooked around his thigh, grinding her sex to his hip with growing desperation. For a second she glanced toward the open doorway. At any moment Greta could walk in on them. Somehow, in this moment, the thought of getting caught having sex with a ghost, with Bruce, only made it more exciting. "Bruce... Oh my God."

Not giving her a chance to catch her breath, Bruce tickled his fingertips down her tummy. Lower and lower until he found the waist of her slacks. "You should wear skirts," he joked. "Easier access."

Carolyn chuckled. "Not in your time. All those under garments."

"In the deep South, do you think women always wore everything they were supposed to under those heavy skirts?" Bruce laughed low and seductively. The pressure of his fingers made Carolyn's tight stomach quiver as he slid his hands beneath the elastic waistband of her slacks. With the smile of a man who knows he is devastating a woman sexually, Bruce returned to her mouth once more. His tongue tasted her mouth with bold, deep strokes full of confidence. He seemed to know he had her. Could have as much of her as he wanted.

And oh how she wanted him. He could do anything, just as long as he didn't stop. Carolyn wanted more. Much, much more.

Easily, Bruce hugged her to him with one arm and lifted her just enough to work the pants down. His kiss never faltered as he arranged her once more back on the desk. Breaking from her mouth, he grinned down at her. "You are delicious. I want to taste more of you. I want to taste all of you."

Laying her back on the desk, his cobalt gaze remained locked on hers. Bruce brought both hands between them to rest on her upper chest. Downward they slid, over her breasts—one still in her bra and one free of it. Then down her trembling stomach, closer and closer to her excitement. Down over her hipbones. At last his thumbs pressed over the front of her milk white panties, making the silk rub delectably over her pussy. Turning his fingers out and downward, Bruce slid between her thighs and the inside of her slacks. The further down her legs he pushed, the more vulnerably naked she became before him. Bruce knelt down and worked one pant leg free, leaving the other gathered around her ankle.

Lovingly, he kissed the inside of one knee and then the other. With gentle coaxing, Bruce pushed her knees apart, giving himself access to her silk-clad pussy. Raising his eyes to hers once more, Bruce licked his way up her thigh. His relentless gaze inspired lustful longings. The cool trail up her skin sent goose bumps blossoming across her flesh. With a gasp, Carolyn reached down and raked her fingers through his hair. Encouragingly, she guided him closer to her center.

With a long, slow lick, Bruce brought his tongue up the seat of her panties. Carolyn could feel his tongue pressing the fabric into her to feel the shape of her through its fragile protection. Her own moisture made the silk tacky against her pussy lips. How she wanted Bruce! She wanted him inside her. Deep, deep inside her warm and quivering pussy. "Yes... Please... Don't stop."

Bruce didn't stop. Hooking a finger inside the leg of her panties, he wedged the fabric aside. The coolness of his breath spilled over her sensitive lips, bringing a shiver that had less to do with the cold than her arousal. Spreading her open with his fingers, Bruce's next lick dragged up her juicy slit. He moaned into her core. The vibration of it telegraphed along every nerve in her body, heightening the experience of pleasure he brought her with each touch.

Delving into her pussy with one long finger, he found the ticklishly sensitive place that caused her to spasm. He stroked her slick inner walls, priming her for more intense pleasure. Only willpower kept her from closing her legs tight around his head. Bruce teased her clit out from beneath its hood with the tip of his tongue. "Oh my God. Oh, God... Bruce. You are so talented. So amazing." Carolyn gripped his hair tighter. Her entire body shook. Giving herself over to him, Carolyn arched back harder. Her pussy pushed demandingly toward him.

Bruce added a second finger, pushing it into her passage. Her muscles contracted around the thickness of him. Bruce chuckled softly at her fragile self control. Every plunge and withdrawal of his fingers sent her into new spasms. As he worked her pussy, he moved lower still. With his free hand, he pushed her thighs wider apart until she could go no further. He bent into her and Carolyn gasped out in surprise to feel his tongue swirling around her anus. Round and round he licked and her hips swiveled with him. Carolyn arched back more, buffeted by the rush of pleasure. Gently his tongue probed at her tight hole, just barely entering her. A second later a finger replaced his tongue. He drove his fingers in and out, two in her pussy and one in her ass, with gentle but relentless force. The dual penetration brought her whole body to life in a shower of tingles.

Bruce opened his mouth and consumed her clit and the soft mound of flesh all around it. His tongue swirled and pressed hard into her sensitive pearl.

Carolyn cried out as the sweetness of his mouth brought her to climax. She convulsed as her cum flowed rich and creamy from her depths. Heat and energy tumbled from her center and throughout her entire body, bringing fulfillment and relief unlike any she'd experienced before. No orgasm in her life could compare to the one Bruce gave her with such ease. The awakening of her body opened her soul and mind like a revelation. Such perfection didn't just happen, of this she was sure. There must be more to this connection she felt to Bruce. More than physical attraction. More than sexual pleasure. He sparked off her very being. The chain reaction didn't stop in her pussy. It cascaded across her mind, heart and soul as well. What exactly it meant, Carolyn could only guess.

Her body spent itself in a succession of trembling jolts. The force of the climax quaked through her until only the echoes of the aftershocks remained.

Then, it was over. Bruce vanished as suddenly as if he'd never been there. Carolyn found herself alone in the study, swaying unsteadily on the table, her clothing in serious disarray. Heated and flustered, she combed her fingers unsteadily through her hair. Could she be falling in love with him? Did sex alone explain her state of euphoria?

Chapter Three

&

Focusing on her work after Bruce left seemed near to impossible. She'd left the chain around her neck, hoping that Bruce might return. Part of her kept expecting to wake up and find that this whole weird day was just a dream. Her intention to ask Bruce about the key, or curse, or deceiver had been forgotten with his fist kiss. Nothing she came across in the records seemed to shed any light on his situation. Close to midnight, Carolyn gave up trying to find the answers and finally dragged herself from her research.

For her own room, Carolyn had selected one of the suites on the upper story. Like Greta, who had a room on the ground floor, Carolyn actually lived in the mansion. Their personal space was, of course, not on the tour.

Carolyn changed into a sleeveless satin nightgown in a shade of royal blue that she loved. The deep feather bed curled around her tired body, welcoming her into its comforting depths. Carolyn snuggled herself into the thick, downy comforter of her jumbo-sized bed. The light beyond the open windows that looked over the widow's walk had faded behind fluttering gauzy curtains. The summer night scents warmed the air in quiet comfort.

Curling up on her side, Carolyn rested the ring on its chain on the bed beside her. With idle fingers she toyed with the antique piece of jewelry to catch glints of moonlight on the facets of the diamond. The gem itself was flawless. Not a scratch or chip or bit of dirt marred its perfection. Each of the diamond's facets gleamed like tiny windows into another world. A world where someone like Bruce could exist, waiting for the right person to reach across the distance and connect with him.

Carolyn snuggled into her pillow with her auburn hair spilling carelessly behind her in a silken tide. She felt safe and utterly at peace. Her hand closed around the diamond without even thinking about it. Having it near her gave her comfort, even though she could not explain why. Perhaps it was the fear of losing the diamond and losing Bruce along with it. Bruce had not attempted to harm her and she no longer worried that he would try. Neither had he made another attempt to trap her, not that being stuck with him would be such a bad thing. It was the stuck for eternity part that worried her. Only, she was alive and could not be trapped the way a ghost could be, right?

In her half-dozing state, she thought she felt the bed shift. The mattress compressed as if someone had climbed in behind her. The pressure was not enough to rouse her, but part of her acknowledged and accepted the information without concern. When the weight of an arm slipped around her waist, she moaned contentedly. A body pressed against her legs and back as someone spooned against her. Carolyn recognized Bruce's mellow scent.

His cool face snuggled up in the crook of her neck, giving her goose bumps. When she stirred to gaze back at him Bruce hugged her tighter. "Just let me hold you," he murmured. "Just let me feel your body close to mine."

Carolyn relaxed into his touch. Her breathing slowed, matching the rhythmic press of his breathing against her back. Ghosts breathed? How odd, she mused. Once again, she marveled at how un-ghostlike he seemed. Maybe it was more from habit than need that his chest expanded and contracted.

Her pillow moved as Bruce slid his arm under her until her head rested on his biceps. The hand that she'd had wedged beneath the pillow reached out. Her tapered fingers interlaced with Bruce's stronger ones. Such simple touching and yet so affectionate. Amazing how Bruce could take her as roughly as he wished one time and then treat her with such loving tenderness another. He painted his lovemaking with a broad pallet of colors, making masterpieces each time.

Lightly, he kissed her cheek near her ear. Just a tender caress of lips. The press of his cool mouth on her flesh brought a soft smile of contentment. The moment was so unhurried. So loving and tender.

Carolyn stroked her fingers up and down the thick muscles of Bruce's forearm as it curled against her belly. Delicately, his finger touched the fabric of her nightgown. As his fingers dragged it up the hem drew further up the curve of her hip. It rode up in the back as well, removing the thin barrier between them. Her heart sang. His delicate touch caressed her as though he treasured her femininity. In his embrace she felt protected and cherished. Bruce bunched up the gown by her breasts so he could lay the flat of his palm on her quivering stomach. His lingering kisses on her ear and neck soothed the excitement stirring in her core.

"You're not wearing bloomers." Humor warmed his deep, breathy voice. With the movement of his hips, Bruce rubbed himself against her bottom. She gasped as she realized that he was nude. His erect member dragged heavily up her butt and across the small of her back with each lazy pump of his body.

She arched to glance back at him, only able to see the length of his side in line with hers. Despite the chill of his form, he looked and felt as solid and real as any living man. The perfect line of his toned tummy, hip and leg extended along side hers so perfectly that it appeared that they had been made for one another. She squeezed his hand, her feelings for him growing with each stroke of his body and every word he spoke.

"I won't hurt you," he promised. Tenderly, he reached down to cup her pussy. Her excitement grew as he massaged her intimately. Her moisture slicked her slit. When Bruce slid a finger between her lips to find her erect clit he chuckled deep in his throat. "You are so wet. Your body is ready. Are you, darling?"

Moving with his infinitely patient pace, Carolyn rode his touch. "Yes," she whispered back. When she felt him shift his body so his cock pressed between her cheeks Carolyn raised her leg slightly to allow him access. Carolyn sighed with pleasure when, instead of sliding into her ready core as she'd expecting him to, he glided his length along her slit, sandwiching his cock between her pussy lips. He rested his forearm on her thigh so she relaxed once more. Her lips wrapped tightly around his thick shaft. Her juices lubricated them both liberally. Even with her body firmly gripping his, Bruce glided easily back and forth. The head of his shaft rubbed over her clit again and again. He kept a hand pressed against the front of her pelvis so that he could push hard against her ass without her scooting forward.

Bruce kissed her neck, awakening all of her senses to him. The sound of his breathing, now marked by quiet groans with each cycle of his pumping body, filled her with joy. Knowing that he enjoyed being with her as much as she enjoyed him made her smile. His long hair tickled her back. As he moved faster, the helmet of his shaft flicked harder against her sensitive clit. Passion swelled within her, like a rosebud packed tight and ready to burst forth with a rich and heavy blossom to fulfill its destiny. Their fingers clenched tighter as a shudder suddenly rippled through Carolyn. "Bruce." She gasped his name.

Her sweet orgasm tumbled gently over the edge, like the crescendo of a symphony when the violins sang in compassionate vibrato. It chimed through her body in echo after wonderful echo. She gripped the diamond in her fist even tighter. The impression of it certainly would remain in her palm for some time to come.

"Give me your awakening. Accept mine in return." Bruce drew back until he nearly slipped out between her cheeks. In a second he'd adjusted his aim and pressed the head of his cock to her anus. Carolyn gasped with surprise. Already well lubricated with her juices, Bruce slipped easily through the ring of muscle. It had come as a surprise and her body had not even had the chance to resist his bold move. Once deep in her ass he held himself there. Carolyn shivered, never having felt this unique and yet wonderful sensation before. It only took her a few deep breaths to relax and accept his cock within her. Focusing on remaining as relaxed as possible, Carolyn enjoyed the glide of Bruce's wide cock in and out of her ass. He moved slickly and easily within her. Little by little, he began to pick up his pace. Carolyn's body accepted him without resistance. She moaned, still high from the orgasm he'd just given her. Banging with more force against her ass, Bruce grunted into her hair. Deep inside her, Carolyn felt his cock throb. His cum gushed in a hot, heavy flow. "You make me give you so much nectar," he growled. "So much. Lovely, you steal my strength. You drain me."

Both of them spent, Bruce held her close, making no move to part from their entangled bodies. The only sound in the night was his deep and even breathing as he drifted off to sleep. As she kept her fingers curled around the diamond ring Carolyn knew she would never want to be parted from it, or from Bruce. Carolyn closed her eyes and gave in to the comfort he gave her. Her feelings for him went beyond compassion or lust. This felt permanent. Unhurried. It felt like forever.

* * * * *

"You are very devious." Bruce's warm voice echoed in the study.

Carolyn raised her eyes to the translucent mist in the shape of a man. The loose blond hair rippled in a breeze she didn't feel. Where the light reflected on the silken flow of his hair it glowed golden but where it twisted into shadow it vanished so the mantle of the fireplace behind him shone through. The right side of him glowed, bathed in a light source she did not see, but his left side faded to merely a misty outline. Neither his voice nor his ephemeral appearance startled her because she'd smelled his deliciously bold scent all morning as if he read over her shoulder. His words did surprise her though. "Oh? How do you mean?"

"I thought only to claim you at first," Bruce stepped closer. "You are fetching and seductive." Another step and he was against the opposite side of the table. "But now I find I want more than just your companionship. I want your affection as well." Bruce stretched his hand toward hers where it rested on the table. His fingertips brushed her wrist and trailed down the back of her hand so lightly that he left chilled goose bumps in his wake. The stirring from the touch cast growing ripples, like a stone's disturbance on the glassy surface of a pond, over her skin. It pulsed through her, drumming in her like a heartbeat. Passion coiled low in her belly, making her gasp.

"Devious," Bruce repeated.

Carolyn breathed, "I never knew ghosts could do so much."

"What do you know of ghosts?" He spoke the words matter-of-factly, as if the concept were an abstract one. As if he himself was not one.

Carolyn rubbed her hand over her chilled wrist. The touch aroused more than just her body. It brought forth a longing for more than just the sexual desires. Looking into his eyes made her nervous. Not nervous the way the living feel when confronted with a spirit but nervous like a woman in the presence of a handsome, attentive man. "Why are you here? Shouldn't you have gone on to heaven?"

"Or hell?" he mused. "I am in both heaven and hell. My beloved home is my heaven and I have become a part of it. However, while I may remain within these stately halls, I am separate from it. Heaven can feel like hell without family and friends to share it with. My heaven rotted into hell a long time ago and yet I remain trapped here."

"Your grandmother's note mentioned a curse. She said there might be some key to release you from your imprisonment. Do you know anything about that?" She reached for him but her hand passed right through his arm.

"Some hag from the bayou shouted some voodoo curse at me because she claimed I built this home on her land. I know that is what my grandmother thought trapped me here. I possess no knowledge of any key."

"What of 'the deceiver'? She thought that the deceiver might know the key."

He shook his head. "I have not a clue who that might be." Bruce turned from her and began to fade. "For me, there is no hope."

"Wait!" Carolyn jumped up and hurried around the table so she could face him. As he had begun to vanish, she physically felt an emptiness forming in the wake of his departure. The very thought of his absence tore a loneliness inside her that she couldn't endure. All she knew was that she needed him to stay. "Don't disappear, please."

"Why not?"

The weight of the sorrow in his expression transferred to Carolyn until she felt the grief as her own. The emotion choked her until tears burned in her eyes. "Such despair." Carolyn shook her head. "Such loneliness." When she reached to stroke his arm in comfort, her hand passed through him again as if he were nothing more than a mist. "I just wish…" She wished he were alive but he wasn't. Reminding him of the obvious would only hurt them both, so she let the thought hang unfinished between them.

Bruce slid his hands, now more substantial, up her bare arms until he cupped her elbows. Gently, he drew her closer to him and guided her arms around his waist. He was solid now. She could feel the fabric flow and fold beneath her fingers, and beneath the clothing, she could trace the definition of his muscles and his spine.

His arms circled her shoulders and pulled her to him. A sense of relief rained over her as Carolyn sank into the embrace. She rested her cheek against his hard chest and breathed in his scent. Despite being solid, Bruce was still cold to the touch as if he'd been out all night in a winter storm. Carolyn shivered but didn't let go.

Bruce rubbed her back so the silk of her short-sleeve blouse massaged her skin. His hands worked upward, claiming ribbons of her loose hair before cradling her cheeks and raising her face so he could see her.

His thumbs stoked over her cheekbone and then back down to trace the line of her jaw. He touched the swell of her bottom lip.

Carolyn examined his handsome features with voracious eyes. He had a strong jaw that drew taut with desire. The blue of his eyes always trapped her, so she avoided them while she memorized the smooth planes of his cheeks, the way his fair hair flared back from his forehead and the full, hungrily parted lips.

Carolyn sighed and her warm breath turned to mist between them.

"Cold?" he asked.

She shook her head but her shivering gave her away.

"Let me try to fix that." Bruce leaned down and kissed Carolyn. His mouth molded to hers as if it belonged there and always had. Carolyn opened to him. They explored and tasted each other as if they were starving. Altering the angle of her head, Bruce deepened the kiss until they seemed to melt together.

When he drew back, Carolyn reached up and removed the ring from the chain around her neck. She slipped it onto her finger and then quickly embraced Bruce once more. Hard and deep, she kissed him with all the love she felt for him warming her heart. Slowly, the world seemed to slip and Carolyn felt a confusing mix of sensations, as if she plummeted backward in slow motion. Carolyn clutched Bruce so his knee slipped between her legs and his hips forced against her center in a desperate embrace.

More than anything, she felt heat between them. The chill melted away and summer returned as if evoked by the sexuality burning inside them.

Carolyn opened her eyes as Bruce withdrew. Thankfully he steadied her, because her legs didn't want to support her. Bruce smiled at her, obviously amused by her state of emotional inebriation. "I'm not swooning," she told him.

"Of course not," he said, but still didn't release her. Which relieved her, because she would slide down to the floor if he did. In which case she'd have no choice but to die of embarrassment.

Carolyn skimmed her fingertips along his warm cheek. Bruce covered her hand with his and rubbed his face in her palm. "You're warm now."

"That's not all." He glanced around the room with a smile and Carolyn followed his gaze.

The study had changed. The antiques that had moments ago showed their age were now shining and new. The friendly blaze in the fireplace crackled and radiated its warmth. Her papers were gone, replaced with leather-bound books and loose sheets of parchment.

"This is my home as I remember it." Bruce beamed down at her. "Too be honest, I never thought anyone else would ever see it as I do. Not until you found that ring."

Carolyn's eyes lit up. "Show me more."

With her hand resting on the crook of his arm, he guided her on a tour of his home. What would be antique furniture in the future shone with newness. The embroidery stitches on the plump cushions were tight and even. No carpets hid the highly polished teak floors that were now free of the scars or blemishes of use. The single item that impressed her the most was the portrait of Bruce by the stairwell. The paint gleamed with freshness and she could even detect a faint whiff of the oils.

"It is all so amazing." Carolyn beamed up at Bruce, thrilled with the treasures he'd shared with her. "And yet, you are so alone." Carolyn took in the magnificent but lonely home and then glanced up at him. "But not any more." Carolyn hooked her finger inside his waistband and tugged Bruce until he stepped closer to her. Lifting her mouth to his she proved her sincerity.

Bruce slid his hands up under her shirt to cup her breasts. His thumbs drifted in light circles over her nipples until they responded, coming to tight and tingling attention. She smiled against his lips, loving the way his touch brought her entire body to awareness instantly. A flush rose from between her thighs and moved upward, like a Louisiana heat wave, until she felt herself blushing. Breathing in his kiss was like breathing in passion. Her awareness and arousal blossomed with every second her lips yielded to his. Her skin burned for his touch. Her soul reached for his in a way only soul mates could.

Her hands flattened against his tight tummy. Wanting to feel more of him, she slid them down until the shape of his swollen cock stopped her. Firmly, she rubbed him through the fabric until Bruce broke their kiss to gasp. Carolyn reclaimed his mouth, not giving him a chance to recover before unfastening the buttons on the front of his trousers. Drawing back for just a second from the kiss, she licked her lips, "I want what is inside here."

Bruce moaned his agreement. His hand slipped up under her hair and brought her deep into a kiss once more. Backing her against the wall, his other hand cupped her bottom and grabbed it hard. Craving his seductive strength, Carolyn opened his pants so Bruce's heavy arousal sprang forth. Even though she wanted to look down at the impressive cock that rested heavily in her palm, Bruce wouldn't allow her to. The thirst in his kiss refused to be denied. Every time she moved to escape the kiss his mouth found hers once more. He drank of her mouth in deep draughts, the desperation in his kiss growing with each quickening heartbeat.

Both her hands cradled Bruce's throbbing cock. Her left supported his tightening sack, rolling his balls gently and getting a breathy growl from him for her efforts. Her right hand circled his shaft and glided up, pulling slightly at the skin. Widening her grip, she rubbed over the head. Drops of pre-cum moistened her fingers, making them slick with his natural lubrication. How was it that a ghost would have such a biological, physical reaction? Was reality in this place so altered that they could both be "real" here? Really real? Like alive real?

Bruce moved his hips with the plunging glide of her hand back down his shaft. He bit her lower lip softly, keeping it sucked inside his mouth even as he groaned with excitement. Bunching his hands in the fabric of her skirt, Bruce gathered it up until her bottom chilled from having nothing but her thin panties covering it.

As Bruce lifted her Carolyn wrapped her legs around his narrow waist. Her arms hugged tightly around his muscled shoulders. With a gasp, he released her lips only to plunge forward once more before she could escape his mouth completely. His tongue drove intimately into her mouth, going deep with bold, unrelenting strokes. Carolyn felt Bruce step out of his trousers with impatient kicks. Once he was free, he carried her to a wide sofa. There he arranged her on her back, her skirt bunched up around her waist, her legs wide to accommodate his body between them.

Carolyn reached up between them, unfastening the line of buttons on his shirt one by one. It fell open to her so she could glide her hands over the smooth bumps and grooves of his torso. Finding his nipples by touch alone, she teased them until his pec muscles flexed.

Bruce rubbed hard at her mons through her panties. Circling her hips, she moved against him so her hidden clit felt the glorious pressure of his touch. Bruce tugged aside the fabric of her underwear, reaching inside the leg to touch her slick center. Two fingers slid between her lips.

Arching back, Carolyn gasped. Bruce didn't let her mouth go that easily, not even to breathe. Every breath was shared. Every inhalation tasted of him.

Carolyn opened her legs wider to Bruce as he pumped his fingers into her pussy. She rode his touch, loving it, loving what he did to her, loving him.

Her eyes opened suddenly at that realization. Frantically, she gripped the sides of his head, her fingers tangling in his soft hair and pushed him back so that she could see his passion-hazed blue eyes. "I love you," she proclaimed. Even hearing those words from herself surprised her. She'd never loved anyone before. Not like this. Not with all her heart. Nothing else mattered in this moment. Bruce was here with her now, however that was possible. Ghost or not, he was the man she loved. The man she felt she'd been meant to find, meant to give herself to, meant to love. Breathless, she begged, "Bruce, take me. Bind me. Claim me. Make me yours."

Bruce gazed at her mouth, intoxicated with desire. His only reply was a passionate moan as once more he bent forward to express himself through the demand of his kiss. He did not to need words to tell her how she made him feel. Not when the melting of their mouths mirrored the joining of their souls. She drew her breath from him like she drew life from his love.

His fingers withdrew from her passage. As he pushed himself back from her, the chill without his body near hers tickled her skin. With quivering anticipation, she watched him rummage through a chest beneath the window until he found a thin and pliable length of rope. His cock remained stiff and extended straight forward as he crossed to her once more. The thick muscles of his forearm clenched as he gripped the rope tightly. With infinite patience, Bruce guided the rope so that the loops barely touched her knee and then glided up her thigh, over her bunched skirt around her middle, along the track of bare skin up her ribs and between her breasts. Carolyn's sigh of surging desire blew out between her pursed lips. She tilted her head away, lengthening her neck for Bruce as the rope traced up her throat and across her cheek.

He knelt beside the sofa and she could tell without watching that he lashed one end of the rope to the leg of the heavy furniture. Wordlessly, he arranged the pillows against the arm of the couch. He stroked her auburn tresses, cupping the back of her head for a second before fisting her hair. Using that to guide her, Bruce forced Carolyn to recline on the pillows. When he claimed her wrists his firm grip, it ignited a firestorm of excitement inside her. Bruce lifted her arms above her head and then had her bend at her elbows so that her forearms reached down the side of the couch. With the speed of familiarity, Bruce secured her hands. Carolyn tugged gently but found little slack in the rope. An excited spasm ran rampant through her as Carolyn writhed needfully against the cushions supporting her.

Bruce returned to look down upon her, still holding the rope trailing from her bound wrists. "You want me to bind you." Lust made his voice hoarse. He bent over her breasts once more, grabbed the bit of fabric bridging the gap between the cups of her bra and snapped it in half with one brutal yank. Carolyn gave a sharp cry of surprise and excitement. Roughly, Bruce gripped one of her breasts around its base and squeezed, forcing her flesh to swell and rise toward him. He looped the rope around the base of her breast and drew it snug enough that he lifted the fullness of it away from her chest so that her breast bulged forward. Squeezing the orb he'd created, he tested the firmness of her constricted breast. The next loop drew it slightly tighter still. This time when he squeezed her firm breast, the intense sensation sparked through Carolyn.

"Ah, yeah!" She struggled to settle her galloping heart rate once more. "Yes." Watching as he bound her other breast as well, she could barely resist her need to move. Her tied wrists held her in place before Bruce. Her legs parted, her moist and sensitive pussy suddenly demanding his attention. Lifting her hips, she rubbed herself against his side as he continued to work around her breasts.

Leaning back, Bruce regarded her breasts. With a flick of his hand he smacked each one firmly. An explosion of pleasure shot through her entire body as she cried out.

Once more Bruce pushed her thighs wide to give him access to her core. She felt the heavy press of his cock to her entrance. He paused there a moment as he braced one hand at the bend between her thighs and her hips. Bruce gripped the crisscrossing harness of rope between her bound breasts. Holding her body steady, he pressed downward with his erection. The long, erotically slow glide of his cock entering her made her body sing with joy. The soft walls of her core gave way to his rigid member only to cling tightly to it once more.

Carolyn hooked her calves behind Bruce's knees. Yanking uselessly on her bound wrists, Carolyn fought to lift her hips to press him even deeper inside her. Surrendering to his demanding kisses even as she gave him her body, a fearful, lonely tension unraveled from her soul. This was love. She knew it. This was fate. Somehow, everything that had happened in her life had led her to this moment of fulfillment. Her heart expanded as if it had been afraid it would never find its destiny. Bruce was here now. She wasn't afraid any more. He completed her. It was that simple. A single tear trailed from the corner of her eye and tickled back into the hair by her ear. Impossible through it seemed, she and Bruce were meant to be. Carolyn refused to believe anything else. It had been the very reason she had begged him to bind her. She didn't want Bruce ever to release his claim on her.

Bruce's fingers dug into Carolyn's hip as he retreated from that first, slow, perfect plunge into her pussy. The next stroke picked up speed, building the ecstasy for both of them.

Carolyn rose to him each time, meeting his pace in a perfect dance of their bodies.

Where the night before had been eternally gentle, the urgency of this moment raged out of control. Bruce's mouth mashed to hers with bruising force. His thick cock rammed hard and deep into her core. His fingers dug into her thigh. Every forceful slam into her body tried to shove her away from him but the harness around her breasts prevented it. Out of control, they rushed to insane intensity. Carolyn thrust her hips up to meet each of Bruce's strikes, forcing him into her depths. Desperately, she ground against his body as much as she could. The building thundercloud of passion exploded between them in an orgasm that ripped a roar from Bruce which echoed through the mansion. His seed gushed deep into her. Carolyn felt the force of it. Her own scream tumbled from her as she gave into her bliss.

Bruce spasmed a few seconds more, the last drops of his cum forced from him. He collapsed on top of Carolyn, not even trying to support his own weight. She breathed shallowly while he pressed her into the sofa. After a few minutes his strength returned and he propped himself up on his elbows to gaze at her. The emotion on his face mixed with honest confusion and concern. Bruce confessed, "I couldn't stop. I had to have you. I felt like I needed to consume you. I wanted to make you mine. You are so sweet and luscious. I had to be inside you. Deep and hard."

Carolyn laughed softly, smiling so widely that she thought she must look a little goofy. "Oh no! Oh you did not hurt me at all. Bruce, darling, you felt so wonderful inside me. Nothing could have been more right." Carolyn feathered light kisses on his jaw. "I meant what I said before. I love you, Bruce."

No expression gave away his thoughts or emotions as he unwrapped her breasts. He released her wrists and then sat her up on the couch and knelt before her so they were eye to eye. "You cannot stay here."

"Here or in the present, where ever we are, we can be together." She stroked his blond hair back from his face.

Bruce gripped her wrists. Gently, he forced her hands away from him. Disentangling himself from her, he got to his feet. "I have nothing to offer you."

"Are you kidding?" Carolyn laughed. She straightened her panties, which had been pushed askew, and smoothed her skirt back down. "You have this! You have yourself. You have your heart."

"Don't you think I want more?" His voice boomed through the mansion like canon fire. He stomped over to his britches and tugged them on angrily. "Don't you think I want you? I don't even have a body! I'm dead! What can I offer you?"

Carolyn ran to him and threw her arms around his chest in an impassioned embrace. "You are real! I can feel you with my hands and my heart."

He gripped her upper arms and forced her to meet his eyes. He opened his mouth to say something, shook what ever thought he considered away and hugged her to him. "You are a stubborn one. I can't deny you even for your own good."

"Good," she laughed. "Because I'm not giving you up."

Bruce hugged her for a long time, rocking her gently from side to side. Carolyn clenched at his shirt and grinned to herself. "One of these times we should get completely naked to make love."

Bruce arched back and gazed down at her. "I thought ladies disliked disrobing completely before a man."

She laughed and hugged into him once more. "Times have changed a lot."

"Then I shall see you properly divested of your clothing when next I ravage your virtue," Bruce teased her. After a long while, he rubbed her back until she looked up at him. Looking down at her open top, he chuckled and then buttoned it closed once more. "Carolyn, I can't make you promises, especially not given the state of things. I can, however, give you this." He collected her left hand and kissed the diamond ring on her ring finger. "That ring belonged to my grandmother. I want you to keep it as yours. I have nothing else to give you, Carolyn."

Beaming with joy, Carolyn smiled up at Bruce. In just a second more he'd admit the words she longed to hear. He'd confess his love for her.

That perfect moment for which she'd waited a lifetime didn't come.

Carolyn felt as if the floor beneath her vanished. She fell into darkness. Bruce, to whom she'd clung so vigorously, faded from her touch like smoke.

Chapter Four

ℬ

Suddenly, Carolyn sat up. She sucked in air and then shook with a violent coughing fit.

"Easy there, sweetie." Greta patted Carolyn on the back. "You're back now."

"What?"

With an understanding, grandmotherly smile, Greta returned to speak with Carolyn. "Time for truth, young lady," Greta folded her hands on her rounded tummy in a matronly fashion. "You had not simply passed out, had you? You crossed the veil. Somehow you penetrated it. You were with Bruce, weren't you?"

"I…" Carolyn knew how crazy it sounded, but it was true. Greta didn't seem to doubt what Carolyn knew had occurred. "Somehow, yes. I believe I was able to cross over because Bruce and I share something. Some connection."

Greta gripped Carolyn's hand firmly, almost too tightly, as though there was some desperate matter at hand. Greta's thumb prodded the diamond of the ring, certainly knowing the significance of it on her left ring finger. Greta's voice held grave concern. "There is something we need to discuss. You must come with me, dear. I need to show something to you."

She still wore the ring and yet she was here and not with Bruce. How could that be? Why had it not kept her with Bruce in his realm? Was the effect temporary? Had something blocked the ring's magic? Pondering over that, Carolyn allowed Greta to lead her outside to the small family plot across the gravel road in front of the house. "Do you see that tombstone there? Can you read the name on the marker?"

Kneeling down, Carolyn squinted at the stone. With her fingers she traced the letters. "Bruce Warren. This is where his body rests."

"So one would think." Greta frowned. "The family placed the marker here but his body was never found. Do you know why?"

Carolyn stilled, watching the grave expression on the older woman's face growing darker with each second. A feeling of unease began to build in her stomach. "Why?"

Greta's gaze moved from the stone to Carolyn's face. Her voice was flat. Lifeless. "Because he didn't die."

Getting to her feet, Carolyn shook her head. "Bruce isn't among the living. Those were your exact words."

"He's not among the living but he lives. He's trapped between worlds." A growing hardness built in Greta's expression. Her mouth tightened, becoming more wrinkled. Her already pale face became ashen. "Not even able to cross this gravel road to where we are, he remains trapped in his beloved home."

Greta glanced back at the house. Carolyn followed her gaze. Bruce stood on the porch, watching and listening, worry and confusion obvious as he heard all Greta admitted. "He is trapped in that house," she repeated. "Right where I trapped him."

"You?" Bruce shouted. "What are you saying?"

Greta ignored him, speaking instead to Carolyn. "You found the key across the veil. True love. If Bruce truly loves you, he will escape his captivity. I won't have that."

With speed and strength Carolyn never could have guessed the older woman possessed, Greta snatched her by her hair and forced her back down to her knees on the plot that had been marked as Bruce's grave. Only Bruce wasn't dead. He'd never died. Greta yanked back Carolyn's head, exposing her neck. Carolyn reached back and pried at the knobby fingers but couldn't loosen their iron grip.

Greta shouted at Bruce. "You challenged me! You built this home on land I claimed. I warned you! I warned you to stay away. Do you finally see the punishment I have laid upon you? Over and over I have changed my appearance and remained caretaker of this home. My home! And forever it shall remain mine!"

"You!" Bruce grimaced in recognition. "You are the hag who cursed me. All so you could torture me and steal my life?" He tried to charge off the porch but slammed into an invisible barrier.

"And so shall it remain!" she shouted at him. From her skirt Greta withdrew a long carving knife. Her focus shifted with deadly seriousness to Carolyn's throat. "All I have to do is keep you from embracing true love more than you embraced your home."

The light glinted off the knife as Greta moved to slash at her. Carolyn stopped fighting with Greta's fingers and reached up her hands to ward off the attack. "No!"

The knife didn't slice at Carolyn. She saw the rush of movement from the corner of her eye. Carolyn's head jerked back as both she and Greta flew back onto the ground. Bruce loomed over them. His hands closed tightly around Greta's throat.

Carolyn rolled free of the struggle. Greta spat something in Creole as she brought the knife down at Bruce. Blocking the blade with his forearm, he prevented her from making good the fatal blow. Hissing, Bruce gripped the gash in his flesh, dropping the elderly woman in the process.

Greta scrambled away and raced back into the house. The door slammed behind her. A split second later, all the windows slammed closed in unison. A screech of pure, demonic evil rattled the building.

"Oh my God!" Carolyn got to her feet and raced to Bruce. "You are bleeding!"

"Which means I'm not dead." He gathered her tightly to his chest and hugged her with his good arm. "Nor am I trapped any longer."

Carolyn helped Bruce remove his shirt and used it to tightly wrap his arm. It would need stitches, she was certain, but the wound was not as deep as she first feared.

Just then the "whoof" sound of a massive fire igniting came from the house. In seconds, flames curtained all the windows simultaneously. "The house is burning! She's destroying it!"

The screams from the house changed from fury to panic and agony. "I think it is destroying her. Her own evil coming back upon her."

"But your home…"

"It is not what matters most to me." Bruce gathered her hand to fondle the diamond ring that had brought them together even before he'd given it to her. "I love you, Carolyn."

She flung her arms around his shoulders. Bruce was alive. Alive and free and he loved her as much as she loved him. Carolyn flattened her body against his, wanting to feel every inch of him pressed against her, so that not even the air separated them any longer. "You've escaped the curse. You can do anything you want now."

"There in only one thing that I want." He tilted her chin back and claimed her with a timeless kiss.

DIAMOND LADY

Desiree Holt

ഇ

Dedication

෨

To my family, who keeps me sane through the insanity. I love you all.

And special thanks as always to my editor, Helen Woodall, who is quite simply the best.

Trademarks Acknowledgement

෨

The author acknowledges the trademarked status and trademark owners of the following wordmarks mentioned in this work of fiction:

Mercedes: Mercedes- Benz USA, LLC

Chapter One
ဢ

Anna Beloit stood on the wide patio of the Danbury Yacht Club, careful to stay as far as possible from the light spilling from the ballroom. The champagne cocktail she was holding was her third, yet the alcohol seemed to have had no effect on her. Probably because her anger kept counteracting it.

Tonight was the last of the big parties before her sister, Shari's, wedding. And as with every one of the pre-wedding activities, she'd been somehow paired with the groom's law partner, John Boudreau. Not that there was anything wrong with him, he was just such a…lawyer. Every conversation turned into a debate or a pontifical explanation of something she really didn't give a shit about.

And if he wasn't debating or pontificating, he was regaling everyone with stories about the top-dollar models he represented and the enormous fees he made from their contracts. Shari, one of those models herself, preened as everyone gasped at the income she obviously brought home.

Big deal!

If there was a moment left over to compliment Anna's thriving bookstore, her pride and joy, she hadn't found it yet. "Anna's little toy," is how the family referred to it.

Well, she was sick of her family, sick of the wedding plans and sick of being thrown together with John who she assumed was to lift her from the level of the plebeian to the exalted upper class. She'd been the dutiful sister for weeks and now the wedding was just around the corner. They could do without her for one night, couldn't they? She loved her sister but one more hour of watching Shari in her model's pose holding court and she'd be headed for the nut house.

Why was it that some women got all the attractive men while others, like her, attracted only the most boring individuals? Was it a matter of hormones or genetic selection?

What she really wanted was to ditch this stupid, boring party and put a little excitement in her life. What she needed was an adventure with a handsome stranger like those in the erotic romances she read when business was slow. One who would help her live out the fantasies that were still just images in her mind.

Fantasies that would shock the hell out of the very proper Beloits, who saw Anna as a recalcitrant child, even at thirty, who need to be brought to heel.

"Damn them. They can all go to hell," she whispered to herself, impulsively throwing the crystal champagne flute into the bushes.

"I didn't expect when I came outside that I'd be taking a shower." The voice was deep and husky startling her with its nearness.

Anna stumbled backward as a tall, well-muscled man in an impeccably cut tuxedo stepped from behind the shrubbery where she'd thrown her glass.

"Oh my God, I'm so sorry." She continued to back away, shaking, as the man moved forward. "I'm angry and acting like a brat, paying no attention to what I'm doing."

He threw back his head and laughed, a low rumbling sound. "Anger is good, if properly controlled." He looked at her from head to toe with experienced eyes. "But I see more than anger in your eyes. I see fire and passion."

"I beg your pardon?"

"If you want to keep away from the light, which it seems you do, I'd stop backing up right about there."

She nearly tripped over her own feet trying to move back into the shadows. "Who are you anyway? And what are you doing hiding out here in the shrubbery? Wait, I know you. I've seen you at other functions that are part of this bizarre ritual

248

my parents are conducting." She shook her head. "I have, haven't I?"

He nodded.

"How do you stand it? Lord. If I have to go to one more party like this and smile at one more jerk-head, I think I'll scream."

"Not my cup of tea either but I do business with the groom's law firm. I guess that put me on the permanent guest list." His eyes hypnotized her, so dark and dangerous. "But I have had my eye on you for a long time, Anna Beloit."

"Y-you know who I am?" She smacked her forehead. "What a dummy I am. Of course you do, if you've been coming to all these duck walks."

He laughed again. "Duck walks. An appropriate name for these events." He winked at her. "Your name is not all that I know. But not nearly as much as I wish to discover."

"You want to learn more about me?" She could hardly believe that this very sexy, very mysterious man, with the enticingly accented voice, would rather go off with her than one of the glamorous females in Shari's entourage.

He pinned her with his gaze. "But of course, *cara.* You are the woman of my dreams."

Her jaw dropped. "Me?"

"That surprises you? I don't know why it should. You're a beautiful woman, full of hidden fire." His mouth shaped itself in a slow, sexy smile. "I would love the chance to bring that fire to life."

Anna shivered as delicious images raced through her mind, images from the pages of the erotic novels she read in a corner of her bookstore. "I-I don't know what to say."

"Say nothing. Just tell me you'd like the same thing."

Well, she'd wished for an adventure, hadn't she? "Aren't you going back inside?"

The sounds of multiple conversations, laughter, the tinkling of cocktail glasses, all seeped out into the night air. He looked through the open doors at the crowd, then down at his dress shirt and jacket, soaked with champagne. Grinning, he gestured toward his dripping clothes. "I don't think I'm appropriately attired to return to the party, do you?"

"Oh lord." She put her hands over her face. "I truly apologize. I was just acting like a spoiled brat and you got all the damage."

He laughed again. "Luckily I have a change of clothes nearby.

Her eyes popped. "You keep an extra tux in the locker room?"

"No, on my boat." He nodded toward the water at the yacht club marina, where boats of every description bobbed in their slips.

"You have a boat." Well, yes, dummy, isn't that what people who belong to yacht clubs own?

He held out a hand to her. "Come. Your penance is to help me make myself presentable again."

"Where are we going?"

"To my boat, *cara*. You will help me change clothes and I will reward you with wine from my vineyards in Italy. It puts to shame anything you can find here."

Anna's heart was skipping like a stone across water. Here was her chance to see if all those things she'd read about were really possible. Her stomach clenched and her pulse skittered. Hadn't she been lying in bed nights wishing just for something like this? Dreaming it? Trying to conjure up an exotic stranger to lift her from her humdrum life?

And now here he was. Devastatingly good looking, in the light spilling out from the club she could see he was at least six feet tall. A thick head of black hair topped a rugged-looking face. Black eyes with diamonds of light reflecting in them looked out from a thick fringe of lashes. A thin scar ran from just over his left eyebrow to below his cheekbone, giving him a rakish look.

He might as well have been flashing a sign that said "Danger". It was all she could do to keep from drooling. And he wanted her. Anna Beloit. Maybe her adventure was about to begin.

"Come, Anna. Let's see what the rest of the evening has in store for us." He held out his hand to her.

She put her small hand in his large, calloused one. The moment their skin touched her nipples hardened so abruptly they nearly poked through the thin silk of her dress. Moisture flooded the crotch of her thong. She walked slowly down the slope to the marina gate, careful not to trip in her high heels. "You know my name. Will you tell me yours?"

"Of course." He flashed a smile at her that made the muscles in her cunt ripple. "I am Dominic."

"Dominic."

"It sounds like music when you say it." He used a key card to unlock the iron gate, then led her along the pier to the last slip. "I like to be as far away from activity as possible. See how quiet it is out here?"

All her senses were on full alert. The spicy scent of Dominic's cologne mingled with the sharp tang of the water. The sky was midnight black, the stars splashed across it like a spray of diamonds, sharp and clear. A breeze so gentle it was almost nonexistent drifted over them.

The boat was certainly more than the simple word implied. Yacht would have been more like it. It was large and magnificent and the name *Diamond Lady* swept across the hull in paint that glittered in the moonlight.

"Is she named for someone?"

He leaned toward her, his breath a whisper against her skin. "How do you know it isn't for you?"

While she was still catching her breath over that, he climbed up a short ladder and opened a segment of the hull that swung inward. Looking down at her, he shook his head. "Shoes like that were not made for climbing ladders. Or for walking on fine teakwood. Come here, *cara*."

He leaned over and placed his hands at her waist, lifting her as if she were as light as a rose petal. When he swung her into his arms the fresh citrus scent of his aftershave teased her senses. He slipped off her shoes and placed them on a table before closing the gate in the hull.

"You must feel the elegance of the deck with your bare feet," he told her.

As he lowered her to stand upright, his hand slid beneath the skirt of her dress, up her thigh and over her hip to lie flat on her abdomen. She shivered at his touch.

If she'd been bolder she would have opened her legs enough to permit him to slide his fingers beneath her thong and touch her dampening folds. She closed her eyes and imagined those thick fingers inserting themselves into her hungry cunt, stroking the deliciously wet inner tissues while she...

Her eyes flew open and she looked up to see Dominic grinning at her, both hands holding her waist beneath her dress, his thumbs caressing her skin.

He winked. "I think we will have a lovely evening ahead of us, don't you? And isn't this wood like satin beneath your feet?"

"Oh yes." Like a child, she wanted to glide her feet over the polished wood, sliding as she'd done in the halls of her house on cleaning day.

"I'll bet your lips feel just as good."

His face was barely an inch from hers. She opened her mouth to say something, then forgot whatever it was as his lips drifted across hers with the softest of touches. He nibbled her bottom lip, drawing it into his mouth and licking it with the tip of his tongue.

She swayed against him, a heady feeling of sensuality consuming her. His tongue was like the flame of a candle, dancing now here, now there, until the entire inside of her mouth was consumed. Yet never once had he increased the pressure of his lips or taken her mouth roughly. He was tempting her with his lips and his tongue, a dance partner beckoning to her. In frustration she wrapped her arms tightly around his neck and pressed her lips hard against his, sweeping her tongue into the warm wetness of his mouth. If she could have, she'd have swallowed his tongue whole.

He lifted his head and chuckled. "I knew there was a hellcat under that proper demeanor. I just didn't know I could unleash it so quickly.

He picked her up again and carried her down a short flight of stairs to the cabin below. Anna kept her arms locked tightly around his neck, wondering if she could trick him into another one of those kisses. Only this time hotter and steamier. God, the man had lips like an angel. Or maybe it was a devil. He certainly made her burn hotter than the fires of hell and they hadn't even done anything yet.

He flipped a switch that turned on recessed lighting and gave the room a soft glow.

She let her eyes travel around the room, trying to take in every detail. "Why, it's almost like a small living room."

"I stay on her often so I wanted to have all my comforts." He set her down and headed toward the built-in bar. "I promised you the finest wine you would ever taste and I always keep my word."

He selected a bottle from a wine refrigerator, opened it and filled two crystal goblets, smiling as he handed her one. "I believe in adventure, don't you, Anna?"

"Oh yes." Her voice had a breathless catch to it. What she really wanted to say was, *You bet your ass I do.*

He touched his glass to hers. "Then to adventure."

"To adventure," she echoed and sipped the clear amber liquid. "Oh my. This is delicious." She looked at the label. "Diamond Lady Vineyards."

"As I said, it's a special blend from my own winery in Italy. This one is a limited edition."

"Are the vineyards named after the boat or the other way around?"

"The boat for the vineyards. The winery had been in the Fellini family for generations. At the end of the first successful year, my great-grandfather bought my great-grandmother diamond earrings. Tiny ones but real stones nevertheless. Each year after that, he gave her something with diamonds. The men in my family have carried on the tradition." He grinned. "I tell my family if the winery ever falls on hard times, we can live out our lives very comfortably on the sale of all those sparklers."

"I don't imagine they take to that idea too well."

He shrugged. "Sentimental, all of them."

"So who have you given diamonds to?" Did she sound jealous?

He shook his head. "Only to my boat so far." His eyes burned into her. "Perhaps tonight that will change."

"Where do you live when you're not on the boat? Italy, where your family is?"

"I live many places. Perhaps I shall take you to see them." He reached for her hand. "That's enough questions for now. Come. You can help me get rid of these clothes. I usually drink my champagne in a glass."

Body quivering, she let him lead her into a bedroom with mirrored walls and the biggest bed she'd ever seen. She couldn't help gawking at it.

"I told you, I like my comfort. When I play, I want a large playpen."

"And are we going to play?" she asked, a slight tremor in her voice?

"I certainly hope so." He guided her to the edge of the bed and gently nudged her to sit down. "That is my intention."

While she watched he removed his clothing one piece at a time, jacket first, next the cummerbund, then the studs and cufflinks from the dress shirt, which he placed carefully on the dresser. His image was reflected in every panel of the mirror and she could see the muscles of his back ripple as he divested himself of his garments. When he reached for the button at the waistband of his pants she started to get up again but he moved to stand directly in front of her.

"I think I'll need you to help me with these. Too much champagne soaked into the fabric. The zipper's stuck."

She stared up at him, heart thumping. Here it was, the place where the rubber met the road. Up until now it was all teasing. Once those pants came off, it was Game On. Was she all talk or did she really want the erotic journey of her lifetime?

"Afraid of me, Anna? No need to be. "His voice was a soft caress. "I won't make you do anything you don't want to. Any time you want me to stop, just tell me and I'll take you back to the club."

She drew a deep breath and her lips curved into a tempting smile. Then, as if they had a mind of their own, her hands moved to the top of his slacks. With fingers that shook only slightly she drew the zipper down, her knuckles grazing the impressive bulge of his erection. She pushed the dress pants down past his hips, her hands caressing his taut skin as they moved over it.

Dominic toed his patent leather dress shoes off and quickly rid himself of his socks and the pants. Then there was nothing between them but snug black silk boxers that left nothing to the imagination. On impulse Anna leaned her cheek against the fly front, the swelling of his cock pressing against her skin. Impishly, she stuck out her tongue and licked the thin material, being careful not to reach through to the skin. Up and down she moved in long, smooth strokes, not touching any other part of him, the moisture from her mouth dampening the fine silk.

He held himself stiff, his thighs pressing against her breasts but when she began to nip him through the cloth, sucking him into her mouth, he threaded his fingers through her hair, pulling her head against him.

"Jesus Christ." His indrawn breath was shaky. "Where did you learn a trick like that?"

"In my head," she teased but only she knew how true it was. Most of her knowledge had come, not from the fumbling lovers she'd barely tolerated but from the erotic romances she devoured in copious quantities. Dominic might think he was the one doing the seducing but Anna had been storing up knowledge for so long if she didn't use it she was afraid her brain would explode. And tonight was giving her just the opportunity she needed.

With a stealthy movement she slid her hands up his thighs, under the silk of his boxers to cup the taut cheeks of his muscular ass. She raked her fingernails lightly across the skin, feeling the baby-fine hair that was softer than satin. As she moved her fingers to the cleft between the cheeks of his buttocks he swore again.

"Enough," he rasped, pulling her head back and stepping away from her. With a soft movement he stripped off his shorts and tossed them aside, his penis rising thick and proud and long from a dark nest of curls. "You should see what it is that's captured your attention."

Anna couldn't tear her eyes away. Every erotic book she'd read described this but she'd yet to see one actually this impressive. How the hell had she managed to get stuck with such losers in bed up until now?

Dominic wrapped the fingers of one hand around his cock and stroked it once from root to tip. "Before tonight is over, Annabella, you will take this in every orifice of your body. If you object, this is your last chance to say so."

Now? Object? When he was standing before her in his glorious nakedness and her arousal was practically running down her leg? Not unless the world came to an earthshaking end.

"No? Then I think one of us is a little overdressed, don't you?"

He stepped forward, reached for the hem of her dress and pulled it over her head, his mouth following the trail of his hands, licking every inch of her skin as he revealed it. His eyes widened at the glint of gold at her navel. Leaning closer he saw a tiny gold book dangling from a thin ring in that dainty little dimple.

"A navel ring," he breathed. "Who'd have thought it. And how beautiful it looks lying against your skin." He rubbed a finger lightly over the charm. "Perhaps after tonight we'll find something even better for that delectable little indentation."

With a quick twist of his hand her thong was history, a devilish look on his face as he felt the sopping crotch. Now he paused at her mound, probing the warm folds with the tip of his tongue. She trembled from the sensations his tongue set off, her legs wobbling, so he lowered her to the bed. When she was naked at last, he wrapped his fingers around her ankles and spread her legs wide, staring at her very wet cunt.

"Sweet Jesus," he hissed, staring at the plump pinkness of her pussy. "Your cunt lips are so wonderfully pouty, practically begging for my mouth. Your glistening tissues are more tempting than a gourmet feast." He stroked the neatly trimmed hair covering her mound. "Very, very nice, bella, but it would look so much better completely naked."

Naked? In her books she'd read about women who waxed their mounds and men who shaved them. Was that what he had in mind?

"I see that doesn't bother you. Very good, then, *cara*. It will be my greatest pleasure to shave you and expose all that skin to my mouth and my hands. Would you like that?"

A tiny throbbing set up inside her hot sheath and more liquid dribbled from her already aroused body. "Oh yes. Yes, I would."

His dark eyes held hers in a gaze that it was impossible to break. "Touch yourself for me," he commanded. "Let me see how you give yourself pleasure with those dainty fingers." He brushed his hands along the insides of her thighs. "You do pleasure yourself, do you not?"

"Yes." The word burst from her mouth, a flush creeping over her body.

"That's nothing to be embarrassed about, my sweet treat. And I want to see you do this. It will help me gauge how quickly you reach each level of pleasure."

Tentatively she reached down with one hand and rested it on her open sex.

"No, *cara,* not like that. Touch your clit. Pull back the little hood that covers it so I can see it in all its glory."

Half embarrassed, half excited, she did as he asked, feeling the cool air on her clitoris as she pulled away its protective covering. "Like that?"

He nodded. "Now rub it with the tip of one finger. Oh yes. What a sensitive body. The lightest touch and your cream releases. Good, good. Keep doing that while I fetch what I need. And turn your head. You can watch yourself in the mirrors. That's what they're for."

Anna looked to her side and gasped at the sight of her masturbating. The throbbing in her hot core increased in intensity and she moved her hand to slide two fingers inside herself. Dominic spotted her in the mirror as he headed out of the room, turned back and locked his fingers around her wrist.

"No, no, *cara*." A tiny smile played at the corners of her mouth. "I have other plans for this succulent pussy. Just the clit for now. Can you do that?"

Catching her lower lip between her teeth, she nodded.

"Good. If you obey me, I have a nice present for you."

Anna lay there in a state of what felt like suspended animation, stroking the tip of her clitoris, feeling the liquid fill her vagina, her body clamoring for more and frustrated at being denied greater pleasure.

In what could have been seconds or minutes Dominic returned carrying a tray with a crystal bowl of soapy water, a razor, a tube of something and three black velvet boxes.

Anna stilled her hand and cocked an eyebrow. "W-What's in the boxes?'

"Presents for you. One for now, the other for when I'm finished shaving you." He set the tray down on the bed and moved her hand away from her clitoris. "Stand up for me for a moment, okay?"

Frowning, she got off the bed, her body still shimmering with need.

"I want you to bend over and close your hands over your ankles. Then look between your legs. Remember, there's a mirror on every wall. See how beautiful you look exposed to my eyes."

She did as he instructed and gasped as she saw every inch of her sex, pink and wet, and the rounded globes of her ass.

"Beautiful," he breathed. "Just beautiful." His hands separated the cheeks of her ass, exposing the puckered rosette winking out at him. "Have you ever been penetrated here, Anna?" He touched the hole with his finger and stroked it idly.

"N-No." She caught her breath at the sensations just that light touch created. "No, I haven't."

"Tonight I will fuck you here and I promise you will love it. And I will prepare you so you will be completely ready for me when the time comes. Now hold still."

He plucked the tube from the tray, uncapped it and pressed it against her anus. Squeezing gently, he forced cool lubricant into the tight channel of her rectum. She jerked at the first sensation of it but his hand on the small of her back steadied her.

"You'll be fine. I promised you would enjoy everything, did I not?"

She nodded, unable to speak.

"Now keep watching."

She saw him insert one finger into her hole, felt him massage the lube around inside her. Then another squeeze of the gel, more stroking of his finger.

"There." His voice was warm and reassuring. "I think you're well prepared. Are you all right, *bella?*

All right? Dark threads of lust were unraveling through her body. She was more than all right. The feel of a man's fingers in her ass was more erotic than any book could describe.

"Yes. Oh yes, Dominic. I'm fine. Definitely fine. More than fine."

He reached over and opened one of the boxes, taking out what looked like a dildo but with flanges at the bottom of it. And sparkles. He held it front of her so she could see it.

"I have these made with diamonds on them, *cara.* I like the way they sparkle when pressed against your ass. Now. I must begin to prepare this gorgeous but tight asshole to accept my cock. We'll work up to it until you'll be more than ready for me. Take a deep breath, Anna. Right now."

She did as he told her, watching him press the tip of it against her anus and slowly but steadily push until it was completely inside her. She slowly let out her breath. Watching him insert the plug in her rectum was as arousing as the feel of it. But then he knew it would be. That was the reason for all the mirrors, so everything was visually stimulating.

"One more little item, just to make sure you stay in a state of readiness for me." He opened a second box and removed a silver vibrator. Setting it on a low speed so the hum was barely audible, he inserted it into her vagina.

Between the vibrator and the butt plug and the stimulation she'd given her clit, she was approaching sensory overload. She had the feeling of floating on a cloud, nothing touching her, every nerve in her body firing from the inside out.

Anna began to shake all over but again Dominic steadied her. "Let yourself get used to it. There. Like that. Concentrate on long, slow breaths."

He helped her to stand upright, laid her back on the bed on a big fluffy towel and arranged her legs so they were bent at the knees, feet planted on the mattress.

"And now we begin."

Chapter Two
🔊

To make sure she didn't try to reach down with her hands and interrupt the delicate process of shaving her, Dominic braceleted Anna's wrists in padded handcuffs. Then he stretched her hands over her head and locked the handcuffs to the headboard. She noted that, like the flanges on the butt plug, they were studded with tiny diamonds.

When Dominic had brought them out and shown them to her, a scene from one of her erotic romances played through her head. The heroine had been handcuffed like this and Anna had found herself aroused and wet just reading about it. The reality was even more arousing and she'd eagerly offered her wrists.

"Do these frighten you, *cara?*" He stared down at her. "I can take them off if they do."

"No. They don't." Her lashes swept down her cheeks as she shyly lowered her eyes. "I…they…excite me."

"Good." He brushed his lips over hers in a whisper of a kiss. "I was hoping you would feel that way. I want you to trust me, to know that at any time this evening you feel uncomfortable or unsure, just tell me and I'll stop."

Stop the adventure she'd been lusting after? Not hardly.

"I'm fine, Dominic."

He knew the combination of the plug and the vibrator gave her a feeling of fullness, of being stretched completely. And the vibrations from the dildo hummed through the thin membrane separating her rectum from her vagina and echoed in the butt plug. Her entire body seemed to be teetering on the edge of a sexual precipice.

"I know you want to come, Anna," he said matter of factly. "I can feel it in the trembling of your body. But we are nowhere near ready for that. There is so much more for you to experience. When you have your orgasm, it will far exceed anything you could ever have imagined."

Dominic refilled her wine glass and held her head up so she could drink from it. "Sip slowly, my love. Yes, like that." He kissed her forehead and her cheeks as she drank the wine, lifting the glass away every few seconds then placing it against her lips again. When she was finished, he put the empty glass on the built-in nightstand.

Anna ran her tongue over her lips. "Mmm. Delicious," she murmured.

"Shall I refill the glass?" he asked, his deep voice as soothing as a caress.

"Yes, please, and she opened her mouth for more.

"I knew you would enjoy it. As I said, we produce a limited quantity of this particular blend each year. I only share it with special people."

She heard the sound of the wine pouring into the goblet, then felt the pressure of the glass against her lips once more.

"Just a taste this time, little one. The effect of the wine can be quite strong." The glass clinked against wood as he set it down again.

He pushed a button on the wall and soft music floated into the air.

Her eyes widened. "*Swan Lake*! Almost no one listens to classical music any more."

"Except for you and me," he smiled.

"This is one of my favorites."

He grinned. "Then how fortunate that I chose to play it."

He hummed to himself as he pulled a short bench over to the foot of the bed and very gently began to apply soapy water to her pubic hair. When he lifted the razor and began to shave her with slow, easy strokes, the pressure of his fingers stretching her skin enhanced the low hum of the vibrator.

When he glanced at her face, he saw she was gritting her teeth to keep her body from responding to the additional stimulation, yet arousal glowed hotly in her eyes.

"I think you are enjoying this even more than I had hoped," he said softly.

"Y-Yes." She barely got the word out but pleasure suffused her face and she licked her lips.

"You wanted this, did you not, my sweet?"

She nodded, giving herself up to the enjoyment.

"But I'm counting on your self-control to hold back your orgasm, knowing what lies ahead of you." He kissed the inside of each knee. "An explosion of senses unlike anything you could ever imagine."

Dominic concentrated on his task, making sure each and every swipe of the razor was smooth and clean. With a soft washcloth he carefully cleaned each area of her mound as he removed the fine curls.

He'd waited a long time for this moment, longer than Anna realized. He was sure she didn't remember the day he'd wandered into her bookstore. He'd glimpsed her through the window as he was striding along the sidewalk and been instantly drawn to her. She was even more mesmerizing naked, a petite doll with rounded breasts and hips accentuated by the soft cotton skirt and blouse she wore. A thick fall of curly auburn hair framed a heart-shaped face and eyes like flaming emeralds. She had been deep in discussion in a conversation corner she'd set up, serving wine to a group of women and touting the merits of a new bestseller. When she smiled and dimples flashed he was instantly hard.

He'd brushed aside the young sales girl who approached him, looked his fill and left. He couldn't remember the last time he'd wanted a woman this badly after seeing her only once. The first thing he did back at his office was to find out her name. Then he'd made it his business to learn every detail he could about the luscious Anna Beloit. The more he learned, the more he wanted her. No, craved her. He had to have her.

It wasn't as if he didn't have his pick of literally any woman he chose. His string of women was embarrassingly long. He'd done nearly everything sexually possible, as often as possible, yet there was still an emptiness inside him nothing could fill. Until he'd laid eyes on Anna.

He discovered the books she enjoyed the most, the music she played in the store, what movies she saw. Who she dated—surprisingly almost no one. She'd parked herself in the shadow of her sister, the high-fashion model, the star of the family. He would bring her out into the light and teach her about life and love. Make her his.

He studied her carefully until he was sure his approach would work. The last thing he wanted was for her to see him as a stalker. Besides, it was more than her body he wanted. Anna had closed off her heart, tired of the men who saw her merely as second best to Shari. As an invited guest at all the pre-wedding festivities, he'd studied her carefully and engaged people in casual conversation about her.

Often he would spot her across the room, standing by herself, perfectly composed but in her eyes a longing that she couldn't quite conceal. He knew women. In Anna Beloit what he saw was a woman secretly desiring adventure. Looking to burst out of her self-contained prison and push life to the edge.

The more he watched her, the more he fell in love with her. Confident in his sexuality, he was sure he could woo her and captivate her. But not in the traditional sense. No, capturing Anna would mean taking her to erotic places she'd never been before. In the end she would be his Diamond Lady.

"How are you feeling, *cara?*" He kept his eyes on his task but he could feel her body humming beneath his touch.

"As if my body doesn't belong to me." Her voice had a shaky quality to it, caused, he was sure, by the multiple sensations assaulting it.

With his thumb and forefinger he pulled her labia taut to give him better access to the fine ribbon of hair. The movement shifted the position of the vibrator and he watched in fascination and more cream gushed from her saturated sheath.

"Keep your body still, my love," he reminded her, as he pulled her labia this way and that to complete his task. When the last curl had been banished, he couldn't resist running his finger around the flesh surrounding the vibrator. He felt Anna's body tighten as she fought to control herself, that ghost of a caress setting of a wave of ripples throughout her body.

His cock hardened painfully, blood throbbing in the thick veins wrapped around it. A tiny pearl of pre-cum beaded at the slit and dropped onto his thigh. He closed his eyes tightly and drew in a long breath. It wouldn't do for him to lose control. He'd hardly begun the evening's activities.

He placed everything he'd been using on the tray and carried it back to the bathroom. When he returned he picked up the remaining black box and kneeled on the bed beside Anna. He stared at her for so long she wiggled and shifted her body.

"Dominic? Is something wrong?"

He shook himself, "I'm just mesmerized by the beauty of your body. Do you know you have the most succulent nipples I have ever seen? Pink and plump, with wide areolas that I can pull into my mouth."

He bent his head and demonstrated, placing his lips fully around one nipple and the surrounding flesh. He pressed the tip against the roof of his mouth, rasping his tongue back and forth on it. He watched Anna's eyes glaze, then spark and her body twitch when he bit down gently.

When he had pulled and tugged on one nipple until it was as hard and full as it could be, he switched to the other one but he didn't neglect the one already aroused. He used his thumb and finger to keep it in a state of swollen readiness. He could tell by Anna's eyes and the limited movements of her body that he was having the desired effect on her.

He lifted his head. "We're almost ready, my sweet thing." He opened the box and lifted out what looked like a piece of jewelry. Two parallel thin gold bars with a waterfall of tiny diamonds cascading from them. "It would be a shame not to adorn these exquisite nipples and only diamonds can do the job effectively."

He opened a tiny screw at one end of the bars, tugged one nipple between them and turned the screw to tighten them. He watched her face to judge when he reached the point of pain but only enough to give pleasure.

"N-Nipple clamps," she said on a breath of air. "I read about them." Her face turned pink. "I actually tried to buy some one time."

One corner of his mouth turned up in a lopsided grin. "Too embarrassed?"

She nodded.

"No matter. I'm glad you're getting your first pair from me." He kissed her breast, then pinched the end of the nipple that protruded. "If things go well, I will be the only one who ever gives them to you."

Her eyes widened at that. "Do you mean…"

"I mean I have wanted you for a very long time. I don't think one night will satisfy me."

"Dominic, I…I"

"Ssh." He touched a fingertip to her lips, then attached the other nipple clamp. He turned back to the nightstand and pressed a switch embedded in the top. The ceiling folded back like an accordion, exposing a giant mirror like those on the walls. "Now, *cara*. You have been a good girl and controlled yourself all this time. I am going to allow you to have the orgasm you want so badly. I will even help you with it. But you must keep your eyes open and watch in the mirror overhead all the time. Do not close your eyes. Can you promise me that?"

She nodded eagerly, even though a faint blush stole over her again.

"Good girl. All right." He took one more item from the black box. "Here we go."

He bent her legs at the knees again, spreading them wide and planting her feet flat on the bed. He knelt between her feet, his wide shoulders preventing her from closing her legs. With a tiny press of his finger he increased the speed of the vibrator, watching her body jerk in response. As soon as he had it set at the speed he wanted, he took the last item in his collection of tricks and toys, a tiny silver bullet, placed it on her clit and turned it on full force.

Her body twisted and jerked, her hips thrusting as much as she could move them. Her entire body was trembling and shaking, a low moan emanating from her throat.

"Too much too much," she gasped. "Dominic, please."

"Almost there, *cara*. Don't fight it."

She tugged on the handcuffs, pushed with her heels and pumped with her hips. He knew the intensity was greater because he was forcing her to keep her eyes on the mirror overhead. Both vibrators were set just high enough to keep her hanging on the precipice of fulfillment. He couldn't take his eyes away from her, the butt plug in her sweet ass, the clutch of her cunt around the dildo, the nub of her clitoris now a gorgeous dark pink. And her body straining, straining, straining for what it needed.

"All right, my sweet. Eyes on the mirror." He turned both vibrators to full, the dual sensation throwing her over the edge.

She screamed his name as she fucked the dildo, desperately trying to close her legs over it, frustrated that she couldn't. But she kept her eyes on the overhead mirror as he'd ordered, the image of herself perhaps the greatest stimulation of all.

He was mesmerized watching her, the pink flush of her skin, the pumping of her hips as she rode the vibrator. The honey scent of her arousal filled the air, making him impossibly, almost painfully hard.

He was awestruck at the sensual nature of this person who hid in the dark corners of her life. He'd sensed it just from that first glimpse of her in her store, the flash of her eyes, the ripple of her laugh. For whatever reason she'd kept a tight clamp on it and he'd become obsessed with opening it up. Releasing it. Now it was exceeding his wildest expectations. He didn't know how long he could wait before sliding his cock into that welcoming velvet grip.

Carefully he stretched his long, muscular body beside her on the bed, stroking and petting her as the aftershocks subsided. Anna lay panting next to him, a fine sheen of perspiration covering her skin. Her breasts shimmered as she dragged air into her lungs, the tiny diamond waterfalls clattering against each other.

Trailing kisses down her face and the valley between her breasts, he reached between her legs, turned off the vibrator and removed it. His hand was covered with her sweet-scented cream and he lapped at it hungrily.

She smiled as she watched him. "You like the way I taste?"

"In a moment you will see just how much." He stroked her arms. "Are the handcuffs uncomfortable for you? I do not want to cause you any pain."

"No, they're fine." She lowered her eyes, a shy sweeping of her lashes across her cheeks. "Actually, I-I've had dreams about this. About being restrained. Does that sound terrible?"

"No." He chuckled. "It sounds wonderful. Tell me what else you dreamed. This is your adventure. I want you to have it all."

She blushed slightly. You won't think badly of me?"

He stroked her cheek with a tender caress. "Anna, nothing you say or do could ever make me think badly of you. To know that you desire to explore erotic sex to its fullest would only enhance my feelings for you. There is nothing, nothing, you could ask of me that would do anything but make my feelings for you stronger."

She wet her lips with the tip of her tongue, a tempting gesture that made his already hardened cock swell even more.

"I dreamed of having my ankles restrained, my legs apart, while you...while you ate my pussy. And did other things to me. And I couldn't get my legs together. The more I tried, the more aroused I became."

Dominic leaned over and kissed her, his tongue sweeping through every part of the dark cavern of her mouth, demanding that hers do the same to him. When he broke the kiss his eyes were smoldering. "Well, my little jewel, your wish is my command. Whatever you would like, I have it here for your pleasure."

He rolled off the bed and strode to one of the mirrored doors. With his hand on the knob, he looked into the mirror and saw Anna's eyes raking his nude body.

"You like what you see, *cara*? I will let you use this body any way you like. But first it is my turn."

He opened one panel and saw Anna's eyes widen at the array of items displayed.

"Are those all yours? I looked up toys like that on the internet. Was that too daring of me?"

"Anna, my pet, I think you have not been daring enough. But we're gong to take care of that tonight." He returned to the bed with a strange device in his hand and bent to kiss her forehead. "I was worried that I would be rushing you. Perhaps I'm not going fast enough."

She gave him a wicked smile. "Perhaps you're not."

* * * * *

She'd seen a picture of the device Dominic held on several of the web pages she'd visited. She'd been amazed at how many pages came up when she typed in "sex toys." This was called a spreader and the picture of it had fascinated her. In reality it titillated her even more.

I'll be spread wide open, at his mercy and he can do anything to me he wants.

She shivered in anticipation.

Her eyes followed him as he moved her bent legs as far apart as possible, then locked the circlets at each end in place around each knee. She'd seen them with ankle restraints but this gave him unrestricted access to every part of her sex.

The moment the last catch snicked into place she felt the walls of her vagina ripple and her own cream lubricate her.

Heat flared in Dominic's eyes as he watched her. "Oh yes. You like this, *cara*. I can see that. There's a lot more beneath that peaches and cream skin than you ever let anyone see." He ran his tongue over her lips. "But you're going to let me see it all, aren't you? All those hot, hidden desires you've been keeping bottled up."

He knelt between her legs and began to lick her newly shaved mound, taking little nips at the bare skin, then rubbing his cheeks against it. The sensation of his freshly-barbered skin against her own suddenly naked pubis shot streaks of heat through her. All the books in the world couldn't describe the sensation she was feeling.

Then gently, as if he were opening a flower, he pulled her labia away from the opening to her vagina and stroked the length of her slit with one wicked caress of his tongue. Anna knew her cream was running out onto his tongue. He hummed in appreciation, the vibrations echoing through her hot sheath and up through her body. Again he stroked and the walls of her cunt rippled in response, begging for something to fill it.

Dominic laughed, a warm sound. "We've barely begun and already your delightfully slick channel begs for something to fill its emptiness. Oh, Anna, what a deliciously responsive body you have. What a treat you are. I could eat you like a fluff of cotton candy."

And he proceeded to do just that. His tongue was like an artist's brush, painting strokes everywhere on her sex—inside her vagina, up and down her outer lips, over that so sensitive area between her vaginal entrance and her anus, back and forth across her clitoris.

Anna hunched and strained against her bonds, excited as much by her inability to do anything as by the wicked ministrations of Dominic's tongue. She remembered suddenly to look overhead and in the mirrored ceiling she could see every movement he made, every touch and stroke.

He lifted his head and when he saw what she was doing paused in his ministration. "Let's make this a little better, shall we?"

He pulled two of the multitude of pillows on the bed toward him and placed them beneath her ass, lifting her so her entire cunt and anus were visible in the overhead mirror.

"Now, *cara,* look to your heart's delight."

And she did, seeing herself wide open, every inch of wet, pink flesh and the movement of his mouth over her as he lapped and nipped and drove her to the brink of orgasm. Watching her body respond heightened her arousal to such an extent she was sure she could come at any moment.

Suddenly he backed away and she gasped with disappointment.

"Shall we add a little something to the fun?" he asked.

"Add…something?"

Her body was so stimulated she could barely think. Her nipples throbbed between the clamps and the waterfalls of diamonds made her breasts heated where they brushed against them. A heavy throbbing in her womb radiated out to

272

every other part of her body even her toes and the ripples in her cunt became so intense she could actually see them when she looked in the overhead mirror. Her clit demanded attention so intensely she wanted to cry with the hunger and need. What could he possible add that would intensify what she was feeling?

But when he turned from the open closet, her breath caught at the sight of the long peacock feather in his hand. Anna felt every nerve ignite with anticipation. In one of the books she'd read the man had used just such a feather to tease the woman to an incredible orgasm yet still left her wanting more. She'd had to masturbate while reading it because the passage turned her on so. And how here was her chance to experience it firsthand.

"Your eyes tell it all, *cara*." Dominic smiled at her. "Never did I expect such a willing pupil, so wild and adventurous. We were made for each other, my sweet."

The moment she felt the first caress of the feather on her clit she raised her eyes to the ceiling mirror, capturing the erotic vision.

The music changed to Stravinsky's *Firebird* and in what was left of her rational mind she thought, *how appropriate*.

And then it began in earnest, the silky feather drifting over her naked mound, brushing her clit, caressing her inner thighs. She tried to arch her hips to urge him to plunge it inside her but the spreader had her nearly immobilized. At last, when she was ready to scream for him to do it, he slipped the feather into her waiting channel and began to fuck her with it.

Anna thought she would go crazy. It wasn't enough, just a tease, coaxing her vagina to clench and pulse but never giving her the satisfaction she needed. She began to beg and plead but the precipice she wanted so desperately to reach hovered too far out of her reach.

"Please," she screamed. "Please, Dominic. Let me come. Now, please."

"Then you shall watch yourself do it," he told her.

Casting the feather aside, he retrieved the vibrator. With one hand he held her pussy wide open while the other ran the vibrator over her outer lips, her slick inner lips and round and round her clit. Her whole body began to shake and perspiration covered her skin. She tugged and pulled on the handcuffs and pressed her knees against the spreader restraints.

Then, with a final burst from the vibrator he tipped her over the edge, holding her vagina open as wide as possible so she could see her orgasm, watch her muscles clench and spasm and liquid pour from her and run down between the cheeks of her ass. She was mesmerized and the longer she looked the more intense her climax grew. The diamonds in the flange of the butt plug winked at her image in the mirror. She threw her head back, the muscles of her neck corded and released a hoarse scream of ecstasy that reverberated in the room.

When her body finally began to quiet, Dominic leaned down between her legs and lapped every bit of liquid she'd spilled, licking his lips and scooping with the tip of his tongue.

"You are so delicious, my sweet. Better than the finest confection I've ever tasted."

He unlocked the spreader and tossed it to the side, then removed the handcuffs. Cradling her in his arms he brushed the damp hair from her forehead and rained kisses on her cheeks and mouth. "Rest a moment," he told her. "Then we will experiment with more surprises.

Anna leaned into him, exhaustion, temptation and greedy sexual hunger racing through her in a tantalizing cocktail.

Chapter Three

ಜಿ

Dominic refilled their wine glasses and raised his in a toast to Anna. "To the most delightful little treasure I have ever found. I may have to find a way to keep you always by my side."

Anna sipped her wine, excited by his words. She'd come looking only for an adventure, a chance to experiment with the things she'd read. Did Dominic mean there would be more to this beyond tonight? She hardly dared hope.

"Where did you get the scar?" she asked, wondering if he was offended by her question.

He smiled. "A souvenir left over from a passionate encounter. Someday I'll tell you all about it. But tonight we have pleasures to enjoy. Roll over onto your hands and knees," he commanded, setting down his glass. "I think we are ready for a new plug in that gorgeous ass of yours."

Anna did as he told her, playfully waving her ass in the air at him.

"Deep breath," he said and slid the plug from its place in her rectum.

She felt suddenly very empty and started to protest.

"Ah, anxious, are we? In a moment that will be taken care of."

He pressed the nozzle of the lubricant tube against her anus, inserting it inside and squeezed the cooling gel into her dark tunnel. Inserting one finger to the hilt he began to massage the lube, rubbing it into her tissues. Shortly a second finger joined the first and when she took that easily he added a third.

"You burn me alive, Anna." His voice was hoarse. "This is the sweetest ass in the world that I have ever possessed."

In response she pushed back against his fingers, trying to urge them in deeper.

"All right, *cara*. Deep breath, now. And turn your head to watch in the mirror."

Her eyes followed his movements as he spread the cheeks of her ass and inserted a plug larger than the first. She held her breath as he pressed it into her slowly, stretching her. The tiny, sharp bites of pain were followed by a flood of pleasure and liquid trickled from her vaginal opening onto the insides of her thighs. Just like the previous plug, the flanges on this one were studded with diamonds that winked in the light.

Anna slowly let her breath out as the plug filled her, then teasingly wriggled her ass at Dominic.

"You are a tease, you know? And teases should be punished, don't you think?"

"P-Punished?" Erotic visions of whips and floggers flooded her brain, just as Dominic brought his hand down on one cheek of her ass in a stinging slap. She jerked, then realized the place where he'd struck her tingled pleasantly.

He bent over her, his mouth close to her ear. "I think you like spankings, my sweet, do you not?"

He brought his hand down on the other cheek just as she nodded her head. "Watch me, *cara*. See how I warm your ass and your pussy."

She tried to anticipate the spankings but he refused to establish a steady rhythm. Now one cheek, now the other, now a pause, then a slap on her bare cunt.

"Tell me how you love this," he demanded.

"Yes, yes," she cried. "More. I want more."

She felt the heat streaking down to the insides of her thighs and through every inch of her sex, especially when he landed particularly stinging slaps on the drenched lips of her pussy. When he hit the base of the plug, she felt the vibrations through every inch of her rectum. Watching the rise and fall of his hand hypnotized her and she wanted to beg him never to stop. When he did she pushed her buttocks back at him, trying to urge him to begin again.

He chuckled. "What a willing pupil you are. And I have so much more to teach you."

Again he refilled their wine glasses. He helped her to her feet and as she stood before one of the mirror panels sipping the delicious creation, Dominic rubbed salve into the places on her buttocks and her outer lips where he'd spanked her. At first the cream was soothing, cooling but suddenly she felt hot tingles every place he touched her. When he scooped some onto a finger and shoved it all the way into her vagina, something happened to her body. She felt as if she were being thrust toward an orgasm without anyone touching her at all.

"You are going to come, my love," he told her. "We both will but not in the way you expect. We will save that for the finale."

She looked at him and frowned, questioningly.

He lifted her onto the bed, placing her on her knees, facing him. Moving her hands behind her, he locked her wrists into the handcuffs so they rested at the base of her spine. The salve was doing its job. She felt as if tiny fingers were stimulating every inch of her sex—her vulva, her labia, her clitoris, her vagina.

Dominic stood in front of her, holding his magnificent cock in one hand. "Open your mouth, *cara*. I have another treat for your."

His penis was thick and long, the head broad and flat and a deep purple. Ropy veins along the side pulsed with the blood pumping through them.

"Dominic, I don't know if—"

"You will take me, Anna. I will help you. And you will swallow my seed. Come. Open your mouth."

She opened her jaws as wide as she could and Dominic slowly eased his cock into her wet heat. Her lips stretched around the broad head and he showed her how to tilt her head back to allow for easier penetration. He worked it in a little at a time, pulling back, then giving more, until, to her own amazement, she had taken nearly all of it.

"Good, good. Very good. And is my magic salve working on you?"

She bobbed her head as much as she could.

"Suck me, Anna. Make me come." He held her head to show her how he liked it and to help the ease of movement. In a moment she was able to relax into it and set up a rhythm that worked for them both. She swirled her tongue around the thick stalk and closed her lips around it, sucking him into her. And all the while he whispered magical, erotic words to her that drove her toward orgasm.

She lost count of time as he fucked her mouth and her own body quivered and shook. She felt him gathering for his climax just before his hoarse shout and she tilted her head back even more. He moved one hand to pinch an engorged nipple peeking through the diamond clamp and as he did so her climax overtook her and Dominic's seed splashed at the back of her throat.

She fell toward him for balance, impaling her mouth further on his cock, until finally she swallowed the last drops and he pulled back and grasped her shoulders.

"My God, Anna," he gasped. "That was incredible. You are a natural at this, do you know that?"

She smiled, pleased at his compliment.

"And you, my sweet? Let's see how well my magic cream did for you."

He reached between her legs and thrust his fingers into her. When he removed them they were dripping and he slowly licked each finger clean. "Better than the wine, I think. You taste like heaven."

278

She dropped her eyes in a shy gesture but then they popped open again. Dominic was still as aroused as if he hadn't just had an astounding climax.

He chuckled. "Yes, some men are like that. Fortunately for me, for both of us, I am ready to fuck you again."

He lifted her from the bed with her hands still locked into the cuffs and carried her out of the bedroom, through the main cabin and up the steps to the deck.

"Outside?" she gasped. "But people will see us."

"We are at the end of the pier," he reminded her. "Up at the prow we are hidden from everything except the moonlight."

"But—"

"No buts," he grinned. "And besides, the threat of discovery only enhances everything." He placed her on her knees on a wide bench at the very front of the boat, stacking pillows under her so she had a place for her head. Then he reached for something resting in a bowl next to her, a rubber ball with straps dangling from it.

"What's that?"

"That, my dear, is to make *sure* we aren't discovered. I love a woman who screams the way you do but only when there's no one around to hear."

He slipped the ball into her mouth, stretching her lips around it and fastened the straps behind her head. Then he reached beneath the cushions on either side of her to reveal manacles bolted to the wood. When he locked them in place around her ankles. She was once again restrained and totally at his mercy. The thought excited her beyond belief. She had read a scene almost like this in her latest book and the reality far surpassed the imagination.

Dominic leaned over and trailed kisses the length of her spine, then licked the cleft of her buttocks above the plug. As she shivered with anticipation, he moved his mouth to the insides of her thighs, kissing and licking every inch of skin until she could barely stand it. Finally he speared his tongue into her vagina, tasting her as he tested her readiness.

"Now, my love," he whispered sheathing himself and slowly thrusting his cock inside her.

She would have gasped but the ball gag suppressed all sound. As he began a steady thrust and retreat, he pressed the base of the plug and it began to vibrate in her rectum. If she had not been restrained she would have been a wild woman under him. If the ball gag had not been in her mouth she would have screamed the heavens down.

As it was she moved her hips as best she could, trying to suck him into her as deeply as possible as the vibrations echoed through her body. Before she realized what was happening, her orgasm took hold of her and she was thrown into space, whirling and spinning, her vaginal muscles greedily milking the penis that was filling it.

Dominic kept up the steady stroke until her spasms reduced to aftershocks. She realized suddenly that he had not come and tried to turn her head to him.

He bent and licked her ear, aware of what she was asking.

"I was saving it," he whispered.

Slowly he removed the butt plug, pulled the cheeks of her ass as wide as he could get them and drove himself into the heated embrace of her rectum.

She screamed silently against the ball gag, every nerve in her body responding once again. Now he increased his tempo, fucking her with hard, rapid strokes, his hands gripping her waist, whispering wild, erotic words to her.

The night breeze blew like a soft whisper of air against their heated skin and the boat rocked gently in the water. Somewhere at the other end of the pier she heard voices and laughter. Dominic was right. The fear of discovery only heightened her arousal.

Her body was matching him thrust for thrust, her ass slapping against his thighs with every movement backward.

The dark spiral uncoiled within her again and when he came inside the slick tunnel of her rectum, her cunt convulsed once more, a climax so shattering she was sure her body would fly apart.

Finally, spent, Dominic collapsed on top of her, catching his weight on his forearms, his heart thudding heavily against her back.

At some point—seconds, minutes, Anna had no idea—he lifted himself away from her, released all the restraints and removed the ball gag. Then he lifted her in his arms again.

"I think a shower is in order, is it not?" He planted a light kiss on her lips.

The shower was much larger than she expected to find on a boat. Spray hit them from all directions with a finely regulated mist. She was thoroughly sated from the sexual activity and pleasantly buzzed from the wine. She could easily have melted into a puddle. It was pleasant to stand there and be ministered to by this man.

Dominic removed the nipple clamps and rubbed lather into her engorged nipples, easing the throbbing caused by the rush of blood after the lengthy constriction. He bathed her thoroughly, as one might wash a child, working the soap into every crack and crevice.

"Your nipples are like ripe berries, *cara*," he crooned, and bent to lick each one. "I could suck on them forever, but I must attend to the rest of this wickedly delicious body."

He rinsed her vagina to remove all traces of the salve so there would be no aftereffects and used a mild enema to cleanse her rectum. Strangely she felt no embarrassment as he ministered to her in this way, only the delightful feeling of being cosseted.

He sat her on the seat in the corner of the shower while he lathered himself and rinsed off. She couldn't stop staring at the perfectly sculpted lines of his body, the thick, black curls of hair on his chest, or his penis, magnificent even at rest as it lay against his heavy testicles. If she weren't so exhausted she'd have coaxed his penis to attention again and started all over.

His eyes twinkled at her, as if he knew what she was thinking. "This is not an ending, *cara,* only a beginning—did I not tell you that? I have many, many plans for us for the future." He shut off the water, leaned forward and kissed her deeply, his tongue licking the inside of her mouth. "Trust me. We will be together for a long time."

He toweled them both dry, then helped her to dress before he pulled on slacks and a cotton shirt. He placed the diamond nipple clamps back in their box and handed it to her.

"Wear these at home for me, when we are apart. Sleep in them and you will think of my hands squeezing your nipples, my mouth sucking on them."

"Thank you." She already imagined herself nude beneath her covers, with the waterfalls of diamonds rustling against the heated skin of her breasts.

"I would tell you to wear them to the wedding but they might not be appropriate for your maid of honor outfit."

"No kidding," she laughed.

He handed her another, smaller box. "So you will wear this instead."

She gasped when she opened the box. A tiny charm in the shape of a boat, completely covered in diamonds, hung from a fine golden chain.

"Oh my God, it's beautiful." She touched it reverently with her fingertips.

"I meant to give it to you as a pendant until I saw the navel ring. Tonight when you go home I want you to put this on instead of the one you have." He pulled her close to him and kissed her with ferocious intensity. Even now his hunger was not completely sated.

"When you see me at the wedding, you will be the only one who knows what's under my gown."

"This is only the beginning, *cara*. One night and I can't imagine you not in my life. Soon you will need someone to manage your bookstore for you because you will be far too busy to attend to it yourself."

"I will? What will I be doing?"

"Why, you will be my Diamond Lady, of course." He grinned at her. "And I will have something besides this boat to carry on the tradition of the Fellini family. Are you willing?"

Anna hugged him tightly. "Of course I am."

He walked her through the cabin and up the stairs to the deck, lifting her easily onto the pier. "I think you'll need a ride home. Your escort has probably long gone."

"And in a perfect snit, I hope. The damn bore."

"It will be my pleasure to drive you."

The ride to her apartment in his Mercedes was smooth and soft music played on a CD. When he pulled up in front of her building, he turned and cupped her face in his hands. "I will see you Saturday at the wedding. Will you be driving with the wedding party?"

"Yes. With my sister and mother."

"Tell them you're taking a long vacation afterwards. Pack a bag and leave it with one of the ushers. I'll have someone get it."

"Truly? We're really going away together?"

"We have not yet begun to explore what we mean to each other. Or the level of eroticism yet to be enjoyed." He touched his lips to hers. "And Anna.

"Mmm?"

"Don't wear any panties to the wedding. We might want to step outside now and then."

She threw back her head and laughed. She was still laughing when she waved goodbye to Dominic and walked into her apartment. Her adventure had turned into something far beyond anything she could ever have imagined, anything she could have dreamed. But the best part of the adventure was about to begin.

HEART DIAMOND

Margaret L. Carter

ℰↄ

Chapter One

සා

The door buzzer cut through the bleakness of yet another Saturday evening. Too late for a door-to-door solicitor. Who would visit at this hour without calling first? Roseanne switched off the black-and-white movie she'd been half watching and trudged to the door. Pausing with her hand on the chain, she said, "Who is it?"

"Just me."

Ted, her late fiancé's brother. She sighed. *I should have guessed*. He was her only friend who never bothered to phone before dropping in. As little as she wanted to deal with him on a weekend night, she didn't have the heart to tell him to get lost. "Yeah, what's up?" she asked, unfastening the chain. Through the door, she heard the patter of a steady rain.

"I've got something important to tell you. Okay if I come in?" His voice sounded enough like his brother's to give her a fresh twinge of sorrow, though they weren't completely alike. Ted's was pitched a little higher.

"You might as well, just for a minute. I was thinking about getting ready for bed." Lucky she hadn't changed into her nightgown yet. The way Ted's eyes roamed over her even in a ratty T-shirt made her vaguely uncomfortable, though he'd never overtly hit on her.

His face always gave her an unwelcome shock. She hoped he didn't notice the wince of pain she tried to suppress. It wasn't his fault that he'd been in the car when his brother died or that the two of them looked so much alike. Strangers had often mistaken them for twins, despite the seventeen-month difference in their ages. They had the same honey-gold hair, which Tim had worn a bit longer and shaggier than Ted's. The same height—six feet two—and they shared a trim, broad-shouldered but not muscle-bound build. Their eyes were different shades of blue—Tim's closer to gray and Ted's profile was a little sharper. Still, any unexpected glimpse of him pierced her breast with a pang of longing and sometimes ignited a flare of need between her thighs, chased by a shadow of guilt. She never considered pursuing that illusion. She knew the inner differences between the brothers too well. Friends with them since high school, she'd dated Ted only a few times before she'd discovered reasons to prefer Tim.

"Mom and Dad asked me to bring you this." He strolled into the living room, lounged on the couch and took a small box out of his pocket. His hair and shirt were damp from the rain.

Roseanne sat down, careful to keep space between them. "What is it?"

"Something Tim left for you." Ted opened the box. It held a silver ring with a blue-tinted, oval-cut diamond flanked by a pair of diamond chips.

She took it from him, her hand trembling and tears misting her eyes. "How—?"

"While the folks were visiting Tim in the ICU, he was conscious for a little while. He asked them to have this ring made for you if he didn't survive. He said you'd talked about it once. Sounded kind of creepy to me."

"Why?" Roseanne's tears made a sparkling halo around the gems. During Tim's lifetime, they hadn't gotten around to buying an engagement ring. "What's creepy about it?"

Ted visibly swallowed, as if working up the nerve to answer. "Because it's made from his ashes. I tried to talk Mom and Dad out of it but they said that was his last wish and he'd been in his right mind when he made it. Personally, I wasn't so sure."

"He did show me the website when he happened to stumble on it. We thought it was cute and sentimental in a weird way. Heartdiamonds.com, it's called." After touching a fingernail to the central stone, she set the box on the coffee table.

"Morbid, if you ask me. Frankly, if I hadn't known our parents would follow up on it with you, I wouldn't have given you this thing. I'd have returned it for a refund and snuck the money back into their account."

After redirecting how much into your own account? She squelched the thought. No matter how tactless he was, he didn't deserve to be accused of greed. Making a profit off his brother's remains, now that would be morbid. "You wouldn't have any right to do that. Tim wanted me to have this ring and it's none of your business."

"How are you ever going to get over his death, staring at this every day?"

Anger flared in her. "Get over it? How can you say a terrible thing like that when it's been less than six months?"

"Come on, Rosie, Tim would've wanted you to move on."

"How do you know what he would've wanted?" She didn't try to hide the irritation in her voice. How many times had she asked Ted not to call her Rosie?

"Sorry, I didn't mean to upset you." He scooted over and draped an arm around her shoulders. "I just want to see you start living again. How about going to dinner with me tomorrow night?"

She shook her head and edged away from him. The arm of the couch didn't leave her much space to retreat. "I don't feel up to that. Thanks anyway."

Inching over, he snaked his arm around her again and squeezed her shoulder. "Come on, hon, give me a chance. You must know how I feel about you."

She stared at him in shock. "No, I don't, and I don't want to hear it." She'd had no idea his repeated invitations, which she'd repeatedly turned down, meant anything other than brotherly concern. Had her passion for Tim and then her grief blinded her so completely that she hadn't noticed Ted still had a thing for her? Had he felt this way the whole time she'd been dating his brother? She sprang to her feet before he could paw her anymore. "Thanks for delivering the ring. You'd better go now."

He frowned, anger clouding his eyes. "You can't leave your heart buried in his grave forever."

"Well, if I ever dig it up, it won't be for you." She stalked to the front door and held it open. "We're friends and that's all. Please don't bring this up again."

He clutched her arm. "You don't mean that. You can't just throw me out."

Roseanne shook him off. "I'm not throwing you out. I'm asking nicely." She chilled her tone enough to hint that "nice" wouldn't necessarily last.

His frown darkened to a scowl. "You're a healthy woman. You need a man. You can't go the rest of your life without getting laid." He grabbed her by the shoulders and pulled her against him. His mouth covered hers with suffocating force.

When she felt the hard muscles of his chest against her breasts and his erect cock pressing on her, a rush of heat dampened her underwear. Both ashamed and furious, she shoved him away. "That does it. Get out of here right now."

Shaking his head, he stomped out. She bolted and chained the door, her stomach churning. She didn't want to fight with any member of Tim's family. Why was Ted suddenly acting like such a jerk?

It must've been some crazy impulse of the moment. If I don't encourage him, he'll forget about it soon enough.

Her cheeks burned with humiliation at the way she'd responded to him for that split second. The reaction was pure animal lust, she assured herself. She didn't even like him that much. She collapsed on the couch and plucked the ring out of the box. The diamond shimmered through the fresh tears that welled up. Though she hadn't come close to "getting over" her loss, she'd started to grow a protective shell. Now this unexpected gift had cracked the shell to let in the pain all over again.

When she slipped the ring onto her left hand, it fit perfectly. Not long before the accident, she and Tim had gotten measured at a jewelry shop and of course he'd remembered her size. She kept it on during her shower, unwilling to lose contact with it for even a few minutes.

With her eyes closed, she relaxed under the hot water spray and imagined Tim standing behind her and massaging her breasts with soapy hands. Yes, she needed to get laid but not by just any man. Definitely not by her dead lover's brother. She'd never have the lovemaking she yearned for again.

As if that hopeless thought had conjured it, a shock like static electricity zapped through her. Had the bathroom wiring shorted out? If so, she couldn't stay under the shower. Just as she reached for the faucet, something looped around her wrist.

She let out an involuntary yelp. Although she didn't see anything, she felt a cool, silken cord wrap around her lower arm. Before she had time to move, a similar invisible length of silk encircled her other arm. Sparks raced along each cord. They didn't hurt. Instead, they raised goose bumps on her naked body and made her nipples and clit tingle. Two more tendrils whipped across her chest to coil around her breasts and flick the nipples. Another tendril, longer and thicker, snaked between her butt cheeks. Her body convulsed with a stronger jolt of electricity.

The longest cord slithered between her legs to invade her slit as well as the cleft of her bottom. The tip vibrated on her clit. She couldn't help planting her legs farther apart, silently begging for more. Tiny electric shocks sparked everywhere at once. The muscles inside her pussy quivered. Leaning with her palms flat against the shower wall, she closed her eyes and surrendered to the climax that swept over her.

The electricity and the invisible tendrils vanished instantly. Heart pounding, she groped for the faucet and turned off the water.

What was that? Am I losing my mind?

Dream. She must have fallen asleep for a minute and had an erotic dream. A crazy, scary one. She staggered out of the shower stall and gasped for breath until her pulse calmed down.

While toweling herself, she took special care to dry the ring, polishing it to a fresh gleam. She put on a satin nightgown and lay in bed with only a sheet between her and the coolness of the air-conditioning. Just before turning off the lamp, she gazed at the photo on the nightstand, as she did every night. It showed her with Tim and his parents' beagle, Grover, on a beach. Roseanne's curly black hair, tousled by the wind, contrasted with Tim's golden mane. His arm encircled her shoulder, fingers almost grazing the edge of her breast the way they never would again. A whimper escaped from her as she switched off the light.

The memory of his smile, his kiss, his touch melted her inside. She pressed both hands to her breasts. The cool circlet of the ring dented her skin. Her nipples hardened in her palms. She squeezed them, though her own touch could never ease the deepest ache. Her stomach cramped with need. Moisture welled between her legs. She kneaded her breasts for a minute then shifted one hand to her mound. She stroked the hair in slow circles, while her thigh muscles tightened and blood-heat engorged her clit and the folds of her pussy.

While pinching a nipple to a firm peak, she dipped a finger into her slit and spread hot cream over the hypersensitive bud. She imagined Tim's fingers on her pussy or better yet, his tongue. Her clit thickened and tingled. She pressed her legs together, trapping her hand. Her other hand wandered from the left breast to the right and back. Every inch demanded touching at once. Frustrated, she arched her hips and stroked faster. Her inner muscles clenched. Shoving two fingers inside, she circled her clit with her thumb.

Never enough. She craved his cock. Fingers, vibrator or a cushion clamped between her legs couldn't fill the void. Yet her body responded anyway. Her vision grayed and all sensation converged on the spot she was rubbing faster and faster. The tingling narrowed to a familiar burning at the tip of her clit. It began to throb and her channel contracted around her fingers. She pressed hard against her pussy while the convulsion racked her.

The pulsations faded all too soon, along with the mindless pleasure they'd brought. Limp, she lay with her tear-dampened eyes closed. Nothing but a physical reflex, an emotionless spasm of nerves and muscles. Would she ever know a lover's warmth again? She had only one refuge from emptiness, the oblivion of sleep. She'd almost drifted off when a word whispered inside her head.

Rosebud.

Her heart lurched. Tim's secret name for her, spoken only while they'd made love. She remembered his lips and tongue teasing her clit when he'd said, "Sweet rose petals. I'm going to sip your nectar like a honeybee."

"Nice line," she'd said between gasps of passion. "But all worker honeybees are sterile females."

His laugh had tickled the hair on her pussy. "Okay, then, I'm a bumblebee with a giant stinger to poke you." After that, he'd called her Rosebud in bed.

"Tim?" She opened her eyes.

Imagination. Nothing but a fragment of dream. The curtains over the bedroom window flapped. *Wind*? Not possible, with the air conditioner running and the window closed. Yet she felt it blowing across her. The breeze raised chill bumps on her damp skin. She pulled the sheet tighter around her shoulders.

A puff of wind snatched the cloth out of her hands and flipped the sheet to the foot of the bed. She lay exposed to the cool air. *Impossible*. Her heart racing, she sat up and reached for the covers. On her left hand, a glimmer of light flashed from the diamond, a brighter glow than any reflection could account for.

A stronger gust of wind shoved her flat on her back. She let out a yelp of alarm. When she tried to move, invisible hands gripped her shoulders to hold her down.

Lie still, Rosebud. Let me pleasure you. I need your climaxes. I need to fuck you until you practically pass out from coming over and over.

Fingers swept down the front of her body, leaving a trail of chills. Her nipples puckered and the still-tender flesh between her thighs tingled. She squirmed. A cold weight settled on her chest and hands pinned her arms to the mattress on either side of the pillow.

I've waited so long for this chance. It's the only way I can be with you. Don't fight me.

Silken cords like the ones she thought she'd dreamed in the shower looped around her wrists. They stretched her arms out on each side and bound them to the bedposts. A second pair of tendrils tangled around her legs to pull them apart and fasten them to the bed's footboard.

While the unseen grip immobilized her, another pair of hands grasped the hem of her nightgown and tugged it over her head. The pressure on her chest eased just long enough for the hands to pull off the gown and toss it to the floor. She bucked against the unseen bonds. Fear sliced through her rising excitement.

Let me go!

Not yet. I need you this way. Got to fuck you until you come. Then maybe you won't scream when I get strong enough to show myself.

That made no sense at all. Yet the breeze wafted the spicy aroma of Tim's aftershave and the salty tang of his skin to her nose.

Okay, definitely a dream, Roseanne thought. *Might as well flow with it.*

Fingers danced all over her body. How many hands? She couldn't count them. They threaded through her hair, cupped her breasts, spiraled around her nipples, trailed down her front to stroke the hair on her mound, massaged her thighs, caressed the insides of her legs until her toes flexed. The pulse pounded in her throat and between her legs. She tried to reach up to embrace her invisible lover but something still shackled her arms. Her lungs felt tight, her breath fast and shallow from both lust and fear.

Don't be afraid. I'd never hurt you.

Let me hold you!

That's not possible yet.

Along with the chill breeze, she felt warm breath in her hair and on her cheeks. Lips grazed her chin and nibbled along the curve of her jaw. She whipped her head from side to side in a futile quest to capture that mouth with hers. A soft laugh ruffled her hair. A tongue fluttered against one side of her mouth, then the other. A moan escaped her. The tongue parted her lips and darted between her teeth. She tasted the single-malt Scotch Tim had often enjoyed as an after-dinner drink.

Her own tongue met and sparred with the invader. So hot. Cool caresses on her flushed body and a searing brand on her lips. The sensation shot down to her breasts and clit like a bolt of lightning. Liquid flooded her slit.

Desperate for pressure there, she struggled to close her thighs. The invisible cords kept her legs splayed against the mattress. The disembodied voice purred with satisfaction.

Not yet. Maybe I'll let you move soon.

Ephemeral touches caressed her neck, breasts, stomach, arms, legs, even the soles of her feet, like a thousand feathers or moth wings. Meanwhile, the invisible mouth kept kissing hers. Every inch of her skin quivered. She felt she might vibrate into a million fragments. Moaning, she arched her hips.

A hot, wet tongue lapped her swollen bud. Yet lips continued to nibble on hers. How could that happen? *Why ask? It's a dream. Anything can happen.*

The next instant, yet another mouth closed on her right breast. No, two sets of lips, identical tongues flickering over both of her nipples. Miniature lightning bolts flashed behind her closed eyelids. Electric shocks radiated outward from her nipples and clit until her whole body quaked. Just as the first pulsations of orgasm surged through her, something parted her pussy lips. An erect cock filled the emptiness. Another firm length plunged between her ass cheeks. She gasped in astonishment and shuddered with the undulating ripples of the twin organs inside her.

The second invasion didn't hurt the way it would have in real life. It only doubled the tantalizing pressure on her G-spot. She raised her bottom and flexed the inner muscles of her pussy and butt to draw the invisible shafts deeper. Their tips generated unbearable friction from both sides on that hypersensitive target. It seared the lining of her pussy, yet without pain. The two cocks thrust in perfect rhythm, while her hips pumped.

More! Deeper, faster.

You want me to fuck you harder?

Yes!

Then say it that way.

Fuck me harder!

He gave what she craved and her whole body shook as she came. She threw back her head and screamed through her release.

When the last tremors faded, the cocks inside her vanished, as did the multiple hands and mouths. A single pair of hands massaged her shoulders and gentle kisses wandered over her cheeks and throat.

"It's all right, Rosebud. I'm with you now."

Wait a minute, that wasn't in my head!

Chapter Two

‰

Roseanne's eyes snapped open. A man's shape lay beside her. A neon-blue glow surrounded it. Tim's face and body, translucent except for the gray-blue eyes. His hand flowed over her like cold water. A shudder coursed through her.

"Roseanne? Don't be afraid, love. I'm sorry I scared you at first." The voice sounded so real, exactly like her memory of Tim's.

"Of course it sounds the way I remember it," she muttered, "because it's coming from my imagination."

"No, it's not," he said. "I'm really here."

She gasped and sat up. When the apparition's fingers trailed down the valley between her breasts, she drew her knees up and wrapped her arms around them to shield herself.

He reached for her again. She let out a half-stifled scream.

He blinked in and out of visibility like a failing light bulb. "Please don't."

A chill enveloped her. "What are you?" she whispered.

"It's me. Honest."

Shaking her head, she squeezed her eyes shut then opened them. He hadn't vanished.

"Why are you afraid?" Lying on his side, he leaned on one elbow and gazed into her eyes. She noticed his elbow and hip didn't dent the mattress. With one finger he touched the diamond. At the moment of contact, his outline momentarily became sharper.

"Are you kidding? Because if you aren't a dream, you're a ghost."

"Well, yeah," he said with a sad smile. "Considering I'm, you know, dead and all that."

Her throat constricted so that for a few seconds she couldn't choke out any words. "Why? How?"

"Why? Because I couldn't stand being torn away from you. I'm able to reach you now because of the diamond."

She stared at the gem, which glimmered in the eerie light he radiated. "You're haunting the ring?"

"If you want to put it that way."

Her eyes roamed over his naked form. "How come I can see you now and not a few minutes ago?"

"I couldn't manifest visibly on my own. I needed energy from you, from your climax. The more I draw, the more solid I can become."

With one finger she poked his chest. The sensation felt like sinking into cool, half-set gelatin. Static electricity fizzed at the point of contact. He reached out to skim over her shoulders and breasts. Again miniature lightning bolts arced in his wake. The hair on her arms bristled and her nipples peaked.

"Please don't pull away from me. I couldn't stand it. Let me love you."

The wistful pleading in his voice made her chest ache. He had to be real. Her mind couldn't have invented all these details.

His shape flickered again. "Don't you want me here? I can't stay if you don't."

If she'd believed all along that his essence survived somewhere, didn't it make some kind of sense that he could appear to her in visible form? In that case, the last thing she wanted was to push him away.

"Of course I want you." The bluish aura around him brightened when she spoke. "Stay. Make love to me." She blushed at the memory of how she'd said it more bluntly in her mind a minute before. He'd never expected those words from her during his lifetime. Becoming a ghost must have broken down his inhibitions. She tried to hug him but again his substance yielded like a viscous liquid. She let out a soft cry of dismay.

"Don't worry about that. Maybe I can become more solid later. Meanwhile, this way has advantages." He splayed one hand over her right breast. The fingers elongated until he was fondling both breasts at once. His other hand drifted down the front of her body, making her skin prickle with tiny sparks. He circled her clit and simultaneously stroked her cleft.

With a sigh, she lay back, spreading her legs. The fingers parting her labia burrowed into her pussy. They lengthened, impossibly filling her. Another finger snaked backward to probe the valley between her rear cheeks. She hissed and jumped at the shock. It seared like ice.

His lips nibbled along the tops of her breasts, then up her neck to kiss her. When his tongue invaded her mouth again, she felt a tug deep in the pit of her stomach. Painless cramps squeezed her insides. The muscles below her rib cage tightened. She felt as if molten lava flowed from her pussy to every point where Tim's ethereal substance touched. She sighed into his open mouth.

Little by little, his fingers and tongue warmed. Within a minute or two, they burned instead of freezing. His body covered hers with no more weight than a cloud. He radiated a whirlpool of energy that sent sparks racing over her skin just as they had before.

"Your passion warms me," he murmured. "It makes me more real, more — here."

"You pulled it out of me. I felt it."

"Did it hurt?" Instead of breath against the hollow of her neck where he nuzzled her, he emitted a tantalizing breeze that wafted over the entire expanse of her bare skin.

"Oh, no." She squirmed under his caresses. "More."

His sinuous fingers tormented her nipples, clit and every opening where she yearned for him to fill her. Meanwhile, his tongue alternately flickered between her lips and stretched to lap her throat and the sensitive spots behind her ears. She arched her spine and tried to wrap her arms around him. They still sank into his rib cage and back as if he were only half real.

But that's just it, he isn't real. If he's not a dream, he's a spirit without a body.

She ordered herself not to think that way. The delectable sensations he incited in her felt real enough. She stopped trying to embrace him, so the strangeness wouldn't distract her from the pleasure. Closing her eyes, she let herself drown in the energy that flooded over her. The hairs on her arms and at the nape of her neck prickled with static. Her clit and pussy lips tightened. The first waves of the mounting climax rippled through her. He filled her everywhere at once. While he strummed her clit, the finger between her buttocks pressed on the base of her spine. As if flipping a switch, that pressure instantly ignited the explosion building in her.

She clutched the sheets in both fists while her hips arched and shocks of ecstasy convulsed her.

When the tremors subsided and she opened her eyes, Tim hovered a few inches above her. His blue aura looked a little brighter. His hands, now of normal size and shape, skimmed from her shoulders to her hips, back up, then down again. They felt slightly less liquid, though still not quite solid.

She lifted one hand and brushed it tentatively over his face. He turned his head to kiss her palm. "Can you really stay?" she asked, barely able to speak above a whisper after that cataclysmic orgasm.

It seemed he hesitated a couple of seconds before answering, "As long as you want me."

She ran her fingers down his chest. The quasi-flesh parted and re-formed in the wake of her exploration. "Can you—can

301

you come inside me?" Glancing down, she surveyed his erection, no less or more solid-looking than the rest of him.

"Just what I hoped you'd ask."

He floated down to cover her. Though she still felt no weight, the tips of her breasts touched his chest, his lower body pressed lightly against hers and his cock probed between her thighs. She opened wider and he slid halfway in.

Incoherent murmurs hummed from her parted lips in time with her rapid breathing. Arching her hips, she struggled to draw him deeper.

Since he didn't need his hands to brace himself above her, they swirled over her shoulders and the outside curves of her breasts while he nibbled her neck and curled around to lap her nipples. "Oh, Rosebud, I love that sound you make when I do this." He yielded to her wordless pleas enough to delve another inch into her channel. "I wish I could feel your pussy."

She contracted her inner muscles around his shaft, which felt more solid than it looked. "What? You can't?"

"Ectoplasm isn't the same as human flesh. I can see and hear but my other senses don't work. I don't have localized sensations in my cock or any other part. I feel your energy all over, equally intense everywhere." He flexed in and out, sending ripples of pleasure through her. Somehow he molded the base of his penis to rub against her clit at exactly the right angle to ease the burn in the nerve endings that clustered there.

Her hips involuntarily humped in rhythm with his too-slow thrusts. "You mean this doesn't do anything for you? You're not getting turned-on like I am?"

"Sure I am." His tongue flickered over her nipples and darted into the hollow of her throat. "Like I said, I feel your energy. Your aura. I hear your pulse beating like a little drum. It's echoing all through me. When you come, it'll hit me like an earthquake."

"Then make me come." She grasped at his shoulders, clenching her fists in frustration when she still couldn't get a grip on him. "Go faster." She swallowed, remembering what he'd demanded of her before he'd become visible. "Fuck me faster."

He pumped faster, harder, until his thrusts felt no different from their most intense coupling in the flesh. No, it was different in some ways—better. His cock lengthened, thickened, filled her beyond anything she'd ever fantasized. At the same time, the root strummed her clit with every stroke. When she closed her eyes, she felt as if she floated off the bed and rocked in his arms like a boat on a stormy ocean. Her head reeled. The phantom wind whirling around her sucked her breath away. She stretched toward the peak—higher, higher—and tumbled over it like a surfer on the crest of a wave.

Tim wrapped around her like a silken cloak, not only with his arms and legs but with his entire self. The shudders that racked her body resonated through him too. She felt them echo back to her, amplified.

At last she floated down to rest, her pulse quieting, breath heaving in and out of her lungs. She opened her eyes and put her arms around Tim. When she tried to smooth his hair off his forehead, it felt more like running her fingers through tendrils of vapor. Yet otherwise, even with the blue aura outlining his silhouette, he looked less translucent, more alive than before, though his skin still felt like cool silk. With a tentative squeeze, she tested its texture.

Her fingernails didn't sink in so readily this time. "You feel different." She wrapped her hand around the shaft of his cock and stroked upward. It grew longer instantly, with a shower of sparks following the path of her caress, but felt as firm as it had in life. In contrast to the coolness elsewhere, that part, like his mouth, felt hot.

"All because of your passion. After you have one more climax, I think I'll become fully solid, at least for a few minutes."

"Another one?" She still had to gasp for breath from the last cataclysm. "No way. I can't come again."

"Yes, you can. I'll prove it right now." He started by kissing her, his hands on her shoulders, thumbs stroking the hollows on either side of her throat, his mouth exploring hers from one corner to the other.

She darted her tongue out to meet his. Again she tasted Scotch and caught a whiff of his spicy aftershave. If she didn't try to hug him too tightly, she could imagine he was alive. Tiny electric shocks danced on her lips and tongue. When he moved from her mouth to her throat and the vee between her breasts, the sparks raced from one spot to the next in his wake. He circled her right breast in narrowing spirals until his tongue reached the nipple and lapped it to an aching peak. Then he did the same on the other side.

She moaned in protest when his mouth left her breasts to wander down the front of her body. Her nipples tingled from the breeze that wafted over the moistened tips. She let out a long sigh of pleasure when he cupped both breasts and skimmed his fingers over the nipples. Meanwhile, he continued downward to nuzzle the damp triangle of hair.

"I wish I could feel how soft this is, the way I remember." His breath hummed against her sensitized flesh.

Fisting the sheets beneath her, she threw her head back and arched her hips in silent pleading. Her clit and the folds of her pussy swelled and tightened. Already the leading edge of a fresh climax rippled along her nerves. His tongue flicked her bud.

"Rose petals and cream. I wish I could smell your skin and taste your pussy." He planted light kisses on the insides of each thigh before licking his way back up to her clit.

"Inside," she whispered.

He lapped the length of her slit over and over, just barely grazing the entrance where the nerves were most sensitive. Her head spun with the sensory overload from his hands on her breasts and his tongue inside her. Her clit started to pulse like a second heartbeat.

"Need to come," she whimpered. "Please." Her hips thrust upward through no conscious choice of hers.

He clamped his mouth on her pussy and his tongue flickered over her clit like a flame. At once the convulsions shuddered through her, on and on, with the vibrations of his energy quaking through her body and driving her to new heights just when she thought she would spiral to completion. He moved upward to lie on top of her. She felt him shaking with the release they shared.

"That's it," he murmured in her ear. "That's what I needed."

Without thinking, she twined her arms around his neck. His muscles felt solid. His scalp felt covered with hair. She opened her eyes to gaze into his. They still glowed and a blue glimmer still sparkled around him but she couldn't see through him anymore. "You feel real."

"Like I said, your passion gives me enough energy to form a solid body. I can't maintain it for long but we can enjoy it while it lasts."

"You mean you can feel things now?"

"No, but that's okay. What's important is how I can make you feel."

He lightly kissed the corners of her eyes, then her cheeks and her throat. His lips wandered over her face until they met hers again. Encircling him with her arms and legs, she savored the taste and smooth warmth of his kiss. If she closed her eyes to shut out the azure halo, she could imagine him alive in her embrace. She ran her fingers through his hair and arched her back to press the length of her body against his.

To her astonishment, desire seared through her again. She yearned for his cock to fill her. The contact with his pseudo-flesh seared her nipples and clit. She rocked her pelvis against his. Liquid gushed between her legs. She whimpered with need.

He nuzzled the side of her neck, his lips branding her skin. "Let me in."

She opened to him and his cock slipped into her sheath, inch by inch. Her hips involuntarily rose to meet him, coaxing him deeper. Cupping one of her breasts with his left hand, he skimmed down her body to the apex of her thighs. He stroked the triangle of hair and probed between the blood-engorged folds.

As his finger circled her clit, she gasped at the sensation, sharpened almost to pain and flexed her hips faster. She quivered all over, helplessly shaken by his touch and the silken glide of his cock inside her. She felt about to shatter with the vibration but the climax eluded her frantic writhing.

His tongue flicked over the hollow of her throat and traced the upper curves of her breasts. "I'm not infinitely flexible this way. Let's try another approach." He pulled out.

With a squeak of dismay, she dug her nails into his shoulders.

He grasped her hips. "Roll over."

She turned onto her stomach. Clasping her inner thighs, he spread them apart and bent her knees to raise her bottom. She invited him inside with an ardent wiggle.

His fingers spiraled around her clit. "Your pussy wants my cock?" The teasing lilt in his voice, exactly like the tone he'd often used at moments like this, only stoked the fire within her.

"Yes! Hurry!"

He swept her hair aside and bit the nape of her neck, the way he'd always done in this position. The nip of his teeth sent a shiver down her spine, straight to her clit. He caressed the bud, finding the spot where it burned most urgently. He surged into her pussy.

She buried her face in the pillow with both hands clutching the pillowcase, fingers flexing in time with his thrusts. The piston strokes of his cock echoed his strumming of her clit. The friction tormented the G-spot deep inside her. Once again, ecstasy flooded over her. She screamed into the pillow to muffle her cries. Above her, Tim's body shook as if racked by the earthquake he'd mentioned.

Turning her head sideways so she could breathe, Roseanne shuddered as the aftershocks of the climax faded. While Tim gently kissed her shoulders and neck, his hands roamed over her back and the globes of her buttocks. He eased off her, though one leg still draped over hers.

She turned on her side to face him. The blue glow still outlined his form. He brushed her hair back from her damp forehead and kissed her there with a flicker of his tongue.

"I wish I could taste the salt on your skin. But that last time was almost as good as real life."

The hand soothing her with long, slow strokes became less like muscle and bone, more like cool water. The color faded from his hair and skin and she could dimly see through him.

"Why are you turning transparent again already?" She wrapped her arms around herself, suddenly chilled.

Chapter Three
‮ℭ‬

"I can't draw but so much energy from you at one time, so I have to conserve it. No matter how it looks or feels, this form is still ectoplasm, not flesh and blood."

"You keep saying that. What does it mean?"

"Ectoplasm is spectral matter, I guess you'd say. Between mundane protoplasm and pure spirit."

Roseanne shivered. "For some reason I feel cold."

He drew the sheet and bedspread up to tuck them around her. "You see what happens when I draw enough of your energy to make myself solid. That's why you've lost body heat."

"I don't care." She clasped his hand, wishing she could keep him from vanishing by holding onto him. "Take as much as you need. I want you to make love to me all night, every night."

He shook his head. "I can't risk hurting you. We have to ration it. Like I said, I'm not completely here, sort of caught in between."

"I would've thought you went into the light, to Heaven or whatever."

"I'm earthbound because my life ended prematurely. At least, that's the best I can figure out. Nobody gave me an instruction manual."

"So why didn't you appear to me before this?"

"I was tethered to the remains of my body. I didn't have any desire to haunt the guys at the plant where they make the diamonds, so I just sort of hovered around. It seemed like an eternity while I was stuck in limbo, waiting until I could touch you again."

She tried without success to visualize his consciousness drifting after his ashes like a balloon on a string. "What about your parents?"

"I was tempted to appear to them but I wouldn't have had enough energy to make them perceive anything except my voice and maybe a glimpse of a shadow. If they hadn't thought they were going crazy, they would've been terrified, the way you were at first." A kiss like a flutter of moth wings alighted on her cheek. "I had faith that you'd be able to accept me."

"Can we do any of the things we used to do together out of bed? Like drink a bottle of wine on the rug in front of the fireplace?"

"You can drink it while I watch. I can't process food or liquid." When her shoulders sagged in disappointment, he said, "Hey, I can still watch the fire and listen to the CD player while I kiss you."

"How about whipping up an omelet for Sunday brunch the way you used to do?"

"I can cook for you, even if I can't eat but not on Sunday morning. Daylight shreds ectoplasm. Why do you think ghost sightings usually happen after dark?"

"So we can't take Grover for walks in the park, either?"

"Since the park closes at sunset, probably not. At most, I could drift along with you as a voice in your head and a shadow out of the corner of your eye."

She rested her head on his shoulder, her eyes blurring with moisture. "You're really dead, aren't you? Even if you're here, sort of."

"Yeah."

"This is kind of like a computer simulation, only with ectoplasm, isn't it? You're not alive."

"No." Sadness muted his voice. "I can haunt you through the ring. I can't come back to life."

"What's the use of showing up like this to tease me with what we can't ever have?" She wiped the back of her hand across her face. "Why did you leave me alone?"

He gave her a puzzled look. "It hurts me as much as it does you. It's not like I had a choice."

"Yes, you did." Furious tears scalded her eyes. "Why did you have to drive that car that night?"

"What?"

She flailed her fists at him and they sank into his mist-like substance. "If you hadn't been driving, you wouldn't be dead."

"But I wasn't. Ted was."

The words hit her like a punch in the stomach. She sat up, hugging her knees. "I don't get it. You were behind the wheel when the police and the ambulance got there."

Tim's form wavered like a smoke cloud buffeted by a breeze. "Now I remember. Ted switched our places."

"He staged it to put the blame on you?"

"Yeah. I remember floating outside my body after I got knocked out in the crash. I watched him haul me into the driver's seat and press my fingers on the steering wheel. He muttered something about being sorry but he couldn't afford another DWI. He shoved my head against the windshield, then wiped the blood off the dashboard on the passenger side. I shouldn't have let him drive in the first place. If you want to blame me for anything, it should be that."

"Why did you?" Roseanne wasn't sure whom she was madder at right now, Tim or Ted.

"He jumped in the car and started it before I could catch up with him. I couldn't just let him drive off by himself, so I got in and tried to talk him into pulling over. He wasn't in a cooperative mood, considering we'd just had a fight."

"About what?"

"You, of course. Don't you have any idea how jealous he's always been over you picking me instead of him?"

"I do not want to know that." She briefly covered her ears. "Why didn't you tell somebody the truth in the hospital? You were conscious for a while there."

"At that point I didn't even remember much of anything about the wreck. I was only thinking about you."

"Well, you should have said something. The police took Ted's word and didn't dig very deep."

"I guess that's partly because I told the other guys in the bar I was going out there to drive Ted home. Nobody saw what happened after I got to the parking lot."

"Did you have to be so damn nice to him all the time?" She clutched the sides of her head, feeling as if it might explode any second. "I knew he pushed you around and took advantage of you, the whole big brother thing. I never suspected he was a total slimeball."

"Shh." Tim's ethereal hands skimmed over her body in a futile gesture of comfort. "It's too late to change the past."

She glared at him. "Ted seems to think lots can change. He was hitting on me tonight. He must think he has a chance, now that you're gone. If he ever tries that again, he'll find out I'd rather be a hermit in a cave living on fried worms than hook up with him."

Just as she drew breath for another blast, a knock hammered on the front door.

Her heart stuttered. "What's that?"

Tim blinked out of existence, then reappeared a second later. "It's Ted. Don't answer it."

Another knock reverberated from downstairs.

"The hell I won't. I'm going to give him a piece of my mind for what he did to you." She rolled out of bed and pulled on a pair of shorts and a T-shirt.

"He's not in his right mind. I don't trust him with you."

"Come on, it's just Ted. He'd never really hurt me. Anyway, if I don't answer the door, he'll wake the whole block." She hurried down to the living room, where she'd left a light on as usual. Tim drifted behind her, vanishing the moment she unbolted the door.

Ted barged in and slammed the door behind him. The rain must have stopped, because his hair and clothes were dry. She smelled beer on his breath. How many had he chugged in the couple of hours since he'd left? When he grabbed her by the shoulders, she flinched. Never before had she sensed any reason to be afraid of him. Had she really known him as well as she'd thought all these years?

"Let go of me! What's wrong with you?"

"I'm sick of waiting around while you blow me off." He shook her. "I'm crazy about you. How long are you going to ignore me?"

"Forget it." She gripped his forearms, trying to pull his hands off her. "There's not a chance. Nada."

With rasping breath, he jerked her closer and snuffled her neck. "You smell like sex. Have you been frigging yourself, daydreaming about him? I think about you every time I beat off."

Fury blazed through her. "Get out of my house. Right now." From the corner of her eye she glimpsed a hazy silhouette, like a cloud of smoke. Tim.

Ted squashed his mouth to hers and forced her lips apart, his teeth harshly scraping her skin. The beer on his breath made her stomach lurch. "Waited long enough. Want to fuck you," he mumbled. She struggled as his hips ground against hers. His erection pressed against her.

Crooking her fingers, she raked her nails across his cheek. With a curse, he let go.

She retreated toward the stairs and scrambled backward, up a few steps. Beside her the apparition of Tim congealed from a transparent cloud into a vaguely human shape.

"Bitch, you can't treat me that way!" For the first time, Ted's eyes wandered from her to the specter hovering next to her. "What the hell is that?"

"You wouldn't believe it." Her chest heaved with labored breaths. "Just go away. It's your fault Tim died. I never want to speak to you again. If you leave me alone, I won't tell your parents and break their hearts all over."

"Tell what? What kind of crap is that?" His voice shook under the bluster, though.

"You lied to everybody. You were driving drunk. If you hadn't been, he'd still be alive."

"How do you know—that's bull."

"Too late to deny it." She folded her arms and backed up another step. "You as good as admitted it right then. You killed your brother. You should be dead, not him."

Ted charged up the stairs at her. "Shut up!"

She raised her arms to ward him off. The ring glowed like a hot coal. Tim brightened into full visibility, though still translucent. Ted froze and stared at him.

"What's going on? That can't be real."

Tim floated down the staircase. Tiny bolts of blue lightning flashed in the sphere of chilled air that enveloped him. Ted flailed his arms and emitted gurgles of terror. "Leave her alone," Tim said. "Don't ever touch her again."

With a scream, Ted backed down the stairs and sprinted for the door. Tim drifted behind him. Roseanne followed, running out the open door just as Ted ran around to the driver's door of his car at the curb.

"Wait!" she called. "You can't drive like this."

Ignoring her, Ted jumped into the car and slammed the door. The engine and lights switched on. The pavement gleamed, still wet from the rain.

Tim, hovering next to Roseanne, said, "I can't let him drive. He's too drunk." He floated through the car window into the passenger seat.

She dashed to the curb and heard him pleading with his brother. "Ted, don't make the same mistake again. Don't be afraid. I won't hurt you. Just turn off the motor and get out of the car."

In a shrill tone of fear tinged with anger, Ted shouted, "Go back to hell!" He gunned the accelerator and the car shot forward.

Little more than a block away, near the playground at the end of the street, the wheels skidded on the wet pavement. Roseanne watched in horror as the car spun out of control, jumped the curb and crashed into a tree. Her heart pounding furiously, she ran to the driver's side and wrenched the door open.

Tim still hovered in the passenger side of the front seat. Cracks spiderwebbed the windshield where Ted's head had rebounded off it. Slumped behind the wheel, he wasn't moving.

She leaned over him to get a closer look under the dome light. No blood but his neck was bent at a strange angle. When she tentatively explored his skull, she found crushed bone on his forehead. Swallowing a spasm of nausea, she fingered both sides of his throat. She couldn't find a pulse.

"I think his neck broke." She gazed up at Tim and rubbed her eyes. "I have to call 911."

"Too late. He's dead." Tim's voice sounded on the verge of a sob. "This wouldn't have happened if I hadn't scared him."

"It's not your fault." Shuddering, she swallowed a lump in her throat and blinked back tears. "You tried to stop him. Are you sure there's no hope?"

"I don't sense his spirit anywhere. He's gone. But maybe—" A glow flared around Tim. He faded to mist. Drifting over to the driver's seat, he shrouded Ted's body like a layer of fog. His substance revolved like a miniature cyclone and contracted to a cone. Beginning with the spearlike point, it poured into Ted's nostrils and gaping mouth.

Roseanne straightened up, lightheaded with shock. The spectral mist vanished into the dead man. A bluish halo surrounded him but seconds later that disappeared too.

Chapter Four

ဆ

A shudder convulsed the body. She knelt to place her hand over his heart. The unnatural glow in the ring she wore burned brighter before dying away completely. His head shifted, aligning itself properly on the spinal column. The scratches from her fingernails vanished. The misshapen spot on his forehead smoothed over. Last, he opened his eyes. For an instant they glowed, then faded to normal. They looked more gray-blue than azure.

"Rosebud?" The voice sounded deeper than Ted's.

"Tim?" she whispered. Ted didn't know that nickname. Her lover would never have shared that secret with anybody, not even his brother. Given Ted's crude habits, especially not his brother.

He hauled himself out of the car, staggering when he tried to stand. She draped his arm over her shoulders and supported him while they walked toward the house.

The middle-aged lady who lived in the unit next to Roseanne opened her door and stared at the wreck. "Oh, my God, what happened?"

"Don't worry," Roseanne said. "He's not hurt. We don't need any help right now. I'll get the car towed in the morning."

She helped him inside and led him to the couch, where he lay down. "It's really you?" After one impossible event on top of another, she felt stunned.

With a slow nod, he said, "Ted's body was empty. He was definitely gone. I couldn't resist the chance to come back to you."

She still trembled from the shock. "I didn't mean what I said. I didn't really want him to die."

"If I hadn't chased him, maybe he wouldn't have. I feel like I've stolen his body. But it was my only chance."

"You didn't make him get drunk or force him to get in the driver's seat. You tried to save him." If she repeated that reminder often enough, maybe she could squash her own feeling of guilt for her part in the fight that had sent Ted running for his car.

As if he sensed her qualms, Tim clasped her hand and placed a gentle kiss on her clenched fingers. "If it wasn't my fault, it sure wasn't yours. He...brought it on himself."

"You're not hurt anymore. I mean, Ted's body isn't. Or yours. Whatever." This development made her head spin worse than the first sight of Tim's ghost had.

"Yes, it looks like the process of entering his body and reviving it healed all damage, including the effects of the alcohol. I'm not drunk the way he was a minute ago."

She noticed he didn't exhale beer fumes anymore. "Neat trick."

He flexed one leg. "That high school football injury Ted used to complain about even seems to be cured."

Kneeling beside the couch, she ran her fingers through his hair, over his shoulders, down the front of his chest. The firm muscles felt familiar, because the two brothers had similar body types. The hair, though the right color, wasn't quite long enough for Tim. Though the voice and eyes were Tim's, he smelled like Ted. Roseanne closed her eyes for a second. It would be easier to accept the change if he wore the spicy aftershave he'd used in life.

His hands wandered over her shoulders, breasts, waist and hips. "I can hardly believe this," he whispered in a tone of awed wonder. "I can feel you. Not just your body heat but your skin, your clothes, everything." He pulled her upward.

She stretched on top of him with her chest against his, her hips cradled between his thighs. When she rested her head on his shoulder, she felt the hammering of his heart. His arms, wrapped around her, trembled. She realized she was shaking too. Tears welled in her eyes. "I can't believe it. It's too much."

"I know." Sobs choked his voice. "More than I could hope for. If only we'd been granted it some other way." He reached under her T-shirt to run his hands up and down her back. He kissed the tears from the corners of her eyes. She raised herself on her elbows to do the same to him. Real skin, living hands on her body, yet not truly Tim's hands. She felt half drowned in a blend of confusion and joy.

"It's almost like he gave you back the life he took from you," she said. "Even if he didn't mean to give it."

Unbuttoning his shirt, she petted the hair on his chest and felt the pebble firmness of each nipple. When she planted a kiss on his collarbone, he sighed and tightened his arms around her. His thighs opened to settle her more firmly between them.

"This may not be the right time to mention it but I actually have a hard-on."

She squirmed against his growing erection. "I think it's the perfect time."

He hooked his fingers in the waistband of her shorts. "I can't change the size or shape of body parts anymore. We'll have to do it the old-fashioned way."

"Sounds great." She rolled onto her side, barely able to fit next to him on the couch and unzipped his shorts.

He touched her hair with a hesitant caress. "Are you sure you're good with this?"

"I'm not good with wishing Ted had died and then having it happen." She rubbed her cheek against his shoulder. "But I'm definitely thankful to have you here."

He stroked her hair. "Amazing. I can feel it all the different textures." He traced the outline of her ear and the curve of her jaw. Meanwhile, his other hand continued wandering over her back.

Roseanne shivered when his fingers trailed down her spine. Again they eased under her waistband at the small of her back. Insinuating her hand inside the open zipper, she fondled his shaft through the briefs.

"Easy," he hissed. He turned on his side to nestle her close to him, face-to-face. His lips brushed the top of her head. He inhaled deeply. "You smell wonderful. Just the way I remembered." After kissing her forehead, he licked her cheek. "You taste like salt. I love being able to taste you."

She nibbled his neck. "Taste all you want, as long as I get equal time."

His muscles tensed under her mouth, while he flexed his hips to press his erection tighter against her. A trickle of heat dampened her shorts. She hadn't bothered with either panties or bra. Tim rolled up her shirt and swept his hands from her back to her waist, then up her sides to the outer curves of her breasts. She folded his shirt flaps out of the way to rub her erect nipples against his chest.

"That's great." He caught her earlobe between his teeth, making her skin tingle. "I can feel your breasts on me. Want to feel more. I can't wait to feel your pussy around my cock." He tugged her shirt off and tossed it on the floor. His hands roamed over her in rapid spirals, as if he yearned to touch every inch at once.

She kneaded his shoulders and upper arms, delighting in the firm muscles. Rolling onto his back, he pulled her on top again. She nipped his neck and shoulders. He kissed her throat and licked his way to the vee between her breasts, while she pushed herself up to give him access. She'd almost forgotten how it felt to have a solid body next to hers, living arms embracing her, warm fingers and lips exploring her most sensitive spots.

He drew one nipple into his mouth and flicked his tongue over it. He breathed on the moist spot, making her shiver. "Look at that," he said. "I have actual breath. And a pulse." Clasping her hand, he held it to his chest. "It's beating like crazy."

"I know. So is mine."

He splayed his palm between her breasts, with thumb and little finger stroking the inner surfaces. "I feel it hammering away. And your skin is like satin."

A lightheaded giggle escaped her. "All that time as a ghost improved your lines."

"It's because I appreciate everything so much more now." While he returned to lapping her nipples, his fingers trailed down to her waistband. "Did I ever notice you have tiny, silky hairs all over?" He peeled her shorts partway off and skimmed over her stomach to the apex of her thighs. "And this hair. Soft and curly. Perfect for petting."

Shudders coursed through her when he tickled the area around her clit. She sat upright to wiggle out of the shorts. "So keep petting."

He did, while she leaned over him with her hands on his shoulders to brace herself. "You're purring. I must be doing something right."

She blushed when she heard the hum in her own throat, a sound she hadn't been conscious of making.

"Keep it up," he said. "I always loved that noise. I'd forgotten about it until right now." He parted the moist folds of her pussy to caress her bud. "I love feeling how thick this gets when you're turned-on."

"Stop," she breathed. "My turn now." She scooted to the floor and knelt beside him. After taking off his shoes and socks, she finished unfastening his shorts and tugged them off. She cupped his erection through the briefs and smiled at the way his breath turned ragged. Insinuating a finger in the fly opening, she ran a fingernail up the shaft. She pulled off the pants and watched his cock spring upright.

With her fingers bouncing his sac and tickling the spot right behind it, she licked up his rod to the tip. He groaned and clutched the cushions under him. When she circled the tip, she tasted a droplet of liquid. Tears misted her eyes at the memories the flavor conjured up, of all the times they'd driven each other to ecstasy this way.

His hips pumped while her tongue flickered up and down his cock, then around it in spirals, first slow, then faster by the second. He grasped the top of her head, fingers tangled in her hair.

"Hold it," he gasped. "I can't stand it anymore. I need to come in the worst way."

"Then do it. Now."

"Inside you. Please."

She scooted up and spread her thighs on either side of his. Raising her hips, she sheathed his cock within her. Her pussy started to ripple with pleasure the moment he began to thrust.

She paused, suspended above him. "I'm not dreaming? You're really here?"

"Yes," he gasped, trembling with the effort of holding still.

"You won't disappear on me?"

"Never."

"Then come on!" She met him with a hard, fast rhythm. Leaning forward, she pressed her clit to his groin and luxuriated in the rubbing of hair against that sensitive spot, the fluid glide of his cock inside her, the almost painful pleasure of the friction deep inside when it thrust up to the root.

"So hot," he groaned. "Your pussy's so hot I can't stand it. Got to come."

"Me too." She dug her nails into his shoulders and rocked still faster to match the speed of his thrusts. Tremors started in her pussy and raced through her whole body. Yet another orgasm racked her. A second later, his explosion echoed hers.

She lay flat on top of him, panting. His breath rasped in her ears and his heart pounded under her cheek. His hands wandered over her as if he still couldn't believe in his own sensations.

When his breathing became more even, he said, "I want to share your bed."

"That's a great idea." She climbed off him. With their arms around each other's waists, they staggered upstairs. Her thigh muscles ached and her clit and sheath felt a little sore. She didn't mind. In fact, she relished the soreness. It proved he'd entered her with a flesh-and-blood cock.

"How about a shower first?" he said as they walked along the second-floor hall. "I can hardly wait to do everything we used to share together."

"Omelets, wine, walks in the park with the dog." A lump clogged her throat for a second. "We'll do it all."

In the shower stall she switched on the hot water and stepped in with him behind her. With her legs trembling, she had to brace herself against the wall. Filling his palms with liquid soap, he washed her back. She arched her spine and let the hum he called a purr vibrate in her throat.

He massaged her shoulders, then spread the soap over her collarbone and the hollows on either side of her neck. In slow circles, he laved her breasts and abdomen. Her thigh muscles quivered, while her pussy muscles contracted and her clit began to swell again.

"I can't," she whispered. "You've worn me out."

Soaping the hair on her mound, he said, "I'll bet you can come once more." A slick finger slid over her clit, which twitched with eagerness for more.

Involuntarily her hips rocked in time with his caresses. She couldn't believe how good they felt, even though every inch of flesh between her legs felt rubbed almost raw already. Hardly able to stand, she leaned back against him.

One of his arms wrapped around her waist to support her, while the other hand kept stroking between her legs. Slowly at first, then faster, the way he knew she liked it. Her clit started pulsing first, then her pussy lips, finally the muscles deep inside. Delirium swept over her one more time.

When her head stopped reeling, she turned to face him. "Yeah, that was a lot like the way we used to do it." She felt her mouth widen in a goofy grin.

He smiled back. She soaped her hands and began washing him. When she reached his cock, it stirred slightly in her clasp but didn't stiffen. "Don't you want to come again?" she asked.

He said with a weak laugh, "I'm a guy. Multiple climaxes are a female thing. A twenty-six-year-old male body has limits." He rested his chin on top of her head. "But I'd still rather have a body than not have one. Give me an hour or so and then we'll see."

After rinsing in the hot water, they stepped out to dry each other. He toweled her hair until no more than damp and she carried a fresh towel into the bedroom to cover the pillow. She stretched out on her back with Tim reclining next to her.

"We've had so many great times in this room," he said, tracing aimless circles on her stomach as if he couldn't bear to stop touching her for more than a second. "I thought I'd lost that forever."

"Me too." She wrapped her arms around his neck. "But not anymore. Let's try to think of it as a bad dream."

"Right. Now we're awake. And I'll never lose you again." He laid his head on her shoulder.

She ran her fingers through the dense pelt of his honey-gold hair. Now that he'd bathed in the soap they always used to wash each other, he smelled like her Tim. With a minor shock, she realized she'd momentarily forgotten he inhabited his brother's body. "I'll have to get used to calling you Ted. Will you be able to fit into his life?"

"Don't see why not. We worked for the same company. I know most of his friends, though I think I'll stay away from the ones he used to get drunk with every weekend. If I slip up, I'll let people think it's because of a delayed grief reaction."

"Are you going to tell your parents you're living in his body?"

He sighed. "I can't. If I try, they'll assume 'Ted' has gone out of his mind. I'll have to be him to everybody except you for the rest of my life."

"To have you back, I can live with that." Trying to visualize the future, she realized that even though his family and friends would never consciously know the truth, they would respond to the shift from Ted's personality to Tim's. Eventually, everyone would adjust to the new situation, as if a different brother had died in the crash. She lifted her hand to contemplate the glitter of the diamond. Life would go on as if some higher power had used the ring to fix what had gone wrong. "I guess we'll have to take it slowly at first. If I got engaged to Ted out of the blue, your folks would freak out."

"As slow as you want in public." His palm skimmed up her side to fondle a breast. "As long as you're all mine in private. We have the rest of our lives now."

"Oh, by the way, could you grow your hair a little longer? And start wearing your old aftershave?"

He laughed. "Sure. Anything to make you happy, Rosebud."

Also by Eileen Ann Brennen

∞

Gamble of a Lifetime
Ghost of a Chance

About the Author

෨

Five years ago, Eileen Ann decided to take a year off from her software consulting business. There was too much to do that couldn't be accomplished between airline flights and hotel stays. Just as soon as she got that garage cleaned, she'd jump right back into the rat race.

Well, the rats are on their own. She still can't walk through the garage, but every day she has a hot date with a to-die-for alpha male-or males!-and hunches over her computer as they fight, angst, or wander through her stories. Multi-published in several genres, Eileen Ann resides in sunny Florida with her husband and one and a half children. (Allegedly, her son is away at school-or so he claims.)

Eileen welcomes comments from readers. You can find her website and email address on her author bio page at www.ellorascave.com.

Tell Us What You Think

We appreciate hearing reader opinions about our books. You can email us at Comments@EllorasCave.com.

About the Author

ॐ

Tiffany Bryan lives in a suburb of Cleveland, where the only thing more fickle than the weather is her imagination. A late life baby, born in the year of the "Dragon" and the youngest of three girls, she found boundaries were something to be tested instead of adhered to. Since she is happily married to a man who provides an inexhaustible amount of inspiration and support, it was a fate-driven step from reading romances to writing them.

A staunch believer of including children in your life and not wrapping your life around them, she celebrates being an empty nester with the same enthusiasm she delegates to any new adventure. After her son and daughter left, Tiffany took the opportunity to do a little wing-spreading of her own and has since attached her scuba diving certification in the deep blue waters of Hawaii and filled the space in the garage where her daughter's car once sat with a shiny new Harley.

Her creativity, coupled with her dare-to-try anything attitude, ensures when you delve between the pages of her books you're guaranteed an entertaining and steamy read.

Tiffany welcomes comments from readers. You can find her website and email address on her author bio page at www.ellorascave.com.

Tell Us What You Think

We appreciate hearing reader opinions about our books. You can email us at Comments@EllorasCave.com.

Also by Amanda Sidhe

&

Summoned by Lust

About the Author

ଓ

Amanda's interests in the paranormal goes beyond paranormal romance. She's involved with Healing Touch, which is a form of healing using spiritual energy. She has gone on ghost hunts and conducted seances. Experiences involving past life regression, channeling, telepathy, precognition and lucid dreams all contribute to the pool of inspiration from which she draws.

Her romances are published by both Ellora's Cave and Cerridwen Press.

Amanda welcomes comments from readers. You can find her website and email address on her author bio page at www.ellorascave.com.

Tell Us What You Think

We appreciate hearing reader opinions about our books. You can email us at Comments@EllorasCave.com.

Also by Desiree Holt

ಏ

About the Author

ഌ

I always wonder what readers really want to know when I write one of these things. Getting to this point in my career has been an interesting journey. I've managed rock and roll bands and organized concerts. Been the only female on the sports staff of a university newspaper. Immersed myself in Nashville peddling a country singer. Lived in five different states. Married two very interesting but totally different men.

I think I must have lived in Texas in another life, because the minute I set foot on Texas soil I knew I was home. Living in Texas Hill Country gives me inspiration for more stories than I'll probably ever be able to tell, what with all the sexy cowboys who surround me and the gorgeous scenery that provides a great setting.

Each day is a new adventure for me, as my characters come to life on the pages of my current work in progress. I'm absolutely compulsive about it when I'm writing and thank all the gods and goddesses that I have such a terrific husband who encourages my writing and puts up with my obsession. As a multi-published author, I love to hear from my readers. Their input keeps my mind fresh and always hunting for new ideas.

Desiree welcomes comments from readers. You can find her website and email address on her author bio page at www.ellorascave.com.

Tell Us What You Think

We appreciate hearing reader opinions about our books. You can email us at Comments@EllorasCave.com.

Also by Margaret L. Carter

ശ

Dark Dreams (*anthology*)

Dragon's Tribute

Ellora's Cavemen: Legendary Tails II (*anthology*)

Love Unleashed

Maiden Flights

Midnight Treat (*anthology*)

New Flame

Night Flight

Tall, Dark and Deadly

Tentacles of Love

Transformations

Virgin Blood

About the Author

တ

Marked for life by reading DRACULA at the age of twelve, Margaret L. Carter specializes in the literature of fantasy and the supernatural, particularly vampires. She received degrees in English from the College of William and Mary, the University of Hawaii, and the University of California. She is a 2000 Eppie Award winner in horror, and with her husband, retired Navy Captain Leslie Roy Carter, she coauthored a fantasy novel, WILD SORCERESS.

Margaret welcomes comments from readers. You can find her website and email address on her author bio page at www.ellorascave.com.

Tell Us What You Think

We appreciate hearing reader opinions about our books. You can email us at Comments@EllorasCave.com.

Why an electronic book?

We live in the Information Age—an exciting time in the history of human civilization, in which technology rules supreme and continues to progress in leaps and bounds every minute of every day. For a multitude of reasons, more and more avid literary fans are opting to purchase e-books instead of paper books. The question from those not yet initiated into the world of electronic reading is simply: *Why?*

1. *Price.* An electronic title at Ellora's Cave Publishing and Cerridwen Press runs anywhere from 40% to 75% less than the cover price of the exact same title in paperback format. Why? Basic mathematics and cost. It is less expensive to publish an e-book (no paper and printing, no warehousing and shipping) than it is to publish a paperback, so the savings are passed along to the consumer.

2. *Space.* Running out of room in your house for your books? That is one worry you will never have with electronic books. For a low one-time cost, you can purchase a handheld device specifically designed for e-reading. Many e-readers have large, convenient screens for viewing. Better yet, hundreds of titles can be stored within your new library—on a single microchip. There are a variety of e-readers from different manufacturers. You can also read e-books on your PC or laptop computer. (Please note that Ellora's Cave does not endorse any specific brands.

You can check our websites at www.ellorascave.com or www.cerridwenpress.com for information we make available to new consumers.)

3. *Mobility.* Because your new e-library consists of only a microchip within a small, easily transportable e-reader, your entire cache of books can be taken with you wherever you go.

4. *Personal Viewing Preferences.* Are the words you are currently reading too small? Too large? Too... ANNOYING? Paperback books cannot be modified according to personal preferences, but e-books can.

5. *Instant Gratification.* Is it the middle of the night and all the bookstores near you are closed? Are you tired of waiting days, sometimes weeks, for bookstores to ship the novels you bought? Ellora's Cave Publishing sells instantaneous downloads twenty-four hours a day, seven days a week, every day of the year. Our webstore is never closed. Our e-book delivery system is 100% automated, meaning your order is filled as soon as you pay for it.

Those are a few of the top reasons why electronic books are replacing paperbacks for many avid readers.

As always, Ellora's Cave and Cerridwen Press welcome your questions and comments. We invite you to email us at Comments@ellorascave.com or write to us directly at Ellora's Cave Publishing Inc., 1056 Home Avenue, Akron, OH 44310-3502.

COMING TO A BOOKSTORE NEAR YOU!

ELLORA'S CAVE

Bestselling Authors Tour

UPDATES AVAILABLE AT
WWW.ELLORASCAVE.COM